CRUEL BETRAYAL!

Lovely, russet-haired Carmody Petrie was sole mistress of Oaklands, the family estate, even before her twenty-first birthday. But though she ran it with grace and wisdom, she could not prevent her brother from losing all they possessed in games of chance.

PERILOUS INTRIGUE!

Soon she was at the mercy of the ruthless Duke of Monmouth, bastard son of King Charles II. Already he had won the deed to Oaklands, and sought to win the throne of England. How soon would it be before he had won Carmody's honor—stealing her virtue as well as her fortune?

BLAZING ROMANCE!

On the high seas and in glittering ballrooms, in chambers of bondage and gamblers' lairs, Carmody defied the raging passions and stormy adventures of England, Jamaica, and the Virginia Colony—drawn to the arms of many men, but to the heart of only one!

The Golden Sovereigns

Jocelyn Carew

AVON
PUBLISHERS OF BARD, CAMELOT, DISCUS, EQUINOX AND FLARE BOOKS

GOLDEN SOVEREIGNS is an original publication of
Avon Books. This work has never before appeared in any
form.

AVON BOOKS
A division of
The Hearst Corporation
959 Eighth Avenue
New York, New York 10019

ISBN: 0-380-00845-9

First Avon Printing, December, 1976

AVON TRADEMARK REG. U.S. PAT. OFF. AND IN
OTHER COUNTRIES, MARCA REGISTRADA,
HECHO EN U.S.A.

Printed in Canada

Book One

ENGLAND

1

THE two riders cantered up the long slope from the sea and reined in at the summit to let the horses breathe.

The man, astride a powerful black stallion that he controlled easily, wore a well-cut riding coat on his powerful shoulders, beautifully fitted breeches, and highly polished boots of a style that the late and sorely lamented King Charles the Second had made the latest fashion the previous winter. All in black, even to his leather gloves, he struck an incongruous and somber note amid the springing green of the Dorset hills.

His companion, a young woman of uncommon beauty, mounted on a high-spirited sorrel mare, was flushed with the exertion of the hard ride. A happy light shone in her eyes, and even a casual onlooker would believe she was desperately in love with the man who rode beside her.

Her eyes, set with an intriguing tilt in her oval face, were the clear gray of the native Dorset stone, but without its hardness. Her fair complexion echoed the blooming pink and white hawthorn in the hedgerows on either side of the lane.

Satisfied that nothing disastrous had happened to Oaklands in the hour they had been away, Carmody Petrie took off her brimmed hat and shook her russet hair. A faint frown shadowed her face as she turned to the man.

"We're more than halfway home, Waldo," Carmody assured her fiance, with a shy smile. "I won't ask you to go with me again. Not to Harriet Paine's."

She was relieved to hear his laugh. "I don't think you'll be asked again," he commented dryly. "She was glad enough to see the last of us, and didn't trouble to hide it."

Waldo turned his horse in the lane, to look back the way they had come. The road slanted down between green borders of lush grass on its gradual descent to the sea, glinting at the horizon like a lost needle in sun-brightened grass.

Reassured by her swift survey of the Petrie lands, drowsily peareful and prosperous under the early June sun, now Carmody was content simply to look at Waldo, to trace with a mental finger the strong bony nose, to feel reassurance at the strength of his jutting chin. Everything about Sir Waldo Rivers was aggressive, thrusting forward, and she thought it was this ambition in him more than any other quality that had attracted her from the first.

Even his thick, black hair, hidden now by his hat, sprang up stiffly from an exaggerated widow's peak, as though it had a bristling, dynamic life of its own. He was a man clearly able to take responsibility for her life as well as his own.

Only a little longer. In ten days her younger brother Ralph would be eighteen, the age when their father once deemed his only son should be mature enough to manage Oaklands, the spreading Petrie estate.

Here where they stood, at the top of the hill, was the highest point of Oaklands, and before her, toward the northwest, lay the farms and woodlands, pastures and cottages, that she had grown to know to the last inch, to know and to love. Her parents' sudden deaths, three years before, had catapulted her at seventeen into a maelstrom of debts and the unceasing demands of managing a large manor.

Both the Cavalier family of her mother and the Puritan Petries had been decimated in the Civil Wars two lifetimes before, and there had quite simply been no one else to take charge. Her father's will, written at a moment when he was unusually well pleased with Carmody, had given her all authority. As it turned out, his will had laid undreamed of burdens upon her, although his intention had been to protect her. If it hadn't been for Yarrow, the estate factor, she could not have managed.

Thinking of Yarrow, Carmody became aware again of the faint uneasiness that had walked with her for the past few days. Would her father, if he could see Ralph today, still feel eighteen was a mature age?

When he had come home last, Ralph had appeared to be what he called, with overweening satisfaction, "a figure of fashion." She could not admire the fawn greatcoat, the newest curled wig, thinking only of how many of the new curly-horned sheep could be bought with the same number of gold sovereigns. But when Ralph returned permanently to Oaklands, she thought optimistically, he would give up his modish Cambridge friends, notably the rakish Peregrine Ashley, and all would be well. A good wife might be the making of him—

"That was a heavy sigh," Waldo remarked, edging his horse Midnight closer. "Don't tell me you have regrets even before we are wed?"

"How could I?" she laughed. "I'll be glad to see the end of Oaklands, and I can't wait to see London again. It's been so long, I fear it will have changed much."

"How wistful you sound!" Waldo rallied her. "Come now, let us stop here. Oaklands can wait a bit longer."

He tied Midnight's rein to a strong tree branch and reached his arms up to help Carmody. She repressed her usual habit of sliding to the ground in a single sinuous movement, and let him place his hands around her waist and set her on her feet just before him. His hands lingered unnecessarily long, she thought. She stirred uneasily.

At once he released her, saying only, "You'll marry me in ten days, Carmody. Yet you still dislike my touch?"

Abashed, she managed a shaky laugh. Seizing upon an excuse, she said, "I still feel Harriet's eyes upon us. Waldo, did you dislike her very much?"

The face he turned to her was bland, even smiling. "Carmody, your unmatched loveliness," he said, putting the ring of sincerity into his deep voice, "puts all other women out of sight. Miss Paine has only her great wealth to keep her company. Let's forget her."

"Willingly."

"Good. Now come, the hedge will keep this devilish wind from us."

The road, worn by countless generations of trampling feet—perhaps the first of them the little dark feet of the Stonehenge men—was, in some places, as much as the height of a man below the base of the hedge. A grassy bank humped up to the roots of the hawthorn, and it was here that Waldo helped Carmody seat herself. He dropped down beside her.

The road would rise and dip once more below this high point before they would be near enough to see the chimneys of Oaklands itself thrusting through the thick green of the trees like reddish stumps in a grassy meadow. Sitting here in the hawthorn's shelter, they were quite alone. Strange, she thought; it is the first time Waldo and I have been away from servants, friends—someone within reach of a shout—since the day we first met at the crossroads.

She had come upon him by chance where the lane divided—one fork leading to Oaklands, the other over the hills, past the place where they now sat, and down the slope to Harriet's. Unaccountably, she marveled, he had stayed to court her, and she still walked in the great wonder of it.

"Three weeks ago," she mused, and turned her silvery eyes to him, "I didn't know you were even in the world, Waldo. And what if I hadn't met you at the fork in the road? What if you had taken the wrong turning?"

Ah, but I did, Waldo protested silently, his disciplined expression reflecting, as usual, none of the sardonic thoughts that filled his mind. On my way to court Miss Paine, the tremendously wealthy Dorset heiress, I was diverted by a pair of bewitching eyes. Pity Carmody's dowry would be so small. Well, he concluded philosophically, maybe there is a way to have both the magnificent wealth of the heiress, and the beauty beside him—

He didn't know that his face had slipped into formidable lines. She had a sudden glimpse of how he would look in perhaps ten years. Would his thoughts still be as hidden from her as they were today? Uneasily, she turned her coat collar up at the back of her neck and shivered.

Instantly, Waldo was all attention. "Are you sure you are all right, Carmody?" he asked. She reassured him with a swift smile.

The wind puffed in from the Channel, shaking the hedge over their heads, scattering white and pink petals over them like a fall of snow. Overhead the fluffy clouds of June swept in from the Channel. Always, in Dorset, near the sea, strong gusts blew on the hilltops. As the winds slid down the slopes into the folds between the hills, they were gentled into garden airs.

This was a dear country. She knew every family who lived in the small whitewashed cottages scattered through the valleys. She was at home, and loved, in the small village which was no more than a cluster of houses around the small church built of Dorset stone, its steeple rising above the squat, ancient yews that surrounded it.

They were silent for a bit. He lay beside her on the ground, supporting himself on one elbow, and looking up into her face.

"You are a beautiful woman, Carmody. Not perhaps as perfect in your features as—as some others I have known, but distinctive. Your eyes are vastly disturbing, do you know that, Carmody? If you ever became aware of the pure havoc you could wreak with them—" He shook his head in mock despair.

Her laugh rang out. "I can never take you seriously, can I, Waldo?" she teased. "What would I do with the havoc? Eat it? Exchange it for—for what?"

His mouth twisted wryly. "Probably some of those stupid sheep. I vow that's all you can think of."

"They're more useful than 'havoc,' " she countered, still in a playful mood. "But after next week I promise I'll forget about sheep, and flax crops!"

"And Oaklands itself?" Waldo quizzed. "I swear I am marrying the estate, and not just a very desirable woman."

"Not Oaklands. That's not mine." She grew suddenly thoughtful. "I'm just realizing it, Waldo. In ten days, I'm losing Oaklands. It's been my whole life for three years, since my parents were killed, paying off the debts and bringing it up to where you see it now. Oaklands isn't tremendously wealthy, but it's providing enough to live on, and comfortably, too."

He started to speak, but instead began to toy with a blade of grass. His long fingers moved restlessly, an unusual sign of agitation.

"It's going to be a great change for me," she confessed. "You'll be patient? But of course London will be diversion enough."

"My sweet," he said at last, tossing away the tortured grass blade. "This is why I wanted to talk to you before we get back to the house. We will not be going to London."

"Not going to London! But why not?"

"I don't want to expose you to the lecherous eyes of our new King."

She stared at him, and then said a little uncertainly, "Don't tease me, Waldo. The King is enormously old, and he would pay no attention to somebody like me. You're joking."

"You have no sense of humor, Carmody. But actually, the new King is a Stuart, and you know the Stuart reputation. No woman is safe from them, and although he takes his vow of chastity, takes it quite often in fact, it is said that he groans in misery until he finds reason to break his vow. And you, Carmody—you could make a man throw away a kingdom."

"But you'd protect me," she ventured. "Wouldn't you, Waldo?"

"Now you're the one who is joking. Me raise an objection to my King? That's no way to collect any plums from the royal household—many a woman has won fortune and preferment for her husband, through the Stuart weakness. And you could do far better than most."

He watched her through narrowed eyelids, intent upon her, almost as though some decision might well hang upon her next words. But she was engrossed in her own thoughts, and he wondered whether she had even understood what he had dared to say, taking a last forlorn chance that she might, after all, make his fortune for him.

Then she glanced sidelong at him from the corners of her almond-shaped, tilted silver-gray eyes. The gesture was flirtatious, but her words indicated that she was unaware of her desirability.

"I don't like talking like this. You frighten me, Waldo."

"Why?"

"I don't know. And that's what makes me afraid, I suppose. But," she added optimistically, "there will be plenty to do in London without warding off our sovereign."

He sat up, digging his heels into the grass of the slope. When he spoke, his voice had lost some of the warmth it had carried for her, almost as though he had moved away from her in another direction.

"I was not joking," he said. "We are not going to London. The situation there is explosive, and I remember the mobs and the rioting when Titus Oates was on trial, only five years ago. King James is little liked as it is. And when the Duke of Monmouth lands—"

"The Duke of Monmouth? Isn't he Charles'—"

"Bastard. Surely he was Charles' favorite, of all his sons. And now he says King Charles actually married his mother, and he is therefore the rightful king. He is coming, so I have heard, to claim the throne."

Awed, she whispered, "That's treason!"

"Depends on your point of view, I suppose. At any rate, he has joined forces with the Earl of Argyle in Scotland, and also, so they say, with Prince William in the Netherlands. The result is that Monmouth is making preparations to invade England."

She thought for a long moment. "Well, Waldo, of course it is your decision. And London will be the better for the anticipation."

"I knew you would understand," he said dryly.

He reached down to help her to her feet, but this time he dropped her hands at once, as though their very touch burned him.

She smiled at him. "Only ten days, Waldo. Have you made the arrangements?"

"Oh—you mean, our marriage? No need for lengthy

planning, Carmody. I have a special license, and when the time comes, we'll appear at the Lyme church and the vicar will marry us."

"In Lyme Regis?"

"Of course. Did you think here in your village? No, the countryside will still be toasting your brother's birthday, and we can slip away. By ourselves."

She stood on tiptoe, looking up into his cool eyes. In their depths, she caught a glimpse of a lurking flame, leaping savagely once before it was gone. She was queerly breathless, as though she tottered on the edge of a deep chasm, the bottom murky in vague, concealing mist. Shakily, she clutched Waldo's sleeve to save herself from falling.

"I think we had better get back to the house," he said. "That cloud looks threatening."

The storm was leaping up from the Channel, high towers of whitish thunderheads growing out of the deepening gray, shot with streaks of unhealthy purple.

The tempest, riding on the rising wind, was approaching so swiftly Carmody could even fancy she heard its galloping feet. How foolish! she thought. It's only that storms always frighten me.

But the hoofbeats persisted. She turned wide, frightened eyes to Waldo. He was staring ahead in the direction of Oaklands, and then, following his gaze, all her fears settled down into place, into the oblivion they deserved. It was only Durward, Waldo's valet, riding hard toward them.

It was obvious that the man was rocked with excitement, bent nearly double over his horse, one arm flailing behind him as he caught sight of Waldo. No accomplished horseman, every bounce in the saddle was reflected in a grimace of pain on his plain face. He shouted something that sounded like "He's here, sir!"

Waldo spoke a short word of reproach and Durward, with an apparent effort, controlled himself. It was odd to watch him pull his accustomed mask of impassivity over the features that a moment before had reflected pain, surprise, and perhaps something more. Now Durward, his servant's expressionless features under control, would pass unnoticed in a crowd.

With a murmured word of apology, Waldo and Durward moved a little apart.

Carmody waited, and wondered. What news could bring Durward so impetuously riding out to meet Waldo? Nothing to do with Oaklands, that was sure. Yarrow, or Pearson, or even Bray the game warden would not have trusted Durward with the time of day, to say nothing of an important message.

And as she waited she was aware of her quickening pulse as she recalled that intimate second of time when she had surprised, as though it were a guilty thing, a depth of emotion in Waldo that he had never before let her see. Uneasily she wondered whether Waldo might prove to be more difficult than she suspected. Unleashed—who knew what he could become?

Waldo now turned to her. "My dear, Durward brings us news that your brother is home."

"But he's not due until next week!"

"But nonetheless, he is here. And Peregrine Ashley is with him."

She bit her lip in dismay. She did not like Perry Ashley, but Waldo disliked him even more. Two weeks before, Ralph had come home bringing Perry Ashley with him, like a bird of ill omen, and the two had disclosed an immediate and mutual loathing. Trust Perry to come and spoil her last week at home, with Waldo on edge, barely civil. And herself trying to keep peace among Ralph and Perry and Waldo.

"I can read your thoughts, my dear. Never mind, I will relieve you of one problem. I will take my leave here, and let Durward escort you home. I will send word when I can come to you again."

"But I don't need an escort."

Firmly he said, "Durward will see you to your home. There is too much unrest in the land. I even feel a bit of it myself. You'll be safe enough."

"On my own lands? Of course."

"By the way, Carmody. Since we won't be traveling to

my house in London, I will need to make other arrangements. We will not have a fixed address, so your attorney won't be able to find us readily. Wouldn't it be well," he suggested smoothly, "to have all the legal business over with before our marriage?"

"Legal business?" She frowned. "I could arrange to have my dowry paid over. Would that help?"

"Immensely." He added with quiet deliberation, "Ashley is totally untrustworthy. I don't look with confidence upon his influence with your brother."

"You knew Ashley from some other place!" she burst out. "I was sure you were old friends, the moment you met!"

"Not friends," he protested dryly. "I think Ashley must be totally devoid of friends."

She nodded wisely. "He's such a popinjay! I couldn't imagine anyone liking him—it would be like avowing affection for a puppet!"

As though to himself, Waldo said slowly, "A puppet, I agree. At least, so he seems. But then, who is pulling the strings?"

Intent upon a train of thought of his own, he stood wrapped in concentration for a long moment. Suddenly becoming aware of her hand tightening on his sleeve, he smiled.

"What do you mean, Waldo? Pulling the strings? You frighten me."

He touched her cheek with his forefinger, and stooped swiftly to kiss her. His kiss was, as always, light upon her lips.

"Nothing to worry about," he said softly. He helped her to mount, and she waved as she rode away, down the slope toward Oaklands. She looked back once to see him standing in the road.

She touched the mare's flank, flicking her into a restless canter. It had been a long time since she felt this irresistible urge to smash things, to run, to ride in headlong flight to the ends of the earth.

Waldo shut her out of his thoughts, and said only, "Nothing to worry about." He changed their honeymoon

plans without consulting her. She would not admit to
Waldo how much she had counted on living in London.
To get clear away from Oaklands, and the sight of her
brother wasting its substance, had been the goal that
cheered her as the days of her guardianship ran out.

Not until she realized that she had lost her escort, leaving Durward jouncing along painfully out of sight behind
her, did she come to herself. He was only doing his best,
she reminded herself. Her innate sense of fair play won
out, and she reined up and waited for him.

She would add Waldo's dowry to the list of things to be
done in the remaining week before the great day—Ralph's
birthday, and her own wedding.

The last thing she would do for Ralph was to give him
a great dinner party to celebrate his coming of age. The
invitations had been sent long before to their friends and
neighbors, and the acceptances were complete. Not a one
was going to miss the chance of seeing what Ralph had
made of himself, she darkly suspected, and she wished she
could be prouder of him.

As Durward came in sight, Carmody put Amber into a
slow trot back to Oaklands. The pursuing clouds reached
the zenith. Without Durward, she could have outrun the
storm. As it was, she resigned herself to a thorough soaking.

Followed at a distance by the valet, she topped the last
rise and looked down into the hill-sheltered hollow that
held the home place. Usually she paused here, to savor her
sense of pride—a pride mingled, to a degree, with pos-
sessiveness. But not this time.

She hardly saw the mellow brick chimneys, the protecting trees, the weathervane atop the stable roof. It was as
though some part of her knew that her peaceful days at
Oaklands were almost behind her, and already the unre-
cognized alteration in her, the fashioning of Oaklands into
merely a memory to warm the heart during the unknown
years ahead, was under way.

Just then the storm clouds overtook the westering sun
and the clear light ahead vanished. Almost before she
could take a breath, the ground-devouring darkness of the

imminent storm engulfed the entire manor house.

Curiously disquieted, she thought that Oaklands itself was passing under a shadow more ominous than a fleeting tempest.

She shivered, and the superstitious fancy was gone. It's just the change in the weather, she decided. Durward pounded up behind her, breathing as heavily at his hack. "Feel the cold air from the sea?" she said. "We had better hurry."

She cantered down the slope, Durward following. She glanced back at him once. She set a hard pace and she doubted his ability to hold his seat.

Overhead the thunder crashed, a great tearing sound as though the sky itself were slit into shreds, and the storm broke ferociously over them.

The first raindrops drummed heavily on the ceiling of leaves overhead, falling weighty as stones, as Carmody dashed across the courtyard and slid like a boy from the saddle.

Lightning flashed, and gratefully she tossed the reins to one of the stableboys and dashed for the shelter of the building. Trotter, the taciturn head groom, held the half-door wide for her and she scurried through it, shaking her head to throw off the rain, feeling her reddish brown hair cascading onto her wet shoulders.

"Just made it, Miss Petrie." Trotter held his words tightly between thin lips, as though there were a fee for each one that escaped him.

She laughed. "It's only water, after all, Trotter."

"Aye," he admitted, "but that's forked lightning too."

"Durward will be along soon," she told him. "Have the boys watch for him. He'll probably come in the back way. But don't stable his horse. After the storm, he'll follow Sir Waldo to Lyme."

She made a move to put up her thick hair, fishing for hairpins, and then decided to let it alone. Unseemly though it was for a grown woman to let her hair hang, undressed, she felt comfortable with Trotter who had, after all, set her on her first pony and picked her, barely holding back her tears, from the ground after her first spills.

With the quiet ease of proven friendship, they leaned elbows on the half-door and watched the storm. She was in a curious mood, unsettled, on the knife-edge of change.

Her childhood, in retrospect one of unalloyed happiness, she had put aside forever three years ago. These last full months stretched back in memory as though they had been lived by someone else, another Carmody Petrie. And, looming ahead, well above the horizon and approaching as swiftly as the storm, was an entirely new person, a changed identity—Lady Rivers.

Misgivings filled her mind. Could she live up to Waldo's strenuous demands on her? She knew his zealous ambition, and she shrewdly suspected that as Lady Rivers he would expect her to play a difficult social role, even the outlines of which were dim and shrouded in her mind. She wished he had not suggested that she could make their fortune by what in plain words was allowing the lustful King to seduce her. Even though Waldo jested, the words still stung.

She sighed discontentedly. She could only do her best. And yet she was vaguely conscious of an absurd longing to stay in this sheltered byway of rural England.

At Oaklands, she was mistress of her own life. But in the wider world—how easily she might be swept away by the currents, and somehow become lost. It was a darkling fantasy, the more frightening because she was not usually swayed by imagination.

Perhaps catching a glimpse of her vision, Trotter was moved to speech. "Aye, it'll be a sore day, Miss Petrie, when you leave."

Jolted back to the present by his rusty voice, she answered, absently, "Aye, Trotter, it will." She wondered whether the source of her uneasiness lay in the unaccustomed, alien habit she had recently developed, of saying, "I'm doing *this* for the last time," or, "I won't be here to see *that* finished."

It was a vicious custom, she decided, and she would rout it out at once. How could she look forward to marrying Waldo when she clung to all these ties to the past?

2

THE storm still raged. The lightning had abated and the thunder roared away inland, but now the rain poured in sheets, rippling in the wind like a pewter-hued fabric whipped by a strong gale.

The dull red bricks of the courtyard paving glistened with running water, and even the pigeons huddled disconsolately in their cotes. She decided Ralph's explanation of his untimely presence must wait.

Belatedly, she asked Trotter if Waldo's valet had reached shelter. Her last sight of him had been at the summit of the last slope down to the manor house, and she had not looked back after the storm broke over their heads.

"Aye, fair cumbered he was," Trotter said with malicious enjoyment. She herself was moved to amusement, remembering Durward awkwardly whipping up his stolid mount, jolting cruelly out of rhythm with the horse.

The rain had stopped for the moment. There was no further excuse for lingering in the stable. She picked up the skirt of her riding dress and ran to the house. The clouds were still lowering, dark and hurrying in the reflecting, patchy puddles—the storm had not finished.

Oaklands was not a great house, even though the building of it started under the last Tudor queen. The Elizabethan Petrie had ideas larger than his income, as indeed had most of the Petries since that time. If it had not been for the infusion of quick-witted and practical Hardie blood from her mother's family, Oaklands would be in a sorry state today.

Voices reached her from the library through the open door toward the front of the oak-paneled hall. Ralph and—she listened intently—yes, his companion was indeed Peregrine Ashley.

Abruptly abandoning her duties as hostess, Carmody lifted her sodden riding skirt in both hands and hurried up the stairs. In the upper hall she met her butler, Pearson.

"Miss Petrie—" he began, but she said grimly, "Not now, Pearson. Send Mercy to me at once."

Even her maid's gentle hands, helping her out of her wet clothes and into her dressing robe, drying her hair, could not soothe her.

She agreed with Waldo. She too mistrusted Peregrine Ashley's influence on Ralph. But what could she do? She could not forbid him the house. She had pointed out to Ralph at Christmas that Perry Ashley was not contributing to his academic progress, but obviously her words had fallen on deaf ears.

For a moment she longed to be as free as Waldo was— simply to fade away at the thought of meeting Perry seemed eminently desirable. And even, she thought guiltily, just to avoid her brother held strong attraction just now.

After dinner Carmody left the men lingering at table, over her father's port, and wandered restlessly into the drawing room. The doors were open onto the twilit garden, and a soft breeze fluttered the heavy curtains. She stepped through the doors, and breathed deeply. The air was fresh, cleared by the departed thunderstorm. The heat in the dining room had been oppressive.

The faint, dewy scent of green growing things surrounded her as she walked in the garden, her pale ivory gown rippling around her like a moth fluttering in the darkness. In a week, just in time for the dinner party, the roses would burst into full bloom. The garden would be so freighted with their musky scent that one's senses would reel, and even the house would be filled with fragrance.

Surprisingly, her thoughts turned to Waldo's warning about the unrest in the land. The Duke of Monmouth had mounted an invasion to claim the throne from his uncle— simply stated, it sounded like something out of a history lesson. She could not picture the Duke. She remembered meeting his father once, at Whitehall. He had been as charming to the tiny girl as rumor had it he was to older ones. All the Stuarts had an eye for a beautiful woman— everyone knew that. She frowned, remembering Waldo's idle banter. It was almost as though he had been sounding her out!

What had he said? Many a beautiful woman had made her fortune, as well as her amiable husband's! Waldo surely was joking!

Well, his jest was ill timed. There was no possible inducement that could be offered to her to make her cast away her principles. But it was the Duke's invasion that was keeping her from honeymooning in London. Where would he land? Somewhere along the Channel, most likely. Portsmouth, Southampton? Lyme Bay?

She looked anxiously around her, ruefully laughing at herself for seeing bulky shapes moving behind every bush. Yet she lingered, reluctant to exchange the balmy evening for the overly warm house.

From the entrance, the parkland stretched as far as she could see, ending in the home woods of great oaks and ancient maples. A magnificent and venerable copper beech stood at the far end of the lawn, an ebony shape in the night. The moon was rising, and her thoughts followed Waldo on his way that afternoon into Lyme, where he had rooms. Soon, soon she would go with him. But first—

She moved with determination toward the house, her mind now on the remarks she intended to make to her brother. She must deal with Ralph, and there had been no opportunity yet to speak to him alone. Perry Ashley had hovered at his side, ignoring her monumental hints that she wanted to see Ralph alone, almost as though he were guarding him. Against his own sister?

She found Ralph alone in the library. She paused on the threshold, seeing without noticing the leather-bound volumes, the heavy blue curtains at the windows, the massive masculine chairs that her father had chosen and which had suited him. Suddenly a vivid, sunlit memory assailed her. Often, as the whim took her, she had run into this room and leaped into her father's arms, to be petted and cosseted. How she missed him! Tears stung the back of her eyes.

Ralph was unimpressive in the chair that their father had filled. She crossed the room to stand accusingly in front of him. "Why have you come home, Ralph?" she demanded bluntly, her rehearsed speech, full of tact and gentleness, flown out the window.

"I came home because I'm through with school," he said, his petulance a sure sign of an uneasy conscience.

"You have more than a week yet until you're of age. You were to stay in school until the day before your birthday. You gave your word. And I'm sure you haven't done so well in your studies that you've finished ahead of time. Besides, you were home only two weeks ago." To borrow money, she thought grimly, but did not say so.

He leaped to his feet and began to pace back and forth. "What would you know of real life? All you think about is dusty farm business—what else? Yarrow and Trotter are the only people you see, except for your fiance! By the way, has he already run off? Where is he?"

"Urgent business," she lied promptly.

"Life's passing me by," he cried, not waiting for her answer, with an air of tragedy. "I'm stuck in a musty old room at school, reading books that don't mean anything, while real life is going on all around."

"Real life is right here at Oaklands, and you will have it all in your hands."

"I'm talking about things you wouldn't understand. Important things."

"Important things?" she echoed angrily. "More important than making a living for all the tenants who rely on you? Keeping them fed and housed?"

"You heard at dinner," he said, as though she hadn't spoken at all. "Perry was talking about King James and the peers that are going to—"

"I heard some sort of nonsense," she interrupted hotly. "But what does young Ashley know about anything? Don't tell me that he sits in on Privy Council meetings!"

"You always scoff at him," Ralph flared. "I know you don't like him, but he's got influence and he's going to help me. That's what kind of friend he is."

Ralph was working himself headlong into the kind of childish tantrum she knew well. She wanted to point out that to all appearances Perry Ashley had done nothing for himself and therefore would not have much influence to spare for Ralph, but wisely she kept silent. Instead, she asked with every appearance of interest, "What is he going to do for you?"

He shot her a wary glance, as though her sudden interest roused his suspicions. "Never mind. It's too soon to talk about it," he said, swaggering a bit and forgetting that he had done nothing all during dinner but talk about *it*, in veiled and irritating innuendo. "There are details yet to work out and it's still very secret. Only a few of us are privy to—what's going on and what's going to happen. But you'll be surprised. And you'll be proud of me."

Ralph stopped in his pacing to face her. She was struck by the mulish determination in his eyes, and she knew he had not changed. Still headstrong and self-willed, fired by the enthusiasm of the moment. She could only hope this frenzy would fade as all the others had done. And soon. Suddenly she recognized his boasting prattle as sheer bravado, hiding a burden that lay heavily upon him.

Her heart sank within her. All the misgivings she had entertained were as nothing, now that the reality was here. She was convinced her brother could not even preserve the gains she had made at Oaklands. Certainly he could not envision the great plans she and Yarrow had begun. She knew the dedication and consuming hard work the land demanded, and Ralph was not yet ready to give it, possibly never would be.

Wisdom deserted her. She said, with sharp exasperation, "You'd better spend your time on learning how to manage the estates. You don't know anything about politics."

Immediately she knew she had blundered. The eyes he

turned to her were alien, cold. "You treat me as though I were in swaddling clothes. I thought this time it would be different. Next week I'll be of age, and I'll have Oaklands. And yet you still think I'm a child."

Knowing he spoke the truth, she took refuge in bluster. "I can remember plenty of times when you were glad enough to have me to come to your rescue. For instance, that time when the vicar almost excommunicated you. It took some doing to get the tombstones back where they belonged, and I had to do some fast promising to get you out of that."

"I might have known you'd bring that up. You never let me forget my sins, do you? But in ten days, exactly— remember that, Carmody—I'll take over my inheritance, and you can't stop me. I might even let Sir Waldo whistle for your dowry. I wonder how long he'd stay in Dorset then."

The blood left her cheeks, and a horrified gasp tore the deathly silence. But the gasp was not hers. It was Ralph's.

"Carmody, I'm sorry," he cried, suddenly a small, penitent boy again, terrified by his own temerity. "I'm sorry, I didn't mean it. No matter what they make me do, I'll—I'll try to get out of it somehow!"

Throwing himself at her feet, he clutched the silk of her skirt with both hands and hid his face in the folds. His voice came muffled, and she began to suspect that he must be more than a little drunk. Her father's port was powerful.

"Please forgive me," he begged. "I'll even send Perry away."

Gently she stroked his hair, pressing his face to her and holding his head, reassuringly, comfortingly, but her thoughts were turbulent and full of wrath.

Somewhere she had heard, "There are no quarrels so bitter as those in the family." Here was the proof. He had wounded her beyond belief, beyond repairing, even without knowing it. She knew she could not forgive him. His hint that Waldo's love would last only as long as her dowry—ah, that was cruel!

But one phrase that Ralph had let slip stuck like a cocklebur in her mind. It demanded explanation, and yet she could not ask him about it—not, certainly, while he was drunk and hysterical.

No matter what they make me do—

And suddenly, as she soothed and comforted her young brother, even as she assured him, mendaciously, that what he had said would be forgotten and forgiven, she realized that he was haunted—haunted by a fear still hidden from her in the secret corners of his mind.

What had Ralph done?

Ralph did not return to school.

A week later he was still at Oaklands, wandering restlessly through the rooms, picking up a book here and setting it down again, not even opened, there. He could not settle to any connected thought, and Carmody, furtively watching him from the corner of her eye, sensed a difference in the younger brother she had protected for so long. Over-protected, if she were to believe Waldo, and perhaps he was right.

But it didn't matter any more, she told herself, did it?

In three days, on Thursday, the eleventh day of June, he would enter into his inheritance, and, as he pointed out waspishly to Carmody more than once, he would then be beyond her reach.

"So that's the extent of your vaulting ambition!" she taunted him once. His aimless mooning about had destroyed her patience, and for the first time she could not reach him with any of her usual methods. The gulf between them had widened until she couldn't bridge it. But he was her only brother, actually her only kin, and she could not shake off the conviction that she was responsible for him.

"Is that all you want?" she goaded, that Monday morning. "Not to see Oaklands prospering, building a good life for your tenants? Not to love every inch of the ground of your forefathers? Nothing so grand, I see. A small ambition after all, and one that requires no effort from you—in three days you'll achieve it by the passage of time." She eyed him, desperately hoping for some sign, no matter how pitifully small, that Ralph was growing aware of his inherited union with the land where Petries had lived and worked for generations.

This morning she had insisted, as a last resort, that he accompany her on her usual rounds, directly after breakfast. They had come as far as the sheep pens. Sooner or later he would have to understand all the improvements made at Oaklands in the last years.

"Escape from your sister," she began again, determined to wrest some response from him. "That doesn't seem an ambition worthy of a Petrie. I'd think you would aim at least as high as Privy Councilor!"

She looked back at the manor house. The great oaks, growing since Plantagenet days, had leafed out almost to their full, and the house was hidden save for two chimneys rising from the green mass, like ancient pilings along the sea edge.

Ralph, knowing her well, followed the direction of her thoughts. "Too bad you didn't inherit," he jeered. She glanced at him and caught the hard mockery in his eyes. "But you'd never get Waldo to settle down here, would you?" he added.

"I never thought of it."

"I just wonder how well you know your fiance," he mused.

Ralph leaned over the rail fence. Carmody always felt a lift of pride at the sight of the sheep in the pen—their curly horns, their bare white faces. But she suspected Ralph hardly saw the beasts. Certainly he was not disposed to admire them. He was engrossed just now in picking out a splinter from the rail that had imbedded itself in his dark red sleeve.

"What do you think of the Dorsets?" she prodded, unwisely.

"Ugly."

She was instantly indignant. "These ugly sheep, as you call them," she pointed out crisply, "are much of the prosperity of Oaklands. A new breed, substantially easier to raise, good wool, and more mutton on the bone." She continued, insulated by her enthusiasm, for several minutes.

The decision to invest in the new breed had cost her many anxious hours, but the event had proved her right. Just now, however, she realized she was babbling on to keep from thinking about Ralph's disturbing comment. "The lambs are already larger than the other breed, at six weeks—Ralph, you're not listening!"

"I'm listening, all right! If you knew how little all this means to me. I've got more important things on my mind!"

"What could be more important than this?" she countered.

He shook his head in exaggerated disbelief. "How do you keep Waldo Rivers chained to your side? Not by your brilliant conversation, you can be sure of that!"

Ralph's words were as salt on a wound she had thought healed. Why *did* Waldo want to marry her? The question was not new to her, but she had forgotten—or hidden away in the recesses of her mind—its frightening insistence. Waldo had given her a beginning recognition of her feminine value, but only a beginning. The tiny seedling was still fragile. Ralph's drunken taunt—*let Sir Waldo whistle for his dowry, and how long will he stay in Dorset then?*—had nearly killed it.

As much in defiance of Ralph, as because Waldo had asked for it, she had had Mr. Hastings pay over the dowry last week, in coin since she had no lands of her own. She wondered if Ralph knew the funds had already been transferred.

She thought not. His secret pleasure in hurting her was hidden except for a telltale quirk at the corner of his weak mouth. How cruel Ralph was to torture her!

The simple instinct of self-defense tutored her now. She could not think of rapier words to stab him with. Only bludgeon words came to her tongue, and she wielded them savagely.

"Your expensive education, paid for by these fields that mean nothing to you," she flashed, "doesn't seem to show. You are wanting in gratitude, and even your manners need mending. But not, my dear brother, by me. I wash my hands of you!"

"At last!" he crowed. "I'll really be of age then, won't I?"

She hesitated for only a second. Then her hand flashed out and struck her brother full on his left cheek. He seized her wrist in strong fingers and held it immobile—while she watched, in horror, five finger-marks grow into scarlet welts on his fair skin—then, deliberately, he tightened his grip cruelly. "For this," he whispered, his pale eyes glittering, "I could—"

Whatever he would have said, whatever threat he might have made, Carmody would never learn. At the same instant, both became aware that they were not alone. Waldo was standing only a few yards away, wearing an expression of well-bred curiosity. As though—the thought passed through her mind—it were a usual thing to find one's host and hostess engaged in physical combat. But there was an unusual gleam in his eyes, she noted with some uneasiness.

Surprisingly, Ralph was the first to recover, and he even managed a travesty of a smile. "A small enough ambition, perhaps, as you say, Carmody," he said with creditable steadiness. "But no smaller than to gloat over a bunch of sheep. Honestly, Carmody, you're disgusting. Look at you! That old spotted skirt, those clumps of boots!"

Carmody forced a self-conscious laugh, and the ugly moment slipped by. But she could not forget it so easily, and knew it would come to haunt sleepless hours of nights to come, when all things loom large in the dark shadows of futile regrets.

"Good morning, Carmody." Waldo spoke evenly, as though her brother, his maroon coat and pale yellow small-clothes, brilliant in the June sunshine, were invisible.

"You're early," she answered, and immediately regretted the foolish redundancy of her remark. Not my brilliant conversation, she remembered, still smarting under her brother's criticism. But what then?

"I have something to tell you, Carmody," he said, and then turned pointed attention to Ralph. "Ralph, aren't you weary of contemplating these estimable examples of livestock?"

Ralph was, in fact, looking restlessly about him. There was nothing as far as he could see but Oaklands. Behind them, nestled in the cup of the valley, lay the glowing brick of the manor house, the kitchen garden, the small herb garden, the broad expanse of lawns and the famous roses of Oaklands. Here in front of them stretched the long sheep pens, and, farther away and partly hidden by the June-budded shrubs, the houses of the more important Home Farm employees—Yarrow, and, farther down the farm road and halfway up the hill, Bray's little cottage, surrounded by Mrs. Bray's crowded garden of hollyhocks, the new name for the Huguenot import that they called "the Outlandish Rose."

The two men faced each other with measuring stares, and Carmody was taken by how different they were. Ralph, not quite as tall as Waldo, was broader in the shoulders but soft, she commented mentally, with already a suggestion of an inevitable paunch, like his father's. If Ralph continued to bolster his self-esteem by resorting to the wine cellar—and, surprised, she could smell now on the wind the sourness of alcohol, this early in the morning—he would soon be grossly fat.

Waldo, only slightly taller, appeared more so. Out of pride in himself, but also because his appearance was an item of his capital assets, he stood erect. His body was hard and muscular. His face was lean, his jaw thrusting forward, clearly a man who knew where he was going, and exactly what he must do to get there.

Expectedly, Ralph looked away first. He laughed slightly, saying, "I understand. The doves want to coo alone. Well, never let it be said, brother-in-law, that I put barriers of any kind in your way."

He sketched a brief salute, made a mocking bow in Carmody's direction, and with the suggestion of a sly grin, left them. He did not return to the house. She watched him go the other way, down the farm road. He was out of sight in moments. She followed him in her mind a little farther, past Yarrow's cottage, past the thatched roof of the Brays', before she turned back to steady her trembling hands on the top rail of the sheep pen.

"Troubled?" said Waldo, covering her hands with his hard brown one. "Ralph's not your responsibility any more. Can't you see that?"

"I see it," she answered honestly, "but I just can't feel it. Not yet."

Waldo watched her thoughtfully for a moment, and then drew her hand through his arm. "Come," he said. "You need a diversion. Let's get right away from these sheds. Doesn't their effluvia offend your delicate nostrils?"

Not too gently, he urged her along a path away from the farm buildings. She accompanied him without question. How good it was to have someone—Waldo—who would take responsibility for her! How lucky she was that Waldo had come along when he did. He saved her life, she thought dramatically. But then a small voice whispered: What if the unexpected visitor that day, the rider who had lost his way in the Dorset hills, had been some other man, and not Waldo Rivers? Could she have loved any presentable man who came to release her from her narrow, sheltered life at Oaklands? Any man? Or only Waldo?

Waldo's voice broke in upon her tortuous thoughts. "Looking sad, Carmody. Sorry? About us?"

Instantly a laugh sprang to her lips. "Are you?" she countered merrily, her eyes brimming with amusement. See, she told herself, you can throw off Oaklands and be gay—be whatever he wants you to be. And how she longed for his approval, for that appraising survey that— more rarely than she liked—told her she was fitting into his plans, reaching his standards.

"Not sorry at all," he assured her, his eyes sending unusual warmth to surround her like a cloak. "Shall we bypass the herb garden?"

He released her hand and let her precede him. She led the way past the herb garden. The sun shone hotly on the growing sage, the new plantings of marjoram, releasing their heady aromas into the air. A whiff of thyme reached her, and she turned to share her pleasure with Waldo. He had stopped, looking behind him on the path, as though to detect whether they had been followed. By Ralph? She thought she could still smell the sour liquory smell mingling with the fragrant herbs.

Sensing her question, he shook his head and caught her arm. Pulling her closer, he whispered into her hair, "Let's go on—farther."

Startled, she queried, "Is what you have to tell me that secret?" He nodded. She withdrew from his arms and turned off the path. The grass was higher here, and cool after the hard-packed dirt path they had been treading.

At last they reached the top of the rise. "We'll be alone here," she assured him. "No one can overhear us."

Truly it was an idyllic spot. A trio of old, bent apple trees, long past their fruitful prime, formed a rough triangle. The meadow grass reached to her knees, pulling at her skirt, and she was suddenly ashamed of the way she was dressed, the soiled skirt that Ralph had scorned.

"My clothes," she exclaimed, dismayed. "I didn't mean you to see me like this!"

"Why not?" he said easily, "since we are to be married in three days? Indeed, we are so close to the happy day— come, sit here beside me."

"A good place to talk," she agreed, hesitantly. The sour mash smell had come with them up the hill, and now she realized it had not been Ralph but Waldo who had been drinking this morning. Something to tell her, he had said—and he needed to fortify himself with false courage!

She sank down in the grass, not too close to him. Leaning back against the corky gnarled trunk of the sturdiest of the decrepit trees, she tucked her skirt around her feet, covering up her "clumps of boots."

From here the buildings were out of sight, and no human sound reached them. The grassy space was cool under the sparse leafage of what had once been an orchard. Dotted at random across the green fabric of the meadow lay the bright embroidery of thousands of wildflowers in bloom—meadowsweet, love-in-a-mist, the prodigal sprinkling of daisies.

"When I was a child, I came here often," she remarked, breaking the silence that had fallen between them.

She closed her eyes and leaned against the tree bole. She

savored the silence around her, murmurous with her own thoughts. How soon her life would be changed! She fought to keep regret from sweeping her.

On Thursday, she would become Lady Rivers. She forced her thoughts ahead, to stalk curiously around that altered state. What would it be like? She had thought often enough of her own house, the parties, the exciting people living glittering, fabled lives in a different, more sophisticated world, although with, sometimes, sinking self-doubts.

What Waldo himself might demand of her, she had refused to dwell upon. She had never refused to perform a duty, unpleasant or not, though her heart might quail.

Strange how her mind ran along that line now. Why? Perhaps her unease stemmed from Waldo's own restlessness—their minds, she believed, marched together surprisingly well.

Then she caught a whiff of sourness cutting unpleasantly across the gentle scent of meadowsweet.

Her eyes flew open. Waldo had inched closer while she had dreamed about the future. His right hand reached out to hold her chin, viselike—so she was forced to look straight into his eyes.

A burning glow turned his cool gray eyes into smoldering red pebbles, and, feeling the warm sour breath on her cheek, she knew he was actually quite drunk.

This, oddly, shocked her more than his hand, releasing her chin and dropping to move heavily over her thin workaday blouse, only exploring at first, then steadily kneading her breast. The tree at her back imprisoned her.

She gasped. "Waldo!" Her heart plunged wildly like a frightened colt under his searching hand, and she knew by the blind expression in his hot eyes that he did not even hear her. He stopped her outcry with a pitiless bruising kiss, his wet mouth stifling her. She could not breathe.

She struggled to push him away, but her writhing only increased his frenzy. His weight bore her to the ground, and he fell off balance on her. The gnarled tree trunk scored her back cruelly. The unexpected pain was real and sharp in a nightmare of fright and madness, and in rising panic she fought back.

She gathered her pitifully small strength blindly. He forced his knee between her legs, and, for the moment, he was off balance. With one desperate thrust she threw herself to one side, away from him.

Scrambling to her feet, Carmody crouched, facing him like a cornered wild thing. He leaned heavily on his elbow, drawing great shuddering breaths, groping for her with clawed fingers.

She watched him warily, her knees trembling too much to attempt escape in flight.

"You don't know," he groaned, finally, "how your eyes invite me. How desirable—"

"*What?*"

She was too aware of her disheveled state to believe she heard him rightly. The rough apple bark had tugged her hair loose so that it hung in heavy chestnut curls on her shoulders. Her blouse was wrenched off one shoulder and torn open to her waist. Desirable? She looked like a hag! But fear, for the first time she could remember, dried her tongue.

"You are so beautiful," he accused her, as though, if he could summon logic to his aid, she would understand. "Those slanting silver eyes—they drive a man mad."

Strength crept back to her, and a touch of hope. Waldo's madness was momentary, and she had escaped the consequences for the time being. She stood up, secretly testing the power in her legs, and—prudently keeping out of arm's reach—said, "Only three days, Waldo? And you couldn't wait?" Then, with returning strength, and Ralph's venom still working in her, she was compelled to taunt him. "Would you have married me then, if you had shamed me now?"

A strange expression crept into his eyes. She turned in sudden alarm and fled down the hillside, through the flower-dotted grass, to the comparative safety of the herb garden. She stopped briefly to fold the torn edges of her blouse to cover her exposed breasts and to tend to her hair, which lay hotly heavy on her neck, and cascaded over her shoulders. She could not be seen like this before her servants.

With swift, practiced hands, she lifted the weight of her hair and piled it atop her head, securing it with the two pins she found still lodged among her curls. The homely, accustomed task soothed her until she stopped gasping for breath, and she thought perhaps her face had lost some of its flaming color.

She longed to linger where she was, simply resting, but a slight sound, as though a shoe dislodged a pebble, startled her like a fawn into self-preserving escape. This time she did not stop until she had rushed headlong up the stairway, and gained the sanctuary of her bedroom. For the first time she could remember, her shaking fingers shot the bolt home, and only then did she feel safe—and private.

She lay down as she was on her bed, staring at the white muslin lining of the tester for a long time without seeing it. Her mind's eye saw only—in ever-increasing detail—the lean face of her dear Waldo, swollen with avid desire. The blind look in his eyes, turned inward toward his own throbbing needs. The astonishing, fearful change in the man she thought she loved for his strong self-control and disciplined restraint.

She lay inert, bruised in body and in her self-core, for a timeless space. At length her thoughts, scurrying like frightened mice in the wainscoting, twisted into a new channel.

How dared Waldo smirch her? she thought, torrid with resentful indignation. But, another part of her said, Isn't it your fault? He told you so. And there was something further, lurking at the fringy limit of her mind. She would not look at that chimera, creeping just out of mind's reach.

She leaped from the bed and rang the bell for Mercy, and hot water, and soap. Plenty of soap, she told her startled maid.

While she waited, she stood before the mirror, trying to see herself as Waldo must. The vibrant chestnut hair—she released it from the pins and let it fall down, framing her face. Clear pale skin, with the golden touch of the sun bringing it to life.

Her eyes, almond-shaped, set at an intriguing slant over high cheekbones, gave her an exotic, almost oriental look. And the color, a gray that could change with her moods into a strange hue like silver, veiled by long, dark lashes.

She studied her face for a long time in the glass. Finally, shyly, greatly daring, she lowered her heavy lashes, and turned her head to peer sidelong at her reflection. Thus, to the best of her recollection, she had looked at Waldo. Then, feeling shamed, abandoned, she turned sharply away, her cheeks hot with remembered humiliation, and new shame.

Mercy came then, struggling with copper tub, pitchers of steaming water, lavender scented soap. Dropping her soiled garments to the floor, Carmody lowered herself into the scalding bath water.

"Take those clothes away and burn them," Carmody told Mercy.

"Burn them, Miss Carmody?" the maid echoed.

"Just do as I say. At once. Now!"

Offended, Mercy marched stiffly from the room, bearing away the tangible evidence of Waldo's abortive storming of Carmody's body.

Carmody scrubbed herself relentlessly, plying her sponge savagely, until her entire body glowed rosy and trembling.

And yet she was not satisfied. She could not reach the monster in her mind, creeping just out of sight, but it now came closer, near enough for her to look squarely at it.

And identify it.

And, somehow, knowing the monster for what it was seemed worst of all.

A new stirring, of springs moving deep inside her, a well of emotion she had never even dreamed of, had been uncovered. When Waldo had laid impertinent hands on her, she had felt a moving, rising, betraying response. Her own body—if she did not carefully govern it—might well turn traitor!

3

LIFE, as a rule, flows on in well-worn channels for count-less days, and then in an hour, without warning, it changes course, rushing into new channels, creaming over hidden rocks, like a Dorset brook gathering itself for a last plunge over the rim of the cliff into the sea. Carmody was not, in the ordinary way, given to fancy, but she was not accustomed, either, to unsettling, disturbing, even outrageous events to mark her days.

That day, she thought ruefully, she would long remember. The scarlet marks of her palm on her brother's cheek, the deliciously terrifying episode with Waldo—

She forced herself to the desk in her small primrose-colored sitting room. There was much to do before Thursday, and she soon immersed herself in the detailed book-keeping of the estate, keeping at her work until Pearson brought her a dish of tea and some biscuits. She was surprised to find she had worked through lunch, and she was ravenous. The butler lingered, opening the curtains, setting the casements ajar to let in the meadow-sweet scent of sun-warmed grass. And with the grassy fragrance came sharp memory of Waldo's mouth invading hers—she closed her eyes against the memory.

Finally she realized that the butler had something to say. She knew she would have to listen eventually, so with good grace she succumbed.

"Pearson."

"Miss Carmody?"

"Stop fiddling with the windows."

"I'm sorry, miss."

"What is it?"

"I don't wish to disturb you." He straightened his old shoulders with an arthritic effort.

"The basic point, please, Pearson."

It was an old game with them. She thought he enjoyed the skirmishing as much as she did, the plucking off of the husks one by one until they reached the sweet kernel of his concern. But she had, today, lost her taste for the sport. And so, it appeared, had he.

"Word has come from Squire Masters. He and Mistress Masters will not be able to come to the young master's dinner party."

"But they said they were coming!"

"Yes, Miss Carmody. But this note came not an hour since."

She sighed hugely. Too bad. She liked Mistress Masters, and respected the bluff, outspoken Squire. She had looked forward to seeing them both.

"I hope they are not ill. Well, Pearson, we'll have to do without—" She stopped short at the sight of his grave old face. "There's more?"

He proffered a salver on which lay scattered at least half a dozen envelopes. She opened one, and another.

"The vicar regrets. . . . Miss Paine regrets. . . . Sir Philip and Lady Crawdon regret. . . . Pearson, nobody's coming!"

Pearson exhibited no surprise. A thought flashed past— by what alchemy did he know what the envelopes contained?

As if reading her mind, he said simply, "The messengers were quite friendly, Miss Carmody."

She hardly heard him. The extent of the catastrophe was slowly creeping into her mind—all her invited guests, with remarkable unanimity, had suddenly, at the last moment, cancelled their dinner acceptances. *All* of them!

But why? All her family's friends from the surrounding areas, all those who had come in years past to revel at Oaklands, in her father's day, in the time of her grandfather and even of *his* father—all were turning away from the Petries. So it seemed.

"Why? Pearson, what can have caused this—this wholesale rebuff?" He would not meet her indignant eyes. When he did not answer, she probed, "What did the friendly messengers tell you?"

"Nothing." But the habit of trusting her was too strong for him, and he capitulated. "All lies and I told them so. Mr. Ralph is foolish maybe, but I've known him all his life and I can't believe it." His old voice took on a pathetically gallant vigor, as he added, "I won't believe it, Miss Carmody. Not of a Petrie. Not if he was to tell me himself!"

Suddenly, she could not press the old man further. He was too close to tears. Vague fear clutched her with chilling hands. Ralph was indeed foolish, she knew well enough. He must have outdone himself this time. Her thoughts ran speculatively over the possibilities. Riding rough-shod over the neighbors' grain fields? Frightening the ewes so they lost their lambs? Burning the Squire's hay ricks again? She discarded them one after another.

None of these could account for the total snubbing that still lay in white envelopes on the pewter tray. It was something else—something formidable this time, no longer childish.

Carmody sighed. She must find out what Ralph had done, and then set it aright. If she could. She suspected darkly that some day he might do something so outrageous that she could never straighten it out. Please God she would be far away by that time—she and Waldo.

"Never mind, Pearson," she comforted him gently. "I'll ride over to Squire's myself, and get to the bottom of it."

Again she sifted through the notes on the salver. The Squire and his lady had been the first to accept Carmody's invitation, and Mistress Masters herself had added a cordial word at the bottom of the note. Now—Carmody read today's note again. Stiff, formal. Almost—she thought, stunned—almost legal in its coldness. Her impression was of someone hastily ridding himself of a guilty association.

She was absent in her thoughts so long that Pearson cleared his throat twice before she looked at him with eyes that saw. "This is too bad, Pearson," she said with creditable calm. "Where does this leave us?"

With the only flash of humor she had ever known in him, Pearson croaked, "With five hundredweight of food prepared, Miss Carmody, and hysterics expected in the cook."

She said dryly, "No doubt you're right. I'll inform cook myself."

Relief spread instantaneously over Pearson. Even though, or perhaps especially because, the cook was Pearson's wife, Carmody could understand his reluctance to bring such unwelcome news to the kitchen where maids had been toiling for days in preparation for the gala.

"According to my reckoning, Pearson, there is no one still coming. No guests at all. Is that correct?"

Pearson coughed automatically. "Except for Sir Waldo."

Except for Sir Waldo—suppose Waldo was not coming back? Suppose she had alienated him, raked his self-esteem so badly he could not face her again? Hurriedly she turned away from the scandal she glimpsed if Waldo did not return to marry her.

"And, of course, Mr. Ashley."

Peregrine Ashley! She had forgotten him. Ralph's dear friend—and, she thought darkly, the worst influence on her brother that she knew.

"We must send word to him at once—" The expression on her butler's face stopped her.

"He has already returned, Miss Carmody. He arrived shortly after noon. He is just now upstairs in his usual room."

But Pearson was, for once, wrong. Perry Ashley was standing on the second step from the bottom of the great oaken stairway which swept up to the bedroom floor. With an instinct honed by long practice, this particular position allowed him the appearance—if one were to come upon him unaware—of just that moment arriving on the scene. Whereas, as happened this time, he had stood there long enough to hear the last part of Carmody's conversation with Pearson, and surmise, accurately enough, the part he did not hear.

Ashley adjusted his ruffled shirt front, apparently absorbed—as befitted a man whose entire life, so it appeared, was devoted to frippery—in the details of his linen. But his acute hearing was stretched in taut concentration toward Carmody's sitting room, whose open door was just out of sight.

"Well, Pearson, I suppose I may as well get it behind me. I'll go to the kitchen at once." She came out into the hall, and caught sight of the elegant creature just setting foot on the last step. "Mr. Ashley! I am sorry I was not here to welcome you to Oaklands. I know Ralph's greeting was warm enough for all."

If there were barbs in her speech, Peregrine did not take obvious note of them. "I thank you, Miss Petrie, for the warmth of your hospitality. How marvelous it is to find something in this world that remains the same, is it not?" His eyes glittered momentarily before he added, "Now my tailor has crossed the border into lunacy, I fear. Just look at this cuff."

As he expected, Carmody dismissed his frivolous concern with a brief, absent word of sympathy, her mind already running ahead to the dreaded scene with cook.

Carmody found the Squire and his lady in their comfortable, dog-filled drawing room. She paused in the doorway for a moment, noting the startled expressions on their faces. Clearly they had not expected such a prompt response to their note. She was gratified—perhaps she could surprise them into dropping their guard.

"Aren't you going to ask me in?" she said into the paralyzed silence. Then she saw they were not alone. Harriet Paine was in a chair next to the hearth, holding a teacup in her hand, frozen in the act of raising it to her lips.

Then Mistress Masters stirred, lifting her billowy bulk out of her chair. "Of course, Carmody, my dear, come in. You just startled us out of our wits, that's all. We had no idea you had arrived. Come, sit down here. Dogs, get off this chair. Scott! Here you are, Carmody—I'll just brush off the dog hairs, that foolish Lady *will* sit in the best chair. . . ."

"Amy, you're babbling," said Squire Masters. His voice rumbled like low thunder. "Sit down, Carmody. I should have known you'd come to ask a question or two."

Gingerly, Carmody sat on the edge of the just-vacated chair, ignoring Lady, who sat on the floor only inches away, reproachful eyes watching her.

"I hardly know what questions to ask," Carmody said presently. "The only one I can think of is—*why?*" She could not ask the question that would bare her dread of whatever Ralph had done.

"Why?" rumbled the Squire. "Surely that is not the point. You already know why."

"On the contrary," said Carmody, "I can think of no reason why you, and the others I thought were our friends, have suddenly decided to wash your hands of us, as though we had acquired some loathsome disease."

Harriet spoke from the corner. "Treason is certainly an odious taint."

Carmody felt the blood drain from her face. Her fear, unacknowledged openly until now, rocked in her stomach, and she clenched her teeth so as not to faint. She was acutely aware of the little things—how Mistress Masters kept her eyes bent upon her embroidery, but she hadn't taken a stitch in five minutes. Squire Masters grunted, angry at Harriet's bald interruption. He himself, no doubt, would have gentled his words.

"Treason!" Carmody's lips formed the word, but she had made no sound.

"Here, drink this."

Mistress Masters was holding a small glass of brandy to Carmody's lips, and a drop of two slid down her throat. She coughed, sipped, and felt better.

"Harriet shouldn't have been blunt about it," said Mistress Masters, throwing a baleful glance at the woman. "It was a nasty shock."

The Squire waited until the color came back into Carmody's cheeks. "Well, now," he said, "I believe you *don't* know anything about this." Outrageously turning his coat, he said, "*I* said all the time you wouldn't be a party to it."

Ignoring an indignant glance from his wife, he said, "It seems young Ralph's got himself into another scrape. Hard to believe he could keep it a secret from you, but there it is. You say so, and I believe you. But you see, the word is all over Dorset that Ralph is raising money for the Duke's invasion. Surely you've heard something about the invasion?"

She summoned up recollection, and finally nodded. "Waldo mentioned it. He seemed to think it was dangerous even to ride out."

"The young fool Monmouth seems to think that the entire West Country is going to rise up and follow him to Whitehall!" exclaimed the Squire, irritation rising.

"You don't mean he's going to invade here?"

"So they say," muttered the Squire. "But no matter what he thinks, nobody is going to join his army. We've had enough civil war in England for our time. Not an estate in this country but has scars to show of the Civil Wars, either Cromwell's destruction, or Cavalier damage. Either way, it doesn't much matter to a man which side kills him, or which side burns his barns."

"Now, Tom," warned his wife, "don't get too excited. Remember what the doctor said."

The doctor was consigned to the nether regions with a word.

"But surely a Catholic king is not what the people fought for?" queried Carmody. She must learn the extent of the mess Ralph had gotten himself into. For she had no doubt that he had been atrociously foolish, even culpably to blame. But a traitor? Never!

"But what matters it?" the Squire countered. "When he dies the throne goes to his daughter Mary, a Protestant princess in the Netherlands. And we'll have no more talk of a Catholic monarch then."

"Of course, you're right, dear," said Amy Masters.

"Besides, James is a cruel man," Masters resumed presently. "His vicious oppression when he was High Commissioner of Scotland shows which way the wind will blow when he deals with men he calls usurpers and worse. I myself wish to have no part of it. It may already be too late. I heard Ralph is already trying to sell your new sheep. But Carmody, I advise you to get him out of this mess. For there will be trouble for all concerned in this enterprise. I fear that anyone who gives so much as a crust of bread to the King's enemies will think better of it before they are through."

Wise counsel, she knew with a part of her mind. And counsel to be followed, except for the one fact. The fact that Ralph was not, could not be, engaged in treason—in any shape or form.

"Not even a crust of bread," she said, and did not know she had spoken aloud until she was warned by the Squire's lifted eyebrow. "I'm sorry," she said, anger growing. "It is just that I know Ralph is not involved in this. He couldn't be. And I'd like to know where such rumors start."

The Squire moved heavily in his chair. He had tried, his attitude said, and found his warnings rebuffed. And since his first duty was to himself and his family, he wished this girl who meant nothing but trouble to him would leave. And he hoped devoutly that no one had seen her come.

Carmody stood, ready to leave. She was dreadfully hurt by what she considered rank injustice. "I thought you were my friends," she said with scornful dignity. "And yet you believe the first ugly rumor that blows across your path. Well, I will not pollute your pure drawing room with my presence any longer. And I do not take it well that you believe rumors rather than Ralph."

Sturdily, the Squire insisted, "Did Ralph himself deny that he was involved?"

"Of course not! How could he? We knew nothing of this—this vicious slander that has clouded our name. There was nothing we knew to deny!"

Mistress Masters set aside her embroidery and rose. "My dear, we are all deeply troubled by this. And if it turns out to be as false as you say, then we will apologize. But in the meantime—"

"You know Ralph well," Carmody cried out in distress. "You don't really believe my brother would turn traitor to his King, do you?"

The silence that filled the room was far more eloquent than any words could have been. Carmody looked first at the Squire, who looked away, his thin lips set in a tight, grim line, then to Mistress Masters, her eyes deep pools of kindness and compassion, and finally to Harriet Paine, who seemed to be gloating over a secret pleasure. Carmody had a sudden dismaying glimpse of how much Harriet must dislike her. But nowhere in the three faces, with such varied emotions playing over them, did she see the slightest trust in Ralph's integrity.

How she had failed her brother! She was to blame, she thought, as much as anyone. She could have done something more to keep him on the right path—but she could not imagine now what more she could have done.

She moved toward the door, and Amy Masters followed her. Standing irresolute on the front steps, Carmody was suddenly loath to go. All her life she had met with nothing but kindness from Mistress Masters, and so it was now.

"I don't want to part with you like this, Carmody," said her friend. "Believe me, if your brother is involved in something like this, he was tricked into it. I don't believe he would instigate something like—what we hear."

"No," Carmody answered honestly. "He isn't intelligent enough, nor capable of a sustained effort in anything. But it's my fault, you know it is."

"I don't see that at all," objected the older woman. "You are unconventional, of course, riding about the countryside without even a groom. Making your own marriage contracts. But that was your father's fault. He left you with an intolerable burden, and it's a wonder to me you didn't sink under it. But, my dear—don't take the blame for Ralph. He is—what he is. You did not make him so."

Swiftly she kissed Carmody's cheek in farewell. They both knew that their ways would not cross again.

Carmody had returned to Oaklands before she was able to sort out all the appalling implications of the news she had heard. A vicious, terrible rumor—Ralph a traitor.

But common sense soon told her that the rumors must be more than idle tavern gossip. They were clearly substantial enough to make the gentry of Dorset turn their collective backs upon the Petries. No matter how hotly she had defended Ralph just now, in her own heart she knew that there was a heavy burden on Ralph's conscience. And the worst thing of all was that she herself could almost believe Ralph was capable of—well, anything.

She cantered into the stableyard. She knew she must look grim and forbidding by the way Trotter hurried out to take Amber's reins in silence, avoiding meeting her eyes. How fast the infection spreads! she thought. She could not be sure that Trotter had heard the ugly rumor, but certainly he could tell that something was gravely amiss.

"Where is my brother?" she asked him, her voice steely with control.

"Sorry, Miss Carmody," said Trotter promptly. "I haven't seen him just lately."

She was suddenly positive that he lied. She remembered now seeing a face at the loft doorway as she came into the yard—saw it for a fleeting instant before the head bobbed down out of sight. She had been too far away to recognize the face—but now she was convinced it was Ralph, hiding from her.

A bad sign. She turned abruptly and went to the house. Just as well, she thought, I need to calm down before I tackle Ralph on this. She had known a confrontation was inevitable, ever since the Squire had said, "Has he denied it?"

In all fairness, she must give Ralph the opportunity to tell her the truth. And if she were angry, that anger would kindle his own and she would have nothing but an ugly scene on her hands.

She passed through the entrance hall where Pearson and the grooms were already busy taking extra chairs back to the rooms on the third floor, used now only for storage. She nodded, approving the prompt removal of all indications that there was to have been a party.

She hoped that, when she finally did have a chance to talk to Ralph, he would not be too drunk to listen. He was drinking these days as though he meant to empty the wine cellars by the end of the month. As she reached her room, Mercy appeared with the tea tray. Carmody was surprised to find it only teatime. This was without question the longest day in the history of the world. Someone, like Joshua son of Nun, must have commanded the sun to stand still. She removed her riding habit, and tossed it over a chair for Mercy to put away. She washed her face and arms in cool water, feeling the hot throbbing of fury in her temples begin to subside.

Her tea was still hot. She slipped on a dressing sacque from her wedding clothes, a confection of pink taffeta over muslin, and took her cup to the open window. She must frame the arguments she would use to Ralph. The question was now far more serious than Ralph's boredom with the estate. Ralph could not be a traitor, she told herself. I must start with that fact. And then she must learn if it was true, as the Squire had informed her, that her, brother was selling the sheep! She began to plan her attack.

She must convince Ralph that selling the sheep would cripple the estate. The hills, with their fast water runoff, their openness to wind, were less productive of crops like clover, sainfoin, flax, woad, and madder. She had tried all of them, but not until the Dorset sheep had been driven in and loosed upon the high pastures did Oaklands begin to enjoy a healthy prosperity. And Ralph had spent much of the income heedlessly at school.

She knew, of course, that she was skirting the main issue—treason. She would not contemplate the possibility. Ralph would deny it, and that was that. But the sale of the sheep was an immediate concern, and one that must be dealt with straightaway.

It's a good thing Ralph wasn't a gambler, she thought wryly. We wouldn't have anything left by now. Absently, her gaze followed a well-worn ritual—to the right toward the great oaks and the drive, and, eventually, down the folding hills to Lyme Bay. Straight ahead toward the south. The warmest airs in winter came from this direction, warmed by the low-lying December sun.

And to the left, out of sight, of course, the line of

stables, barns, and the newer sheep pens, the sandy road passing them to rise, curving gently to follow the easier grades, till it met the crossroads near the village.

Still roaming her lands in her mind, she realized she had been hearing voices somewhere below her. Not intending to eavesdrop, she was caught before she could draw away. The voice that reached her first was lightly masculine, and she recognized it at once. Perry Ashley.

"Come now, Ralph, you can't be quite that innocent. You knew that you were gambling with *men*, didn't you? And did you really believe that it would all go away? Like a bad dream?"

Carmody had the impression that the discussion had been started elsewhere—perhaps the barn loft—and had only now reached a point which was clearly serious. She could not define the exact timbre of Perry Ashley's voice, but instinctively she shrank away from it, hoping the flowered curtains at the window would shield her. Without knowing how she knew, she was convinced that it could be dangerous to overhear this conversation. Yet, rooted by curiosity, she could not move.

She clutched her robe to her throat in a futile attempt to keep from shivering. Perry's voice rose again. "Well, it won't. And think of the advantages. All the promises you believed—"

Only a few more sentences were spoken before the two below the window moved away, out of earshot. But they were more frightening yet.

Perry's voice, full of chilling menace, carried well. "Don't try to weasel out of this, Ralph. You're tied up tight as can be. It wouldn't be healthy to change your mind."

If Ralph said anything in response, Carmody didn't hear it. She was shocked by the totally new facet to Peregrine Ashley's character. She would not have believed his affected drawl could change into an incisive steely knife, cutting so sharply that the wound would not bleed, not until later. Perry was, unexpectedly, a formidable force.

How could she have been so mistaken in him? But at least her judgment was sure when it came to Ralph. The question was clearly about money, and there was no question of—*the other*.

In happy relief she hurried to dress. She must never let Ralph know she had almost—but not quite—been persuaded by the Squire. Almost, but not quite, lost her trust in her brother.

She had scarcely settled pale green muslin squarely on her slim hips, straightening the collar where it rode on her shoulders, reaching for the belt, when she heard a strange noise in the hall. A heavy, thumping noise, just beyond her bedroom door. Holding up her full skirt with one hand, she ran to open the door.

Ralph stood outside. She screamed lightly, her fingers clamping over her mouth to silence the cry that rose in her throat at the sight of him. He looked at her dumbly. She thought at first he was dead drunk. But the dull opaqueness in his pale blue eyes was new, and the awful gray pallor of his unhealthy skin told her he was cold sober.

"My God, Ralph!" she heard herself say, before she reached out to pull him into her room. She glanced briefly down the empty hall. Where was Perry? She half expected to see him dogging Ralph's stumbling leaden footsteps.

She turned back into her room. Ralph was standing exactly where her forceful push had propelled him. He had not taken a step from that spot, nor, she considered after glancing at the wooden figure, would he be likely to for a measurable space of time.

She paused, then turned back to bar the door against untimely interruptions. "We don't need Mercy bursting in on us," she managed to say with laudable steadiness. Ralph had brought with him an aura of desperate fear. Carmody's heart thudded unevenly somewhere near her constricted throat.

"Carmody?" he croaked in a strangled, unrecognizable voice. "Save me."

At once he was five years old again and she, rising eight, had found him atop a shed with the only way of getting down from his precarious perch barred by a billy goat of fierce habits. Carmody had beguiled the goat away that day, and the small boy had scrambled to safety.

"Tell me," she said simply, breathing a silent prayer of gratitude that he had turned to her at last. Flitting through her agitated thoughts was the hope that he would be willing to listen to her, to heed her plea on behalf of Oaklands. Rapt in her own relief, she hardly heard what he was saying.

"Carmody, I've given away Oaklands—to Monmouth."

"No, Ralph, nothing can be as bad as you think—" Her voice trailed away into silence. Between them there was only a empty space, filled with nothing but the appalling enormity of his flat statement.

"You've *what*?" Even as her horrified exclamation shot out of her like a bullet, she knew that he spoke truth. This was the basis for the ugly rumor. The reason for Squire's revulsion. And Peregrine's cool assurance as he spoke, unaware of her presence, under her window.

With a calmness she didn't feel, Carmody said, "Best tell me. How could you do such a thing? It's not like you."

Had he become so enamored of the glory of great armies marching, the honors to be won in some battle as neat and bloodless as a tapestry of Crusader and Saracen?

"You don't know what is *like me*. Where did you think all the money went? I've gambled ever since I went away to school. I didn't want to go there anyway. I knew I wouldn't fit in. But you made me, Carmody." He lifted his eyes to her stony face. Blaming his folly on her was easy. He had done this many times before, and always it had proven beneficial to him. She seemed unmoved this time, and he drew some small courage from the fact. Perhaps it would turn out to be not so disastrous as he dreaded. Even mention of his gambling had passed without the upbraiding he had expected.

There was a telltale throbbing in the bluish vein at his sister's right temple, the only sign of her unbearably chaotic thoughts, but Ralph did not notice. He went on with growing confidence. Maybe it would be all right, after all, and once again—although he did not view it quite that precisely—he might escape the consequences of his folly.

"But I fell in with a splendid group," he explained boyishly, as though if he told her everything, she would certainly applaud. "They liked me, and I tell you, Carmody, we had great times." His eyes sought hers for the approval he expected that she would give him—she always had. Carmody's stomach writhed. "But this last year, somehow, it all changed. It wasn't so much fun. Then somebody told me about a game going on in town."

At least his woodenness had vanished, Carmody thought with brief irritation, although his mood, his unbelievably childish narration, nailed down her certainty that her brother was woefully miscast as the heir to a substantial estate.

What was she to do? She could not continue as the guiding force behind the sinews and muscle of Oaklands. It was Ralph's inheritance, not hers. And, of course, he exaggerated when he said he had given it away.

Her own destiny lay far afield—with Waldo. Remembering him, Carmody's skin kindled, as though it lived separately from her self, glowing like dry tinder touched into flame by a burning glass. Only the faintest glow, so far. Waldo's touch was the spark. The fire was still hidden, but—it was there, smoldering, ready to burst into raging fire. Her senses had—she thought uneasily—taken the bit in their teeth.

She realized with a start that Ralph was still confessing, baring his soul to her, who had no power of absolution for him. She felt she had been absent a long time in her thoughts, but he had moved forward only inches in his toilsome tale.

The game going on in town, as it developed—slowly, haltingly, with Ralph going off tangentially in his narrative like a retriever loping the uplands in search of a mitigating circumstance to lay at her feet—the game was for higher stakes than he had expected, than he really could afford.

"But at first, don't you see, I won. I really won a great deal," he told her virtuously. "I see now that it was a trap. Oh, I've learned a lot, Carmody. I'll never make that mistake again."

But there will be others just as bad, she prophesied dismally, in silence.

"Then," Ralph went on morosely, "my luck started to change. I began losing, and I lost everything I'd won. Oh, they let me win once in a while, small amounts, just to keep me coming. But I lost more than I won."

Carmody bent her mind to what her brother was saying. She longed simply to run out of the room, leaving him to his conscience, which was obviously becoming mollified by his confession. But he had come to her for help, and she could not deny him.

"How much did you lose, Ralph?"

The strangled note in her vocie at last alerted him. He glanced up quickly, anxiously. "You're angry, Carmody." He stated the obvious fact. "I don't blame you."

"How much did you lose?" she insisted.

The answer, when it came, was direct—and worse than she could have possibly guessed.

"Everything."

"Everything? To Monmouth?"

He nodded. She regarded him for a long time in stony silence. She did not trust herself to say the slightest word to him, for fear the formidable grip she held on her angry tongue would slip and, once loosed, would release a flood which would sweep them both away into disaster. Apparently Ralph had now unburdened himself of all that his small soul struggled under. The yoke bruised her shoulders.

"The land itself, Ralph? You had no right to gamble that away."

"Well, of course, I know that," Ralph said, with humble virtue. "I just meant everything else."

Disaster whirled around her, like logs floating in a stream.

"Such as?" When he did not answer, she began again, carefully. "The sheep? The harvest? The flax?" He nodded to each. Remorselessly, she continued, "The horses? The contents of the wine cellar?"

That was why he was drinking so heavily, she thought

with sour humor. He wanted to dispose of as much of the mortgaged assets as he could before they were removed.

He turned impatiently to her and thrust out his hands in an awkward gesture of supplication. "Don't make it worse for me, Carmody. I told you how it was. Everything. Even the tenants' furniture. Our furniture. Even—your dowry, Carmody."

With rare malice, she said nothing. Time enough for him to find out that Mr. Hastings had already paid over her dowry to Waldo. A fortunate decision she had made there, she reflected briefly—born of her assessment of her brother's moral fiber. She was right—he was indeed capable of refusing to honor his obligations.

"My dowry," she said coldly. "And I suppose," she added with purposeful exaggeration, "the clothes on my back?"

Appallingly, he nodded. "But don't think too harshly of me," he said with baseless cheerfulness. "I don't think they'll collect."

"Why not?" Her question came like a shot. "Don't try to fool me, Ralph. I heard what that nullity Ashley said. He didn't sound forgiving to me."

"Oh."

The monosyllable was short, but it was as eloquent as a sermon. Ralph had thought, even now, even in the abyss of his shame, that he could cozen Carmody. If she had not overheard that vicious note in Ashley's voice, Ralph would not have told her everything. He would still have kept a shred of covering dragged over the last bare degradation.

"When are they coming for it?" she intoned. "When will the bailiffs come to drag away everything our family has amassed over the generations? When will they take our mother's bed? Our father's desk, his books? Will they let us live on in this house bare to the walls? Perhaps I can smuggle a ragged shift out of the house to cover me as I stand begging in the roads of Dorset!" She had never felt such a towering passion. Sheer rage dropped a red veil over Ralph's face, blinding her. The walls behind him were shot through with red, the color of blood, and she blinked away the red film in her eyes.

"*When, Ralph?*"

Unconsciously she took a step toward him, and he shrank back. Suddenly he was sidling along the back of the settee, and she twitched her fingers, itching for physical contact, to claw the scant beard from his fuzzy chin, to scrape his skin raw until that helpless, charming, boyish *idiocy* no longer mocked her.

She moved after him, stepping with feline suppleness, stalking him as though she were a lioness, terrible in her fury.

"*When?*"

"It's for the Duke, Carmody. We'll get it all back." He dropped the words like sops before her, hoping to divert her merciless approach. He was honestly afraid of her.

"*When?*"

"When he wins the throne."

"What did they promise you?"

He stared, his pale eyes darting into the corners of the room, anywhere away from his sister's merciless eyes. "Wh-what makes you think—"

"Oh, Ralph, don't be so stupid. You've done nothing the past week but drop crass hints about the great days coming! I can't believe that seeing Oaklands bare to the walls and the fields fallowed would come under the heading of glory, even to you!"

He edged away. He mumbled, "They said I had the makings of a shrewd politician. *You* never gave me credit for anything."

"A place on the Privy Council, perhaps?" she jibed. He did not answer. With increasing suspicion, she regarded the head hanging guiltily, the white soft hands writhing restlessly—and guessed rightly that she had hit the mark. Ralph a Privy Councilor, in Monmouth's government? He could not even hold onto his own patrimony! It was laughable, in a lunatic way.

"So when you owed them so much you couldn't pay, they promised you great things, an easy way out, if you signed certain notes. Is that it?"

He nodded.

"You *stupid—traitor!*"

Too late, she saw that he had edged too near the door for her to stop him. With a spasmodic jerk, he lifted the latch and opened the door. Still in the doorway, but with escape assured, he managed one last inspired offering.

"The notes I signed—they're made out to the Duke of Monmouth. And if he's lost at sea on his way to England—"

He let the sentence hang in the air, like a fluttering pennant to signal her attention. He slammed the door shut behind him. The sound coincided with the crash of a half-full pitcher against the inside of the door. Carmody was a second too late with her shot.

She sank into a chair and covered her face with shaking hands. It was a long time before her angry shuddering ceased to rack her body. A long time before she realized, with a bitter taste in her mouth, that the happy days were gone, and nothing but acrid *stupid* misery lay before her.

Somewhere inside her mind, optimism, cruelly battered to the ground, seized upon one phrase that might somehow help. *If the Duke is lost at sea—*

The English Channel is both a great rampart, standing boldly between England and the jealous continent, and a broad highway leading into the heart of the island as well. A highway traveled, among others, by Angles and Saxons, Romans, William the Conqueror from Normandy, and Queen Isabella and her dark star Mortimer.

The wind decided which face the Channel wore—the west wind, born somewhere in the blue immensity of the Atlantic, roaring in from the Western Approaches and beyond, kept sails filled to make easting, and England needed no greater fortification.

But the east wind! The east wind was a traitor, opening up harbors from Dover to Mounts Bay, inviting foreign hulls to cross, if it suited their purpose, if they had courage high enough, if they dared risk the treacherous sea.

For the Channel could smile one moment, and then a cloud, no bigger perhaps than a man's hand, could turn within an hour into a raging gale from the west.

So Medina-Sidonia had learned, a century before,

watching his proud, gilded Armada turn into an unparalleled collection of matchsticks almost before his sick old eyes.

But so far, in early June, 1685, there were only light but steady breezes from the northeast, romping down the Channel and bearing before them three small ships built in the round Dutch fashion, seaworthy in storms, but with a regrettable tendency to wallow in the trough.

The uneasy movement of the foremost ship seemed to have no effect upon the man standing in the bow. He was not much more than middle height, but his figure was neat and powerful, and he moved with a certain dancing grace. Black bars of eyebrows over lively eyes. Full sensual lips.

At the moment, he stood with both hands on the bow rail of the *Helderenburgh*, peering ahead of the ship into the hazy distance. He knew this section of the Channel, the narrows that washed the shore of his beloved England. No matter how often his father banished him to Amsterdam—the jumbled city of tight little houses where he was born—the bastard James Scott, Duke of Monmouth, longed with an avid aching in his soul for the green hills, the gentle land of England.

And now he was on his way home—the Netherlands would never be home to him—for what was the last time. This time, there would be no indulgent father to chuckle in his private closet over his first-born's wildness, to crow with delight over his victories in foot-races and wrestling matches. A spasm of grief crossed the handsome Stuart face, so much like his father's.

His dead father. Charles Stuart, second of that name, had suffered a stroke four months before, and succumbed in a decent Christian fashion in two days. Rumor had insisted that not only was his father's death Christian—it was also a "closet Catholic" death. It was said that a priest, summoned up the back stairs, had received Charles into the Catholic faith moments before he died.

But—who really knew? The only witness was God, though mere men were the creatures who whispered, who sent rumors flying from St. Michael's Bay to the mouth of the Tyne. His younger brother James, now the king, and second of *that* name, was out and out leaning toward the Catholic faith, and did not bother to hide his convictions. In a Protestant country, a land which had gone desperately to war over religion—and taxes—only a generation before, James the King was brave, if not overly wise.

James' nephew, now watching the gathering haze on the far horizon with a knowledgeable eye, considered that his uncle's honesty would avail him nothing. He himself was known as the Protestant Duke, and he was the leader, or figurehead, of the rabid Protestants—a group which, believing what he wanted to believe, he considered to be most of England.

James Scott's thoughts now turned along Stuart lines. His wife, Anne, in a marriage made for him by his father, had gone to her father's manor. He could no more live without women than his father could. In that, he was a thorough-going Stuart. But, surprisingly, there was no woman aboard this ship carrying the Duke of Monmouth.

Colonel Prydgeon, the man who stood in confidence closest to James, had warned him. "No women on this expedition. We'll need all the concentration we have to pull through this."

"Prydgeon!" James had laughed, in amused disbelief. "You can't mean that. You know I can't concentrate without—" He stopped short. His aide's expression, reflecting the severe misgivings that had driven him to criticize his master, did not waver in its gravity. "Not a laughing matter, I see. Well, if I must be celibate, it will make a change, at least. But I warn you, when I get to Whitehall—"

He had made a gesture with his hands, the long well-shaped Stuart fingers graphic, that left no doubt of his meaning. Whitehall would out-Stuart the Stuarts.

Now, he was alone on the deck.

James had sailed the Channel before, from his birthplace in Amsterdam to his birthright—according to his own reckoning, not universally shared—in England. Sometimes his crossing was blessed by a royal invitation, and sometimes—regrettably often—his father's anger rode at his back, sending him eastward again into exile in Holland.

Impatiently, he projected himself now, in spirit as he would have done with his body, could he have arranged it, ahead of the slow-moving ship, down the Channel, past the Isle of Wight, where his grandfather Charles the First had sojourned—trusting his friends, a fatal error—past Southhampton Water, past the rising hills of Dorset.

After this foray, England would be his in fact, rather than on paper, especially since the document bearing his mother's marriage lines had never been found.

The haze in the distance thickened. Fortunately, James, who was standing in the bow of the ship—his scarf, bearing his flamboyant device of a heart pierced by two arrows, surmounted by a plume of feathers, with two angels bearing up a scarf on both sides, whipping sharply in the wind—possessed a stomach not easily turned by the waves, rising now into a distressing chop.

He had chosen a small bay for his landing. Even though his great friend the Earl of Shaftesbury had died, his words stayed with the young man. Again it was strange that James remembered, because usually advice passed through his mind leaving no more imprint than sunlight on the sea.

He was in a rare mood of recollection today, James thought. That was the curse of sea travel—nothing to see, just time to be endured and waited out. He was never good company for himself. He was so charmingly good-natured that he rarely was alone, and he had had no need to develop the habit of solitude.

The picture of a library came into his mind—where would that have been? Not the Earl of Shaftesbury's own country seat. The Earl was too cunning to entertain the controversial Monmouth except on neutral territory. Chichester, it must have been. James had gone there often, and in fact it was his last visit there that had caused the King his father to bundle him hastily off to exile again. Not Chichester in itself, but the fact that the King had expressly forbidden him to go there. That was one time Charles had been really angry, and, surprised, James had wisely decided not to charm him. That was the last time he had seen his father, angered and sorely disillusioned.

The brown hand folded abruptly into a fist and pounded the teak rail. Regrets he had in plenty—but no way to rout them.

The library, he remembered—dark oak, paneled. Brown leather bindings on the shelves. James had looked around him in simple wonder that anyone could be so lost to the delights of the world as to read book after book.

But Shaftesbury, on the occasion presently filling James' mind, had ignored the books. Instead they had sat over some excellent white sherry, and while James could not remember much of what his mentor had said, one thing came back to him with the force of a commandment, when he, Argyle, Prydgeon, and a few others had mapped out the plan for their invasion of England.

"A small harbor, a few men," Shaftesbury had advised. "Then the countryside must rise. Englishmen always sympathize with the underdog, remember that. A few men, and you'll need help. If you don't rouse the countryside *then*—"

The implication was clear, even though neither man put it into words. If the country itself was not behind the invader, then he had no chance.

James insisted on landing in Lyme Bay. He had overridden all opposition, not really knowing why he felt that his luck depended on that particular inlet. Shaftesbury's home had been nearby, but that was not enough to sway him. No, it was something more, something his Scottish ancestor, Mary, could have understood. A fey persuasion, a mystical conviction—that had once been enough for his royal ancestress Mary, and so it was enough for James.

He looked forward with the utmost cheerfulness. He had had his way on this, and he took that as a good omen. The countryside would hail him at the very moment of landing, and his small army would become a conquering host marching to London.

By this time, Argyle, landing in Scotland, would have raised the clans, and Scotland—always eager to lift the claymore and sound the pipes—would be well over the Tweed and marching savagely into the northern shires.

The late twilight grew out of the haze in the west, and

the soft English evening fell upon the three ships, making gamely and unmolested toward Portland Bill.

James huddled against the sea chill on the seat he had made his own. How good it was to see England again! How long he had been away!

He regarded the gentle hills, amethyst in the sunset, turning to a deeper blue the color of lapis lazuli, and still holding, on the hilltops, the last apple green and saffron of the western sky. His thoughts skittered, shallow as always, ahead to the morrow.

Perhaps there would be a woman in Lyme Regis—or even more than one. A smile stole over his handsome face, and he was content.

4

THE morning after Ralph's purging confession, Carmody rode—in haste and bitterness—to Lyme Regis. Her only hope, she had decided during a night of chaotic sleeplessness, was Mr. Hastings.

The pounding rhythm of Amber's flying feet on the dusty road managed, through sheer physical monotony, to soothe her. She pulled up at last, her grooms Ham and Wat far enough behind her to escape the whirling dust clouds.

They were at the top of a height looking down on the village of Lyme Regis. Lyme, one of the larger communities along that rocky coast, was a niggardly collection of narrow lanes passing for streets, leading up cliff and down dale to the sea. A mean little cluster of houses, but Mr. Hastings lived in one of them, and there she must go.

The harbor was enclosed by a long dark finger, a stone pier said to have been constructed by order of one of the first Norman kings, to make a haven for fishermen, but not a harbor deep enough to accommodate men of war. The harbor held two fishing smacks now, one unloading at the wharf at the water's edge. The other was even now setting out to sea, nets festooned in dark scallops over the rail, ready to be dropped in deep water.

With a word to her companions, Carmody put her mare into the road down into Lyme Regis, and made her way to the office where Mr. Hastings spun his webs of legal writs like a benevolent spider.

His clerk she knew slightly. She smiled at him, scantly noticing the youth's reaction. He was a reedy young man, probably no more than twenty, and tall. His height shamed him so that he tried to disguise it, and, sitting at a desk, he developed a habit of bending his shoulders so that he was nearer the stature of his fellows.

But, unconsciously, at the sight of the friendly smile on the lovely face of Miss Petrie, he rose to his full height and squared his thin shoulders. *She would find in him a worthy servant* ran in confused fashion through his susceptible brain.

"Griswold? Do I have it right?" she said charmingly. "How good it is to see you again. Is Mr. Hastings in?"

He would have given his world to produce Mr. Hastings then and there, but facts were facts. "No, Miss Petrie," he said, stammering slightly, "he has gone to Axminster, and won't be back."

Disappointment struck like a knife. "Not ever?" she said gently, holding her rising panic in check for the moment.

"No, n-no," he said in confusion. "Tomorrow. He'll—I mean he'll be back in the morning."

She had not known how greatly she had counted on Mr. Hastings. The useless folly of her impulsive journey stood out baldly in her mind. "Whatever shall I do?" she said, pitifully. "Tomorrow is too late."

"T-too late?" Then, in a burst of rashness, Griswold came from behind the counter. "I'll ride over and get him," he offered, grandly ignoring the distance between the two towns.

With difficulty she dissuaded him. Finally, she told him the inescapable truth. "Tomorrow my brother will be of age, and nothing can be done."

She turned away, shoulders drooping in spite of herself. She had been hare-brained even to come. A mad optimism had told her that Mr. Hastings could, on her behalf, make void the notes, showing that they were signed while Ralph was still a minor.

Now, slowly, she drew the papers from her pocket. Copies of the notes, Ralph had said as he gave them to her, with a virtuous air of having attended to all details in an exemplary manner. And now she read them carefully, Griswold breathing heavily across the desk.

And then she saw what she should have seen before. "Look," she said hollowly. "Look at the date!"

Obediently, the clerk followed her pointing finger. "June eleventh," he said, obligingly. "Tomorrow."

"My brother's birthday. He—or they—dated these notes ahead to the day he comes of age."

Griswold may have been impressionable, even innocent of custom when faced with beautiful women, but he was not stupid. He had, in fact, an acute mind, and the problem Carmody held in her hands was almost as stimulating as the faint perfume of lavender that rose from her clothing when she moved.

"Nothing to prove he was a minor when he signed," he said, regaining some of his usual crispness. He caught sight of something else on the papers, and exclaimed, "The Duke of Monmouth! Does Mr. Petrie really know him? I've heard," he leaned over to whisper cautiously, "that he's already sailed from Holland."

With sudden malice, she cried, "I hope his boat sinks!" And then she asked Griswold, as though he were a man of experience, "What happens if the Duke's invasion fails? What of these?" She shook the papers.

Griswold did not answer at first. But, under the steady regard of those silvery eyes, he crumpled. "Burn the copies, at least," he advised. "Their very existence is proof of treason," he said simply, and wished he had cut his tongue out before he had to tell her.

Crushed, she left the office, turning away so he would not see her sudden tears. But, suddenly wiser than he had been before Carmody Petrie crossed his path, he knew she was crying. He knew, too, that Ralph was not worth a single tear. "Not one tear," he repeated aloud, fiercely slamming a vellum-bound lawbook back onto the shelf, and gave himself over to daydreams in which, sword in hand and lawbook under his arm, he could rescue the silver-eyed lady from the dragon, whose head, predictably, was Ralph Petrie's.

Unaware of the fantastic drama being enacted in the office behind her, Carmody emerged from the dark corridor of the building and blinked in the sudden brightness.

From anywhere in the town, one could see the flat, dimpling surface of the bay. Now both ships had made their way past the long Plantagenet pier, out into the fishing deeps, and the harbor lay empty.

How many times, she thought, mindful of her own russet hair, had the inhabitants of this strand watched anxiously to sea, dreading the inevitable spring visit of the long, snake-headed ships bearing the wild Vikings in their exuberant search for loot, for fat stock, grain and women. She touched her reddish hair with both hands. Somewhere, back in the mists of time, one of her own ancestors must have watched with cold fear in her heart, running, perhaps, not fast enough, not far enough. And bearing afterward the memory of hot breath on her face, suddenly bared flesh, under bruisingly cold armor—for no Viking in war or in pleasure dared risk a dagger in his unprotected back.

Did she remember, this ancestress, with mixed emotions? Did she stand, perhaps on this very place, the next year, watching again? This time with a secret, longing ache instead of cold fear? Holding a small, copper-haired bundle in her arms, pridefully?

"Miss Carmody?" It was Ham, diffident, anxious, bringing her back to the present. "Shall we start back?"

"No," she said on impulse. She could not bear the thought of going back to Oaklands, not just yet. She needed to be alone, to get accustomed to the idea that Oaklands would be violated, that unclean hands would rip away her mother's linens, her own chiffon gowns, even her shifts trimmed with hand-made lace. She groaned. "We'll stay here the night, and start back in the morning. I must inquire about an inn."

She made sure that Ham and Wat were suitably housed, and the horses stalled with fresh straw, and oats for their supper. Her own supper sat before her in the candlelight in the private room of the *Green Swan*, untouched. She scarcely saw it, the visions in her mind far more clear and detailed.

No one could help her. The disaster was complete. Ralph would be of age tomorrow, and so would the notes. There was nothing to keep the bailiffs from seizing everything of Oaklands, everything except the buildings themselves and the land beneath them. The land had fed Petries for six centuries, and before that the Saxons who had found England so fair they refused to return to the forests of the Elbe. And, if Ralph objected, there was the mortally worse charge that could be—and would be, without doubt—brought against him.

The breeze came up from the sea, softly, carrying the stirring scent of sea wrack on the beach and brine lapping at the wooden posts of the wharf. Her thoughts turned then, away from Oaklands, to the Duke.

Still the faintest of hopes stirred in her. The Channel often suffered violent, unpredictable tempests. Perhaps, far out on the Channel, the winds had been chaotic enough to sink the little Dutch boats in which the Duke would set sail.

The weather could be his worst enemy. She breathed a fervent prayer that it might, it must, be so. With an optimism unconsciously rivaling her brother's—and at least this time with as little basis—she took comfort at the thought that the Duke might have turned back.

She read carefully the documents Ralph had given her. They were merely copies, but, as young Griswold had pointed out, copies prove the existence of original documents, and even the copies revealed treason—financial support of the King's sworn enemy—in fact if not in intent.

Slowly, Carmody fed one corner of the first paper into the candle flame and watched it burn. She did not move from her chair until all the papers were soot and ash.

She sat long afterwards at the window until her thoughts calmed, watching until the moon silvering the water rose high, and made only jet shadows along the shore. It was a mysterious scene, earth and sea, wind and wave, and over all the ancient, inscrutable moon.

For a mystic moment she felt kin to all this, felt the blood in her veins pulse in the same harmony as her unknown ancestress must have felt, when the earth was young. She could sleep now, she knew.

And as she slept, the *Helderenburgh* and her two smaller escorts slipped on the dawn tide into the protection of the harbor, let their cables slip through the hawses, and rode comfortably at anchor, aloof and enigmatical, on the quiet surface of Lyme Bay.

Carmody woke to bright sunlight. The day was Thursday, the eleventh of June. Her brother's birthday. He was eighteen years old now, she thought, lying in bed, looking at the ceiling. The age at which her father had thought Ralph would be capable of caring for the Petrie estates.

Her own wedding day—and she knew it was significant that she thought of that only a poor second. Waldo had not returned. She should feel something more about Waldo's desertion—not a word since she had fled from him in the orchard. But Ralph's troubles were so pressing, so tragically devastating, that her own were half forgotten. Waldo's business, she had learned, often took him away for days at a time, and she decided his current absence was only to be expected. But her mind was filled with Ralph and with Oaklands. Waldo said she loved the estate better than she loved him. Perhaps he was right—certainly the coming loss of Oaklands struck an arrow into her heart.

She could not believe Ralph capable of true treason. Even with his pathetic claim to future glory, his signature on notes that proved sweeping, all-embracing contribution to the Duke's cause, Ralph had quite simply been tricked by his devious friends, and fallen into their trap.

And there was no way now by which she could extricate him from the snare.

When she got back to Oaklands—

She didn't know when the idea first occurred to her. She would not go back to Oaklands! She counted the small coins left in her purse. For the first time in her life, she realized that money, these small florins, were all that lay between her and an unknown alternative. Waldo would help her!

He would come to her as soon as he knew she was here in Lyme. But now it was time to start her day.

She was sipping her second dish of tea in the private dining room when Waldo found her. She looked up when the door opened, expecting to see the scurrying waitress who had served her, and she gasped in happy surprise.

"Waldo! How glad I am to see you!" she exclaimed. "Come sit down with me. Can I offer you——"

"Nothing at all," he said, his pleasant voice unbelievably welcome in her ears. He crossed the room and stooped to kiss her lightly on the cheek. Somehow, it was not what she had expected.

"I met your servant on the street," he explained. "I gather there is trouble at Oaklands."

"Trouble? Do you know," she said shyly, "seeing you makes it fade away. Nothing can be as bad as I think, if you are here."

She reached out to touch his hand. "Waldo, do you know what day this is? Our wedding day."

"It was to have been," Waldo agreed, cheerfully. He glanced at her, with carefully concealed speculation. "We will see. Perhaps tomorrow. But just now, my dear, you must tell me what is amiss."

"Waldo," she sighed hugely. She was on the very edge of begging him to marry her today, at once—carry her away from the rotting memory of Oaklands, make her so happy that she would never look back. But she said only, "I fear that Ralph has gambled away his inheritance. I don't know how it could have happened, but——"

Waldo's fingers tightened on hers, but that was the only outward sign of his thoughts. He listened while she told him—Ralph, feeling alien in his school, had been made much of by a group he considered fashionable and powerful. They had led him into gambling, and when he began to lose, took up notes for staggering amounts. She still could not tell him the whole.

"It will take all of the movables of Oaklands to satisfy his creditors."

"But he was a minor—they could not pursue him."

"But the notes—now see how clever they were—the

notes were dated June eleventh, his birthday, the day when
he achieves total control over his assets. So he is not a minor, not from this day."

The scent of Waldo's shaving soap came strongly to her,
pleasant and masculine, and strangely disturbing. Suddenly
she could feel, as strongly in recollection as though it were
now happening, his demanding mouth on hers, insistent, not
to be denied. She looked away, unable to breathe.

Waldo eyed her with misgivings. Her cheek, fair and
cool in repose, now bore the faint flush of stirring emotion. He had, he realized, not misread the face she had
turned to him from the first moment he saw her. Innocent,
beguiling, childlike, he had thought—her unutterable
beauty had reached out to impel him beyond his rigid
self-control. Her eyes, holding promises she did not yet understand, sometimes silver and sometimes an intriguing
slate color, had ensnared him. But it was her sweetly
shaped lips, giving hint of sleeping passion, that had
brought him to that moment in the orchard.

The moment, he vowed anew, that she would pay for—
she was to blame for his loss of control, for his wallowing
in the stews of unbridled passion. She was the only person
who had witnessed his groveling. And she would regret it.

Her own thoughts returned from that moment to Oaklands, still heavy on her mind as it had been unceasingly
for the past three years. One does not cut out one's heart
without a struggle, without some lingering ties left to
snatch at one's attention. Her thoughts, in spite of knowing that there was nothing to be done any more, that it
was Ralph's problem, still returned to linger caressingly
around the hills she knew, the village, the people who
had, with her, formed their own threads in the tapestry of
living in her corner of Dorset.

"What about the Duke?" she said, startling her companion.

"The Duke?" he asked warily. His own recent, and very
secret, transactions in Whitehall were so large in his mind
that he wondered whether Carmody was in fact a witch,
reading his mind, even foretelling his future.

"I should think that the notes are worthless, unless the Duke lands. Am I right, Waldo?"

"Not as long as they exist. In themselves they are proof of treason, no matter what the outcome."

She did not know how close she came that moment, he thought, to a repetition of the incident in the orchard. He had never been so moved by anyone in his life. Her eyes were like silver pools in a dark forest caught in moonlight, he thought in a poetic strain totally foreign to his nature. And she was, even indignant over her stupid brother's mistakes, eminently desirable. Not like Harriet Paine—

With determination, he mastered his thoughts. If he were to think of that other woman, ugly, forbidding and cold in her manner, but so rich, so rich!—this witch before him, sparkling in animation and lively in her gestures, might read his mind, might guess that he never had intended to marry her, but merely to get her dowry in hand. Now he had that, and was free to pursue the wealthy Miss Paine.

"But the Duke *has* come," he said calmly. In fact, although he did not tell her, he had already sent secret word of this to a certain officer of King James, who paid well for such advance information.

"What?" She was taken aback. The last faint possibility of reprieve had taken possession of her, the night before, and with unreason she had clutched it to her as more than even a probability. She stared at Waldo. "How do you know?"

He rose to his feet and stood looking down at her. Carmody was conscious of something new and frightening in his expression.

"The reason I believe the Duke is here, my dear," he said, with an approximate return to the indolent, assured way of speaking that was habitual with him, "is obvious, if you will just look out that window."

She flung the casement wide. The *Green Swan* was halfway up the hillside that rose to the northwest of Lyme Regis. The town itself was built like a great jumble of steps, with narrow alleys climbing the cliff like castaways trying to escape the sea below. The Dorset coast was rocky, and in places wild, and when the storms swept in from the Western Approaches, past the Scillies, past Land's End, and into the broad indentation in England's coast that was called Lyme Bay, the first fury of the waves and wind flung itself on the Dorset bulwarks. Little Lyme Regis was old, old as William the Conqueror, who built the long cobbled pier to make Lyme Regis a safe haven for fishing boats.

From the window, Carmody looked down onto the huddled houses along the steep streets, down to the shore. Out in the harbor, at the very end of the long dark finger of the Plantagenet mole, called the Cob, lay three ships, rocking to the swell of waves on the shelving bottom. "But they're merely fishing boats!"

"They do look so, don't they," Waldo mused. "But you see, they are built in the Dutch fashion, and the Duke has been living in exile in the Netherlands. I am told that the largest of the three boasts twenty-six guns, neatly hidden. And what its cargo is, one may surmise."

"Arms?"

"So it is said."

She could see no movement aboard any of the three ships. No flags drooped from the mast, no sails were set. From here she could even see the slanting cable that anchored one of the ships.

"Is it truly Monmouth?"

"No one really knows. But look."

The narrow street below was filling with people. Windows banged open up and down the lane. Carmody leaned out, balancing precariously over the sill, eager to catch the gabbled words echoing up the inn walls.

The three boats were not known to Lyme Regis. Anything not known was a cause for alarm. Even yet tall poles stood along the coast—sturdy poles with barrels fixed at the top, and inland, so she had been told, there were others like them at stated intervals. In the days of her grandfather, the barrels were constantly filled with pitch, and sentries watched night and day for signs of an invading fleet. The burning pitch would send up Biblical warning—flame if by night, smoke if by day—and the first inland watchtower would send the message on inland in the same way. No invader had set foot on England's shore, unwanted by at least a portion of the people, since the fierce dragon ships of the Vikings had rounded Portland Bill.

Following the pointing fingers jabbing skyward from the milling groups below, she saw on the clifftop, high above, little dark knots of people, all looking seaward, and, from their puzzled gestures and irresolute running from group to group, none of them any wiser than Carmody herself.

She turned impulsively to Waldo. "Shouldn't we go up there to see better?"

Waldo, amused, said, "Are you that curious?"

Tartly, she retorted, "If that is really the Duke, then he is to be the new owner of much of Oaklands, and I do have an interest."

Halfway to the door she turned and said, "Perhaps I could persuade the Duke to burn the notes. Do you think I could?"

Waldo caught his breath. As she looked then, he thought, her strange eyes lit by an inward fire, standing almost on tiptoe with hope and eagerness, she could persuade any man of anything.

Any man, he amended, except himself, who had a desperate need to be made secure in his life, a security that, to Waldo Rivers—son of an impoverished curate in an obscure Nottingham village, winning his title by means he did not wish to remember—meant, quite simply, a great deal of money. And, fortunately, he had the personal attributes to secure his goal—a great deal of charm, a handsome face and graceful figure, and a total lack of scruples.

"I think," he said, reflectively, "perhaps—"

He left the sentence unfinished. But Carmody did not care. Already she was thinking ahead. If the Duke were anything like his father, he would be kind. The late King had been gracious to a small frightened girl, once, lost in the halls of Whitehall when she had run away from her mother, who had been conversing with Queen Catherine.

If the Duke were like his father—maybe she could explain to him just how weak Ralph was, and how much Oaklands meant to the Petries. Loyal to the Duke's grandfather through the Civil Wars—she thought up all the points she could collect to weave into an argument to convince James Scott, Duke of Monmouth.

Waldo and Carmody, along with what must have been the entire human and canine population of Lyme Regis, scrambled up the alleys, the track up the cliff—made for goats, Carmody thought crossly, turning her booted ankle painfully—and clustered like bees hiving on the stunted, wind-whipped furze.

Speculation ran like flickering flame along the clifftop.

"Yon is naught but a fishing smack," said one old mariner, weathered to mahogany brown by wind and weather.

"Too large for that," said another, spitting carefully to leeward. "The Dutch don't sent out boats like that just into the Channel."

"On to India, aye, I know that."

There was more, but Carmody noticed that not a one of them mentioned James Scott, Duke of Monmouth, the late beloved King's bastard son. It was as if they feared to be disappointed, as if they hid their deepest hopes under a casual mask. Did they want Monmouth, or not?

Someone said that the two Customs officers, who had rowed out as was their duty to examine incoming ships, had not returned. The two officials were—according to first one and then another—in chains in the hold, having a bit of Holland gin in the captain's cabin, or taking their pick of great rubies from Burma, as a bribe. But a bribe for what, no one seemed to know.

"Surely they could think up an engrossing reason, wouldn't you think?" Waldo murmured in her ear. She flashed a smile, and would have answered but just then something happened that stopped, effectively, all tongues.

A boat lowered from the larger ship. It was full of men, and at once it began to move toward the shore. Carmody could see the rhythmic cadence of the oars, and knew instinctively that only men used to boats could achieve such unison. They were not, then, an army.

But then Waldo pointed. Another boat was lowered, and another, and another.

In the end there were seven boats, lowered from the

three ships. They turned away from the town, rowing toward the half-moon of sand and shingle just below the cliff where the crowd stood.

The first man leaped ashore from the leading boat. He was athletic—no other could have leaped the space between the prow of the boat and the shingle without falling. This man, clad in leather jerkin and doublet, half boots with pale cuffs, and long curls over his shoulders, laughed aloud, one would guess in sheer exuberance, and waved his plumed hat in a gesture to the men following him.

"Come ashore!" he cried, his voice rising along the cliff face like spray from a wave.

Fascinated, but for different reasons, Carmody and Waldo both watched the disembarkation. One after another, boat after boat, man after man—none of them taking quite the same leap as their leader—until eighty men stood in rough formation behind the first-landed, at the foot of a trail leading up from the shore to the top of the cliff.

The leader made a gesture almost regal and, as one man, the eighty dropped to their knees. Then, kneeling himself, the leader led in prayer. He spoke clearly and with volume, apparently trying to reach the people on the clifftop as well as his Divine Protector. The Duke had indeed landed in England.

Carmody broke away from Waldo and started back down the cliff, the way they had come. She was alone on the path, moving slowly, like a sleepwalker. Waldo would marry her, of course, tomorrow, or the next day. Or the day after. But what would happen to Ralph? Her mind refused to take her beyond the loss of Oaklands. Ralph a traitor? Hardly. Nor even a conspirator. But the notes, the originals, said otherwise.

Behind her, like the tramp of a conquering army, like the booted feet of Roman legions, came a marching rhythm that shook the ground.

She looked up. The men from the shore had already topped the cliff and started down the path that she was on. There was hardly room for two to pass.

She shrank against the face of the cliff, making herself as small as she could, and watched the men come.

They could knock her over the edge, she thought, and the idea filled her with terror, widening her eyes, and making her face pathetically pale.

She looked up—into the eyes of the leader.

He hesitated, breaking step for a fraction of a second. For that fraction, he saw terrified silver eyes in a beautiful oval face. She saw a flicker in his dark eyes, a flicker that, later, she would recognize.

But all she could do now was to stammer, "I—I'm sorry!"

He smiled at her, slowly, with kindly warmth, and reached out as though to touch her. But he dropped his hand, and said only, "Sorry? I'm not!" before he went on.

She stood numbly until the last of the eighty men had passed, as well as a good share of the tumbling, eager, excited population of Lyme Regis, and Waldo found her.

"You know that was the Duke?" he asked, taking her possessively by the arm and helping her down the deserted path.

She nodded. It was the Duke, and something had passed between them. Something she did not like in the least.

"Yes," she said, "the Duke has begun his invasion."

Waldo fell silent, but the look on his face spoke of furious thought.

Silence stretched between them until they were in sight of the *Green Swan.* "There's no hope for Oaklands now," she said mournfully.

Waldo stiffened. "You have a mind that is like one of your own Dorset roads," he told her, only half amused. "You've traveled along the same path so long that your concern has trodden all else into a deep rut, until now you can't see over the sides."

"Waldo?" She could not make out his meaning.

"You have thought of nothing but Oaklands, and that half-witted brother of yours, for so long—you can't even think of me. You're no more ready to marry me today, or tomorrow, than you are to—to join this army!" he finished.

"That's not true!"

"My dear, you don't see yourself. All these weeks, I have heard nothing from you but Oaklands, Oaklands. What can I do to help my brother?" His uncanny mimicking of her voice was cruel. "You have no idea of what is going on in London—what politics are in the air, what will happen to England if the Duke fails, or even what will happen if he should win."

"You did not tell me you wanted a—a Portia!" She spat out the words. She felt her thin grasp on her temper slipping away. She could not hold it in much longer, but she dared not quarrel with Waldo. She needed him, and not just because he represented her future. She needed his calmness, his clear logic—and she tried to say so.

"Waldo, please. Don't scold me. I'll try to be what you want, believe me, I will. I don't think"— she paused to swallow the lump that threatened to emerge, sobbing, from her throat—"I don't think I could bear it without you. You are such a steady person."

Her voice died away. She looked beseechingly at him in her need, and all he could think of was that he was standing within hand's reach of her, and she was pleading with him, willing, melting—and her very forlornness, naked of defenses, promised more to Waldo than she knew.

For a long, long moment he hovered—balanced on the knife-edge between seizing her, as every fiber of his throbbing body demanded, and following the road laid out by the desperate determination of his stony will. Long afterward, he wondered, as many a man does, what would have happened, along what road would his life have traveled, had he taken the other fork.

Just now, he said, a trifle unsteadily, "Carmody, I must leave you now." Wildly he improvised, "I must find out what I can of the Duke's plans. Maybe," he added with a happy triumph, "maybe I can get an appointment for you to see him, so that you can put the case for your brother to the Duke himself."

The happiness leaping in her eyes nearly unmanned him. But the moment was past, and he now had a firm grip on himself. He knew that he must at least follow through on this suggestion, and the effort might well have advantages. If he could get first-hand knowledge of the Duke's military strength, for example, his friend in London might well bestow a bonus on him.

Monmouth's headquarters staff—hardly deserving of such a grand title—were housed in a small hostelry in the center of town. From the entrance, the Duke could look down into the harbor and see his three ships riding at anchor in the full June sunlight. While the ships were there, the Duke had a rear door open, so to speak, a means of escape from this enterprise. If he needed it. It would not be the first time he would have fled England. The Stuarts, as a clan, seemed unusually prone to flight, to secret escapes. Monmouth's father had slept all night in a tree at Boscobel, to elude pursuers. Monmouth kept his ships at hand.

It had taken Waldo two hours to return to Carmody, but he had an appointment for her with someone high on the Duke's staff. Carmody was freshly bathed, to take away the dust and dirt of the cliff path, and she dressed with great care in a pale gray gown shot with glimmerings of yellow like daffodils smiling through the dirty snow of March, and a matching yellow shawl. She piled her glossy hair high upon her head, letting its glorious burnished color serve as its own adornment. She was pleased by Waldo's reaction, and they went out together into the crowded streets.

News of the Duke's landing had spread quickly and already men from the nearby countryside had come to join him. Some stood in the street outside the inn. Others, dressed higgledy-piggledy and armed indifferently, mostly with pikes, wandered, half drunken, around the square. In just a few hours, the Duke was already possessed of an army. Carmody was a few steps ahead of Waldo when one of the men fell into shambling step beside her, his clothes stiff with sweat and his breath strong with spiritous fumes.

"One of the ladies down to see a real army, hey? Tired of your bread and milk men, dear?"

She stiffened, feeling the beginnings of fear touch her

cheeks, uncurl in the region of her stomach. Her heart pounded in her ears. If he touched her—!

A hand under her elbow made her scream silently, and she was only dimly aware that the ragged soldier was mumbling something like a frightened apology and Waldo was beside her.

"My dear, I'm so sorry. Come away inside," he said, pulling her hastily through a door into the dim interior of a building. He peered anxiously at her. "Did you suffer any hurt? No? I would have killed him if he had touched you. That's the kind of soldier Monmouth expects to win his crown with."

Waldo's quiet intimate voice was calming her. At length, she was able to give him a fairly normal smile. "I'm all right now."

She cast a darkling glance toward the closed door to the outside, half fearful still of the rough men lounging idly beyond it. In spite of herself, or perhaps because of the sudden coolness inside the building, she shivered and drew her yellow shawl close.

The room where they were to meet Colonel Prydgeon, the officer in charge of supplies—including Oaklands!—was obviously an inn's taproom. It was paneled in dark oak, blackened with the smoke of a generation of fires. The mantel held brass tankards and a metal tray. The trestle tables had been removed and stored away, all but one, apparently used as a desk. The occupant had apparently just stepped out, for papers were strewn over the table and a pen lay where it had been dropped in haste. The long bar stretched across the opposite side of the room. Only a yeasty memory remained in the air, reminding Carmody forcefully of the brew house at Oaklands where the household ale was made.

"I'll find the Colonel," said Waldo. "You'll be safe here."

He left Carmody sitting on the long bench beside the table. She was used to the half-light now, and she could see that the sheets of paper appeared to contain lists, of whatever kind she could only guess. Shoes, and flintlocks, she supposed. Horses? The army would need horses to ride,

animals to carry supplies, pull wagons. Perhaps—the
thought made her cringe—even an inventory of Oaklands
lay there somewhere in the disordered pile. What would
happen to Amber? Would her beloved high-spirited mare
fall into the hands of some rough-handed clod? Someone
like the drunken soldier who had accosted her just moments ago?

The light peeping through the shutter slats lay in regular
bars across the bare boards of the floor. Somewhere a door
opened and voices rose, cut off sharply when the door shut
with a slam. But no one came.

She noticed for the first time a door on the interior wall.
It blended into the paneling so closely as to be invisible,
even though she could see now that it was ajar. A private
sitting room beyond, probably.

Where was Waldo? Why couldn't he find the Colonel—
Pigeon? no, Prydgeon. She stirred restlessly on the hard
bench.

Someone entered the room next door. She could hear
footsteps, muffled as though on carpet, and a voice, deep
and pleasant, although there was something odd in the in-
tonation that caught her ear. It seemed not quite human,
not the ordinary rise and fall of normal conversation.
Struck by the strangeness of it, she half rose from her
bench, staring at the door.

Her question was answered. A swift little foot-patter,
and through the door, so close to the floor that at first she
did not see it, came a tiny dog. He stopped, lifting his
muzzle, inquiring news of the air, and discovered Carmody. In a moment he was at her feet, imploring with all
his wriggling body to be picked up. Captivated, she
stooped to lift the animal.

Suddenly, she was four years old again. Her mother's
hand was on her shoulder, pushing her into a deep curtsey,
and saying, "Majesty, my daughter Carmody."

And she herself looking up a long way into the heavy
face, the long curling hair, and the sad eyes, and saying,
"May I see your little dog, sir? Please?"

Then the King had placed in her chubby hands the animal, so small it could hide in his sleeve. So soft, the toy

spaniel had been, as soft as this tiny beast now attacking her fingers in miniature frenzy. She was so unexpectedly delighted that she laughed aloud.

She spoke foolishness to the wriggling beast, and heard her own words in the same cadence that had puzzled her moments before. Suddenly she felt the prickling of the skin that told her someone was watching her. Startled, she looked up and saw the man standing in the doorway to the parlor. He was eying her with frank approval.

"No wonder my dog scampered away from me," he said. "It was certainly not to see the Colonel. Pepe abhors the Colonel. Very good taste my dog has. I mean, of course, in taking so strong a liking to you."

She felt no awe in the presence of this royalty—if the Duke were indeed royal, as some seemed to doubt. But she must not trouble him with her affairs. Waldo had taken pains to get her an appointment with the Colonel, and she should not take matters into her own hands.

"But what is it?" the Duke persisted. "I can see that you are not easy in your mind. You did not come to see me?"

"My lord, I must confess—"

"Such beauty as yours has no need to confess." The words slipped off his tongue so easily, so practiced, that he could send them forth while thinking of other, more important things. But this time, he was thinking only of the ravishing copper-haired, tremendously lovely, and—he would have sworn—untouched woman of quality standing before him.

He looked with narrowed eyes at her. This, he knew, was what Prydgeon had warned him about, what would cause Ferguson to give vent to lurid curses in half a dozen languages before he would clamp his lantern jaws closed, in deference to rank.

No women, they had told him. Not until they captured Whitehall. But not even his dear mistress Henrietta could match this beguiling creature. Lady Wentworth was practiced, too practiced, and the Duke was intrigued, for the moment, by innocence.

Monmouth, with a rebellion to lead, a kingdom to win, even his life at stake, reached out to take Carmody by the hand, and smiled, winningly, reassuringly. Rising anticipation bubbled inside him, as it always did with a new challenge.

"I remember you, my dear, from the cliff path," he said. "Come into my poor sitting room and let me see if I can't help you."

The touch of his hand was gentle, and she trusted him. He would do what he could for her, she read in his dark, frank eyes, and perhaps—just perhaps—there was a chance for Oaklands, even yet.

Caution spoke in her ear, and was ignored. She would have died rather than admit that the Duke held more than Oaklands in his careless hands, that he had obscurely touched the thread that Waldo had begun to unravel. And who knows, she thought recklessly, what may lie at the other end of the string?

"My lord," she said, curtseying, and preceded him into the inner room.

The Duke's parlor was only a little larger than the sitting room at the *Green Swan*, but it was far more luxurious. There were three large chairs, a round table, and a pair of doors opening out onto a terrace beyond. The paved area of the terrace was narrow and irregularly shaped, fitting the side of the hill on which the inn was built. One end of the pavement disappeared into the rock wall of the hill, and a parapet of fitted flat stones served as a boundary. From where she stood at the open terrace door, she guessed that beyond the parapet lay nothing but a sheer drop.

Overhead was a latticework of wood in the new pergola style, and a rampant vine rioted over the structure, making a sort of dappled sun-and-shadow design on the irregular pavement.

"Lovely," she said, turning back into the darkness of the room. The Duke was close, far too close, to her. She stepped away, and he did not follow her. There was only half an arm's length between them, and she glanced nervously at the door, measuring her escape route—if one were needed. But the door through which she had come, dismayingly, was closed. She thought, how very stupid I am!

The Duke watched her with amusement. She was so like a curious kitten, he thought, exploring her surroundings with interest, and he made himself stand very still so as not to frighten her. He read the thoughts passing over her face, with practiced ease. Innocence, belated apprehension, and alarm. He had little doubt that if he were to make an ill-considered gesture, she would fly through the door and be lost to him. He could not take the time to seek her out, he thought, with a rebellion to lead, but he could benefit from this moment, and, if he were very careful—

She had reached the stage of standing on tiptoe ready to fly, when he spoke. "Don't be afraid. I won't hurt you. And I don't know your name."

"Carmody Petrie." It was a whisper.

"You did not come here to pet my dog," he said dryly.

She could not look at him. Suddenly she did not know how to proceed.

"I must go. Waldo will be anxious."

"Let Waldo—whoever he is—wait. Look at me." She did not move. "Carmody Petrie, look at me."

There was sufficient authority in his voice to make her look up at him. Her fear stood in her eyes, but she could not help it. Shyness kept her from leaving, a paradox that was hard to understand, but quite simply, she did not know how to leave the presence of a royal duke in a graceful manner.

He did not move, did not make so much as a finger's gesture toward her. But his eyes were bold enough. He searched her face, and then, slowly, his gaze moved downward, over the slim, boyish figure, with only a soft, slight swelling to tell him otherwise. The slim waist, no bigger than a man's two hands would encircle. The flat hips—

She followed his every thought, vaguely, and not in as much detail, but the category in which they lay was unmistakable. She felt uncomfortably warm—strangely, she fancied, the color of sunrise tinted her thoughts, a warm, promising rose, of a fleeting sweetness that would soon be gone. And she could not keep her thoughts from showing in her face.

"Don't be afraid," he repeated. "Tell me, why did you come?"

"It's my brother," she faltered, and if he were disappointed, he did not show it.

"Your brother? He wishes to enlist in my army? He must come to see my colonel." He was talking considerately, to put this lovely nymph—so he thought of her—at ease. Her beseeching eyes had, without either of them being aware of it, stirred something deep and forgotten, from the youth he had never had, akin to the young spring of the world. And he was suddenly loath to lose this. He was like a boy with a package tied in fancy ribbons for his birthday—speculating wildly about what lay inside, eager to open it, and yet enjoying the suspense. Yes, this package, he thought with grim determination, was his—his very own, and he alone would open it, in his own good time.

The fancy pleased him. He would, a little longer, enjoy the curiosity, the wonder.

"Tell me," he commanded, his voice sweetly insistent.

And she did. She told him about her struggle at Oaklands to bring it into prosperity. Her efforts, her determination, to make of her brother a gentleman in manners as well as in birth—not like the clods that most country squires were, not having the means or the inclination to rub off their crudeness at court.

And the debacle!

Ralph's enormous gambling losses—the notes signed, and due today.

"This day," she told him, finishing what had seemed a long, wearying story, and yet one from which his interest never seemed to waver. "And the notes are payable to you, my lord duke. Which some folks say proves treason against my brother."

"To me?" His surprise appeared genuine. Then, as suspicion came to him, he asked, "Who drew your brother into the gambling parlors?"

"Peregrine Ashley."

"Perry," the Duke said, nodding slowly. "An overly ambitious young man."

"You know him?"

"I know him. He seeks to gain advancement, in ways that I would not approve. My dear Carmody, you must not believe that I condone this kind of debauchment of a juvenile. It is a great shame for a young man to gamble away his inheritance. If I were King, I should see to it that Peregrine Ashley and his kind should suffer for this."

He set his lips, and glanced at Carmody. The slight flush that meant she had hope was vastly becoming on that fair skin. He toyed with the thought that, illumined by passion, she might well kindle a light that would fill his whole world. For a time. But the game, he thought facetiously, was worth the candle.

"Then you'll cancel the notes?" she cried ecstatically.

"If I were King," he repeated, "I should be glad to. But as you see, I am not. Not yet. And, in the meantime, I need certain things."

Certain things! Carmody's fears returned in greater force than before. What were these certain things? Before she could ask, his pleasant voice continued, "Arms, ammunition. Supplies for the men, blankets, food. Horses. I have a man at Taunton bringing men and horses—but horses eat, as well as men, Carmody. So you see?"

"I see," she said, unable to hold back the welling tears. "I see that you gave me the belief that you would be generous, as I have heard the Stuarts are. But—maybe the Stuart blood does not flow in your veins, after all." She spoke heedlessly, meaning only that his mother's blood, as so often happens, might be the dominant strain in him. But, tensing under his sudden silence, she glanced at him and then stood, transfixed under the terrible glare from his dark eyes.

They had turned threatening as thunderheads from the Channel. He crossed the intervening space in one stride and crushed her shoulders in a savage grip. "Never say that again, or—I may kill you," he said, spitting the words out between clenched teeth so that she was not sure she understood.

He shook her, as a rat terrier shakes his victim. Her hair slid out from the confining pins, and she felt one heavy tress on her shoulder, cascading over his hand. He grimaced as though the bright color burned his skin, but his reaction was involuntary. He was in the grip of terrible anger.

"My uncle"— it was impossible to believe the venom he put into that word—"my *uncle* says that the King was not my father. And when I get to London, I'll make him crawl through every corridor in the palace, on his knees. I'll make him kiss my mother's picture. That foul swine!"

He trembled with words that could not be said, strangling him, engorging him until the veins stood out on his forehead. His fingers closed cruelly on Carmody's shoulders, bruising the skin through the thin cloth. She cried out in pain.

Slowly his gaze focused on her again, and he came back from what seemed a long, long distance away. "I hurt you, didn't I?" he apologized. "I'm sorry. But you don't know how much you hurt me."

He seemed to have forgotten for the moment why she had come, and his driving anger, for lack of proper outlet, diverted itself abruptly into another channel. The pupils of his eyes widened, and his hands on her shoulders, while less painful, were still strong.

He drew her to him, and slowly pressed his mouth down upon hers, hard, insistent, letting his anger flood out upon her like a river in spate.

The silver eyes that reproached him, when at length he drew back and shuddered, were not the same eyes that had intrigued him before. He read in them disgust, fear, and revulsion. He had spoiled something that could have been very precious by that damnable anger that swept him very rarely. And of all the times to let that bile sweep up to his tongue—the ancient canard about his mother that James Stuart, brother of Charles the King, had set current. The jealousy of the late king's brother would destroy him, the Duke thought, but not in the way his uncle planned. He groaned with old, remembered pain.

"Now you see me for what I am," he told her, not even

sure she was still in the room. He spoke aloud, not daring to look up lest she read what was in his eyes. "A stupid, stupid fool."

Carmody was so shaken that she had to hold onto the door handle. The terrible storm that had shaken him had, for different reasons, had its echo in her—as a storm out at sea, sending fine ships to the bottom, has its echo in the waves crashing upon the rocky cliffs of Dorset.

She had to leave this room. She could not stay penned up with the Duke any longer. Feebly, she asked, "What about my brother's notes?"

The bald statement was so outrageously incongruous that he stared at her. He was still flushed with passion, and his breath came fast and shallow. He leaned both hands flat on the table, supporting his weight on them. Suddenly, he experienced a pendulum swing of emotion that, in other times, had been one of his greatest charms. He laughed. He stood upright and laughed so uproariously that she was alarmed anew.

At length, he stopped, abruptly. "All right, Carmody Petrie. I owe you an apology for my unthinking grasp of you. I am not always so rough, believe me. I will find other ways to supply my army—supposing always that I acquire one. And your improvident brother can retire to Oaklands—is that the name?—to contemplate his stupidity. But—" his dark eyes took on a glitter—"you know my price, Carmody."

"Price?" she echoed feebly.

His smile turned one-sided, the right side of his full lips lifting in an odd quirk. "Shall I show you again what I mean?"

Her hands moved convulsively on the latch. "No, no," she protested faintly.

"Put up your hair," he advised her, "before your Waldo and my colonel misunderstand."

Automatically, watching him fearfully to catch the first sign of movement toward her, she released the door latch and set both hands to capturing the burnished curls and pinning them back into place.

"I must tell you, my lord," she said, her voice admirably

controlled, "that the price you would exact for my brother's patrimony, which your minions stole from him, is excessive. There is not any possible circumstance under which I would yield to your disgusting terms."

"None? You might learn to like me a little. What then?"

"You—you're joking with me, my lord duke. And I consider that an unhandsome advantage to take of me. But I can assure you, that is as remote as—" she recalled nursery tales of Robert the Bruce, from her old north country nurse—"as if Scotland would conquer England."

She opened the door and, controlling her urgent desire to run, stepped with commendable poise through the door. Waldo rose jerkily to his feet and Colonel Prydgeon eyed her with grave misgivings.

"What happened, Carmody?" Waldo demanded. "Don't tell me. On second thought, I don't want to know. Let's get out of here."

"I found the Duke most sympathetic," she told her fiance. The quivering of her chin took away some of the grace of her statement. A groan rose behind her, but the Colonel's face was bland when she turned.

"I don't have any idea of what you both are thinking," she lied calmly, "but I think I accomplished my mission. The Duke is a—gentleman."

The word was not the first one that came to her lips, but it sounded better than the short one that occurred to her first. She led the way out of the colonel's office. Waldo was vibrating with unasked questions. Carmody was still shaking inside.

She held Waldo's arm, the only tangible solid in her world. Once away from the inn she stopped short. Words spilled from her lips. "Waldo, you have a special license. Marry me today!" And keep me safe, she begged silently.

"Not today," he soothed, as he would a child. "Carmody, people are watching us."

"Waldo, when?"

"When this is all settled," he told her. "I'll come back to marry."

"Truly?"

"Word of honor." Marry, yes, but not, deuce take it, to Carmody.

As he parted from her at the door of the *Green Swan*, he said, "You have a passionate nature, Carmody. I hope one day you will meet your match. In the meantime, if I were you, I would give careful thought to the reason why you spurned the Duke. Many a noblewoman has thought it no sin to ease a king's needs. Are you afraid, Carmody? Afraid of yourself?"

Behind her, back in the Duke's sitting room, the Duke was undergoing relentless questioning by his colonel. The existence of the notes did not surprise Prydgeon. "More than one of these out," he said shortly, rapping the table with his knuckles. "How do you think I paid for those ships? The cargo of guns that they're going to unload as soon as we have soldiers to give them to? These things cost money." As an afterthought, he added, "My lord."

"Oh, I agree," the Duke said slowly. "But it is possible—"

Suddenly he gathered himself into the picture of a leader of an army. He had had years of genuine success in military endeavors, and in fact, if he could have been a soldier for the rest of his life, he would have been happy. But there were others to consider. That decision had been made, and he was here in Lyme, a town that offered him more than ordinary benefits.

"I agree completely, my old friend," he said, flashing the smile that could atone for much. "First, I want those Petrie notes in my own hand. Next, here's what I want you to do."

He gave certain orders, and after he had finished, both men looked at each other with companionable smiles—one in understanding and admiration, the other smile one of happy anticipation.

5

CARMODY reached the sanctuary of her room at the *Green Swan*, tossed her yellow scarf on the floor and dropped exhausted into the chair beside the narrow window. She threw the casement wide, to catch the slightest breeze from the sea.

She had been assaulted in her most private thoughts by a man who was, at best, a stranger. Only the mischance that he held the fate of Oaklands in his hands had brought her to see him at all.

She leaned her feverish forehead against the frame of the window. Below her the narrow cobblestone lane was nearly lost beneath the overhang of the inn and of the building opposite. Her window was set at a slant so that without moving she could catch a glimpse of the Bay. The Duke's three ships still rode at anchor.

She could only think of the Duke's monstrous offer.

Oaklands was on one pan of the scale, and the Duke had told her what was required in the other pan to make it balance. But she would not pay that price. Never, never, never.

There was only one thing left to her. Go home to Oaklands, and pray for a swift finish to the Duke's business. Only then could Oaklands rest easy—only then would Waldo come back to marry her. Some way, there had to be another chance for her brother.

She ordered horses for the morning. "Tomorrow," she

told Ham, who was sullen with worry, "things will look better."

"I don't like it here, Miss Petrie. I fear this place."

"I, too, am anxious to be away," she assured him. "We'll not linger here."

In the morning, in the act of leaving Lyme, she was buoyed up with the faintest shred of hope. At least she was doing something, rather than standing in one place, while her thoughts ran in a squirrel-cage. Amber too seemed glad to be on the way again, and exhibited such high spirits that Carmody was hard put to control the sorrel mare.

After half an hour of hard riding, she pulled up. No need to gallop all the way, she thought, and turned to say a word to Ham. He was looking back over the way they had come, and he seemed uneasy.

"What's the matter, Ham?" she said, instinctively speaking in a whisper. She edged Amber closer. Wat sat his plow horse a little distance away. The three of them waited in the roadway, alert, listening, and now Carmody could hear the clop of horsemen coming.

"More than one," she remarked. "They're in more of a hurry than we are."

The riders came into sight at the bend in the road. There were six of them, and she did not like their looks. Burly men, they rode their horses as though they were used to them, but not, she thought without knowing why, as gentlemen rode.

She felt a prickle of alarm, and saw a real fear in Ham's eyes. They were no match for a half dozen armed men. Their only recourse was to run, and she left it too late to give the order. The men beyond sighted them, and the leader gave a cry of triumph. She wheeled her mare and pricked her hard with her heels—but though Amber bent into it, it was no use. In moments, the men had overpowered Ham and Wat, and the leader had overtaken her. He put a burly hand to Amber's bridle.

Furious, she screamed, "Get your hands off!" She raised her arm and brought her little riding lash down across the man's dark face. His heavy lips contorted with pain, and she saw a mad red gleam in his eye that frightened her.

In moments, it was over. With incredible strength, he wrenched the high-strung mare to a halt, and sidled his horse over to Carmody, knee to knee, panting heavily. His breath was tavern-laden.

She told him as much. And as much more as she could readily think of, and for a little space he looked at her, the anger turning from red hot to white, and more dangerous a man she had never seen.

And then she turned and saw Ham and Wat, lying on the ground near their horses. "You didn't have to kill them!" she screamed, raising her whip hand. This time, the ruffian had warning, and with a gesture so easy that it could hardly be seen, the whip was in his hand, and her wrists were clamped in his enormous sausage-like fingers.

"They'll be all right," he said. "Boscomb, pile them on the saddles. We'll have to take them back, I suppose." He turned to Carmody. With a grotesque change of manner, he became overly formal. "Miss Petrie? I'm sorry to discommode you, but I must insist that you return with me to town."

"Why?" The word came out like a bullet. She wished it were.

"Because, Miss Petrie, you are riding a fine mare that is not yours."

"Not mine? This is Amber, my own mare. I raised her from a colt!"

Fumbling with one hand, still imprisoning her wrists with the other, he fished out from some recess in his clothing a folded paper. "Read it," he advised her.

Unbelieving, and yet with a dreadful conviction that would not be denied, she read the paper. Her worst fears lay open before her, in black and white.

"And—and you're the bailiff?" she faltered.

He bowed in mock courtesy. "As you see. I am empowered to take the stock back to Lyme. In payment of debts, which I don't know about, but I am sure you do. Yes," he added, after a searching look at her stricken face, "I see you do. Now I also have instructions concerning your person. But nothing about your men."

She held herself rigid. "And what are your instructions about me? And who gives you your instructions?"

"The answer to your last question should be no mystery to you. But my instructions are to bring you back to Lyme, safely. You need not fear me or my men."

"I will not go."

"You wish to be set afoot here, miles from anywhere?"

"If I must."

He glanced at her, gauging her measure of determination, and shrugged his shoulders. "Very well. We will take the mare." She sat defiantly still, until he added, "With or without you." Hastily she dismounted. What manner of man was this? More than a bailiff, she was sure. He had some breeding, an air of command, overlaid by a rough, semi-martial bearing that, like an ill-fitting coat, sometimes gaped open. There was steel beneath his manner, and the Duke's army, marching down from the clifftop, came to mind.

She stood in the roadway, holding herself together by sheer force of pride. She dared not say a word, lest all her control slip out through the opening of her lips. She watched in mute trembling fury, while two of the men dismounted and bent to pick up Ham. They tossed him, face down, across the saddle before she could reach them, her fingers clawing at them, screaming unintelligible syllables of defiance. She scratched one face, her nails leaving lines like a rake down his cheek, and turned toward the other man. She was grasped from behind around the waist and lifted off the ground, and set, still kicking, before the men who called himself bailiff.

"Now then," he said sternly, but with a touch of lurking admiration, "that's enough. You're quite a wildcat—and I sure wish I had the taming of you. You are going back with me."

"I thought I had a choice," she sobbed. Now that the tears had started, she could not stop them.

"You have," he said dryly. "You can go back to town,

in front of my saddle. I'll admit you'd be quite an armful. I might even forget my instructions."

She stopped in the middle of a sob, and cried, "Never!"

"Or you can go back riding the mare."

"My mare," she snarled, but her defiance lacked conviction.

Mounted on Amber, she was hemmed in on either side by her tormenter and one of his men. She huddled forlornly in the saddle as they jogged back to Lyme. The leader had finally tipped the scale, gaining her reluctant acquiescence, by telling her that her men were going back to jail for riding stolen horses! *If*, that is, she did not come willingly herself.

Her whole life seemed to have descended into a series of unpalatable choices. If you do not give up something, then dire things will happen to those around you. If you do not ride Amber back to Lyme, your men will be jailed. If you do not prove agreeable to the Duke of Monmouth, with his cruelly bruising fingers and his rapacious mouth, then Oaklands, all the people you have loved and cared for—who count on you, have trusted you and your family back to the dim mists of the time when the first Petrie took over this land—all those whose lives depended on Oaklands would be reduced to penury.

Without the sheep, the grains, the livestock—the tools for plowing, the stores of marrows for the winter—without all the means of scratching a livelihood from the soil, there was no way they could endure until the spring to come. And she was a small sacrifice weighed against such calamity.

She could not sacrifice herself. She could not literally hand herself over as the premium to redeem her brother's disastrous notes.

She was freed when they reached the edge of town. Ham and Wat had recovered some measure of consciousness, and, as she watched helplessly, they were given a choice too. Jail, or the Duke's army. Ham's reproachful look lingered long in her memory. She trudged past the Duke's blue standard in the market square, and up the hill toward the *Green Swan*, the inn she had left in such good spirits that morning. Then, she had been going home to abide the unknown outcome of Ralph's sins. Now, the outcome was no longer unknown. But still, she did not yet know the worst.

The door of the *Swan* stood open. The landlord was engaged in fierce conversation with another man. When he saw her coming, he cried aloud, "There she is! Miss Petrie, tell this man I don't know where you are! Except now, of course, I do. I mean—"

"Never mind what you mean, landlord," the man said. "I see Miss Petrie." He stepped forward and touched his hat. "Miss Petrie? I have bad news."

She stared at him, uncomprehending. She was covered with dust from her fast, futile journey, and she was growlingly hungry. But she could not think of eating, not while that great lump sat in her throat. "Bad news?" Her voice was a whisper. What more bad news could there be?

"Your brother," the man explained. "He sent me to bring you to him."

"Bring me?" At last she stirred. "Why doesn't he come himself? I was on my way to Oaklands when—" She glanced at the inquisitive landlord. No need to tell the world, she thought, that she was penniless, or nearly so. "Bring me? Where?"

She went with him. It was a short distance. She wondered idly whether she was right to trust this man, whom she had never seen before, but there seemed to be no choice. Besides, any choice she had had lately had been, in the last analysis, no choice at all.

To her astonishment, her escort stopped before the jail. The man guided her through the barred door, into a dim foul-smelling interior. The door clanged behind them. She gagged at the stench. She thought no longer. Instead, an atavistic self-preserving defiance surged up from the depths of her being.

"No!" she screamed. "Not that!"

She turned to flee. Quicker than thought, her guide's hand shot out to encircle her wrist. "You're wrong, Miss Petrie!" he cried, trying to calm her. He could have been a twin of the bailiff who had confiscated Amber. His grasp held her where she was. "You're not arrested!"

She tugged vainly at her imprisoned wrist, trying with the other hand to pry loose his fingers. "Then let me go!"

"It's your brother who's a prisoner."

It took a moment for his words to penetrate. Then, resistance oozed out of her. "My brother? Here? *In jail?*"

Ralph was alone. She stood outside, looking into the cell through open bars. She had expected this dungeon-like stone cubicle, not as large as the smokehouse at Oaklands, but there, there was air stirring. Such as it was. The smell was compounded of old urine, old, and human filth—for the first time she understood the true meaning of *noisome.*

But the straw was fresh, her guide told her—changed just last week. She glanced at him, in time to catch a momentary sympathy in his eye. Ralph lay huddled in the corner, as though he were a bundle of dirty rags tossed by a careless hand.

"Carmody?" Ralph's voice was a hoarse rasp. It came again, a raven-croak, before she believed that it had come from the figure sprawled on the straw. He crawled to the bars, and pulled himself up until he was looking into her face. The look in his eyes shattered her.

"Carmody. Help me. Get me out of here. They said you wouldn't come. But I knew you would." His voice slid upward into a whine. "You'd come and get me out. Carmody, I'll die in here."

It was the simple truth. Not only as Ralph saw it, but—the truth. Already he was hovering on the knife-edge of lunacy. And he had been here, so her guide told her, only since the night before.

"They came to Oaklands and took me away," Ralph said, in childish wonder. "They said they'd let me see you."

He repeated all that he had said, in varying ways, and varying tones. Sometimes with anger, other times with vague sounds like an infant's mewling.

"I've seen enough," she said, grimly, to her guide. She did not look back at the simple creature groveling on his knees and howling after her.

"Why is he in there?" she asked with desperate calmness.

"Didn't you know? This is the debtors' prison."

Debtors' prison. It was not enough that the bailiffs seized Amber, were confiscating all the movable assets of Oaklands. Weren't they satisfied until they took Ralph's blood?

"But he's going to be tried, isn't he?"

"So I understand. But of course the town government has come to a stop now. The Mayor has run off, and everyone else is caught up in—"

"In the Duke's affairs," she concluded bitterly. She had been innocent until now, but no longer. Even she could see that the Duke's shadow moved behind today's events. Only the Duke had the authority to confiscate, to jail, since only the Duke had Ralph's notes.

She stood irresolute on the pavement in front of the forbidding stone prison. She wished she could faint, and gain a little surcease for her miseries. Even Ralph, at least now and then, could forget his sorrows, even if the alternative was a short period of lunatic oblivion.

She walked toward the *Green Swan*, not even surprised when she realized that she was alone. Her guide—whoever he had been—had disappeared from her side and she had not noticed him go. She climbed the stairs to the room she had had before, and bolted the door behind her. Surprisingly, her boxes were neatly stacked along the wall. Someone—again the shadow of the Duke moved—had taken care to bring them back.

She sat at the window, and looked out across the harbor. There was but one end to her thoughts—she had to get Ralph out of jail, before he lost his weak mind altogether. She was his sister, and she could not walk away from him. Oaklands in the balance had not been enough—not quite enough. Now Ralph's life had been added. She was defeated.

She sat as though carved from the gray Dorset stone. The sun westered, and began to sink toward the Devon hills beyond the bay. Once someone tapped on the door, but when she did not answer, the footsteps padded softly away.

The bay turned to molten orange, and the far hills grew deep purple in the twilight. From the beach at the foot of the valley, a boat set out toward the larger ship still anchored in the harbor. One boat only, with four men in it.

Even from this distance she had no trouble in recognizing the Duke—he stood in the bow of the boat, self-assured, confident, regal. She could see, in her mind, the warm brown eyes, hotly surveying her. She could feel, and stonily remember, his harsh grip on her shoulders, his avid mouth on hers, stemming her thoughtless accusation that he might not be a Stuart.

Holding herself rigidly, like a sleepwalker, her face cold and closed against the world, she rose from her stool, and, her destination fixed in her mind, set out on her way to save Ralph.

Carmody stood at the top of the rope ladder, left conveniently over the rail of the *Helderenburgh*, the largest of the Duke's minuscule fleet. She was not experienced enough to be certain, but she thought that there should have been someone on deck to challenge her. For all anyone knew, she might be an emissary of King James, with a smoking petard in one hand.

She gave the lack of a sentry no more thought. She was in a curious dreamlike state. One part of her—like an outer shell—walked, and, when occasion arose, would talk. She was aware of boats and oarsmen, even of their curious glances as they rowed her across the fulling tide to the ship. But an inner part of her lived and had its being entirely separate from hands that drew her cloak closer, from feet that slid on wet rope rungs.

That inner part was enclosed in a covering as hard as ivory. She still saw before her, with every breath, the pitiful, pathetic, mad face of her brother, his sanity nearly gone in less than a day in prison. Was he sunk in remorse? Not likely. Simply given, by malicious fate, a lifetime of duty that forever would be too heavy.

She did not work her way then to the deeper fact—that

he was shallow enough so that nothing struck very deep. His emotions were violent as waves in a basin, and as easily stilled. But this—this terrible imprisonment— This he did not deserve, she thought.

She stood on the deck for a few moments. She did not know what to do next. The deck of a ship was as strange to her as the streets of London. The ship moved like a thing alive under her thin-soled slippers, and she reached both hands to the rail to steady herself.

The part of her that was alive and moving saw that the bay had turned to turquoise under the shadow of the Devon hills, holding the light of the sun on their topmost ridges, and turning the land on the far shores to a plum-colored shadow. Here, where she stood, the gentle rose of the sun-touched clouds reflected on her face, showing the deadly pallor that had marked her since the color drained to her toes, back in that noisome jail.

The sea breeze was gentle, lifting one careless curl and dropping it again without even disturbing its coil. She did not need her cloak, she thought, and reached a hand up to her throat to loosen it. But on the way back to land, the air might be cooler.

The way back to land—a strangled sob caught in her throat. What kind of person would she be when she went back to land? What would the next few hours hold?

She closed her eyes. She could not envision the next small space of time. Eyes open or closed, Ralph's face, gray, the beginnings of a blond beard appearing already on his chin, the hopeless eyes, haunted her. But now, on the canting deck, slightly atilt with the gentle rollers from the bay, she did not even know which way to go.

Waldo would have known—but then, if Waldo had not abandoned her, she would not be standing here now.

Then she heard the voices. They seemed disembodied at first, coming out of the air around her. Or, she thought, from the bottom of the sea. Puzzled, she looked over the rail. There was nobody below. The surface of the sea, in the deep shadow cast by the ship, looked oily and murky. The smell coming up the side to her was full of brine, decayed fish, and things she did not want to know about.

But no boat rode there, waiting for her. She had sent her oarsmen back. It was wiser not to allow any retreat to stand as a last resort, in case—

After a moment she saw in the dark waters a lighter splotch, and finally recognized it as the light from one of the small windows almost directly under her feet.

That was where the voices must be coming from. The Duke must be in the cabin below. And, thankful for the respite, she knew he was not alone. Looking about for a means to descend to the cabin, she discovered a small ladder leading downward from an open hatch. The ladder was not as perilous as the rope ladder over the side, but none the less she blew out the breath she had been holding when she found there were no more steps beneath her feet, only solid floor.

The darkness was nearly total. At last she saw a thin line of light near the floor, stealing through beneath a closed door. In the narrow aisle, she could reach her hands out and place her palms on the bulkheads on either side. The voices here in the confined space were louder, and angrier, than they had been on deck. She recognized neither of them, but she supposed one must belong to the Duke. Her lips tightened to hold back the bile on her tongue.

One of the voices sank to beseeching tones. "But, my lord, you saw what the man did. Dare is of no use to you—he will be nothing but trouble."

"While you, I suppose"—it was the Duke speaking—"have brought me none? What is this, then? You've killed a man, my good friend, and while this may not matter in the stews of Amsterdam, the mood here is less violent."

"Less violent! Then, I suppose, my lord, that that mob you call an army was after me to shake my hand?"

The Duke laughed. "I am glad to see your wit is not changed. Fletcher, you'll be the death of me yet!"

There was a sudden silence, heavy with implication. Then the Duke added in a serious tone, "That was a bad choice of words, wasn't it? I trust it wasn't an omen. Do you think it was, Fletcher?"

"No, my lord duke. If I could do anything to save your

life, you know I would. I will never betray you—you know that. But—"

"Yes, I know. Given a high enough price on my head, I could count on the fingers of one hand the men who would not betray me. And, perhaps, one woman."

Fletcher was evidently moving something heavy on a wooden table, judging from the sounds that reached Carmody, who was still leaning against the wall in the obscurity at the bottom of the steps. A scraping noise, followed by a series of light thumps.

"I have all my gear, my lord," Fletcher resumed. "I'll leave the cabin to you."

"My thanks," said the Duke. "I may have need of it."

Footsteps sounded near the door. Carmody shrank back. There was no hope of escaping notice, once the door opened and light from within poured out into the corridor. She retreated, stumbling, halfway up the steps.

She was just in time. The door opened, below, and the light probed as far as the bottom of the steps. Fletcher, apparently, stood in the doorway for one last word with the Duke.

"My lord?"

"Yes, Fletcher."

"Is there any message—for anyone, in Utrecht?"

A short silence. Perhaps the Duke was enamored of someone already, thought Carmody. Somehow the tone of Fletcher's question lent itself to that surmise. If so, perhaps the Duke would be too faithful to that one to look at Carmody again. Perhaps she had mistaken his import, and all this was in vain!

Her breath caught in her throat. What would she do then? She did not know. Fletcher gently reminded the Duke, "My lord?"

"No message, Fletcher. Not even that she is in my thoughts now. For in truth, Fletcher, such a kind message from me would be a lie."

Fletcher stumbled over his words. "A great general has many things on his mind, my lord."

"My good Fletcher, a good general is the best I am. But

even a poor general is none the less a man. No, Fletcher, thank you. No message."

Fletcher walked down the narrow corridor. There must have been cabins beyond, Carmody thought, because Fletcher did not come her way. His footsteps died away in the distance before she moved.

Now that she was actually within reach of the Duke, her courage failed her. No matter what happened, she thought miserably, she could not take a step toward the Duke. Not even Ralph's bleared features, swimming vaguely unfocused in her mind as though seen through blinding tears, had the power to make her take one step.

Ralph had gambled, not Carmody, one part of her brain, struggling to the surface, pointed out severely. You're already too late to save Oaklands, then why? Why should Ralph, already taking so much of you—taunting and cruel, outrageously insulting—require more?

The debate raged feverishly in her brain. The floor beneath the steps on which she huddled was still lit. The Duke's cabin door was open. Now there was only the sound of the ship's timbers, straining at the anchor cable as the tide came in. The tilt of the step beneath her swayed gently, like the soothing motion of a cradle.

The orange-yellow rhomboid of light lying on the dark floor of the corridor before her suddenly changed shape, as the irregular shadow of a man flickered over it. The occupant of the cabin had come to the door.

What could she do? There was no place to fly, even if her knees had not turned to pudding. She stifled a whimper born in her throat.

"Come, Carmody, out into the light where I can see you."

She could not move, no, not if her life depended on it. She was as mesmerized as a rabbit before the dogs.

"Carmody?"

He came to her then, pulling her to her feet. The touch of his hand was fire on her fingers, and without knowing quite how it happened, she was drawn into the cabin with him.

He closed the door behind them, and, after a second's

reflection, dropped the bar into place. "Now then, Carmody," he said, "we will be able to talk at leisure, with no rude interruptions."

Her ears rang with pounding blood. She hoped she did not disgrace herself by being sick, and then, she thought, that would be a novel escape from ignominy. But she was too sturdy.

"You did come here to talk, did you not?" The Duke asked, a faint frown appearing between his fine dark eyebrows. "Or," he continued, leaning forward, hands on the table, "did you come here for, shall we say, something else?"

"M-my brother—" she began.

"Your brother?" he asked with an appearance of sternness. He was enjoying this encounter, nibbling away at the edges of her armor, tearing it away piece by piece even without her knowing it so that, eventually, she would stand defenseless before him. This was gallant sport, and he did not care how long it took. The outcome was inevitable. It had taken planning, and a certain amount of ruthlessness, but the rewards, he thought, his lip-licking glance traveling over his prey, would be great indeed. He would be sorely disappointed if they were not.

"Tell me about your brother," he coaxed." Is he quite well?"

His bantering tone was insulting enough. Even if he had not been the instigator of such brutal rending of the substance of the Petries, as she knew he had been, she would have taken umbrage at his callousness. And suddenly the outer shell of Carmody cracked with a rending noise that she thought surely must be heard on deck. He gave no sign.

Now, she was angry. Resentful. Furious—*wild.*

With the rage that had held her in an icy grip for hours now welling up, she rose to her feet from the settle where she had dropped when she came in to the cabin. "My lord duke," she said, leaning on the table in her turn and facing the man squarely, and speaking in a low clear voice that her servants would have recognized with trembling, "you are playing with me as a cat plays with a mouse. I

would have thought you above such clod-like, ungentle-
manly behavior. You are the master here. You have the
power to release my brother, and set him back in his
proper place at Oaklands, and to return his notes."

He had not moved. He was so close to her, his face and
hers nearly touching—so close that she could see the
bronze flecks move in his brown eyes, and feel his breath
hot on her cheek.

"Is that not right?" She invested the next words with
scorn. "My lord duke?"

The touch of amusement that she was able to add to her
tone, she was pleased to see, nettled him. She did not
pause to think that it might be a dangerous sport to taunt
a royal duke. Suppose he succeeded in his rebellion?
Then—King?

His breath was coming faster. "You have come here to
upbraid me? It seems to me that the fault lies in a foolish
young man who gambled more than he could afford to
lose."

"But he was enticed into the game by your agents. By
those who had the right to act for you. Do you deny
that?" She added, just enough later to underline her insin-
cerity, "Sir?"

"I do deny it."

"And your name was on the notes merely by chance?
Oh come, now." She knew her retort was feeble—not in
its correctness, but in the force with which she said it. For
the scent of the man's shaving soap reached her—a smell
compounded of leather, and woolens, and an indefinable
something else, a combination that touched a hidden spot
inside her consciousness. It was to her usual lavender as a
lion *passant* was to a kitten.

"I am a man, my dear Miss Petrie, who will seize any
benefit that comes his way."

His meaning was unmistakable. But she must be careful
to exact the benefits, herself, that she was to pay for. *What
does the price include?* She had bargained before with
him, to save Oaklands. Now the stakes were higher, much
higher. Her mind seemed to be her own again, taking
charge, and she was content to follow its lead.

"But you are willing to give up this benefit of my brother's little estate." She contrived to look puzzled.

"Your brother's little estate, as you call it, is worth—a certain amount, to me. Have you seen my men? The army that is rising to serve under my standard?"

"No, my lord duke," she said with elaborate courtesy. "I have been otherwise engaged, visiting my brother. In his elegant town lodgings."

"Ah, Carmody, you're a worthy foe—no, not foe. Opponent is a better word. For you will not be my enemy. Not tonight."

Her eyes glittered warningly. "One thing more. Let us bargain directly, my lord. Let me tell you what my price is."

"You're not in much of a position to bargain," he chuckled. "You came here on your own. I have no doubt the oarsmen who brought you are just this moment regaling their friends with the story. And it is you, Carmody, who has sought me out." He sighed hugely, concealing a smile. "As so many do."

Fiercely, she strove to regain her advantage. "No one who knows you—"

His mood suddenly changed. "Very well. Anyone who knows me knows that I am a man of my word. Before you throw that lamp, Carmody, consider what would happen were the ship to catch fire. There is no place to run to, except the harbor. And the tide will turn within the hour."

She set the lamp back in its gimbal. She had not realized she held it. How angry she was! She must clear her mind!

But the Duke was suddenly tired of his game. He spoke brusquely. "Very well, Carmody. I told you I would return the notes. Now I am saying, too, that I will see that your brother is freed." He measured her with his eyes, and ventured, "But first—"

She shook her head. The riband around her hair slipped with the movement, and one lock of bronze hair slipped down to her shoulder. The Duke watched it fall, and took an involuntary step toward her. "First," she said, her breath coming in little gasps, "free my brother."

"You bargain? *Now?* Carmody, don't you have any emotion? You feel nothing? Your blood doesn't throb in your head, as mine does? Your body doesn't burn to be fused with mine?"

He touched her hair, smoothing it back from her shoulder, and letting his hand lie warmly on the thin dress. Smiling gently, he loosened the riband and dropped it to the floor. Automatically, she reached up with both hands to gather her flowing hair into a semblance of shape, and the movement pressed her against the Duke. His hands moved on her back, pressing her close to him so that she could not escape. The rising force of him pressed hard against her, and she shrank back in panic.

"You feel nothing?" he murmured into her hair. "Carmody, you are lying if you deny it."

The inflaming nearness of him, the surprising river of passion that suddenly rose to meet his, frightened her. It was instinct, a revulsion against the imminent invasion of her privacy that caused her muscles to flex of their own accord and, with a mighty, desperate thrust, shoved him backward.

"You little—!" the Duke snarled. No longer was he the polished Stuart bastard who charmed his women into willing compliance. The beast in him—she thought—raged rampant.

Too quick for thought she reached for the oil lamp and held it, shaking in her trembling hands, before her. "One more step," she hissed, "and I'll drop this. I don't care what happens."

"Carmody, you're a fool!"

"Not fool enough, maybe," she said. "Send word to shore. Set my brother free this hour."

Her unwavering gaze gave him pause. He had seen such a look before, but never on a woman, and he knew that she would not hesitate to drop the oil lamp. He had no wish to die a remarkably unpleasant death in the stinking harbor, not for any woman—or man—in this world.

She wasn't worth the candle, he thought, amused at the way his thoughts ran. Rather, he corrected, not worth the oil lamp.

"As soon as we get on shore," he temporized, but her look did not waver. He had no idea how much desperation lay behind that basilisk stare, but he had no wish to probe it to the depths.

With a muffled curse, he snatched pen and paper from the open shelf behind him, and scratched a few lines on it. He thrust the paper at her. "Read it," he gritted.

The words leaped from the paper. "Ralph Petrie's possessions are to be restored to him in full. He has satisfied his obligations to me. He is to be free within the hour."

"The notes?"

"I don't carry them with me. When we get back to shore. Satisfied?"

She nodded.

"Wait here." He disappeared through the door. She the sound of wood on wood, of a boat scraping the side of could hear footsteps on the deck above. Then voices. And the ship.

She anticipated the progress of the small boat to land. ter—and before the tide could finally turn to the ebb, Ralph Prydgeon—she had seen that name on the face of the let- Then the letter would go to the hands of Colonel would be free to walk the streets, possibly a sane man. What would he do?

What *could* he do? He could go back to Oaklands, secure in the possession of his estate. Mercy Holland would be safe, old Tom could live out his days in peace. Pearson, Yarrow, dear Mrs. Bray and her hollyhocks—Oaklands would go on just as it had always done, she thought, to the limit of what she could do for it.

And what would happen to her?

The answer came through the door at the moment. "You heard? I've sent the note to Prydgeon. You can trust him. Even if you don't trust me."

She could only nod. Her lips formed the words Thank You, but her mouth was too dry to make a sound.

"You can put the lamp down, Carmody."

She glanced at it, unaware that she was still holding it. He talked on, gentling her. He had moved too fast, he knew, like breaking a fractious horse that feared the bridle.

His impatience allayed for the moment, he held a tight rein on himself. But she would make it up to him, he vowed.

He stepped toward her. "You are a lovely woman, Carmody," he said, "but tonight I will make you even more beautiful. Give me the lamp."

Without resistance she suffered him to remove the oil lamp from her nerveless hands and place it overhead in the gimbal. "Would you really have dropped it, Carmody?" he coaxed. "Tell me the truth."

She heaved a great, shuddering sigh, as though awakening from a bad dream. She had succeeded. She had won Ralph's freedom, little though—a small voice told her—he deserved it. He should have been left to pay for his own excesses. But—it was not entirely his fault. She had paid for him so many times that he had no coin of strength in him to meet his own debts.

She glanced at the Duke, a mischievous gleam in her eyes. Relief at her success bubbled in her like a fine wine, until she could not contain it.

"I don't know," she said honestly, more to herself than to Monmouth. "Probably not. You still hadn't freed my brother."

The Duke smiled. The appealing woman with the strange eyes who stood before him now was unawakened, full of great promise. But the woman that Carmody had been a few moments ago, the woman with the oil lamp in shaking hands—that woman scared the Duke right down to his polished boots!

"Just to remove temptation," he said. He reached over her head, contriving to pin her against the lower bunk as he did so, and blew out the flame.

She gasped in the sudden darkness.

"My lord duke—" she faltered.

He took her off balance, the edge of the bunk behind her knees betraying her. She fell heavily onto the hard bunk. Her world narrowed to a small intense space— warm, arousing hands stroking every inch of her skin, kindling every nerve into clamorous tingling.

Warm moist lips, mouth fusing with mouth—someone

sobbing in rising ecstacy. Without knowing when or how, her dress was no longer between her and the rough scraping blanket beneath her, and she had no more defenses left. Instinctively, she lifted her arms to encircle his neck, and the gesture arched her—most pleasurably—against the duke's moving body.

The throbbing in her temples kept her from thinking. She was no longer aware of herself—only of the inevitable moment when the last scrap of privacy, of wholeness, would be torn from her and she would no longer be herself but would be half of a melting coalescence. Her treacherous senses ruled her, clamoring for the fusion that was moments away, seconds—

There, on the night of Friday, June twelfth, in the stuffy dark of the captain's cabin, the door that Waldo Rivers had set ajar, the door to an unsuspected dominion of bliss, was opened, full wide and with exuberant zest, by the royal bastard.

6

THE Duke of Mommouth rode at the head of his army. He set a slow pace, since the road wound up across the cliffs, and down into small dells hardly dignified by the name of valleys.

Inland, he knew, the country would grow more prosperous, and—he devoutly hoped—more receptive to his cause. His reception at Lyme had been loud, noisy, and cheerful. But enthusiasm had not been backed by money, by weapons, or—more vital than the hard stuff an army uses—by local gentry support.

He had need of money, but even in Amsterdam he had need of money. Sometimes he wondered whether there was enough money in the world to buy all the things he wanted. He knew—once in a while, in rare honesty—that what he really wanted was for everyone to say, There goes the legitimate heir. But his mother had been more generous than far-seeing, and if the missing little black box holding her valuables ever came to light, he had a horrid conviction that Lucy Walter's marriage lines would not be in it.

In the meantime, since he could not have his heart's desire, he indulged himself in smaller things. They owe me this, he would say—gambling, fine clothes, women, jewels—and he helped himself liberally.

Now, he was not sure how he found himself heading an invasion of England, claiming the crown from his uncle, the anointed King. Surrounded in the Netherlands by

Fletcher, and Ferguson, and Gray, and Argyle, it seemed somehow easier to say yes than to resist. It always seemed easier to say yes.

Argyle had been the one who carried the most weight. Head of a powerful group of Scottish exiles, and himself under sentence of death in Scotland, he bristled with a fierce insistence for justice, as he saw it. And he was at this very moment raising the clans against the King. At least, Monmouth had not heard otherwise.

But now, on this sunny morning of June eighteenth, the larks sang overhead in the illimitable blue, the chaffinches flickered in the hedges, and all was well in his world.

He pulled up at the top of a fell, and looked about him. Gray moved up on his left. "Nothing but more of the same country we've been going over, my lord," Gray complained.

"And all of it empty," said the Duke. "Thank God."

Gray glanced nervously sideways. "One would think that you did not want to meet the King's forces."

"You mean the usurper," the Duke corrected mechanically. "You are right. With this army? Gray, you know how feeble this force is. You, of all people, should know."

Gray looked away. The memory of last Sunday was still festering in him, and it would take a touch no heavier than a goose feather to break his wounds into the open. Only the Duke could have spoken even thus gently to him. Gray had taken his cavalry to meet the first troops of the gathering Devonshire militia. His cavalry! He could have cried when he inspected them for the first time, and he had told the Duke so. Raw plow hands, untrained artisans, matched with horses that only lately had passed, nodding their great sleepy heads down the fields, their most exciting hour of the day when they were turned toward barn and feed.

That Sunday, with untried peasants on their backs, horses and men went out to their first battle. First battle! Gray thought, biting his lips with fury. It was the first *shot* that did it. Horses plunged, terrified. They shouldered each other, maddened with the acrid smoke of gunpowder, and flailed out with hooves at anything that stood in their way.

The plowmen could not control the panic-stricken horses, and, in fact, Gray suspected darkly, the men were as insensate as their mounts. But it was not fair to man or beast to put them under fire at such disadvantage. The encounter had been an unqualified rout.

"Poor Gray!" murmured the Duke sympathetically. "You should have had real Brunswickers behind you."

"My lord, we should be nearing London by now," Gray said simply, "if that had been the case."

The Duke looked behind him. His army toiled up the rise. There were his good men from Holland, half of them. The other half were far out of sight, behind the last stragglers of the foot soldiers, behind the miscellaneous carts and wagons, of food, ammunition, and other items of value to the men. The Duke was not one to impose austerity.

A faint smile flickered over his face. "Gray, we'll reach Taunton tomorrow." He turned to the woman on the sorrel mare who sat quietly, a few paces removed. "How far is it to Taunton, Carmody?"

On hearing her name, she turned. Her strange gray eyes looked at him without interest, but she said, pleasantly enough, "I do not know."

She looked away, as though the question had no interest for her, as though she were far distant in thought, and only by chance her outer shell was here in this place, at this moment.

The Duke looked thoughtfully at her, a faint frown appearing between his eyebrows. "All right, Gray, we'll go on." Gray cantered back along the line of march, leaving the Duke alone with her.

"Come, Carmody," he said, moving his horse forward until he was knee to knee with her, "can you not give me a smile? Surely you are not suffering?"

"Suffering?" she said, thoughtfully. "No, I don't believe I am. Except for your inability to produce my brother's notes, as you agreed to do before you left Lyme."

"You have any complaints for me?" he insisted. "Your lodgings last night, for example? Were they comfortable?"

She flashed a molten silver glance at him. "Comfortable enough, my lord duke, but hardly private."

A smile touched the corner of his full mouth, but he said with every appearance of solemnity, "Since you mention it, I agree. I must have the guard posted farther away. I had no idea that you longed so for seclusion with me that even a guard out of sight would distress you. I must see to it, my dear. Tomorrow, we will be at Taunton, and I shall see to that we are housed within walls, most privately."

She sat Amber stiffly. She would not yield an inch to him who took everything without permission. He was insistent, masterful, and, no matter how she begged, without mercy. She had expected to give herself to him once, in return for the disastrous notes. But the Duke claimed he could not find them and insisted that she accompany him while he searched for them in his possessions. An excuse, she knew, but what could she do? As long as the documents existed, she had accomplished nothing. And if she derived any pleasure from the Duke's company, day or night, she vowed he would never know of it.

They made camp that night in a valley not far from Taunton. As was the usage, servants rode on ahead, and on the spot chosen by Gray set up the Duke's tent, and tents for his officers. Dinner was already cooking over a hundred small campfires in the early twilight between the folding hills, as Carmody rode down the last slope.

The amethyst twilight gathered in and the little fires winked like amber in the dusk. There was warmth ahead, and hot food, and ease for her aching muscles, weary from days in the saddle. If she could only have a hot bath, she thought.

The Duke dismounted and came to stand at her stirrup. "Tired?" he said gently. She felt tears starting behind her eyes at the concern in his voice. Imperceptibly she swayed toward him. Then she caught herself. She could not allow even the appearance of weakness to show.

"No, my lord duke," she said, more sharply than she intended.

"You are a beautiful liar," he told her. "Nevertheless, I've a surprise for you."

Unreasonably, she snapped. "You're sending me home."

To her irritation, he laughed gustily. "No such luck, Carmody Petrie," he told her. "And one of these days you are going to tell me that you like me a little."

She was hot and tired, and covered with dust and, she felt, a grime that was more tarnish than dirt. She was soiled, body and mind, and the worst was that she no longer cared. He could do nothing worse to her. No one could, so she thought. She would remember that, one day.

"Come, Carmody, you'll do much better if you don't fight me."

"I can dismount by myself," she said, sitting stubbornly without loosening the reins, staring straight ahead.

"I didn't mean that," he said wickedly. He reached up to set his hands about her slim waist. He stood so, looking at her until she turned, startled, tinglingly aware of his touch on her, and looked at him. His face, so familiar to her now in light and in darkness, was calm, good humor touching the corners of his full mouth, his eyes containing a lurking twinkle as of a secret amusement. In spite of herself, she had to smile.

"Much better, my darling," he said. "Now I'll show you my surprise."

He set her on the ground, and held her, hands still circling her waist, close to him. She was burningly conscious of the sly gaze of his officers—the men she had come to know in recent days. Colonel Prydgeon, Gray, even that vulpine Ferguson whom she loathed without knowing why. "My lord duke, everyone's looking," she protested faintly.

"I've told you, my name is James."

"Yes, my lord duke."

"You will stay here just like this until you say my name."

She had no doubt that he would be as good as his word. She could not keep from burning with the flush that crept upward to cover her cheeks, and she knew that he could read her mind as though it were an open book. The laughter in his eyes rose to bubble over into a throaty chuckle.

She had heard that sound before, and she hastened to comply with his wish. "Yes—James."

"Good."

He turned her then, dropping his arm across her shoulders, and led her to the tent. Lifting the flap, he ushered her inside. Her surprise rooted her to the ground.

Instead of the usual furnishings of the tent—a wide cot with a pallet laid on top, a Turkey rug on the wooden floor, and a pair of simple chairs—there was a copper tub, clearly borrowed from one of the laundresses in the rear of the army column, and two great steaming ewers of water. Her small case of toilet articles was laid out nearby on a chair beside the tub.

The cot was shoved back against the tent wall, the rug rolled up beside it.

Her eyes filled with grateful tears. "Of all things I've longed for," she began.

He dropped the tent flap behind him. "Grateful?"

She truly was. She was aware in the recesses of her mind that he had been unusually good to her. She rode at his right hand, and she had the respect, at least outwardly, of those around her. Although she was only dimly aware of something else, yet it had its influence. For the first time since her father died, she was being taken care of. For these past three years she had borne more responsibility than she wanted—the entire estate, all the men and women and children of Oaklands looked to her, and while in some ways it was satisfying to know that such authority lay in her hand, yet it was a constant erosion of the feminine part of her. She had to be strong for Ralph—much good it had done her!—and instinctively she had known not to cling to Waldo.

Now she could let someone else care for her. Even though this might only last a short time—certainly if the Duke won through as far as Whitehall, her presence could only embarrass him there—yet, it was a useful reprieve. She did not know, consciously, how much she was changing—but she did suspect that she would not be the same again.

James—she must remember to call him that, since it

pleased him—was still looking down at her, that quizzical
expression in his eyes that at times irritated her, at other
times probed and found a matching response in her.

"Grateful?" she repeated. "Oh yes, I am. Thank you."
She took a step toward him. "James," she added.

She was in his arms in a moment. His hand pressed
hard in the small of her back, arching her to fit his hard
body, and her own senses accomplished their final betrayal. His eyebrows rose in agreeable surprise, and he
lifted her quickly and carried her the two steps to the pallet. His hasty hands bared her shoulders, tugged at the thin
cloth covering her breasts, and his lips were murmurous
and demanding on the hollow at the base of her throat,
moving over her.

She had forgotten Ralph as though he had never existed, and Oaklands vanished as well. There was nothing but
the thrumming in her head, the hammering along her
veins, the gathering fiery force somewhere within—

James left her. The bath water was still tepid, and she
stepped into the tub and let the relaxing water steal over
her. She soaped lavishly, and scrubbed away the dirt of
the road. She could not help but remember that other
time—when she had scoured her skin, scoured Waldo's
defiling touch away in the fear she would never again be
clean.

She was not one to look back, and now she told herself,
If ever you exercised that talent of forgetting the past, this
is the time. And yet, she dared not look ahead.

She lived, just now, in a little bubble in time, floating on
the surface of life, cast adrift—but it could be worse. She
had yielded to the Duke to save Ralph, whether he was
worth it or not. In the doing, she had lost something of
herself. And yet, in the losing, she had discovered the vast,
compelling domain of her senses.

After her solitary supper, after the moon had risen and
set, the Duke came back from his hours-long conference
with his staff over the news that had arrived by a hard-rid-
ing messenger from the east.

Parliament had voted an attainder of the Duke of Monmouth, for high treason, she learned later, and offered a reward of five thousand pounds for his person.

She heard his footfall behind her, where she sat on the ground before a small fire. Only embers remained, and she had been so lost in her thoughts that she had not taken the effort to add more wood.

She looked up when the footsteps stopped before her. His face—perhaps by a trick of the firelight—looked drawn and gray, and without volition she stretched her hand up to take his.

He pulled her to him, still without a word, and led her into the tent. "Shall I light the lamp?" she asked.

"No." He took off his doublet and dropped it on the chair, careless for once of his clothes. The tub was gone, and the soft woolen rug covered the wooden floor. He sat on the chair and pulled off his boots.

"James?" She dropped to her knees before him. "What terrible thing has happened?"

He did not answer for so long that she slid between his knees and put her hands on either side of his face. He smiled at her then, a queer, lopsided smile. "Are you mothering me?" he said with a broken laugh. "A mother is not what I need, believe me."

Stung, she leaped to her feet. "I've had enough of mothering," she flung at him, shamed by his spurning of her shyly offered comfort.

She crossed to sit on the edge of the pallet, as far away from him as she could get. She put her cold hands up to cool her burning cheeks. She had thought, this afternoon, that she had advanced a long way toward liking him. That he would meet her happily and draw her with him into a new excitement and wonder. And now—

She felt him in front of her. He put his hands on hers, and drew them away from her face. He had discarded his shirt, and he pulled her up to stand with him, holding her so closely that they seemed one. "Don't fight me, Carmody. Not tonight."

Shyly, feeling awkward and yet losing herself in his quivering need, she reached up to pull his head down and pressed her lips to his. In a moment, she pulled away and said, "I won't fight."

Later, his hands tender on her bare hips, he murmured with that throaty chuckle she knew well, "What a pitcher of hot water will do! If I had known that, I would have raided the galley of the *Helderenburgh*!"

For the first time since she had met the Duke, she laughed. Once started, she could not seem to stop, and silent laughter shook her. James stiffened beside her. His hands moved quickly over her quaking shoulders, up to her face. His fingers moved lightly over her cheeks.

"You're not crying?"

She stifled her laughter into a gurgle, and said, "No, James. Not crying."

"You're laughing!" he said with wonder in his voice. "This is the first time you haven't turned away from me and sobbed yourself to sleep."

She couldn't find an answer to that—there was no way she could put into words the change in her feeling for him, and instinctively she knew that this bubble-like iridescence between them would vanish under a serious examination. But James seemed content with his own discovery, and did not press her to answer.

Instead, he stopped her mouth so that she could not have answered had she wished to, and soon all her worries about what the future would bring them were lost in a new tidal wave of wonder and delight that swept her farther than she had ever been carried before.

Taunton was a lively and prosperous town.

In the late morning light, the beautiful Perpendicular tower of St. Mary Magdalene rose above the fertile valley full of orchards, and pastures, a valley full of green lushness.

James had high hopes of Taunton. It was a seat of great Whig sentiment, and Presbyterian persuasion. By all accounts, the Protestant Duke would be welcome here. James expected the countryside to flock to his support.

Taunton had stood fast for Parliament in the Civil

War, and even after the Restoration of the Stuarts, a generation before, Taunton had held to their old sentiments.

The Puritanical spirit had reached the notice of the government at Whitehall, and Charles the Second, a forgiving King for the most part, had lost his amiability when it came to Taunton. By royal edict their moat, protecting the town against the Royalist army of his father, was filled up and grass planted on it. The city had been walled, but the wall was destroyed. Not even a trace of the old foundation remained now.

Charles the Second's son, at the head of an invading army, pulled up at the last rise and looked down into the valley. He edged his roan toward the sorrel mare. "I promised you that tonight you would sleep within walls," he teased Carmody softly, so that no one else could hear. "I keep my promises—at least to you."

James reached out to take her hand. "Come, love, let us see what Taunton has to offer us," he said with a lazy smile. She smiled back, and together they cantered down the last slope to the unwalled town.

As they drew near, the blue standard fluttering just behind them, Carmody pulled up. "Let us not offend them," she murmured. She was not sure he heard her, for something was taking place just ahead of them, and every eye in the vanguard was intent. It reminded her that this was not a mere picnic outing, but a serious, warlike advance, dangerous and impudent.

From the town, past a point where there must have been a gate in the wall that once surrounded it, came a small procession. First came a flag, held in uncertain hands, dipping and wavering, embroidered, so Carmody learned later, with symbols of royalty. It was hastily put together, and some of the lilies seemed bunched together, but the thought behind it was sincere.

The procession following the flag was made up of schoolgirls, young and fresh—innocent, so Carmody thought wryly, as she herself had been not more than a week before. She yearned over them—sending blessings for long and good life silently over the Duke's shoulders.

Garlands of fresh flowers crowned their bare heads in

long draping lines from the first to the last, and the girls came singing.

It was charming, heart-touching, innocent.

Ahead of the procession marched a woman—possibly their school mistress. She looked back from time to time, to monitor her following, and then stepped out again with firm step and head held high.

Carmody was too far away to hear the meeting. The Duke cantered ahead, his groom at his heels, and—making a great ceremony of it—he dismounted and advanced on foot. The lady curtseyed, the little girls curtseyed. The flag dipped precariously, and the Duke put out a hand to steady it. It all took place in pantomime—the Duke and the lady, the flustered children.

The wind blew fitfully here in the valley, and once in a while it carried a few words to the riders stationed behind. Edging forward, Ferguson's curiosity moved him within earshot, and Amber too moved ahead, so that Carmody heard the last of it.

The lady held something out to the Duke, who took it with an appearance of great reverence. A small Bible, covered in white, with gold threads catching the light as the object changed hands. The Duke stood for an impressive moment, with bowed head, and, finally, simply, said, "I come to defend the truths contained in this book, and to seal them, if it must be so, with my blood."

The incident had turned too solemn. Carmody shivered, feeling a shadow pass between her and the sun. She glanced up, but there was not a cloud in the sky.

Their arrival in the town was a triumph. Every door, every window had its wreath of fresh flowers. The men wore sprigs of green in their hats—the badge of the Protestant cause. Men fell in behind the vanguard, shouting slogans, carrying their weapons.

By nightfall, the Duke looked from the windows of the inn which he had made his headquarters, to see a street full of soldiers. Newly recruited, they were rough and undisciplined, and small fights broke out sporadically on the fringes of the mob. The army that had come from Lyme were seasoned veterans compared to these jostling hordes below the window.

"My army!" he said, bitterness on his tongue. "Where are the peers of the realm, Ferguson? Where are the Protestant gentry that you promised me?"

"Wildman promised you, not I, my lord. I never trusted him, myself." Ferguson's accent grew broader, more Scottish, the more persuasive he became. He was tall and lean, stooped to a point of deformity. His great jaw was too heavy for his face, and his sharp little eyes were lost beneath his wig. His perpetual rash was more pronounced now in the firelight. Carmody held herself stiffly, not to betray her loathing of the man. She suspected, rightly, that he could be a dangerous enemy.

Just now, he was a dangerous friend, but the issue was still hidden in the mists of the future. "But, as I say, my lord, they are not going to jump at the chance to put their heads on the block."

The Duke looked somberly at him. "We all have done as much."

"Aye, but we know what we're fighting for. We know you'll set up your royal standard when the time is right."

The Duke watched him, unblinking. Carmody had the impression that this was an old argument.

"And I say the time is right now."

"You want me to claim the throne, say I'm King right now."

"Aye." Ferguson cast his little eyes around the room. "Gray there, he'll agree with me."

"By your leave, my lord." It was Nathaniel Wade. He was, or had been in happier days, a lawyer in Bristol. His views were ardently republican, and he was suspected of having a guiding hand in more than one insurrection against the throne. "We already have a king, if a king's what's wanted. But that's not the way of it. What we need is a new form of government. The old one's brought us naught but trouble, and expense. The people have rights, and they want a republic, a right to govern themselves. That's the new thing in the way of the world. A king's out of march with the times."

Gray exploded at once, and others came to Wade's support. Carmody noticed that Ferguson, having set the argument in motion, now retired to the sidelines, watching keenly, but holding his tongue. The Duke frowned. He let the antagonists go on until their voices raised sufficiently to be heard in the street.

"Quiet," he ordered firmly. "Do you want our new recruits to know that we can't agree among ourselves? There's nothing more damaging than for a soldier not to trust his leaders. I want to hear no more of this argument."

"But—" Ferguson began, but under a quelling look from the Duke, he subsided and made an excuse to leave. One by one the others departed, and James and Carmody were left alone. She watched him warily. She thought he had forgotten her presence.

He stood at the window looking down into the street. Flares from below flickered fitfully on his face, making it seem more expressive than ordinary. His face, oddly, was not lined. Instead, it was as though his thoughts etched themselves somewhere inside, upon his soul, perhaps, while his smooth face showed to the world only what he chose that it show.

Her leg cramped suddenly and she moved involuntarily to ease it. She made the slightest of sounds, but James heard her.

"So, Carmody, you have not left me? I should like to think it was because you could not bear to see me alone." He turned from the window. "Is that true?"

"As you say, my lord duke."

Suddenly angry, he crossed the room to her, seizing her by the shoulders. "What did I tell you? Say it!"

"J-James."

"Why do I have to force you to treat me like a human being, Carmody? Don't you know I have fallen completely—" He stopped short, and smiled oddly. "I never thought I'd say it—at least, say it and mean it."

"Say what?" she prompted after he fell silent. She had not lit the lamp, so that the deep purple from the window was the only light in the room. From where she stood she could see the blue deepening on the great tower of St. Mary Magdalene, in deeper shadows in the vertical tracery, the perpendicular lines making the tower stretch in an illusion of endlessness toward the infinite.

When he spoke, it was on a changed subject. "Light the lamp," he told her. "My thoughts are dark enough as it is."

For the first time he spoke to her as though she were a person, as though there was more to her than a delightful means of easing his urgency. "You heard the arguments, Carmody—shall I declare myself King?"

"James, I am not instructed enough to know what is right. If the question were about the rot in the flax fields, then I would know. But Waldo tried to explain politics to me, and I guess I am stupid because I never understood what he was talking about."

"Waldo!" James snorted.

She lit the lamp and set it on a table closer to the window. She, too, wanted to banish the dark. The welcome today to the Duke had been tumultuous, and was still riotous, judging from the sounds of revelry outside the open window. But despite that and the stifling heat, she had felt cold ever since the shadow that was no shadow passed over her on the sunny hillside that morning.

She could not shake off the depression that gripped her, and she recognized that much of the same depression held James in thrall.

"Come here, Carmody," the Duke said. He had dropped into the only easy chair in the room, a great hulking piece of furniture that more properly belonged in an abbey refectory, she thought. In fact, it had once held the abbot of a nearby priory, and on the dissolution of the monastery by a Tudor edict, the chair, as well as other valuable furnishings and plate, had vanished. No one asked questions, and the chair had been unearthed particularly to lend honor and grace to the Duke's rooms.

He pulled her down to sit half on his lap, half beside him in the narrow space between him and the oaken arm of the chair. He pulled off the riband binding her magnificent hair, and let the tresses slip downward over her shoulders, spreading out over his chest. Idly he toyed with a ringlet, twisting it endlessly around his square-tipped fingers.

"Did Waldo ever smooth your hair back, thus?" James said. "Did he ever—"

"No!" she cried sharply. "You know, James, you were the first." How could he have mistaken that? she wondered. But then, he often teased her thus. Strange, she thought, I have known James—this well—for less than a week, and I am saying to myself, He often does this, or he always does this. How well I have learned his ways! But then, she added silently, I have nothing else to do but to study him. James still held the notes that Ralph had signed, and while he still held them, she was still captive.

In a gilded cage, she owned honestly. But still a captive.

"Poor Waldo," James said softly. "How much he missed by not taking you on sight. And I cannot see why he didn't. That first day, Carmody, do you remember? There on the side of that cliff, you looked at me. Right then, I made up my mind."

She could not have escaped. One way or another, she thought, he would have pursued her, unless she had been able to fly to the New World.

The lamp flickered, and nearly went out in a sudden gust of wind. "James, let me close the window," she suggested.

"It's hot enough to fry in here," James said. "Superstitious, Carmody? Let's make the lamp an omen. If it stays lit, then we'll talk, a while. If the wind blows it out—"

"I'll light it again," she told him tartly.

His arm tightened around her shoulder, and she knew she could not move unless he chose to let her. Full of guile, she coaxed, "James, tell me what the quarrel was about? You are the rightful king, aren't you? Then why make a great thing about it?"

"Because, my child, some of these men are supporting me because somehow they believe I will depose my uncle, and call an election to name a new government."

"Not you as King?"

"So they think."

"And why do they think that?"

"My darling Carmody, I would guess," he said, laughing, "that they believe what they want to believe. From some hint that Ferguson dropped, perhaps."

"I don't like him."

"No more do I," he said softly, "but it will not do to make an enemy of him."

The lamp cast misshappen shadows into the corners of the room, moving and changing shape with the flickering of the flame. She squirmed from his embrace and gained her feet. "Too many shadows," she told him, "they're getting on my nerves.

It was hot in the room, and she blamed the heat for her restlessness. "Really, James," she said with soft laughter, "the tent was cooler." She did not think he heard her.

Her eye fell on an object on the table. "Where did this come from?"

"The lady at the head of the schoolgirls gave it to me." James came to stand beside her. "It's a handsome thing, isn't it? And I believe I spoke handsomely in my turn." She picked it up and turned it over in her fingers.

"Such beautiful embroidery work on it," she commented. "White satin covering. This is French weaving. And the golden threads—" She stopped abruptly. She had opened the back, looking at the inside covers to see how cleverly the material had been put together. Her fingers had explored, because the light was dim, and she had found something bulky inside the back cover.

"What is it, darling?" he asked, touching her shoulder. "Something wrong?" For answer she held out the open book to show him. "Ah, something inside the cover? How interesting. Perhaps it's a note from old Somerset, telling me he's bringing me an army. Open it, Carmody."

She tugged at the thread and it gave way. The contents of the hiding place, inside the back cover of the small Bible, slid out into her hand, cold and smooth.

"It's coins, James! Sovereigns. Two golden sovereigns."

He uttered a short exclamation, and took the coins from her. Together they examined the Bible, but it had yielded up all its secrets. James tossed the heavy coins in his hand, deep in thought. "How good they are," she ventured, "to give you this."

He nodded. "They've given me more than they know, Carmody." Suddenly he laughed, a boyish cheerful laugh. "Superstition, again. Sovereigns! That's an omen, Carmody. I am to be King, that's what it means."

He picked her up by the waist and whirled her around the room, laughing all the while. "Now, then," he said, setting her down. "You take these. No, don't argue with me. I can't give you a great deal, but these are my own, and I want you to have them." His mouth twisted. "With all my worldly goods, Carmody. Take them."

There was no way to refuse without hurting him badly. She managed a faint thank you, and left to find her small case. She would find a better place to hide them tomorrow, but now the case would have to do. She had just fastened the case again, and looked back at James. He was watching her with amused intentness. "You think I'll take them back?"

"Oh, James, no!"

"You're good luck for me, Carmody," he told her, suddenly sober. "It was my lucky day when I—met you. Well, it's settled. I'll have to do some ground work, convince a few people, but before I leave Taunton, I'll be King."

He pulled her close. "What a nuisance this army is," he murmured. "Always, when I want to think about you, to make love to you, Prydgeon or Gray come in with some nonsense." James was edgy, irritable. She bent her head to lean her forehead on his shoulder, smelling the faint pleasant aroma of clean linen.

James's dearest wish was to be king, and yet he hung back, almost as though he were afraid. She stirred, and felt the circle of his arms tighten around her. "Perhaps we could buy a gypsy wagon," he said, "and travel through France and Italy, and never come home. Would you like that, Carmody?"

Trying to match his mood, she said lightly, "Just you and me?"

"With those eyes, my dear, you will draw me wherever

you will. You've cast a spell, and I'll never be free of you."

She did not answer at once. But when he insisted, she said, "I don't want to think of the future, James."

Slowly, he agreed. "The present is all we have, Carmody. So come, love, and make the present something to remember."

A sudden gust of wind came in the window. The lamp flame flared high, and brightened the room momentarily. Together, the two of them watched the flame. It flared twice more, and then was gone. The wind had been too strong for it.

"Another omen, Carmody," said James, laughing, as he picked her up and took her into the inner room. "No more talking, my darling. Not tonight."

7

FOR a man who had just been proclaimed King, Carmody thought, watching him secretly through the doorway to the inner room, James did not look exhilarated. Indeed, she thought, he seemed more like a man in sore need of comfort than one strong enough to bear a kingdom on his shoulders.

On the contrary, it was the loathsome Ferguson who was in such high spirits that finally, in disgust, James had sent him away. James did not confide in her, exuding instead a morose aura that preyed on her own mind. She could not shake off the gloom that descended on her like a cloak from James.

She packed her few things and touched the waistband of her skirt, feeling the two round coins sewn into the lining. Touching the golden sovereigns might bring her luck, she thought, borrowing for a time James' own superstition. They had been given in love, she justified herself, or what passed with James for love, and so carried more goodwill than some of the other things surrounding her.

As they marched out of Taunton, taking to the road again like the Children's Crusade centuries before, she felt her spirits rising with the sheer physical pleasure of being once more on horseback, once more riding all day in the open air.

It was a short day's journey to Bridgewater. And there, for the first time, she began to believe she was indeed traveling with a royal personage.

122

They were met some distance from the town by the Mayor and the Aldermen, dressed in official robes, walking out to give them welcome. The officials, after lengthy and pompous speeches—which served to cheer James—led the way as the procession wound through the streets to the high cross. There, as Carmody fell back to lose herself in the throng, James was welcomed as true king.

Heartened by the support that had come to him in Bridgewater, James began to revive. When they left Bridgewater, he looked back at the army unwinding along the road behind him with a sense of pride. These men were giving up everything to follow him. They knew the risks—his uncle had already put a magnificent price on his head—and yet they followed him. He heard again in his memory the cries of applause when he made his previous tours—in his father's reign, but against his father's wishes—through the West Country. It was those journeys, the pleasant recollections of approval and enthusiasm, all expressions, he thought, of the great love his people had for him, that had brought him to claim the throne upon his father's death.

At first, after landing, he was sorely disappointed at the meager number of recruits that flocked to his banner. Ferguson had said that the entire countryside would be raised in his behalf. Instead, James thought darkly, even the Mayor of Lyme Regis had scuttled off somewhere, and sent word to Whitehall of the Duke's landing.

The lack of enthusiasm had dismayed him. He still thought his own presence would provide the magic touch that would make even stones rise up like men and follow him. The only surprise that Lyme had offered was the delectable woman he had found to accompany him. It had taken longer with her than with some others—longer to work his own urbane spell. Even yet he was not entirely sure that she was eager for him. A frown appeared between his eyebrows. There was always that first stiffening under his hands, always the resistance that was almost a shudder. It piqued his vanity. Before he was through with her, she would run to him, ardent and breathless, even begging. It was a small triumph to look forward to, but it was one, in his boundless conceit, he was sure of.

There were perhaps seven thousand men in James' train, and a sorrier excuse for an army had never existed. So he said.

"Look at the cavalry, Carmody! Farm boys on cart horses. One shot from Feversham's cannon and they won't stop till they're munching hay in their own stables. I vow there's bound to be more broken bones from falling off horses than from enemy fire!"

The army had to make its own weapons, since for unexplained reasons, whatever arms had come in the three ships had also returned to Holland, still in the ships' holds. The most wicked-looking of the handmade arms was a scythe blade fastened to a strong pole. It was a murderous affair, and Carmody shuddered when she saw the first of them. But even scythes were in such short supply that many men were turned away from the recruiting stations, simply because there were not weapons enough to arm them.

The army trudged wearily from Bridgewater to camp within sight of Bristol, and then moved on to Glastonbury and Bath. Bath, calmly and coolly, closed its gates and retreated into silence behind its walls. It was then that the army began to melt away. It was clear that there would be no chance to swing their scythes, they told each other. Might as well be back in Axminster—or Taunton, or Lyme—where there's a bit of fun at night, they said, and there isn't so much rain.

The rains came heavily, and continuously. Never stopping by night or by day, the rains soaked tents, bedding, clothing. The rains dampened the kindling, and, if by chance a small fire could be built from miraculously dry wood, kept tucked away in the baggage, the rains fought it to a standstill.

And by the time they reached Bridgewater—the second time, in retreat now—the army was weaker by at least four thousand men, who were there of an evening and not there at dawn.

It had been two weeks, plus a day, since Carmody had

been rowed out to the *Helderenburgh*. She was drained of emotion. This night she refused to sit near James, as he wished, while his generals gloomily discussed their plans with him. She retired into the tent, and firmly closed the flap behind her. Tonight she did not even light the lamp. There was no copper bath to wash away the mud of the road. The army was exhausted from slogging through mud up to their knees from the constant driving rain. And she was numb from exhaustion.

Her riding skirt was stiff with mud, and she reluctantly laid it over a stool. By morning it would be dry enough to brush into pathetic respectability. But nothing would help her boots any more. She stood them on the floor beside the stool. Her shirt followed the skirt, and she found the shift she kept for covering at night. The damp crept into the corners, and even the pallet that covered the wide cot was damp at one corner where it had been carelessly uncovered during the day.

She shivered. She pulled a covering from the cot and huddled it around her shoulders. She did not know how long she sat there, lost in nameless misery, her mind blank.

Later, lying awake next to James, hearing the muffled whinny of a cavalry horse, the soft thumping of the bodyguard's boots, she could see nothing but dark shapes ahead, dark monstrous forms rising in the mists of the future.

James stirred restlessly and turned toward her. She edged out of reach, taking care not to rouse him. But the small movement had disturbed her train of thought, setting it into another direction. And she decided that she did not want to know the future. Not even tomorrow.

Tomorrow, when it came, was like the others, riding across the countryside, but this time the forty soldiers of James' personal guard rode closer together, forming something of a shield with their bodies, and for the first time she realized that she might actually be killed. No matter where she rode in the column, a bullet could find her. After the first *frisson* of terror, she began to think that perhaps that was the way it was meant to end. Except that—she realized—the notes still existed with Ralph's signature.

As the rebellion fell apart, as the invading forces faded away, James depended more and more on her soothing presence. There was hardly a moment of the day when she was not aware of his desire for her. Instead of waning, as she had cynically supposed it would, it seemed to grow, and grow.

So it was that he did not send her to a place of safety, the night of the twenty-sixth, even though, she knew later, there had been no safe place.

That Saturday, early in the morning, she heard her first real shots of the rebellion. Feversham's advance guard, under James' bastard half-brother the Duke of Grafton, appeared at Philip's Norton, and the battle was joined.

The first victory fell to Monmouth, but only because Feversham did not wish to commit his troops until his artillery arrived. The rebels made a good showing, and Monmouth was heartened.

The fighting at Philip's Norton lasted sporadically throughout the day. Carmody moved restlessly from the tent to the space in front, where James sat with Prydgeon, Ferguson, and the others. She hardly thought of herself. She had passed a point where she thought of escape. Now all she longed for was that the whole affair come to an end. Whether she followed James—follow was not the word, she thought with a grimace; he would not let her out of his sight—whether she accompanied James to London, in victory, or whether the rebellion would die here in the mud and the rain—she did not care.

She was hardly living, as it was. And either way—victory or defeat—there was no escape from James, until he tired of her and, fulfilling his promise, gave her the infamous notes.

She stood, restlessly, in the doorway of the tent. James was listening with apparent attention to Colonel Prydgeon, speaking dryly on some supply problem. But then James glanced at her, and she knew his thoughts were not concentrated on the dwindling supply of bullets. Cheeks hot, she turned abruptly back into the tent. She hoped none of the men had seen that look of James', but then—what did it matter, when they all knew what she was?

It was that moment that decided her. She would get the notes back from James, stealing them if she had to, and then she would leave, preserving the tatters of such self-respect as she had left. She did not care what happened after she had destroyed the notes, but she must make sure that the last two weeks had done some good.

There was no chance to put her plan to get the notes into action that night. As soon as twilight deepened, the army marched again, this time to the south, and, at dawn, arrived at Frome. Frome was enthusiastic in their reception, but the cupboard was bare, thanks to the prompt action of the Earl of Pembroke who had disarmed the inhabitants only three days before.

The army was exhausted. The night's march, on top of the alarms and skirmishes of the day, had drained them all. The rain had fallen heavily, relentlessly, and the roads were mud to the knees. July 4, 1685. Sunday again. The army lay where it sprawled, exhausted, unfed, mud-covered.

Carmody spent a sleepless night. She sat just inside the flap of her tent, watching the fires die down, the ragged soldiers on the ground, pulling whatever shreds of clothing they could find over themselves to guard against the feared night air.

The lesser fires of the stars grew brighter as the nearer flames died, and she watched them wheel overhead, marking the progress of night.

She had thought James was a strong man, and only circumstances could defeat him. But with the clear insight of early morning, after a sleepless night, she saw that it was his weakness that led him to listen to advisers who seemed to fade away like shadows at noon, to believe what he wanted to believe—that he was so loved that England to a man would rise to give him the throne.

Well, she had come this far with him. Forced at first against her will, she had discovered charm in him, an appeal that was magnetic, and the glimmerings of the devotion that the Stuarts seemed to compel. And—she would go on with him. Not, she thought realistically, because she was consumed by belief in his cause—not at all.

Simply because there was nothing else to do.
surprise attack on his uncle's troops, he too was blinded by

Far across the valley of the Frome rose the hills around Bridgewater. So close had they come returning to the tracks they had made going north. It was retreat, nothing else. And she believed she could ride as far as Oaklands as she herself withdrew. And then?

She stirred, feeling the cold mist creeping up from the river. Far away a sleepy bird stirred, protesting against the coming dawn, and close at hand a horse whinnied. Her vague planning took a new turn, sinister and chilling.

She was, certainly in the eyes of the law, as much a traitor as Ralph. Aid and comfort to the enemy, she thought it might be called. Aid, not at all—but comfort, perhaps. And if she returned to Oaklands, she would bring upon her people a dreadful fate, carrying it with her as one does a miasma of plague.

She could never return to Oaklands.

The Battle of Sedgemoor routed what was left of the army after James' indecision, the rain, the mud and the darkness, and a great yawning ditch opened up before his lack of food, had taken their toll. In the night of James' men, unseen and unreported by his scouts.

James, ever a man of omens, seeing the dawn about to break and knowing his high adventure was finished, took horse in flight, grabbing up Carmody on the way, thundering away from Sedgemoor as though the devil followed.

The haystack was the strangest of all places to spend a night. And when she woke, early in the morning, she had dreamed she was back at Oaklands, in a happier day when her parents were both alive, and she had no duties except to enjoy sunshine, the wonderful world of fields and meadows, streams and trees. The same haunting scent of hay, and far away a rooster crowed.

She glanced around, still half-dreaming. How had she got here?

A movement next to her startled her into total and painful awakening. "You all right?" said James Scott. No longer King Monmouth, she realized slowly. Now only a traitor to the Crown with a massive price on his head, hunted all through the day yesterday like a desperate fox.

The whole sorry bungling mess came down on her head in that moment. She had reached the lowest ebb of her life, made doubly poignant by the sweet nostalgia of the dream she had just had. "I'm fine," she lied.

He took her arm with a strong hand and looked keenly into her face. "Those eyes," he said. "I'll never know what lies behind them. Mark my words, Carmody, you'll find your strange eyes will either make your fortune, or ruin you."

"They have ruined me," she said, "and I never knew how it happened."

He loosened his hold on her arm, and she became aware that he had forgotten her existence. She had seen him look like this before, when he needed to think of his next move. Usually, after such concentrated thought, he would turn to her and tell her what he had decided, asking her opinion. Now that she thought about it, seldom did anything she say change his mind. She waited now, letting her thoughts disappear. If she thought, put her thoughts into pictures, she could not bear them.

But this time James said nothing to show what he had decided to do. He simply said, "You'll be all right, Carmody. You will fall on your feet wherever you go."

"That sounds like a farewell."

"Didn't you know?"

She did not answer at once. She had known, of course. She had believed that separation was inevitable, but a bridge to cross at another time. But now the bridge was before her.

"I've sent word to my cousin William, in the Lowlands, to send ships for me. I can get off at Southampton, or close enough, and get back to Amsterdam."

"And what happens to Colonel Prydgeon?" she asked.

"And Fletcher? And Gray?" She did not ask, *What happens to me?* Her pride kept her from that folly.

"What? Oh, they'll make their way the best way they can. But I cannot take you with me." He smiled, a travesty of his ordinary winning smile. "You'll do better on your own."

What his words meant, she knew, translated, was that he would do better on his own. The Stuarts were not noted for loyalty to their adherents, except in instances so isolated that they were remarked. And even Charles the First, James' grandfather, had given over Strafford to Parliament rather than risk his throne. Only when the question came to the throne itself had Charles stood firm, firm enough to lose his head.

James gave her a last kiss on the forehead, a sort of benison, and even while she received it, murmuring appropriate words of farewell, the scales fell from her eyes.

James Scott was an actor *manqué*. He filled his role on the limited stage of his own understanding, and as long as others read their lines correctly, all was well. Nor did he care what happened to the cast after his brief hour on the stage.

"You have forgotten something," she pointed out.

He frowned. He disliked an importunate woman. He hoped she wasn't going to spoil this idyll for him. "I told you, Carmody, that we must live for the day only—"

"And you have, my lord duke," she said, hardly able to keep her voice from trembling. She was numb inside. No longer could she hold anger—it spilled away from her as though held in a leaky cup. But she was determined that these three weeks would not be in vain for her.

"The notes," she said firmly. "You promised me the notes my brother signed."

She held her hand out imperiously.

"How very beautiful you are," he sighed. In that moment, if he could have simply taken her hand and walked away from his troubles, keeping her with him, he would have asked for nothing more from Providence. But his only chance to preserve his neck from the block—and a very slim chance it was—was to travel alone. He thought obscurely that his travel would look much like headlong flight. Call it what they would, it was his neck, and he had an understandable wish to keep it intact.

"The notes, my lord duke."

"Ah, Carmody, I failed with you. You have not the slightest feeling for me at all, do you?"

She dared not answer. At last, with a sigh, he reached into a secret pocket in his jacket. He pulled out a small packet, wrapped carefully in silk. Opening it, he took out a dark blue riband, a golden round object like a rising sun—"Order of the Garter—that goes into the first river I cross. Ah, here are the notes. I cannot condemn your brother for his stupidity, Carmody. Otherwise I should scarcely have gotten you to share my bed. Would I?"

"No, my lord duke."

"Tell me, Carmody—" The bantering look was entirely gone from his face, and instead there crept over it the be-seeching look of a small boy, hoping for a word of praise. "Wasn't it worth it?"

She thought for a moment of what lay ahead of him—she had listened with profit to the men talking in low voices outside her tent. There would be flight and ignominious exile in a foreign country the rest of his life—if he were lucky. For a man who loved England as James did, this was dire punishment.

And if he were not lucky? There were no illusions in her mind—James would mount the steps and lay his head on the block, and that, as King James had proclaimed, would be "justice done right speedily."

She could not, even now with the notes safely in her hand, turn her back on James. He had, after all, treated her well according to his lights. No man could do more.

"Thank you, James," she said softly, "for everything."

Not exuberant, but it would have to do, she thought.

Carmody slipped to the ground, cautiously. Already she was taking on a new character, a hunted prey of the hounds. Her country sense stood her in good stead now, since from the contented whinny of the horses in the nearby stable, and the cooing of doves on the roof, she knew that no alarm had been raised.

She stole through the barnyard, taking care to keep the haystack between her and the thatched house beyond. At the bottom of the sunny meadow ran a small stream, which she waded, boots in hand. Beyond the grassy slope rose to a coppice of trees at the top, crowning the hill, a remnant of the ancient forest. She made her way there.

She found a hiding place under the roots of an old oak fallen victim to some long-ago storm. She would stay here, she decided, until—

Until what, she did not know. She had now reached a point where she must wait upon the inspiration of the moment. She had thought only hours before that a sign would show her which way to go. The sign had not yet come. Until then she must simply wait, and watch.

She huddled under the roots. From here she could see the haystack, and knew the moment that James left the stack. He waited until the farmer had cared for his stock, and then gone off to work some fields. It was hay-cutting time, and presumably last night's shelter would soon be augmented by a cartload, the size of the empty cart the farmer pulled with him as he left, disappearing around the far side of the barn.

James cautiously thrust one foot after another, and with consummate stealth and infinite slowness disappeared down the road in the direction opposite to that of Lyme Regis. He was going toward the New Forest, to hide himself as he made his way to William of Orange's ships at Southampton. He had no doubt that William would come to his rescue. William hated King James, his father-in-law, she knew from what her James had said, and he would let no opportunity escape to irritate his brother monarch.

Carmody stayed huddled under her shelter long after James had disappeared. At length hunger drove her from it. With the tightness of her belt around her empty stomach, she remembered—she still had James's two golden sovereigns, given him by the lady of Taunton. Well, it was small enough reward. As long as the two gold coins were sewn into the waist of her skirt, she was not penniless.

She could not afterward remember the next four days. When she was given time to reflect, with the hope of death upon her, she could not remember. But somewhere there was a small fire, and she fed Ralph's notes into the flames, as she had done once with the copies. She remembered nothing more, except the empty feeling that her mission had, at last and at what cost, been accomplished.

There were hills and valleys. A shepherd, wordless as his sheep, but with pity in his faded eyes, gave her his bread and cheese. She walked, mostly by night, by late moonlight or early starlight. If it had not been for those days of hard riding and hardy camping at night, she could not have done it. But her body had fined down until it was as muscular as a young farm woman, and it now served her in good stead.

She thought she remembered four sunrises before she reached a high point where, in the far distance, she could see a silver line that old experience told her was the sea. She propped herself against a great oak, and unwrapped the last square piece of cheese left from the shepherd's munificence. The neighboring region of Cheddar had long been known locally for its cheese, and it formed a staple of ordinary diet. It had never, on her own table at Oaklands, tasted as delectable.

Breaking off the tiniest possible pieces, and letting them linger on her tongue, she was able to sustain the illusion that she was eating a meal.

Before her was spread the slanting saucer-shaped valley that led down to the sea. The far mouth of the valley, where it opened out upon the shore, held a settlement of houses. She thought she knew the town, but it must be the stuff of dreams, because she could not remember how she had reached this place. She wiped her fingers on the grass, rather than her skirt, and thought with a mad chuckle that she was still fastidious.

That was the last of the cheese. The last of anything. She settled herself more comfortably against the tree, and set herself to consider the town beyond. Somewhere in that town she must find help, food, some hiding place. She had reached a point where she was conscious of only the needs of an animal. Food, shelter, safety.

And clothing—she noted ruefully that her pale gray gown, worn for the first time the evening she went aboard the Duke's ship, was almost fog-like in its wispy fringes. There were rents in the muslin, torn by berry branches, odd sticks, and other nameless accidents.

But—she fingered the coins at her waist—she was still not destitute.

Below was the church, with its familiar square-topped steeple. The church at Lyme Regis, where, once, she had planned to wed Waldo. And, if she looked with the eyes of imagination, she thought she could see the very inn that had sheltered James.

It took two days to reach the edge of Lyme Regis. Happily she arrived as the light of day was turning imperceptibly into sea-tinged twilight.

The sea beyond the town threw back the silver light of the evening sky, tinged with lemon at the horizon, and saffron streaks above. The steeple was darkly silhouetted against the sky and the sea, and she felt a flood of relief washing over her like a spring tide.

As she had descended the valley, her half-formed plans crystallized into a clear-cut design. She would go to Waldo's apartment, and throw herself on his mercy. He might not have an over-supply of that virtue, she thought, but he would certainly help her on her way. He had loved her once, and perhaps he still did. Perhaps.

The streets of Lyme on that July night were hot and stifling. The tall crooked buildings lining the cobbled streets kept out whatever breeze came up the hill at nightfall from the sea, and all the residents of the poorer section of town seemed prepared to spend the night in the streets.

She mingled with them, making her way as unobtrusively as possible, trending ever toward the street where she expected to find Waldo.

One or two men accosted her, but she flung her arm out at them, silently, and her very silence seemed to repel them. One, indeed, called her a witch, but his fellows, in fear, reduced him to muteness, and she passed on without harm. She dared not speak for fear of giving herself away. Her speech was not that of the people of the streets.

At length, she arrived in the block where she knew Waldo lived. Her luck, having deserted her for the past weeks, now returned. Good luck, she thought at first.

A carriage drew up in front of the building at the far end of the row. She could not tell whether it was in front of Waldo's door, but there was no doubt about the man who emerged from the vehicle, and then sprang lightly up the steps. It was Waldo!

Someone passed her, eyeing her suspiciously. She became aware then that she had passed the region where she was inconspicuous. This was a better part of town, one where she felt at home. But in looking at her dress, she realized that she was alien now. She must not embarrass Waldo. But what could she do? She had counted on Waldo's help. There was no place else to turn, no one to seek out. Nobody but Waldo, and she could not go to him.

Suddenly she thought—Maybe I can. There must be a back entrance to this building, and if I can find it—

It took quite a while, but eventually, among piles of garbage, some sinister-looking tumbledown outbuildings, and quite a few gaunt cats, she found the back of Waldo's apartment building. The same maroon curtains showed at the back windows as had been visible from the front, and there was a lamp on a table just inside the open window. There was a shed, a lean-to affair, just under the maroon-curtained window, but the sill was too high for her to reach.

She sought for and found a door, unlocked. She entered a dirty, narrow hall, smelling of yesterday's cabbage and last week's fried fish, and dimly lit by reflected lights from other rooms.

She made her way to the stairs, ascended, and at length stood outside Waldo's door. She heard voices within, and one approached the door.

Quickly she stepped back into the shadows. The door opened. Durward stepped into the hall and swiftly ran down the stairs. Elated at the confirmation that she had found Waldo's apartment, she hurried to the door. Should she knock? Better surprise him.

She stepped through the door. Blinking in the sudden brightness, none the less she could see Waldo, tobacco-pipe in one hand, leaning over to snuff the one candle on the table.

"What did you forget, Durward?" Waldo said, faintly irritated.

~~ When there was no answer, he looked up. When he saw her, in her wraith-like gray rags, he must have thought she was a ghost, for he stared at her in sheer astonishment, and the color drained down from his cheekbones until his face resembled the tallow candle.

Putting all her resources into one last effort, Carmody said, with a creditable attempt at well-bred civility, "Good evening, Waldo."

The room swam about her.

She felt Waldo's hands on her arms, felt a chair placed behind her knees, and she sat, leaning forward, holding to the edge of the table. A glass of brandy was at her lips, and she sipped gratefully.

"Now," Waldo said, his eyes watching her intently. "Where is the Duke?"

"I don't know," she said. Some obscure impulse to caution made her add, "He went into the battle, and I didn't see him afterwards."

Could anyone prove otherwise? She recalled the darkness of that night of the fifth of July, when James thought he could surprise Feversham's men, and instead was surprised himself. He had come back for her in the dark, and the two of them had run, stumbling, sensing people around them, but knowing each was intent on his own escape. No, no one could have seen them escaping the field of Sedgemoor together.

"Sure?" Waldo insisted.

"He left me." It was a simple statement of fact. Let him make of it what he could.

"How did you get here?"

The heat of the room was making her giddy—that or the unaccustomed brandy, or the lack of food.

"I don't know. I walked, mostly. I don't remember. Waldo," she ended with a wail, "I'm *hungry*."

He rummaged in a cupboard and came back with some cold meat and a bit of bread. She fell wolfishly on it. He let her eat in silence. She looked up once to catch his eyes on her, but he did not seem to see her.

Finally, he said, "Why did you come here?"

"For help. Believe me, I am not presuming on our engagement. That has long since, I assume, been broken. Neither one of us wishes for marriage, I am sure. But— Waldo, you did receive my dowry, before I left Oaklands. Could you not help me in consideration of that?"

"Of course, I will help you," he said, with a smile. "Just wait here while I make some arrangements."

He was gone a short time, and she had leisure to look about her. There was on the table before her the one candle, its flame wavering in the fitful breeze from the open window. The empty plate, cleaned even of crumbs, on which her small supper had been served. The half-full brandy glass, and a book of some sort. At the far end of the table lay a few coins, a snuffbox, a leather tobacco-pouch, a gun. A pistol, she thought absently, and noted with mild surprise that it looked loaded. Waldo no doubt could protect himself well against footpads and brigands.

When he came back, he brought with him a cloak, dark blue, made of badly woven, stiff material.

"Borrowed it from my landlady," he said. "You will need this. Your clothes, Carmody! Abominable."

"Yes," she agreed. This dress had been one of her wedding clothes, she remembered, but wisely decided not to mention the fact. "Waldo, I need to know what to do. Should I take ship for—the colonies? Can you buy my passage?"

"With what, my dear? I have little money, you know."

"You have my dowry. Have you spent it all so soon?"

He refused to look at her. "My dear, you know that the Duke needed funds. And presumably, you have had your share of it."

Certain words she had heard in the Duke's quarters now took on meaning to her, certain little pieces of puzzle fell into place. "But they said you did not give him any funds at all. It was remarked that you had not supported him, in spite of your great interest in his activities. It gave rise to some suspicion, Waldo."

"Oh, that Prydgeon," Waldo said, shaking his head in recognition of the follies of men. "He must have lined his own pockets with the money."

"Colonel Prydgeon is an honest man!" she retorted hotly.

"And you are such a fine judge of men," Waldo said mildly.

Disconcerted, she rose to her feet and began to move at random. She was much restored by the food she had eaten, but she still kept the palm of one hand on the table lest she feel faint again.

"You refuse to help me?"

"On the contrary," Waldo said with a winning smile. "I have made all the arrangements necessary for your future."

Then she heard the noise. The sound of heavy boots in the street. They stopped just outside the house, and she could hear them begin again as they approached the front door below.

"Waldo! The soldiers are coming! Where shall I hide!"

"You will not hide, my dear. I have sent for the royal troops, and they will take you away."

"You!"

"Of course, my dear. Did I not say that you were a peerless judge of men? Let me amend that a bit. You see what you wish to see. In me, as in everyone else. The Duke, Ralph—"

"Keep quiet!"

She was near hysteria. The boots were on the stairs, and there was not a moment to spare. Waldo kept talking, talking, and she could not think. She must escape. She must—

"Waldo, keep away from me!"

He had started toward her, to hold her for the soldiers.

The paralysis that had engulfed her suddenly left like the breaking of a shell. She could move. She darted to the end of the table. Without volition, she picked up the pistol. "Keep away from me!" she screamed.

In her dreadful panic, somehow her fingers moved convulsively on the trigger. The report filled the room to bursting.

Waldo's eyes smiled no more. Instead, they looked puzzled, then widened as they fastened on her in disbelief. "How could you—"

She could barely hear his faint accusation. Still moving mechanically, all her senses screamed at her that it was time to leave. Help was coming for Waldo. There would be none for her.

Snatching the blue cloak that Waldo had dropped over a chair, she scuttled to the window. She paused long enough to draw the maroon curtains together, before she slipped through them and perched precariously on the sill.

It was fully dark now. Shapes moving at the end of the alley were indistinct, and she was sure she could not be seen where she was. But she could not stay. In the room behind her, soldiers burst through the door, exclaiming loudly as they saw Waldo, wounded, and fallen to the floor.

She threw her cloak, the borrowed cloak Waldo had brought her, down in front of her, and heard it thud unexpectedly near. She had forgotten the existence of the shed just below the window. If she were careful—

She let herself down from the window sill, and dropped the last couple of feet, landing on the buffer of the cloak. She heard the voices from Waldo's window. Someone had discovered her means of escape. Quickly she threw the cloak over her mist-gray attire, and huddled on the slanting shed roof close to the wall. She hid her face in the folds of the cloak.

The cloak was rank with relics of grease-fried mackerel. She could barely breathe. It was at that moment, hunted, a murderess, a traitor, with no home, no family left, no future, that she accepted death as an open door to be reached without trouble. Ralph had long since disowned her, she supposed, and her loss would not even ripple his mind.

But her body, left on its own, still functioned automatically. She stayed crumpled against the wall, a dark pile of rags no different from the shed roof beneath her, until the questioning heads of soldiers were withdrawn into the interior and she heard them clatter down the stairs. Some stayed behind to tend Waldo, she supposed, but as to the rest—the hunt was up.

She did not know what she did the rest of that night. She was still enveloped in the cocoon of numbness, addled slightly by the brandy she had drunk on an empty stomach, and ravished by the horror of having killed a man.

Waldo, the man she had thought she loved, who was to marry her and take her into a life of happiness and ease—now dead in that apartment, and by her hand. It seemed a strange thing, when she considered it, and had, so it seemed, little to do with her.

Her senses took over, and began to act on the principle of self-preservation.

Through this alley, into that doorway while the troops marched by. Huddle in this shed, cringe behind that fence. Always seek the open country beyond Lyme. This meant going either to the seashore, or up the valley the way she had come.

She was hungry again by morning. She had not slept, not daring to stop. She was walking along the shore of Lyme Bay, to the west of the town, when daylight came. The first pink streamers fanned over the bay, looking as though the town were the center of the radiation. The sun was far northeast now, when it rose. Her own shadow stretched far along the shingle before her.

She begged a bit of fried fish from a suspicious fisherman's wife, and kept going. She had lost all sense of caution now. Death, she believed, would find her, if not tonight, then tomorrow, and she longed only to lie down and sleep, not to waken again.

How far from Oaklands she had come! Less than a month ago she was at home. Now—she looked down at her rags. The shredded gray muslin barely covered her.

She clutched the waistband, seeking reassurance. The coins were still there, but worthless to her now. Her feet were bare and cut, bleeding where the salt water reached her wounds.

She would sit in this hollow in the sand, she thought, and think about Oaklands. It had been long since she thought about her home, drowsy with bees, with the breeze stirring the heavy oak leaves. The cooing of doves. The shouts of the stable boys.

The shouts continued, sounding more real than the other sounds she remembered. At length, she looked up, and there were the soldiers.

They surrounded her in a semicircle, a petty officer and his patrol of six men. "Here's one. Camp follower, has to be. Lots of them loose yet. But this one won't get away!"

Somewhere deep inside her, disbelief stirred. They were making jest of her. Surely they knew who she was. Surely they must know that they had found Waldo's murderess!

She had gone as far as she could go. There was nowhere left to run—she did not want to run. The soldiers spoke to her, but she did not heed them. The voices in her own head were far more insistent, far clearer.

All she wanted from anybody was mercy. Mercifully to be left alone to die in the dunes, to starve to death upon the hills—mercy.

Without knowing it, she had spoken aloud. One of the men reached down and took her arm, pulling her to her feet. "Mercy?" he demanded roughly. She nodded.

"Mercy what?"

And by a trick of her subconscious mind, recently absorbed in dreams of Oaklands, she said, "Mercy Holland."

They half-carried her back to town, and thrust her into the already packed jail. The heavy iron door swung shut with a blood-chilling clang, and she fell to her knees before she lost consciousness.

It was a long nightmare.

Sometimes Carmody thought she would wake up soon, must wake up to the scent of roses at the bedroom window, and Mercy bringing her hot tea. But it could not be

Mercy. Because she herself was Mercy, wasn't she? They all said so.

The cell was crowded to bursting. The straw underfoot became noisome and slippery with unnamed filth. Mercy found a corner of the cell where she crouched, all day and all night. There was no difference in the cell. There was no light in the daytime—merely a lesser darkness. And there was one meal in the daytime. None at night.

She lost track of time. It could have been two days, two months. Eventually—in fact, only a few days passing—a pattern emerged, based on Winchester, a town nearly a hundred miles away.

James the Second had allowed years of pent-up hatred and jealousy of his nephew to fester, only to break out now in his appointment of Justice Jeffreys to try the conspirators in the "Monmouth Plot." The incident was not even dignified with the title insurrection, or rebellion. It was simply a "plot," and as such could be treated with vicious retribution.

In due course, Carmody, still clinging desperately to her new name of Mercy Holland, was taken from Lyme Regis across the hills to Hampshire, there to be lodged in the Winchester prison.

This jail was even more crowded than Lyme. Carmody could not eat the jail fare—her cellmates accused her of being too fancy to eat plain food, but in fact, she would have been glad enough to eat if she could have removed the lump in her throat. The lump was the memory of Waldo—the great explosion and the acrid smell of gunpowder filling the room in a blue cloud. The odd change in Waldo's expression as he realized what she had done. His dying accusation of her in his eyes—

The moment she confessed her true name, she believed, she would be taken out and hanged for murder. Waldo must have given her right name when he sent for the soldiers. But, even though she told herself that this was what she wanted, she could not bring herself to speak. So the days went along, Carmody in a state of half-sleeping and half-waking, wrapped in numbness, consumed by doubts, and keyed-up by unreasoning fear.

Jeffreys was condemning people out of hand for treason, comporting himself on the bench, so it was said, like a man taken leave of his senses. The trials of the conspirators were mockeries. Men who had done no more than dress a soldier's wounds far from the scene of battle were condemned to death. A poor old woman who had done no more than share a crust of bread with a fugitive was sentenced to an unholy execution.

A lethargy fell upon Carmody that nothing could penetrate. Days came and went, and she did not rouse. She fell ill, and by the time her turn came to be taken into court, to face Justice Jeffreys, she was unrecognizable as Carmody Petrie. Her reason had departed, and only a shell remained to be sentenced.

Death was near that day. Of the dozen prisoners who stood before the judge, ten were to be taken out that very day and executed. One other was to be whipped, once a year for seven years, through every market town in Hampshire.

"And you," sneered Jeffreys, looking at the pathetic figure before him, dull red-brown hair, eyes half-closed, thin as a fence post. "What's your crime? Never mind, probably more than I want to hear. Now then—what's your name?"

Make it quick, thought Carmody. Let me just get this all over with. No one cares, not even I, what happens. Just be merciful—

She spoke half aloud—"Mercy."

The judge consulted a list on his desk. "Oh yes," he said, "Mercy. Holland, I see. Well, Mercy Holland, this is the end of a long day. I feel weary of all this, and that is lucky for you. Mercy Holland, I sentence you to penal servitude in the West Indies. For life. I understand that won't be long under the conditions out there."

Carmody slid, unconscious, to the floor.

Book Two

JAMAICA

1

THE sun, directly overhead, shimmered hotly down upon the sea beyond the harbor mouth, picking up little diamonds dancing along the tops of the gentle swelling waves. Great white clouds piled high, like foam on a Dorset stream in spate, mounted into towers along the southern horizon. The clouds at their castellated summits gleamed white, but in their shadowy depths lurked the pastel colors of the rainbow. Pale lavender, shading into violet, outlined the rounded hills of clouds against the fleece-white higher mounds.

Rose-gray along the lower parts of the clouds, the faintest of pale tinted reflections on the sea followed their majestic progress along the horizon. The boundary separating sea and sky was full of mystery and yet familiar. Carmody Petrie, now called Mercy Holland on the ship's register of convicts, took a last long look at the sea, the limitless waste that separated her from all she had once known. She turned away, to face the harbor of Port Royal on the island of Jamaica.

She could not have told how long the voyage had taken. There was little, in the stinking hold of the convict ship, to mark the passage of days. Only, too frequently, the removal, without ceremony, of a body too frail to last the voyage, and better off dead, most likely, than those who survived, for a short life to be spent in the steamy cane fields on the island.

A different motion now stirred beneath the keel of the

146

ship. The long dipping and rising rhythm of the open sea had become, in the past weeks, a second nature, familiar as a pulse beat, a condition of life like the ever-blowing wind, the singing of the wind in the shrouds, the creaking of the working timbers. Now the ship jerked, choppily responding to the shortened waves of the harbor, answering to the sharp movements of the helm.

They had arrived at their destination.

Carmody took a last long look at the freedom of the sea she was leaving behind her, with as much regret as she could summon. Like tilting an empty cup, she thought, to let the last lingering moisture run together to form a drop—one drop—of liquid. All the emotion she had left, now, would not make so much as that one drop.

"Come now, Mercy," said a voice in her ear. "Pluck up now, and look at where we've got to. A heaven like they tell about. Heaven on earth. I *don't* think."

It was Lucy—Carmody never learned her last name. Possibly as false as Mercy Holland, and what difference did it make, after all? Lucy had been kind to her. "Might as well do something," Lucy had said stoutly, soon after the voyage began, "as sit here and rot. Pluck up heart, Mercy, thee's doing no good in the corner there." Cajoling and scolding in turn, Lucy had forced her to her feet in the disgustingly foul hold, made her help to do what little was possible to care for the ailing and the wounded, all dumped together in the hold like straw dropped from the barn loft onto the floor.

Carmody had developed a real affection for the stout countrywoman, who had quite probably saved her life, Now she willingly cast aside her own unpleasant thoughts, and joined Lucy at the rail.

The harbor seemed pleasant enough, full of shipping, smelling, as all harbors do, of tar and old ropes, fish and brine. The buildings, surprisingly, were white, giving a crisp neat look to the settlement.

Behind the houses rose mountains, abruptly, bluff-like, covered with trees of various kinds, producing variegated stripings of green on the mountain side, their branches so thickly leaved they appeared entangled and matted.

The pigmy houses seemed one or two stories high at most. The overshadowing mountains seemed to reach to the sky like a painted screen, so tall that their summits shaded into misty blue, mingling with low-flying clouds.

In spite of her numbness, Carmody could not restrain the stirrings of curiosity at the new land before her. What kind of settlement was this? What sort of people lived here? What products could this hot, damp, oppressive climate raise? Nothing like the cool cleansing climate of the Dorset downs—but she must never remember. Never again. Her hand had killed a man, and she was forever set apart, forever banished from her home.

Lucy, at her side, was prosaic. "What kind of masters shall we have, do you reck?" She peered along the waterfront. "Suppose they's all pirates along here? Boats look like it." Her eyes grew round with fright, although Carmody guessed shrewdly that a good measure of hopeful excitement lay in Lucy's thoughts as well as alarm.

"Well, we'll soon find out," the woman sighed. "I heard captain say he wanted to unload us right soon, before the harrycane comes. What do you suppose is a harry-whatever?" Carmody could not enlighten her.

The ship was anchored, the sound of the cable running out through hawseholes accompanied by the heavy tramp of sailors' bare callused feet on the holystoned deck, and the downhaul swish of canvas. The last few days the prisoners had been allowed up at intervals from the hold. There was less chance of losing them overboard now than in the rougher seas to the north, and exposure to the sun would bring color to the cheeks and sparkle to the eyes, to fetch a better price at the market in Port Royal.

As always in any group the size of this batch of prisoners, one or two men were surprisingly well informed. So Carmody knew that Judge Jeffreys, in his insane greed, had contracted with those at Court to turn over numbers of convicted prisoners to certain privileged persons, for a sum of money. Arrangements were made then for the reselling of the "batch" to ship captains, for a substantial profit, and the captains in their turn conveyed their human property to the slave markets of Jamaica to be sold.

Just so, thought Carmody wryly, had she purchased her curly-horned sheep. God send her a deliverance as happy as theirs!

"What will they do?" said Lucy. Now that the time was so close, now that even from the deck they could see, in the square on the waterfront, a raised platform that stood above the surrounding streets, even practical Lucy began to quail.

A sailor, passing from the capstan where he had finally secured the anchor cable, overheard her question. Flashing broken teeth in his sun-dark face, he stopped and grinned evilly. "I tell you what they do. They take you ashore to yon platform, see? That's the slave block. They shove you up the ladder and ask for bids."

"But we're not slaves!" protested Carmody.

"Might as well be. That's the way they sell the rights to you, anyway. I wish I had the price," he added, his eyes lingering hungrily on Lucy's sturdy body, "I sure wish I did."

Lucky flinched, but she stood valiantly. "You need a cook, do ye? A woman to scrub up your filthy rags?"

"Nay, not that," he said, his grin spreading. "But I'll be there anyway, just to see the fun."

"Fun?" cried Carmody, doubting she had heard him rightly. Selling humans like beasts of the field—*fun*?

His eyes never left Lucy, even though he answered Carmody. "Aye, fun. Yon platform is high above the crowd, see. So to give us all a good look. And the buyers will want to know what they're bidding on. Only reasonable, you might say, to see what you're getting. Without all the fancy wrappings."

Lucy's plodding wits caught up with the sailor's meaning. She blushed, from the deep scooped neck of her single garment right up to the roots of her vigorous, springing brown hair.

"Aye, I'll not miss the sights! And sometimes, you even get a chance to feel—" He wheeled, laughing, and left them.

Carmody thought, if she considered at all, that she had already reached the lowest pitch of her life. Nothing worse could happen to her—she remembered thinking that on the heights above Lyme Regis, when she was well-fed, well-clothed, riding her own mare, and shamed by James Scott's greedy eyes.

Or later, in that hideous nightmare that showed her a man's blood on her hands.

Now, she could feel Lucy shuddering next to her. To feel rough hands crudely pulling off her sole covering in full sight of men like the sailor just past, even worse, of men who judged as a livestock buyer judged—

Involuntarily she took a step toward the rail and looked down. What would it be like to plunge into that roily dirty water, floating with spars and rotten bananas, and other, unnamable filth? And lose herself forever in the depths?

No worse than—that other.

Lucy was first to recover. "Nay, Mercy," she murmured, "that's a sin. Though I wouldn't blame you. Pluck up, now. Maybe he just made sport of us."

Maybe. And the worst moment was past.

"Too bad to waste the extra food the captain brought out the last few days for us," Carmody said, straining to add a light touch to banish the darkness in her mind. "Even you don't look quite so thin."

"Nay," laughed Lucy ruefully. "You should have seen me at my best. Full ten stone I weighed, and I could work in the hayfields right along with my man. God rest his soul."

She spared a tear for the man whose inpetuousness in joining the Duke's army had led to her own capture, even though Lucy herself had never set eyes on the Duke, nor had she encouraged her husband to join the army. "But a man will have his will, mind," she said philosophically, "and he'll only fret his life away if you cross him. Look yonder."

Lucy pointed to a small boat crossing the harbor, heading directly for their ship. By now the rest of the convicts were coming up from the hold, a few at a time, the women first. The ship's officers clearly felt that the danger of revolt was past, now that they had anchored at Port Royal, under the guns of the King's forts, and the unfortunates blinked and shaded their eyes from the blinding glare of the fierce tropical sun.

The boat drew steadily closer. Besides the two oarsmen, it held only one man. He sat uneasily on the seat in the stern, as though anxious to get to his business. He was dressed in dark clothes, of a style outmoded by ten years, even according to Lyme Regis standards. Against the light colors of the cloud-reflecting waters, the bright hues of the clothing of persons walking along the waterfront, the white houses behind, ranged along the semicircle of the harbor, this man looked larger than life, perched like a brooding raven on the seat.

As he drew near, he removed his broad-brimmed hat and lifted his eyes to the persons lining the rail. Carmody realized with a shock that this rookish man was handsome—exceptionally so. His brows were straight across and heavy, his features were regular, his chin was strong, with a cleft in it. His upper lip was perhaps too thin, as though it clamped a rigid discipline on the voluptuous penchants revealed by the full, sensual lower lip. An interesting face, a contradictory set of features—

The convicts, huddled together in shaky self-protection, reluctant to leave the support of their fellows with whom they had existed for weeks, were afraid even of the light of the sun. The visitor's gaze passed slowly, measuringly, insolently, from one to another until it stopped for a brief moment when his eyes fell upon Carmody. He moved no muscle in his face before he shifted his gaze from her to Lucy, and then on to another. But Carmody had looked directly into his eyes under the heavy brows, and she didn't like what she saw.

The newcomer apparently knew the captain, for they greeted each other on deck with the familiarity of old acquaintance.

"Tolliver!" cried the captain. "Haven't you had enough of these trashy riffraff? Come to buy more? I tell you the price will be higher this time. Supply's getting scarce back home."

"You'll make your expenses and then some," replied

Tolliver in a surly fashion. "More than I will. That last batch—half of them got away."

"Escaped from you? A rare feat!"

"Not for long. Caught some of them. Now then, let's get to business. Remember, what I buy you won't have to feed until market day."

Their voices faded as the two men disappeared down the hatchway that led to the captain's cabin. Whatever bargaining was done was over soon. When they reappeared on deck, the captain was wiping his slack mouth with his sleeve, and the yeasty smell of liquor came with him. But Edward Tolliver seemed unmoved, and even in his dark clothing looked as cool as when he had come aboard.

"Five convicts," the captain was saying. "Your choice."

He looked eminently satisfied with his bargain. Carmody guessed that Tolliver must have paid very well indeed. She wondered why he did not wait until the auction to buy his convicts, for he might save money in the long run. But to get his choice without interference must be worth dealing with the captain, and, most probably, the bribe that allowed him to be first on board.

Carmody felt pressure building up in her lungs, in her heart. The blood pounded in her head as she realized that Tolliver was to make his choice at once. She fixed her eyes on the far horizon, noting with odd clarity the King's fort made of strange-colored stones, the sharp outline of the guns pointing out to sea, smelling the throat-tickling fragrance of coffee and allspice.

The waistband of her skirt stuck to her slim waist, with the heat of the sun pouring down making her skin glisten with perspiration. She was suddenly conscious of the fact that she could not remember when she had bathed last. Was it before she killed Waldo? She still wore the same misty gray shreds she wore then, the useless golden sovereigns still sewn into the waistband.

Strange, she thought with intensity, while Tolliver came closer and closer, picking the convicts he wished to buy—"That one. No, not him, he looks unhealthy"—strange how she could not quite remember Waldo's face, neither the face distorted by lust that day in the meadow, nor the face that looked teasingly down on her as they planned their wedding. She could recall only the shocked expression in his eyes, as the ball from his pistol, the pistol held in both her hands, had penetrated his body.

And then Mr. Tolliver was standing before her. The silence about them lengthened, and it seemed to her that all the world stood still except for the gulls screaming mindlessly across the harbor, low above the water.

"Look at me."

She obeyed. Looking up past his waistcoat, past his loosely knotted neck scarf, the chin—with that unusually deep cleft. His eyes. She must have been mistaken, she thought, in what she had seen in his eyes before. Now they were impersonal, glittering with coldness, boring into her own.

"Your name?"

"Mercy Holland."

"Can you cook?"

The truth faltered on the tip of her tongue. But she and Lucy had discussed certain possibilities, and Lucy nudged her now. "Yes," Carmody lied.

"Sew?"

Another lie. "Yes."

Say yes to everything, Lucy had advised. The best way to get along is to do whatever they ask, or say you can.

"Those hands never scrubbed a floor."

It was a bald statement. She could not think of the right thing to say. But perhaps her silence was best after all. His stare persisted and for the first time, she thought, I'm glad I'm not as beautiful any more as James thought I was. I'm scraggly, ill-kept, dirty, and even my skin is scaly from the terrible food.

She thought he was going to pass by, and she felt relieved. Even the auction would be better, she thought—the auction, and whatever else happened to her were no more than penance for the irrevocable sin. She must submit, submit.

She steeled herself now, thinking of the auction to come, and she was surprised to feel the rough hands of the sailors on her arms, thrusting her into Tolliver's boat, shoving her forward to stand in the prow, with four other convicts. Lucy was one.

"What happened?" Carmody breathed.

"You didn't hear? He said, 'I choose her, and the one who poked her to give the right answers.' I didn't think he saw me do that."

"Then we'll be together?"

"So it seems," said Lucy. "At least for now." But she would not explain what sudden memory made her look sad, as though the enormity of what had happened to her, one of the hundreds of innocent victims of the Duke's ill-fated rebellion, had just now been brought home to her. Nothing Carmody could do or say could comfort Lucy. She had, in truth, little comfort to give.

The Tolliver plantation was situated only a few miles from Port Royal, along the low-lying land at the foot of the mountains. The range of mountains ran east and west like a backbone in the center of the island, and ended almost abruptly in cliffs and bluffs, seamed by ravines and splashing streams, leaping from waterfall to waterfall until the water reached the flat, exceedingly fertile miles between the bluffs and the shore.

The vegetation along the road from Port Royal to the plantation was thick and deep green. Strange scents came from the lush greenness, the smell of moldy earth, of nameless rotting things at the heart of the jungle, and, over all, the spicy scent of Jamaica pepper, the ginger that grew wild, and, in fitful gusts on the breeze, the strong smell of fragrant coffee.

The wagon clattered and creaked along the fine dust of the road, lurching in ruts, throwing the five convicts against each other painfully. But they were not chained, a privilege that Carmody was grateful for. She had been chained in the prison in Winchester, and she thought she could never again be rid of the panic that seized her if someone accidentally clasped her ankle.

A burly black man drove the team of mules, and another trudged along at the rear of the wagon. Each was armed with a wicked-looking whip. There was little temptation, besides the fear of the whips, to escape, at least along this road hedged in by unpleasantly thick shrubs and rapacious vines. Who knew what lay at their roots?

Insensibly, the sound of the squeaky cart, rhythmic and regular, lulled Carmody until she swayed in her place in a merciful lethargy.

Bits of pictures floated across her drowsy mind, like the swift pink reflections of passing clouds upon the sea, too fleeting to catch hold of.

There was, surprisingly, small memory of James, of Waldo, even of Ralph. It was as though all those men moved and breathed in another world, with another Carmody Petrie. She hardly knew that girl, any more. That person had lived in sunlight, looking ahead to happy vistas, all on the surface of life like a water beetle, skimming on the surface of a stream, heedless of deep pools and dark currents beneath it.

All those days might never have been. Carmody thought of them as faraway, lost dreams.

The reality was Lucy, kind, doggedly cheerful, beside her. And the jolting wagon, and the three men, silent, sullen, their hands bound.

The jolting stopped as the wagon turned into a smaller road, away from the sea. A turning, and another turning, brought them to a clearing, and the buildings of the plantation.

Carmody opened her eyes in amazement at the blasting brilliance of color. The calm turquoise of the sea and the vivid green of the roadside brush were replaced by the scarlet flowers of a vine climbing upon the pillars of the outbuildings and along the roofs. The great falls of lilac-colored flowers, white lilies, and the overpowering scent of mimosa combined to assault her senses.

Descending from the cart, she staggered, and would have fallen but for the strong hand of the guard. "You'll get used to the land under your feet," he assured her in a liquid voice, sounding like English, but overlaid with the lilt of a foreign tongue. Spanish? African?

She smiled her thanks. There were others there to see their undignified arrival, watching with expressions that

seemed bereft of all emotion. She had expected, if she had
thought of it at all, to be overwhelmed by a pity from
them that she did not want—she had deliberately chosen,
for reasons that seemed vital at the time, to go with the
Duke on his rebellious invasion of Dorset. She had compounded that sin with the worse one of murder, and whatever came her way was simply the atonement she would
have to make. And she would reject sympathy.

But pity was not evident on the faces, the color of sun-
dark mahogany, around her. So might they have watched
the unloading of so many barrels of flour. A simple fact of
daily living, to be noticed and then forgotten.

But there was one pair of eyes that held more than she
expected. Just before she and Lucy were led to the dark
hut they were to share, built of some wood that was rough
and brown, the same color as the dirt of the trodden yard,
she felt someone watching her. She looked involuntarily
around her.

At the edge of the green lawn belonging to the great
house behind him stood Edward Tolliver, watching the unloading of his purchases. His eyes, cold as the sea and as
unfathomable, lingered longest on Carmody, and, suddenly
prickling with trepidation, she hastened, following Lucy
into the dim interior of the hut.

She wished she had not lied.

Her plan—shared by Lucy and inspired, it must be said,
by Lucy's Somerset practical sense—had been to say Yes
to everything. But when it came down to the truth, in the
slaves' compound on the Tolliver plantation, Carmody
could do none of the things she had claimed.

Cooking? Never in her life.

Sewing? Well, yes. A little embroidery now and then,
but when it came to patching heavy work clothes, she had
not the first idea how to start.

Bonwit, the black man who was chief of the household
staff, surveyed her helplessly.

"Mercy, what am I to do with you?" His soft voice had
a deep echo in it—like listening to the shell, she learned

later, of the great conch. "The master said to put you to work, but—"

He shook his great head sadly. The cook, Ascar, had brought Carmody to him. "Look, Bonwit," Ascar had said. "Her poor hands, and a sorrier mess she's made of vegetables for the table I never saw. Those scraped knuckles—I swear I don't want her bleeding into my chicken stew. Mercy's her name, but mercy's what she needs."

Carmody sat on a three-legged stool while a spirited discussion raged over her head. Ascar fought her battle for her—the obscenely fat cook, her dark hair oiled into submission, bristled in defense of Carmody, and compassion was clear in her flashing liquid eyes.

Carmody did not even care what happened to her next. What difference did it make? She was in prison here, too. The only difference was she would die more slowly here than she would have in England where the prison damp and the fever would have carried her off.

She was not supposed to have an easy atonement for taking a life, she knew in some obscure corner of her mind. But the only aim in her life now was simply to endure. To move *here* when she was told, or *there* when someone gave her different orders. To try to scrape the skins off vegetables, to study the rough sewing work, and wonder how that silly Daphne, the linen maid at Oaklands, had managed to take fairy-like stitches with her great reddened hands.

"Mercy! Can you?"

It was Bonwit's voice in her ears, and she realized that he had been talking to her for some moments. "I'm sorry," she said quickly. "I did not hear."

Ascar exclaimed, "See what I told you, Bonwit? That girl just dreams all day long. I don't know what we're going to do. The master—"

Subtly the atmosphere changed. She had noticed this from the first. When Edward Tolliver was mentioned, an alteration came upon his slaves. It was not abject fear, as she might have expected, remembering those cold light eyes of fierce blue. It was more in the nature, perhaps, of considering him an alien, a creature who was not to be understood, but certainly avoided, and even—she thought once—to be pitied in a way.

But she must have been wrong about that.

"Can I what, Bonwit?" she repeated, caught by the intense concentration in his eyes. He had thought of something. She was anxious to cooperate with Bonwit. The servants had been kind to her, and even, she suspected, covered up her obvious ineptitude after Lucy had been sent away to work in the fields.

"I have no wish to shame you, Mercy, but I must know the truth this time." She cast about wildly in her mind. What could he want? And the question, when it came, was so simple she nearly laughed aloud. "Can you read?"

"Yes."

Bonwit looked at her steadily, obviously reflecting on the other talents she had claimed falsely. From a shelf, he produced a dog-eared book, the edges of the thin pages torn and badly foxed from dampness and much use.

"Read," he commanded her.

Obediently she opened the book at random and began to read. "Hearken, O daughter, and consider; incline thine ear; forget also thine own people, and thy father's house . . . ."

The Psalm betrayed her. She choked on the words, and her eyes, brimming, blurred the pages so that even the book was lost to her sight. Wordlessly, she shook her head and handed the book blindly in the direction of Bonwit. He took it from her.

After a moment of silence, he said softly to Ascar, "She can read. I'll speak to the master. You take care of her."

Carmody could not stop crying. Gentle hands on her shoulders urged her from the stool and guided her toward a cot at the far end of the two-room shack which served the plantation as kitchen. She dropped gratefully on the hard pallet and abandoned herself to misery.

"Forget also thine own people. . . ." It was an arrow aimed straight at her inner fortress, the shell she had erected to save the small spark of Carmody from violation.

Oaklands, she would never see again. She wandered in

her mind back to Oaklands, her father's house, the house that she would never see again. Her dear father, the hard years after he died, the three weeks when she had allowed her person to be degraded, but Oaklands was saved—

What had Lucy said, one night when they crouched in a corner of the crammed hold, whispering to keep the nightmares of the dark away? That what happened inside of you was the most important—Lucy had said—and what did it matter what men did to your outer husk? And Carmody had found it so, in a way. But something had also happened inside her that terrible moment when Waldo's eyes had looked inward upon his grievous hurt and seen his death approaching.

Oaklands was dim, Ralph's features were vague, and even James had faded in her memory—but she would never be free of Waldo's eyes.

When she rose from Ascar's cot, it was late. The tropical twilight had spent its brief moment gentling the air, and now the soft night was lit with torches, and the slaves, sleeping through the heat of the oppressive day, came to life. The kitchen reeked with the smell of allspice, and burnt coffee. Carmody was content to sit on the edge of the cot, watching the flickering shadows cast by the torchlight and the cooking fire across the walls of the shack. She felt as though she could never move again, and then the obscure thought came to her that she was dead, and the flickering flame—

She cried out.

Ascar's voice, creamy and rich as satin, answered. "You awake, girl? Bonwit's been here I don't know how many times, and always you were sleeping. I told him, Bonwit, I say, she needs the sleep. Crammed into that coffin of a ship. I mind how it was. Eight weeks in a dead calm for us. But you won't need to hear about that. Bonwit's got a surprise for you."

Ascar stood beside her, holding a bowl of frothy liquid in her dark hands. "Come now, girl," she coaxed, "you're going to want to look your best. I'll comb your pretty hair and fetch a dress you can fit into, but you drink this first.

Mind, I'm going to stand right here until you drink it down, every drop."

Carmody never knew what was in that magic bowl, but it accomplished a minor miracle. By the time she stood before Edward Tolliver in his living room, she felt almost ready for anything.

Bonwit led her into the room, and stood beside her, his great bulk reassuringly solid. Tolliver nodded dismissal, and when Bonwit vanished, silent as a dark shadow, she took an involuntary step backward. But, almost forgotten, her Petrie blood stirred now, and she remained where she was, standing straight, and waiting with every appearance of respect for the master's words.

"Bonwit tells me you can read. Is that true?"

"Yes." A little late, she caught herself and added, "Sir."

"I hope this is truer than other accomplishments you have assured me you can do." He surveyed her, seemingly impersonal, but a small muscle twitched at the base of his jaw. "Oh, yes, don't think for a moment that I don't know what happens in my household. Some men think it is beneath their dignity to know what their slaves are doing. But I am watchful. I know what is said about me." His eyes flickered toward his left, but Carmody did not follow his glance. She dared not miss a word of this man's speech, lest she overlook a clue to her own future.

"My wife always saw to that. That the slaves had plenty of news on which to feed their incessant gossip."

He jerked to his feet and began to pace back and forth on a small space of rug between the leather chair he had been sitting in, and a small table holding a tray with a glass bottle and a single glass.

"I suppose you have heard much about me?" He stopped in his tracks and glared at her. "That I am cruel? That I—" He was brought up short by the bewildered expression on Carmody's face. "No," he added, more reasonably, "I don't think you have. Well, that is all to the good. My wife will have a clear field in which to indoctrinate you. You will enjoy that, my dear, won't you?"

He turned and spoke over his shoulder. Startled, Carmody saw for the first time that they were not alone. Surprisingly, as if by sheer force of will power, he had brought to animation a doll sitting in a chair.

"My wife," he introduced bleakly.

Carmody saw a woman thin to emaciation. Her skin seemed simply to be brought tightly over not flesh, but bones—very fine bones, though. Her cheekbones were high and her nose was straight, an aristocratic face at its best.

But it was the woman's eyes that caught Carmody's interest—dark, velvety brown, with unexpected flecks of honey dancing in them, like sun dappling the bottom of a shallow stream. The face was clearly that of a woman who suffered a good deal of pain, without cease. The beautifully shaped lips were tucked in tightly, so as not to betray emotion. The eyes, strange and yet humorous, looking levelly at Carmody. The face of a beauty who, no matter what had happened, had strength of character to overcome tribulation.

And she had known tribulation, undoubtedly, for her terrible thinness, and her look of suffering, shouted the fact aloud.

"My wife, Mercy," repeated Tolliver. "Bonwit tells me you can read, and although he often lies, perhaps this time he is telling the truth. I do hope so, for his sake."

"I can read."

"Aurelia, this is the convict I spoke to you about. She may be able to amuse you, since I no longer can."

Aurelia spoke for the first time. "Edward, you never amused me."

A spell hung in the air, a threat given and received, a menace unsheathed like a cat flexing her claws, and then it was past before Carmody could be sure of it.

Edward turned to Carmody. "I will leave you two to get acquainted. Later I will tell you how my wife came to be crippled. She may wish to tell you some other tale, but you will know which is telling the truth."

He left the room in two strides, without a backward glance. Carmody was uncertain what she should do. He had not told her what her duties were to be, nor, in fact, whether she was to have duties. Perhaps she would, after ten minutes, be removed and thrust back into the single hut that had been home to her for the month since the convict ship had docked, and she had been chosen by Edward Tolliver—because she would sew and cook!

The silence lengthened between the two women until Carmody thought it would burst asunder in the air. She longed to sink through the floor, or to flee. Truly, she might have turned and run, except, as so often seemed to happen to her, there was no place to run to.

"Come here, Mercy," Aurelia said, at last. "He will not come back. Not tonight."

Carmody advanced as she was bidden, a step at a time. At last she stood directly in front of the woman. As close as this, she could see that the woman's dress was of fine silk, and the golden chains around her neck, falling in jingling lengths over her insignificant chest, were of exquisite delicacy.

Edward Tolliver apparently did not stint his invalid wife.

"Edward has said you will read to me, and take care of my needs. Are you willing?"

Aurelia's voice was pleasant and low-pitched. Suddenly Carmody felt irresistibly drawn to the woman, her courage in suffering, her kindness. "Yes," Carmody said with a rush. "I—I hope I can do as well as you wish."

"I am sure you will, my dear. But not tonight. I am weary, suddenly. Please tell Bonwit I am ready to go upstairs, and bring your things in the morning. You will stay in the house, next to me."

Carmody had been with Aurelia ten days. Her room, a narrow, cell-like space which suited her need for atonement, adjoined Aurelia's suite of rooms, and she evolved a real affection for her mistress. It did not take long for Carmody to find that however humorous, however in command of her suffering and her emotions Aurelia might be, it was only in the absence of her husband that these merits appeared.

For when he stepped into the room on his regular visits, his light eyes glittering as they surveyed the room with one sweep—Carmody was sure he took an inventory of every visible item, and even perhaps some tucked away inside drawers—Aurelia seemed to become somehow diminished. And Edward, whether by design or not, seemed to exude more life, more vitality.

As though he drew certain vital elements from his wife, to increment his own.

At first, Carmody feared every visit. She would stand, nervously pleating her full skirt, gathered peasant-fashion by a lined straw belt into which she had sewn the gold sovereigns, and pose as though looking at the floor. But through her long lashes, she would look at the filtered image of Tolliver. She soon learned to assess his moods, not as well as Aurelia could, of course, but sufficiently to know when it was possible to stand unnoticed like a carved statue of teak, or when it was wise to sidle toward the door, and choosing a moment, ease through it out of sight.

She began to relax with the onset of familiarity with her situation. Aurelia liked her, and Edward did not bother her. Lucy was away in the fields, and Carmody could not have spent time with her even if she had worked in the kitchen.

Aurelia thrived on a regular schedule, and Carmody soon adjusted to it. There was only an hour or two a day that she had to herself, the time after lunch, in the heat of the day, when all others, too, took their naps to avoid the heat of the tropical sun.

Carmody thought she had found, here with Aurelia, a safe haven, undeserved, but appreciated.

One day, a week and a half after her arrival in Aurelia's rooms, Carmody happened to be putting fresh linens away in the chest in Aurelia's bedroom, while Aurelia sat in her sitting room at an open window to catch what breeze she could.

Edward Tolliver came to see his wife. Carmody heard his unscheduled arrival in the sitting room. "So. Deserted by your maid, I see," Edward said, his voice loud and rasping. "I wonder you don't complain about her to me. You complain about everything else."

Aurelia's voice was a mere murmur, and Carmody could not distinguish the words. Silently, she stepped closer to the door. There must be a reason for this unusual visit, Carmody thought, excusing herself for eavesdropping by deciding she needed to know about anything that might upset her patient.

"Is it possible that you are satisfied with your new maid? I am glad to hear it. This is progress indeed. Perhaps God's punishment on you has run its course. Perhaps He will forgive you for—what you have done to me. And now, possibly, you will even learn to walk again."

What punishment could he mean? Obviously, he referred to his wife's invalidism. But punishment for what? Aurelia had told her that she had fallen from a horse, and had injured her spine so severely that she was never free from pain, and never would walk again.

Surely the pain was sufficient to bear, without Tolliver's goading? Carmody wondered whether she should cause a diversion by entering the room. She pictured what would happen if she did so, and she decided she could do no good. She had never seen him in this mood before.

"Let us hope it is so, my dear," he was saying. "If you can walk again, we will see what lessons you have learned. Will you run right after him again? I wonder."

This time, Carmody could hear Aurelia's reply. "You think that was all my fault? Think again, Edward."

"It *was* your fault, Aurelia. Your fault, and you tried to laugh away the terrible damage you did to me. Tried even to blame me!" Tolliver's voice rose, grew louder, and a touch of rage entered it. "I will show you. I will take the rights that belong to me. If Abraham could, then I can. And—I'll prove to you whose fault it is. I'll make you watch!"

Carmody couldn't understand what he meant, but she was very sure that it would not be wise to probe. Edward Tolliver was incoherently verging toward uncontrollable anger, right then, and she wanted nothing so much as to flee. But she could not desert Aurelia.

She remembered, then, something that Aurelia had told her recently. Don't anger him, she had advised Carmody.

For my sake, she had added. Now Carmody understood. Tolliver would take out his anger on his helpless wife. Something must have gone wrong somewhere on the plantation, and he had come to vent his frustrated rage on his wife.

Carmody hardly dared to breathe. She was so intent upon not making a sound herself that she did not hear the footsteps crossing to the door at her hand. Not until she saw him in the open doorway did she realize that Tolliver had moved.

"Listening. I thought as much. Well, I don't have time to take care of you now. But I will. One day, mark my words. If you don't understand me, ask your mistress. She knows what I mean, well enough!"

He was gone in three strides, and they were left alone to stare, white-faced, eyes wide and dark, at each other. What did he mean? Carmody could not perceive anything other than a vague menace in him.

And Aurelia would not tell her. She would only say, "He couldn't! He couldn't really—*do* anything to you. That's the trouble, you see!" Aurelia was nearing hysterics.

"What couldn't he do?" Carmody asked, pouring brandy hurriedly. Aurelia didn't answer.

"Leave me alone," said Aurelia, gulping down the fiery liquor. "I'd—just like to be alone."

Thus bidden, Carmody, exhausted by the recent storm of emotions she had witnessed, stepped through the verandah door onto the long balcony that ran the length of the house. She liked this porch, away from the busyness of the ground floor, almost as high as the treetops. The lacebark trees, and the palms that were called royal, stretched above her head, making the porch shady and cool. From the sea came a steady sea-wind, and the stiff palm leaves clashed endlessly, like a medieval tournament heard far away.

It was still mid-afternoon. She could catch a glimpse of the sea itself. The delicate shading of the waters delighted her—aquamarine to deepest blue, passing through green and turquoise. The white-tipped waves rolled steadily in, as though there would never be an end to them. Only once, Ascar had said, "Them waves get big as a house when the wind whoops up out of the south there."

Maybe she would see that awe-inspiring sight sometime.

Just now, the trees, the wind, and the sea—all untouched by human misery, the petty little threats of petty little men—cast a numbing spell over her, and she thought that Tolliver had merely been taking out his spite on her. Aurelia was used to it, probably, but Carmody must learn to live with such an uneasy state of affairs. But if worst came to worst—

She remembered some talk she had overheard down at the shacks. Some slaves had escaped from Tolliver's plantation—before she had arrived in Jamaica. And there was a woman in the mountains, a woman called the "healing woman," and it was thought that the escaped slaves had made their way to her. Perhaps, if things got too bad—

But they wouldn't. She was sure Aurelia wouldn't permit anything to happen to her. Aurelia had even promised, *he couldn't*. Aurelia had spoiled it then, by adding, *That's the trouble*. It sounded almost as though her mistress had conceived some ill-will toward her. Carmody decided she would be best off to forget it all.

It was a good thing, she concluded, that no one had overheard that terrible conversation. Much could be made of it, no doubt. At that moment, she felt that someone watched her now.

She knew that eyes were upon her—she could sense the force of a considerable intelligence focused upon her.

She stiffened and then deliberately relaxed, so as not to betray her sudden awareness. Little by little she turned her head to search the surroundings, but there was no one—

He stepped away from the shelter of a giant yucca and looked up at the balcony where she stood.

The stranger was tall, and blond, and handsome. He frowned, a worried expression that had nothing to do with her. But as their glances locked, she saw in him a dawning look of intentness, as though, all in a moment, an entirely new train of thought had opened to him.

He smiled faintly at her, and sketched a brief wave with

one hand. And then, without a sound, and as though she had ceased to exist, he moved toward the garden, and the path that led to Tolliver's small office building set beyond the bamboo hedge.

2

CARMODY felt as if she had in truth become two persons. One was the Carmody she had known a long time ago, assured, loved by her people, and even—although she knew better now—secure in the love of Sir Waldo Rivers.

The other was the person standing on a verandah in Jamaica. Mercy Holland, jailed because she had followed the army of the rebel Duke. A girl of a lower class, used to hard labor—so they all assumed—and possessed surprisingly of an ability to read. Clever with her hands in a sickroom, familiar with the fussy details required by a lady of her maid.

The more she could bury Carmody, the more she could forget Waldo crumpling slowly to the floor in an interminable deliberate motion, the better off she would be.

Safety was here with Aurelia Tolliver, on a forgotten plantation along the south coast of Jamaica. Serving her sentence—that is, Mercy's sentence—and avoiding Carmody's fate, which would surely be execution for murder.

All these thoughts went through her mind faster than the flickering of the fireflies, while she watched the broad shoulders of the stranger disappear. And before he was entirely out of sight she had whirled from the railing and started down the stairway at the end of the verandah, descending into the garden, just where the man had stood when she first saw him.

Not quite knowing why, she followed along the path he must have taken. Through a growth of small palmettos, avoiding the oyster shell paths where her step would crunch, she hurried. She could not explain, even to herself, why she suddenly felt she needed to see this man again. Mere curiosity, she supposed. The man was the first visitor to the Tollivers since she had landed.

She lost him in the dense growth of the tropical garden.

A flicker of movement, brief as the flickering of a lizard's tongue, told her where he had gone. The pendulum swing of a great palm leaf still marked his passage. She crossed the garden, carefully. She paused at the far edge, where the leaf had now stopped moving, to get her bearings again. She had never been in this part of the grounds before. The slaves were forbidden to come this far, and she would have no defense if she were caught.

The big house lay to her left. The verandah where she had stood was at the front of the house, and she was now opposite the rear of the building.

Ahead of her stood a hedge of bamboo. It seemed impenetrable from where she stood only a few feet away, but— there was the telltale palm frond just this side of the hedge, and the man was certainly out of sight. There was no place else he could have gone.

She should have turned back. Part of her knew that, told her so insistently, but she stepped forward, reckless of the consequences.

She halted in mid-step. Voices erupted almost at her right hand, surprisingly loud and clear. The one was Edward Tolliver's—the other must be that of the stranger. The first words she heard from Tolliver arrested her.

"Come to beg again?"

The stranger was slow to reply, as though he dared not lose his temper, but the effort was difficult. "Beg? That is a strange word to use, Tolliver. You give nothing away, not that I ever heard."

"Why should I?"

"No reason. But a man who has everything, as you do—" A vague, taunting note appeared in the stranger's voice.

"Take care, Vickery," warned Tolliver. "Don't overstep

the bounds of my patience, or you'll never get another farthing."

"You're not the only one on the island who lends money, you know."

"But I'm the one you come to. And I know the reason, too. No one else will give you a penny. You've already gambled away not only your own plantation, but all the money you could borrow, besides."

"I'll get it all back."

"Your plantation, too, I suppose? Then I shall not waste money trying to improve it."

"The plantation, too. And I have your mortgage in writing, so you cannot refuse to accept my payments to reclaim my own land."

"And what does that mean? That I'm not a man of my word?"

Tolliver's voice faded, as though he had walked away from the window, and Carmody took an involuntary step forward. She could not say why she stayed. She forced a way through the hedge.

She was in a neat clearing, with a small square white building in the center. The building had one window in the side facing Carmody, and it was, as most windows in Jamaica were, open, to catch the faintest sea breeze. It was through this window that the voices came to her, and she guessed that the men were standing just inside. If they were to look out, they would certainly see her.

She edged along the hedge to her left, until she could not be seen from inside. Certainly Tolliver, when he spoke again, was still intent upon Vickery, and not an eavesdropper.

"You'll never get enough money to get your plantation back. And if I lend you the money you want now, you'll throw it away."

The lazy drawl of the other man cut across Tolliver's clipped accusations. "But if you don't lend it to me, you'll never get anything back, except the plantation. The land is still there, but everything else is gone. And even the land is in bad shape—it will cost you more than it's worth to run it. Better let me have the money, Tolliver."

There was a sudden stirring inside, as of a drawer opening, and the interview was nearly over. Vickery would get the money, and the sordid little transaction would be done.

Silently, Carmody backed away, out of sight of the building, and made her way by devious paths until she emerged at the back of the slaves' quarters.

Ascar caught sight of her from the open kitchen doorway. Carmody felt a rush of affection for the enormously fat woman who had tried so hard to teach her kitchen ways. She smiled, but Ascar, surprisingly, looked too worried to smile back.

"Thought you'd be the healing woman," Ascar said shortly.

"Healing woman? Oh, the one from the mountains?"

Ascar nodded. "Sent word. Iletha's baby's bad."

Iletha was the slave who had worked beside Carmody in the kitchen. She had been three days ago delivered of a great-boned child. and Carmody had taken her turn that night after Aurelia Tolliver was asleep, to watch by the bedside of the moaning girl. Only at dawn, when Carmody had needed to slip back to her own bed so as not to be missed, Iletha's baby had still not come.

Now, three days later, Iletha's baby was ill.

Sending for the Healing Woman meant the trouble was serious. Carmody offered., "Can I do something?"

"What about Mrs. Tolliver?"

Carmody shrugged. "He came in, made trouble. She sent me away."

Ascar nodded, not surprised, and led the way to Iletha's cabin. Ascar's broad back shook when she walked. The interior of the hut was dark and evil-smelling, compounded of dirt and old unhappy things. The smell struck Carmody like a blow and she stiffened, but swallowed the lump rising to choke her and breathed again.

"Iletha?" she called softly, "It's Mercy." She dropped to her knees beside the pallet. Iletha's dark eyes turned to her in wounded pain, like a sick animal. Suddenly Carmody was carried back to Oaklands in her memory, a treacherous trick, but serving a purpose after all. For she remembered the times with Yarrow at her side, and Bray standing behind, when she had nursed sick lambs from their sniffling nameless weaknesses, until they could stand alone, butting their soft woolly heads against their mothers in a greedy instinct for food. An eating lamb was a well lamb, Bray had always said.

"The baby won't eat?" Carmody guessed.

Iletha nodded. Wordlessly she moved so that Carmody could see the tiny infant, held lovingly in the crook of her mother's arm. Carefully, Carmody lifted the tiny body, carefully keeping her hand supporting the lolling head.

"I won't hurt her," Carmody promised, and snuggled the infant close to her, warming it with her own body while she took it out into the light.

Ascar watched her solemnly. Carmody had sudden doubts that shook her deeply. Suppose she could do nothing for the baby? Suppose the infant died in her arms? Certainly the baby looked dreadfully sick and weak.

"Do you have any milk? Hot, with brandy?"

Ascar sent a boy to the kitchen to fetch what Carmody wanted. Out here in the sunlight, Carmody took a long look at the baby. She was tiny, lighter in color than Iletha. A child of mixed blood, no doubt. She concentrated on stirring up the mixture from the ingredients the boy had brought. Just before she tried to coax some of the warm fluid into the infant's mouth, she stopped. She looked up doubtfully at Ascar.

"I don't know—" she began, but Ascar stopped her.

"I know," she said firmly. "Bonwit, tell her."

"I've seen it before," he said. "Trouble like this don't get cured. Just like the white blood wants to make trouble for us."

"Iletha?"

"She'll get along. She never wanted it anyway, at least until she held it. It's white man's trouble, that's all. White man took her, once, on the mountain trail. But this little thing ain't to blame for that."

Encouraged, Carmody soaked a piece of cloth in the liquid, and inserted the cloth, nipple-like, into the slack mouth. Gently, gently. Squeezing it, getting a few drops down the throat. Why hadn't Ascar done this?

Ascar had sent for the Healing Woman—and if fate sent her, they would be content. But if fate willed the child to die? Shrewdly Carmody surmised that none of these slaves would cry. Who wanted the issue of a white man's detestable rape? But the helplessness of the infant tugged at Carmody.

So intent was she on the child, the struggle which was literally between life and death, that she forgot her surroundings. A trick of her mind insulated her. She could think only of each breath, each struggling, gagging swallow, somehow forcing death's moment away, a step at the time. And suddenly, she was sure she would win.

Finally, the baby began on her own to make little sucking noises. She even seemed to have grown a little, her wrinkled skin filling out slightly.

Remembering where she was, Carmody looked up into the black faces around her. They had been kind from the moment she had arrived among them, but they had withheld their trust. Now they had altered, giving her approval and letting her see that a bond had been forged between her and them.

Wordlessly, feeling the unspoken current of understanding flowing between her and Ascar, she held the baby out. Ascar took the child, her great bosom dwarfing the infant. "She'll want her mama now," she said and took the child into the cabin.

Ascar's full rich voice floated outside to where they waited, overriding Iletha's faint protests. But in the end, inevitably, Ascar's belief that the baby would live prevailed over Iletha's fears. When Ascar came out to the silent group waiting, all willing the child to eat, to live, she nodded. "She'll do now."

Carmody was unutterably tired. Who was the baby's father—Edward Tolliver? She thought it possible. But then she remembered that Iletha had come to the plantation only six months ago from some other owner. The secret of the baby's father must lie in her previous home. As though it mattered. Carmody was learning fast.

The state of slaves, and of course of convicts, was one of property. She owned nothing, not even the gown she wore, not slippers on her feet. Tolliver had furnished them, and he could take them away. The same with Ascar, Bonwit. He could take the infant away from Iletha, if he chose, and dispose of it as he would.

The only real hope any of them had was that Tolliver was mindful of the cash value of his property. Carmody, as a convict, was on a slightly different footing—Tolliver could not take her life without accounting for it to the Governor. But she knew that accidents can happen. Aurelia Tolliver had been thrown from her horse. And an accident to Carmody of whatever kind could easily be contrived and the slaves could not legally witness to the truth.

"Thank you," said Bonwit. "Best get back to Mistress."

Carmody nodded. "I suppose so."

Aurelia Tolliver had been an invalid for only six months. She had grown up on the island, knew everyone. Her father had been a high-ranking government official, and she had lived in a great house in Port Royal itself.

When her parents had died within six months of each other, she was left alone with insufficient money to live on. Marriage was a necessity, and while up to that time she could have had her choice of men, since her father's position gave her great standing in the colony, after she was left alone suitors seemed to vanish. So she told Carmody.

"And Edward came to the rescue." She gave a little choking gurgle, and Carmody realized that it was the first time since she came to take care of her that her mistress had laughed.

"He still loves you," Carmody said, automatically. She was brushing Aurelia's hair with long slow strokes, trying to fill up the time until she would put Aurelia to bed. Aurelia retired early, but Carmody found the hours between then and the time she herself grew drowsy to stretch interminably at times.

She lured Aurelia into talking about—about anything, really, anything to keep her awake longer.

"Loves me? I wonder," said Aurelia. "I thought he did, once."

"He still does," repeated Carmody, her mind far away.

"Have you ever been in love, Mercy?"

"No. Not really. I thought I was."

"Well, then you just don't know what it's like. Not to know the fire that sweeps through you at his very touch, the pounding in your brain when he's near. How he clutches your very vitals and turns you into a whimpering animal, begging him to hurt you, to ease the burning fire that rages—"

Carmody paused in her brushing, holding the brush suspended in the air. Suddenly she was not on this torrid, decaying island—but instead, the winds of the high downs, clean, scouring, flapped the canvas tent and James was coming toward her, his eyes amused, hands sliding from hip to breast, his lips suddenly fierce and bruising—

"Mercy? What's the matter?" Aurelia's voice sounded fretful, breaking Carmody's bubble of memory into nothing. But Aurelia didn't wait for an answer. "I suppose someone of your class wouldn't know what I mean."

I'm better born than you, for all your fine airs! screamed Carmody silently. Aurelia, as her illness worsened, was losing the humor that had sustained her for so long. And Carmody realized that she could learn to hate this whining woman.

"No, Mistress Tolliver, I'm sure I wouldn't." With an effort she began to brush again, this time as much to soothe herself as Aurelia. "But I'm sure your husband still loves you."

"I wasn't speaking about my husband," Aurelia said crossly. "Now I want to go to bed."

After Aurelia had retired, Carmody was too restless to sleep. Aurelia had opened up old wounds that Carmody had thought were safely healed over. Now she knew that they had only been festering below the surface.

She stepped out onto the verandah. The wind was soft from the sea, rustling the palm leaves, clattering them noisily, bringing the wet feeling of surf on the shore, cool waves.

How James would have loved this place! she thought. It was strange how well she knew him. And even knowing how fickle he was, how sure she was that he would go back to his Lady Henrietta, how despicably he had forced Carmody herself into his bed, none the less there was his powerful Stuart charm that wound a spell light as gossamer, strong as iron, around all those who were exposed to it.

And she had been exposed to that charm more than most. Days together riding companionably over the downs, nights exploring the farther shores of love—

She clenched her fists on the iron railing of the verandah until she gasped with pain. How James would laugh at her for, almost, believing he loved her! And then, more darkly, how Waldo would taunt her with her maidenly behavior in the old orchard—seeing what sly betrayal her senses were accomplishing now!

Her thoughts were too dark to be borne. She had the sudden impression that she was as delicately balanced as a *bomba de fuego*, a Spanish ball of fire that exploded on contact, spewing terror and disaster over a wide area.

She knew she would not sleep, not this night. She had no desire to slip down to her friends—Ascar, Bonwit, the others. There was nothing they could say to her that would ease her fretting. And yet, if James stood beside her now, she would feel nothing for him. She was over that fever of the blood that had risen from stepping deliberately into the trap he had laid for her.

No, the fever now burning in her was for something she had not yet known. She would never find an easing for it—and that, she thought, was probably the ultimate punishment for her sin, the sin of murder. Waldo could not live, breathe, assuage his desires, eat—

So his killer could not reach out her hand to grasp the things that same hand had ruthlessly snatched from him.

It was folly to go over and over things past. She had managed for a while almost to forget them. But Aurelia had brought it all back, and now she could not rid herself of the haunting.

She went down the verandah steps. There was a cove not far away, where the slaves had told her the sea lay gently upon the shore, and the shadows were kindly sheltering. Perhaps she could find it. She remembered snatches of description.

She slipped through the thicket that hid the house from the road. There was an opening where the driveway breached the hedge, and the moonlight, turning everything miraculously into ebony and silver, showed her the shell drive, lying like a dim white ribbon threaded through the opening into the road.

She paused, remembering that the cove lay to the left, away from the way they had come in the cart from Port Royal. She walked along the road, slowly, because even at midnight, with the moon high, the air between the jungle thickets that lined the road was breathless and oppressive.

Then—the road curved and the silver cove opened up to her. The air was still, except for the palm leaves constantly in motion. The road edged along the inner point of the cove, and the sea lapped gently at the sandy edge of the roadway. It was an enchanted place upon the earth. She almost looked for Merlin, who might have conjured this vision up for her to see, but not touch.

Could it be touched?

Fearfully, almost afraid to breathe upon this vision lest it vanish, bubble-like, she left the roadway and stood upon the beach. The sea at her feet was cool, cool. In a moment she removed her slippers and stood with bare feet upon the wet sand. Almost unthinking, as though a force stood outside her and directed her movements, she lifted her gown over her head, dropped it, and stood marble-white in the moon's light, letting the air play upon her hot fevered skin.

Beyond the cove, the vast southern sea stretched, the moon bright upon it, silver and shadowed. The colors of the day—rose, turquoise, green—were all wiped away in the ghostly light of night.

Here in the deserted cove, with no one around, she felt almost free again. As though Carmody Petrie were alone in a world freshly made solely for her.

The sea was irresistible. She stepped in, feeling her way upon the hard sand of the bottom, splashing her hands suddenly in sheer excitement. How lovely this was—the haunting ghosts repelled, and only this moment for living.

The water reached her waist. She scooped it up in cupped hands, letting it fall over her uplifted face, streaming down her neck onto her shoulders, her breasts—

She could have laughed aloud in sweeping delight!

A slight sound made her look up. Someone was watching her. A cloud drifted across the moon, shadowing the cove, darkening her happiness. Eyes watched from the shore—

And suddenly, as she covered her breasts with shaking hands, she felt the sudden emptiness, and knew she was alone.

But the ecstacy of that unexpected moment in the pristine moonlight had vanished beyond recall.

Carmody did not leave the house again, not for a long time after that night. The experience was dismaying, like lifting up a lovely leaf on a rosebush and finding an ugly slug battening on the stem.

Besides, Aurelia seemed to demand more and more service from her, and was restless whenever Carmody was out of her sight.

The sick woman's moods were strange, and Carmody could not be sure of her from one day to the next.

One day, Carmody, massaging the invalid's wasted limbs, conceived the idea that there was still some strength in the withered muscles.

"See how much fuller they are now than they were," she said, trying to coax Aurelia out of a lethargy she had adopted that week. Carmody thought, disloyally, that Aurelia was only playing at being crippled—to avoid Edward's marital demands, perhaps. Or to avoid the running of the household, or even to console herself for some loss, something she dreamed of yet, but which was forever out of her grasp. And yet the wasted legs were real enough.

Leaning back on her heels at Aurelia's feet, Carmody studied the woman. "I am surprised," she began deviously, "that the doctor does not come regularly to visit you."

"I don't need a doctor. I know I can't walk. I don't need him to tell me so."

"But see how much better your legs look than they did," Carmody said again. "They seem warmer to my hand, and I think there's real life in them. Wouldn't you like to walk again?"

She held her breath. She did not truly think that Aurelia could recover completely, or even partially, but certainly she believed that to have the hope of it, to work at something, would be better than sitting day after day without hope. Carmody could have told her about the desolation left behind when hope has flown away.

Aurelia turned her dark eyes on her. "I wonder. I wonder, Mercy, whether it would make any difference?"

"I don't understand. I should think walking, even if it were slow, would be better than staying pent up in this room. I remember—"

"What do you remember, Mercy?"

Carmody bit her lip. She had been about to say that she remembered riding Amber across the tops of the downs, racing along the clifftop with the wind taking her copper-colored hair and trailing it behind her, to the scandal of Mistress Masters. But Mercy Holland came of a class that would never have ridden a blooded mare. Possibly a slow plodding carthorse—but Carmody had almost betrayed herself.

"I remember taking long walks," Carmody said, not quite lying. "They gave me a chance to think."

"I have sufficient opportunity to think," said Aurelia bitterly. "About the mistakes I made, about the man my father wanted me to marry, and I thought there was plenty of time to choose. But there wasn't." Carmody worked a little longer, kneading the withered muscles, kneeling at Aurelia's feet, before the woman spoke again.

"Did I ever tell you how I fell?"

"Riding, and your horse stumbled," summarized Carmody briefly.

"But has Edward told you why I was galloping along the mountain trail? I was running away from him."

"Running away?" Carmody echoed.

"I was in love," Aurelia said, suddenly caught up in a mist of recollection. "We used to meet in a little cove down the road, not far, but Edward never came there. A perfect little place, magical. But it wasn't very private, after all."

Carmody stifled an exclamation. That cove? Could it be the same one? It hadn't been very private for her, either.

"He found me there once, waiting for—my lover. And—"

The silence was prolonged. "What happened then?" Carmody whispered finally. She was still on her knees, her hands idle in her lap. She had not wanted to break the spell that wrapped Aurelia.

"Yes," spoke a voice from the doorway, hard, brutal. "Tell her what happened then. I am sure you remember."

"Edward!"

Carmody scrambled to her feet and stood, her heart pounding. She was in no danger, she thought—his anger seemed concentrated on Aurelia. What had he done when he found his wife waiting for another man? Beat her?

His upper lip clamped tight over the lower one, and the lines of torment formed white taut brackets around his mouth. At this unguarded moment, Carmody could believe nearly anything of him. But if she were careful—She began edging toward the door.

Edward's eyes, sharp and cruel, impaled her where she stood as swiftly as a flung lance. Something went wrong with her breathing. With a conscious effort, she made herself breathe in, long breaths, trying for calm.

"Come here, Mercy," said Edward.

It did not occur to her to defy him. He held her gaze riveted upon him, and she moved forward, step by step, as a bird obeyed a serpent.

Step by step toward him. She could see his hands clenching into fists, and she steeled herself against the blow she expected. She stopped a yard away from him.

"Come here, I said."

Another step, two. She was so close now that she could see the roughness of his skin, the thinness of his upper lip with the beads of perspiration on it. The contrasting, almost ugly, fullness of his lower lip, speaking of self-indulgence, or sensuality that could not always be controlled by the tightened upper lip.

In another step she would touch him. Nothing could make her take that extra step. She smelled the heavy lye-soap smell of his ruffled shirt, the sterile cleanliness of his light jacket.

What did he want of her?

"Aurelia," he said, not taking his eyes from Carmody's, "you have chosen to deny me the rights of a husband. For half a year now. Using your accident as an excuse. Like Hosea the Prophet, the wife I have, for my sins, was free, even lavish, with other men. But not to me."

"Edward—"

"I will not be denied any longer of what is rightfully mine. Aurelia, make ready to receive me as your husband. At once."

Aurelia cowered in her chair. Carmody could not think what to do. He was going to force his wife to his will before he left the room—so much he threatened. Could he be so indecent?

"Edward, you—you know I can't. Edward, don't make me. You'll kill me like this. I'll die if you touch me! I wish you had never come after me that night—"

Aurelia's babbling slid into incoherency. Her eyes were fixed on her husband's face, but Carmody, from the corner of her eye, guessed that her mistress for the moment was not quite sane. She made an involuntary gesture toward Aurelia.

Tolliver's fingers on Carmody's arm, just above her elbow, nailed her to the ground. "Aurelia," he said icily. "Look at me."

"Y-yes, Edward. Yes, yes, yes, yes—"

"You refuse me. I will therefore be justified in forcing your handmaiden to take your place."

Carmody quivered from head to toe. Her knees turned to water as she took in his intention. Outrage galvanized her into defiance.

She threw her entire strength into breaking away from his iron grip, but in vain. Worse than vain, for it stirred him to action. The glitter in his eyes boded her no good. She could not believe that he intended to attack her, right before his wife's eyes!

But his breathing came quicker, shallower. "Wait!" Carmody cried. "This is—"

"See, Aurelia?" Tolliver gasped. He forced Carmody closer to Aurelia's chair. "See? She's got to take your place. And you're going to watch!"

He reached with his free hand to the neck of Carmody's gown. With a wrenching twist he tore it open to the waist, where her straw belt held fast. Her eyes blurred. He was so close she could see only his heavy eyebrows, feel his hot short breaths upon her cheek, feeling his crushing fingers painfully kneading the breast he had bared—

Aurelia pummeled with her fists on any part of her husband she could reach, fruitlessly, until she landed a telling, lucky blow that fetched him groaning, doubling up in pain.

And Carmody was free.

She was thrown backward against the wall, and sagged against it. The scene before her was tangled, confused—

"You—you beast!" Aurelia sobbed. "You terrible monster, you poor excuse for a man—"

Carmody did not stay to see any more. She fled through the door to her own room, and moved the small chest in front of it.

She crouched until she heard his heavy footfalls leave Aurelia's room, and plod down the broad steps to the first floor. Then, for the next hours, she tried to calm Aurelia's hysterics. She did not have time for her own.

But after she had got Aurelia to bed, and sat beside her until the drops of laudanum had taken effect, she remembered one clear phrase from Aurelia's hysterical babbling, after Edward had left.

"He couldn't do anything. He's not capable of really hurting you."

"Hurting me?" Carmody had echoed. "I've had a demonstration, thank you, and I must decline to believe you."

Not much of a statement, as far as defiance went, but it

had brought on a fresh outburst of Aurelia's hysterical laughter, and Carmody remembered it for that reason.

Edward Tolliver's moment of lunacy apparently spent itself, for he did not return. Carmody wondered how she should act when she saw him again. Or, even worse, how would he behave?

The answer came the next day—he acted as though nothing had happened. He nodded briefly to her in the hall, as she shrank trembling against the wall as he passed. He might not even have remembered who she was, she thought later.

Little by little the ugly episode faded away. Aurelia would not talk about it, nor, when she was calm again, would she explain that strange comment. "Did I say he couldn't do it? You must not have heard correctly," she said crisply. Carmody dared not insist.

Carmody did not return to the cove, no matter how hot the weather was, nor how much she longed to immerse herself in the cool silvery water. She was positive that someone had watched her that night, and she feared that it was Edward Tolliver.

She spent time with the slaves whenever she could spare a minute or two. She was cautious, though, and left Aurelia's protection only when she was sure that Tolliver had left the plantation.

Iletha's baby grew fat, and the girl thanked Carmody shyly every time she saw her. Bonwit said very little, but suddenly Carmody realized that he was often nearby when Tolliver was at home. Was Bonwit guarding her?

She stopped him, one day. "Bonwit, I've noticed—"

"Noticed what, Missy?"

Suddenly she could not put her suspicions into words. She could not speak of the degradation Tolliver had inflicted on her. She looked appealingly into Bonwit's soft brown eyes, and spread her hands helplessly.

Bonwit understood, and smiled. "Don't fear, missy. We're all watching. We all watch for each other."

That was all he said, but the assurance he carried to her was like balm to her lonely nights. They all watched for each other, and they included her in their vigilance. She did belong somewhere, after all, with people who cared a little about her. She slept more soundly after that.

It was several weeks later. With the assurance that Bonwit had given her, and the determined reticence on Aurelia's part, the ugly episode faded away. Her straw belt still held the golden sovereigns that were worth more as a souvenir of a mad three weeks than as money. Where could she spend a sovereign here in Port Royal? No one would believe her if she told where the coin had come from.

She could imagine the interrogation: "So, the Duke of Monmouth himself gave it to you? To Mercy Holland? Why? He had a companion already, the murderess Carmody Petrie—"

She lined the straw belt anew, securing the slight protruberances that were the coins. The belt itself she wore every day, and it had stood her in good stead the day of Tolliver's lunacy. So she referred to the episode in her mind.

She relaxed her vigil somewhat. Aurelia would not even try to walk. Even though she never spoke of that terrible day, Carmody was sure it was constantly in her mind. For one thing, Aurelia seemed to have little spirit left in her. Edward visited briefly, Carmody fleeing to the next room, but all he did was ask his wife how she felt, and left before he received an answer.

Until one day when Carmody saw him ride out. He was going to Port Royal, he told Bonwit, his saddlebags full of papers and business to be transacted. After that he was going to visit his upland plantations, a new tract of land that he had obtained. He would be gone, so he said, for at least four days.

Reveling in the peace she felt, knowing that Tolliver was far away, she put Aurelia to bed the first night, near midnight, and stepped out upon the verandah. This luxury had been forbidden to her recently, for the balcony stretched the length of the house, past all the bedroom windows. Once in a while she smelled the faintly pleasant aroma of a cigar, and knew that Tolliver sometimes walked upon the balcony. She could not afford to chance his seeing her.

But Tolliver was far away tonight. From the verandah she could hear sounds of a guitar from the cabins down the hill. Apparently the master's absence lifted a yoke from other shoulders as well.

She really should try to sleep, she thought. But the night was warm, the breeze caressed her cheeks and her bare arms. Far away through the trees she could catch glimpses of silver where the sea breathed in the soft night.

The cove lured her, but she would not go. She was quite often reckless, she knew, but foolish? No. Suppose it had not been Tolliver watching her that night.

She must find something to divert her thoughts, and decided to read. The books were in a room off the living room, where she had first met Aurelia.

The moonlight was bright as day on the upper landing, and she descended the stairs surefootedly, and turned through the open door into the living room. The windows were open, and she started as she thought she saw a shadow move across the porch. But no, it was just the dappled moonlight making constantly moving patches on the floor when the palm trees moved. She chided herself for being silly.

In the library, she found the candle, the wax smooth under her fingers. She fumbled for the tinder, and accidentally struck the candlestick with her hand. It made the smallest of noises, sliding on the surface of the desk, but it sounded excessively loud in the silence, and her heart pounded, even though she knew there was no one to hear. From the cabins she could hear bursts of laughter, and once in a while a snatch of song.

And then she heard something else—

Someone was breathing, very close to her. Her own panicky gasps, she thought, and forced herself not to breathe for a moment—but there was a definite sharp exhalation, as though a breath could not be held any longer.

The shadow on the porch had been real, she thought. A scream rose to her throat, and she wheeled to run to the door. But the intruder was faster.

And then strong arms were crushing her. She could feel the hard stuff of clothing bristly through her thin dress.

A bruising mouth stifled her outcry, and she knew she could not escape this time. The scoured smell of lye-soap told her that Tolliver had returned, against all odds.

This time Aurelia could not rescue her.

Carmody could not breathe. She was drowning, sinking away, losing consciousness, and suddenly she was released and thrown against the desk. She felt a sharp pain in the flesh of her hip as she struck the sharp edge, and she gasped.

But he pinned her still, against the desk, moving against her. Tolliver whispered, hoarse and sobbing in her ear, broken little tortured phrases. "It's Aurelia's fault. She said I wasn't a man. But with someone else, I will be. Already I can feel it. I wish she could see me. Hurry, Mercy— Feel? Against you?"

Then suddenly someone spoke from the moon-silvered doorway of the front verandah. "Anybody home? Tolliver? Are you here?"

"Vickery!" Tolliver's voice was insensate with fury, and he pushed Carmody away from him.

The intruder said, "You weren't down at your office. I need to see you."

Vickery had come just in time. Another moment, and it would have been too late. With trembling hands Carmody struck the light. The single candle showed Tolliver's eyes, hollowed, shadowed, like blinds drawn in an empty house.

The two men left the room, ignoring Carmody as though she weren't there, except that Howard Vickery turned at the door and looked back, and—outrageously— winked at her!

She did not know how long she stood there, absently rubbing her bruised hip, licking nervous lips, feeling sick at heart. She thought fleetingly that even Justice Jeffreys would be satisfied at her punishment. Maybe she could get Aurelia to send her away, send her to work in the indigo fields. She was vague about field work, but she knew that she would not live long under such harsh conditions. But that would be better than to live like this!

She must thank Howard Vickery. The urge presented itself to her and in her confused and desperate state of mind, rapidly became an obsessive need. She must thank him—

The men had left the house, heading for the office at the other end of the garden. She made her way there, keeping to the shadows, hoping to waylay Howard when he left. She must be careful. From the cabins came snatches of pure melody, and then voices joined in harmony—Where had they been when she needed them? she thought wryly.

Tolliver had planned this ambush, she was convinced. Why? I'm not even a person to him, she argued. He doesn't know me, or what I think—I am simply a collection of bones and flesh that serves his need. Like a pen when one needs to write. Like—

She reached the hedge outside the office building, just in time. Howard was leaving.

His voice was still urbane and unruffled, but his words were desperate. "You know you're my last chance, Tolliver. And on your head be whatever happens to me." Tolliver's answer was inaudible. "Just a simple loan, that's all, and you refuse me. You'll never get any of your money back now."

Tolliver had come closer to the door, apparently, for his words were clear. "I've got your plantation, haven't I? And some of those slaves you're so fond of? That girl you attacked—she and her baby are down there singing right now. One woman wasn't enough for you, I suppose! While you're in jail you can think about what happens to your women." Then Tolliver laughed, a blood-chilling sound of pure malice and spite.

Fortunately Howard came out of the office alone. He was half across the garden before Carmody even saw him. She hurried to catch up with him, and she had to tug at his sleeve before he was aware of her.

"Oh," he said, "you! Aren't you taking a chance? That mad dog will be storming out of there and what happens to you then? I can't protect you forever, you know. I'll be in jail by morning."

Jail? The vision of Ralph in the prison at Lyme Regis

swam before Carmody's eyes. The Winchester prison, and the heavy galling chains on her ankles. Suddenly she could not see this smiling man who had saved her in such a terrible place.

"You need money to save yourself from that?" she whispered.

"It's a long story, child," said Howard, kindly. "And nothing to worry you with. But it's true. He's already got everything I own. And balks at a bit more."

Suddenly she knew how she could repay him. Swiftly her fingers fumbled with her belt. "Let me—"

"Come now," Howard said. "While you are exceedingly attractive, there's no need to offer me so much."

She understood him at once. "I am grateful to you," she said coldly, "but not that grateful. I will give you only what I can well afford." She added, with a touch of bitter amusement, "My master sees to all my needs, and even more."

"I noticed."

She undid the lining of her belt, and held the golden sovereigns in her hand. "Will these help?" she asked, letting him see the coins, dark on the palm of her hand.

His glittering eyes told her the answer. "They will make all the difference."

"Then take them. In gratitude for your timely interference."

He considered her thoughtfully. "I will accept them, as a loan. And whenever you need them, come to me. I'll repay you even if I have to steal the money."

He smiled, and touched her cheek with one finger, running down her cheek, along her jaw, and down to the hollow at the base of her throat. "Tolliver has a discerning eye, I'll say that for him."

And then, suddenly, he was gone. She looked after him for a long time before she remembered Tolliver. Then she picked up her loose skirts and ran to the house, and didn't stop until she had reached the haven of her bedroom.

3

SHE heard no more from Howard Vickery for a long time.

She had not expected to, of course, but her days settled into a prosy routine that made one day seem like the next, and all Carmody's senses deadened to match her days, slipping away as though gathering dust on a shelf, to be discovered anew one day. Or perhaps not, as it might happen.

The only change was in Aurelia. From that terrible moment when she had thrust with her whole pitiful strength between her maid and her husband, she seemed to fail. It was as though the purpose of her life had been accomplished, and now there was nothing left but to let her life ebb away, to die with as much dignity as her crippled body could manage.

Tolliver himself was away from home much of the time. He had acquired a large new plantation, and he needed to spend all his energies putting it into good production. Bonwit told Carmody about it. "They is Mr. Vickery's plantation, that he foreclosed on. Mr. Vickery, he got bad luck, but they do say his luck took a turn up lately."

"Oh? When was that?"

He told her a date that coincided with her gift of the two sovereigns. She remembered, oddly, that James had said the sovereigns were an omen—*they mean me to be King*, he had exulted, swinging her around the room. Bad

189

luck they had been to him—and to her upon whom he had bestowed the coins.

But now, clearly, the luck of the coins was good for Howard Vickery. She was glad that the coins had done him some good. She had no need for them. Her sentence was for life, and only rarely did she hope it might be a long life.

It had been, now, three years since the day that she had stepped aboard the *Helderenburgh*. She hardly ever looked back. Now that the coins were out of her hands, the tangible reminder, always under her fingers, was gone.

Even Lucy had gone—died, Bonwit had told her—and her last link with England was no more.

Aurelia depended more and more on her, and she was restless now whenever Carmody was out of her sight. Once in a while a new slave, Jassy, came to sit while Carmody escaped for an hour.

Jassy was young, tall, slender as a tree, with skin the color of spring honey, and eyes like a cat's. She moved sleekly, and Carmody did not particularly like her, but Aurelia tolerated the girl, where she could not abide Iletha.

One day, after Carmody had slipped down to watch Iletha's baby toddling gleefully across the beaten ground of the slaves' quarters, and listen to Ascar's comfortable laugh that shook her whole body like ripples in a pond, she found Jassy waiting anxiously for her. Jassy closed the door to Aurelia's room behind her and faced Carmody on the landing.

"You know that lady's dying." Jassy's words were a statement, not a question.

"Oh, no!" whispered Carmody. "What happened?"

"Nothing new," said Jassy. "But you see it coming, don't you?"

Carmody knew the girl was right. Little things about Aurelia she had noticed from time to time, without considering their deeper meaning. The increasing vagueness of her glance, the rejection of one interest after another, as though she were deliberately withdrawing herself from life. But it took Jassy to put it into words.

"What can we do?" It seemed natural to turn to Jassy. She might be young, but there was wisdom in her eyes, a look as though the yellow eyes had looked upon everything, and nothing more could shock them. She had come lately as a part of Tolliver's acquisition of the Vickery assets, as had Iletha years before, when Vickery's luck first forsook him.

Suddenly Carmody recognized that she and Jassy were deeply alike—both had to endure a life that had been forced upon them, a life not of their own choosing. What would Jassy be like, if she could do as she pleased? Where would she go? What kind of days would please her?

Carmody almost spoke then, recognizing their kinship, but she knew she should not. There was little left for either of them except their own dignity, their own bit of privacy, and, as she would not want to give up one iota of her own, so she would not pry the lid from Jassy's.

"Nothing *to* do," said Jassy, her voice flowing gently like honey on a hot muffin, "nothing but go with her far as you can."

Jassy slipped fluidly past Carmody, and with a heavy heart Carmody entered Aurelia's room.

It took longer for Aurelia to leave the world than Jassy had prophesied. Carmody made up her mind that Aurelia would not die.

She coaxed Aurelia to eat, she coaxed her to talk. "Tell me how it was when you were at home," she begged. "Tell me about Lord Bellenmore's ball again. You wore a peacock blue gown, I think? Or was that the time you wore the pink damask—?"

And as Carmody forced Aurelia to talk about the past, she soon became so familiar with Aurelia's childhood home that she could have walked there herself in the dark—and no Tolliver to leap out of the shadows at her.

Aurelia's wardrobe and Aurelia's suitors—Carmody, in her concentration on Aurelia's past, let the present grow vague and shadowy. It came as a shock to see Bonwit's face as he brought up a tray, or when the boys came to move Aurelia from chair to bed.

But in spite of Carmody's heroic efforts, there came the

day when Aurelia refused to leave her bed. She clutched Carmody's hand, pitifully clinging to her.

"Mercy. You're just like your name," Aurelia said faintly. Her words came one at a time, with long pauses between. "You've been so good to me." She closed her eyes, and for a moment Carmody thought her next breath would not come. Fearfully, her tongue dry, she loosened the thin fingers for a moment, long enough to run out to the landing. It happened that Jassy was passing through the hall below, and glanced up.

Carmody couldn't speak. A lump of grief rose in her throat, and although she could make the shape of the words, she could make no sound.

Jassy nodded at once. "I'll send for the master."

Back with Aurelia, Carmody pulled a little stool close to the bed and took the frail hand again in hers.

She sat there beside the bed, listening to the labored breathing. Each breath seemed the last, and then Aurelia would breathe again, a ragged doleful sound, and Carmody herself breathed again. She began to think ahead, to go with Jassy's messenger to find Edward Tolliver. He would not be grief-stricken, she guessed, and then decided she was wrong. Whatever shame he had heaped upon Carmody had been aimed specifically at torturning his wife. And hate was the obverse side of the coin of love.

Aurelia had spurned him, called him "not a man." And Aurelia had assured her that she had nothing to fear from Edward.

His fatal impotence had led them all to this. Aurelia knew, and Carmody guessed that all the slaves knew— their strange pity of him made sense to her now.

Aurelia opened her eyes and looked at Carmody. For a moment strong affection flowed between them like a river, before Aurelia closed her eyes, and sighed once more, and then breathed no longer.

The room seemed suddenly empty, as though the soul of the house itself had fled. And yet that was foolish, for Aurelia had not animated the household for months. It was simply that Aurelia was Carmody's reason for being here in this room, going—as Jassy had said—as far as she could with her. Now Aurelia had traveled beyond that parting, and Carmody must go on alone.

Carmody was too numb to think, then, about what might happen to her. She was lifted from beside the bed, by hands she did not know. She knew only that the room was suddenly stifling, crowded with doctor, vicar, Jassy. At the last, she saw the grim face of Edward Tolliver in the doorway.

It was the sight of his tormented face, the passion-filled expression of a man who has ridden hard and purposefully, that prodded her into action. She allowed Jassy to lead her to the small cell-like room she called her own.

Carmody closed her eyes and leaned her aching head against the frame of the window. She had not slept for two nights, and very little in the days before that. She could not take in the fact that Aurelia was gone. She lay down on the narrow cot, but she was too tired to rest. Her thoughts raced down unfamiliar corridors and her head throbbed. Where had Aurelia—the substance that was truly the woman—gone? Was she standing, sympathetic and troubled, in this room with Carmody? In the next room, watching Edward's hollow grief?

Carmody believed his grief was fraudulent. How could any man truly love his wife, and yet persecute her daily with torturing words and even, that fateful day, with the savage obscenity of his barbarous lust for Carmody?

"Come now, Mercy."

She woke to find Iletha gently holding her wrist, and she sat up in alarm. For a bewildered moment, she could not think what catastrophe could have brought the girl this far into the house. Then it all came back to her, the feel of Aurelia's hand inert in hers, the sudden little sigh that said she was gone.

"Come now, Mercy," repeated Iletha. "Don't let your shoulders sag like that. The mistress is dead, and that's a release for her. You fought for her, all of us know that, the same you fought for my baby. But it wasn't to be." Soothing little platitudes, but nonetheless Carmody's quick ear could hear the real concern behind them, and was in some wise comforted.

She stayed in her room the rest of that day, too numb to move. Little things that had made up her daily routine—soft powder to ease a hot back, mending of thin muslin dresses, cleaning brush and comb, the scented soap—

All were useless now, and with her purpose gone, Carmody's energy too flagged. She wondered idly what would happen to her. Tolliver had plantations in plenty now, fields of sugar cane, plantings of indigo—all needing callused hands to work them.

She knew she would sink under such toil, but her thoughts turned to welcome it. Anything would be better than this aimless convict's existence. She was only an item of property, merely a possession to be counted at the yearly inventory—"Mercy Holland, life convict."

And she would be glad for an end to it.

The end came sooner than she thought, and in a way she did not expect.

Aurelia's funeral was held in the church in Port Royal, where she had attended services when she was a girl. The slaves, of course, did not attend.

Carmody watched the procession drive out of the gateway, the black hearse with nodding sable plumes on the sides, the black horses bobbing their tired old heads, and saw Tolliver himself follow the hearse dressed in black, his shoulders rigid, his hands held oddly in front of him until Carmody realized he would be carrying a prayer book.

Carmody hurried to set her own things together. She must, before Tolliver returned, escape to the little hut she had shared with Lucy when they had first come. She stopped in mid-air, holding her night shift folded in her hand, as she realized she did not know where Lucy was buried. The news had come of Lucy's death at a moment when Carmody was distracted by that terrible scene with Tolliver, and she had felt genuine sorrow, but she had never heard how Lucy had died. Of the fever? Of overwork? Now she could ask Bonwit.

As it turned out, she never asked Bonwit. She had her few simple possessions stacked in a pile on the bed, a scarf spread beneath them ready for tying. Briefly, she remembered the great stacks of her trousseau clothing piled on the bed at Oaklands. Now, she had one shift of coarse cloth for night wear, and two day gowns, one of which she wore now. Once she had had three, but Tolliver had ruined one of them.

Her lips tightened. She must remove herself from the house before they came back from the funeral. She would lose herself in the slave quarters, and if he did not see her, he would forget her. She resolved to avoid Tolliver as long as she could.

She tied the scarf, folding its corners toward the middle and making a knot. She took one last look around the room, to see whether she had forgotten anything, and then she heard a noise next door.

Someone was moving around in Aurelia's room. One of the slaves, perhaps, already cleaning away the last traces of the mistress. A great hurry to tidy up, Carmody thought, to erase Aurelia's memory, but it was not her affair. The only way out of her room, though, was through Aurelia's sitting room. She decided to wait a moment, hoping the person would go.

Footsteps approached the connecting door between the rooms. It was strange, she thought later, that she had had no presentiment of trouble. The footsteps came closer and the door was thrown open, smashed back against the wall.

"Mercy," said Edward Tolliver, "come in here."

There was no escape. He stood impatiently at the door, and she had to pass him close enough to hear his ragged breathing. She held her knobby parcel in one hand, and with the other held her skirt away from touching any part of Edward Tolliver.

She glanced at him after she had passed, and saw with dismay that he had seen her aversion even to his garments. She moved casually across the room, apparently aimlessly, but actually she was scheming to take her stand near a door—to the hall and the stairs, or the other door leading to the verandah.

"Here, Mercy," he ordered, "Come here, next to the window."

She had to obey. He stood, whether by design or not, between her and the doors. She would have to pass him to get out of the room. And he was far too big, far too close, for her to take that chance.

He eyed her for a long time. She steeled herself against his stare, as repellent as though he had put his hands upon her body.

In an attempt to divert him, she faltered, "May I extend my sympathy to you?"

"She was no good," Tolliver said calmly. "She broke God's laws and He punished her. That is all there was to it. She refused her husband. Locked me out. Went whoring after another man. She was punished. Enough of her."

Carmody looked past Tolliver, gauging the distance to the door. She began to edge, imperceptibly, to her right. Possibly she could gain the hall door—

"You will need a new dress, I suppose. Choose one to your liking from *her* closet."

Startled, Carmody forgot she was inching away from him. "New dress?" she echoed. "For what?"

"For your marriage. I still have some regard for appearances, you know. A handmaiden should be treated with civility."

Carmody seized upon the one word that terrified her. "Marriage?"

"Yes," Edward Tolliver said, turning his strange, fanatic's eyes fully upon her. "No need to edge toward the door like that. I can stop you any time I choose. You will make ready for your marriage tonight."

"Tonight!" Aurelia was barely in her grave, and her husband was going to marry again.

"Never!" spat Carmody. "I will not do it."

"You have no choice. You are my possession, and I take care of what is mine. You will never get away. Aurelia didn't. You must realize that I am offering you an honorable state. I could simply take you, you know. Right here, on the floor, if you defy me any longer. But I want heirs, and they must be legitimate."

Carmody's eyes darted back and forth, seeking escape like a hare fascinated by a leveret. It was as hopeless, she knew, but every instinct in her rose up against the infamous proposal of this terrible man. She was convinced, wildly, that if he touched her, so much as touched her arm, she would faint.

"In fact," he was saying, outrageously, "perhaps I had better give you a sample, right now. And after you're ruined, you'll beg me to marry you."

He advanced toward her and she backed away, step by step, keeping pace with him, until the wall behind her stopped her. Instinct dictated her next move. If she moved toward her left, she might reach the verandah door, but she must divert him.

"Beg you?" she snarled at him. "You will never see the day that I will beg you for anything. Marry you? I'd rather die first!"

Inch by inch. The low chest of drawers, a step away. She kept her eyes fixed on Tolliver, crouching ready to throw herself away from him. Quickly she summoned a picture of the surface of the chest—a candlestick, a small ink holder, a book or two, nothing to serve, except—

There was no more time. As she reached her left hand out to grasp the brass letter opener, he was upon her.

She fought him. She bit the fingers that he tightened over her mouth, she lunged out with her knee. But he eluded her.

She reached clawed fingers to his face, and felt savage satisfaction as the skin of his cheek yielded beneath her nails.

"You devil!" he panted. "You—"

She knew only that he was cursing her, steadily, with vicious words that she did not even understand. She planted both hands against his chest, and shoved with a supreme effort. He staggered back. But she had angered him now, without inflicting much damage.

His eyes blazed redly, like a wolf's in the night, and saliva ran disgustingly from his ugly lower lip. She was determined to defend herself. With his great strength, he could do as he pleased with her. But he would not find it easy.

He lifted his hand and struck her on the side of the

head. The blow was unexpected, and she fell to her knees. She cowered away from the blows she saw coming, but to no avail. He rained his fists upon her head, upon her shoulders. She cringed from him, and fell at last to the floor.

Someone was suddenly crying out. "You'll beg me to marry you!" The words came in short panting jerks.

She knew she must save herself soon. His fury gave no sign of waning. She scrambled on hands and knees, sheltering under the low table for a moment. Her skirt was in her way, and with one hand she hitched it up above her knees. With the other hand she overturned the table. One corner must have struck his thigh for he grunted briefly.

On the instant's respite, she staggered to her feet. Her knees failed her and she fell heavily against the low chest. Blindly reaching behind her, she touched something cool and metallic. She had found the letter opener. Her fingers closed around it, and she crouched threateningly, like a cornered wildcat. Her russet hair had come unpinned, and hung heavily on her shoulders. Her eyes blazed like molten silver, and she gasped for breath.

"Touch me," she warned, "and I'll use this."

He stopped for only a second. Then, that insane light still in his eyes, he taunted, "You can't kill me!"

Kill—kill! Waldo's face, surprised and crumpling, swam before her eyes, and she knew she could not kill again. The letter opener fell from suddenly nerveless fingers, and she stared at her assailant with wide frightened eyes.

He was mad, there was no doubt of it in her mind now. His eyes were wild and unseeing, his fury raged growlingly in his throat.

His fingers closed upon her wrist, tightening his grip. In another moment, he would break the bones. She cried out—

"Beg!" he said, the word coming through lips slit-thin. "Beg, damn you!"

She did not answer, saving her breath for one last effort. He would kill her, she realized, his desire somehow transformed into the senseless need to batter, to smash, to destroy. He twisted her arm, until she fell again to her knees. "Beg!"

She shook her head. Her lips formed the word *Never*, but he did not hear it, for she made no sound. Only a vague whimpering that she realized was her own animal voice. She could not stop.

She looked up at him—to see his clenched fist descending upon her. Her hands flew up to cover her face. A blow, and she heard something snap. Another blow, and another—and then came the darkness.

And with the darkness, mercifully, peace.

She wakened, at last, with a need to learn where the strangely loud humming came from, a great swarm of bees that had somehow hived inside her head. She longed to move away from the distracting noise, but the darkness came again and with it a strange moaning.

Somewhere far away—she was in a serene meadow, the bees swarming and sheep bleating upon the cool hilltops. Then it all changed again, and darkness sped over the hills and the valleys. Somewhere there was a safe harbor, if she could just get there. She tried to open her eyes, to blink away the darkness, but she could not.

She lifted hurting fingers to her eyelids, to force them open, but her touch revealed only swellings that, throbbing, had nothing to do with eyes.

Her eyes were swollen shut. Little by little she began to remember—but she could not explain what had happened to her. She remembered—the last she remembered was riding Amber into a valley, and there were lights like fireflies over the floor of the valley. Campfires, and there was a man—

James. She must remember his name. He insisted that she call him James. It was all so fuzzy, and somehow she knew that she was in terrible trouble, but James could not help her any more.

She must leave this place. She knew, and did not know how she knew, that there was a door into a hall. Help lay beyond that door. She inched herself over the floor. All was darkness, and she felt only the rough straw matting beneath her fingers. She was crawling—

Fresh air on her face. She must have reached the door, then. The floor—it must be the hall?—felt strange beneath her fingers, cool on her palms.

Palms! She could hear them plainly now, clattering in the wind. And she crawled on her hands and knees across the cool floor. Until she put her hand out ahead of her and there was nothing there. As she lost her balance, and began to roll over and over down the steps, she knew she had found a door at last—

The wrong door.

Waking and sleeping.

Voices, pain. The black cloak of darkness over her face.

Bouncing along like a ball. Trying to tell someone about it. Make the ball stop bouncing! she cried, but she heard no sound. At last, mercifully, she slept.

"Better for her," said a dark, rich voice that she would have recognized.

"Bonwit, is she dead?" said Ascar.

The faces around her were heavy with worry. "Got to take her away. Got to take her *up.*"

There was no need to explain. All those around the bruised body on the ground knew what *up* meant.

"Who's going to do it?" demanded Jassy. "You know that devil's going to start looking for her."

"We don't know nothing, you understand me."

"I'm not dumb. But all I say is, you leave here, he's going to want to know where you gone, that's all."

"Poor child, poor child," crooned Ascar, and in her voice was all the bewilderment of one who sees cruelty and cannot fight back against it.

"We're going to get her *up* there," said Iletha, suddenly, full of determination. "She save my baby. Now we save her."

Bonwit nodded approvingly. "We all got to stick together. He's a *devil,* that's what he is."

Solemn heads nodded, attesting to the truth. While none of them had witnessed what had taken place in that room upstairs, they were wise in their study of their master, and when he hurled down the stairs and away down the driveway, as though a thousand demons howled at his heels, they began to skirt around the outside limits of the house, of their grounds, looking for whatever needed to be found.

So they discovered Carmody, doubled up and moaning, unconscious, at the foot of the verandah steps. More than the fall, they judged, noting the swollen, livid eyes, the bruises already turning leaden in color, the broken hands. And with the secrecy that meant, in their troubled lives, security, they lifted her gently and bore her away to their quarters.

"I can't do no more," said Ascar. "She needs the Healing Woman."

And thus they decided to take Carmody *up*. Up the mountain, through the tangled network of ravines marked by secret symbols, alongside rushing streams.

Up through the forests of mahogany, of satinwood and ebony, past the rocks that formed the backbone of the island. It was a terrible trip for the inert figure on the rude canvas stretcher. Feet slipped on mud, slueing the stretcher sideways, and more than once, one of the bearers nearly fell.

She moaned, once, and the stretcher was set carefully on a nearly flat place along the secret trail.

"Mercy," came Bonwit's strong whisper. "Can you hear me?"

He was answered by a moan.

"We're going to get you safe, now. Going to get you right away where you'll be safe." Purposely, he repeated words he knew she needed to hear. "Can't nobody hurt you. You'll be safe. Just trust us, Mercy, trust us."

She sighed heavily, and lapsed again into unconsciousness. He held her wrist—the one less badly bruised—his thick finger feeling the slow, shaky rhythm pounding just under the skin. "We'd best wait till moonrise," he said, worry whittling at his voice. "She can't stand much more."

The moon rose, silvering the tops of the trees below the place where the four men rested, their backs against the mountain. When the road before them took on a faint, luminescent clarity, Bonwit nodded, and the four of them lifted, once again, the stretcher bearing Carmody.

Carmody knew nothing of her journey up the mountain. She dreamed, faces she knew and faces she did not know. In her dream, Lucy was there and Carmody could not remember where she had seen her last. But Lucy was dead.

James was there in her dream, dressed, oddly, with a turban around his head, laughing at her, his strong white teeth flashing in his gypsy face.

And when she tried to wake up, tried to open her eyes, she could not. She cried out in panic, "I can't see!"

And always, then, came a cheering voice saying, "Thee will see, in the right time. Drink this."

She drank, and slipped into dreams again.

When the dreams at last slipped away, vanishing like fog under a sunny morning, she opened her eyes, and she could see. She lay on her side for a long time, just as she had wakened, not moving, savoring the blessed gift of sight.

There was half the world, as she saw it, made of intense blue sky, studded with scudding, high-piled clouds. Close at hand there were rocks and beaten ground, and, incongruously, a small battered kettle lying on its side.

She could not think where she was, or how she had arrived at this strange ledge-like place. Something very unpleasant lurked just out of sight at the limit of memory. Perhaps she had died and been placed here on this shelf until they decided what to do with her. She considered that possibility seriously, and felt not the slightest emotion.

Except that she could not be dead. She hurt too much—her head, her face. Cautiously she tried to flex her fingers, one by one. She could not move them. It was as if they were made of stone.

She must have cried out. Suddenly there was a dark-faced woman kneeling beside her. "So. You have returned to us from your wandering."

Carmody hesitated. Her dreams had been vivid, but she could scarcely believe she was not still traveling among the wraiths of her mind. "Where is this place? And what's happened to me?" Her faint voice was taut with panic, and she tried to sit up. Not a muscle obeyed. "My hands—what is wrong with me?"

The woman said, "You were brought up here to me. You had a very bad time. Do you remember?"

Carmody considered. Finally, she confessed, "I don't remember much. Except someone—you?—said I would see, in the right time!"

She could see—but she hardly remembered the time when she couldn't. Only the voice, promising her.

"Yes." It was a plain statement, full of assurance. "And now you see."

Carmody struggled to her elbow. Something else emerged from the shadows. "You—you're the Healing Woman?"

"So they call me. But we will talk of this another time. What do you remember? Try to tell me."

Carmody tried. She looked at her hands, lying on the blanket that covered her. Scraped raw, covered with an evil-smelling salve. The little finger of her right hand was bent at a strange angle. Nothing she could remember could account for these injuries.

"The last I remember," she said slowly, lifting an exploring hand to her face, which felt strangely melon-like in shape, "was James and he was worried about the battle the next day. We are at Bridgewater, aren't we? But no, the clouds don't look right!"

Panic was rising in her. She couldn't remember what had happened after James left her, and rode out to look at his troops drilling in the meadow in front of a marsh, called—what was the marsh called? Sedgemoor?

She must have lost hours after that, and where could she have gotten these terrible injuries? She turned hysterically to the Healing Woman. "Where is James? What happened? Where are all the soldiers?"

The woman's eyes held a kind of worried pity. Carmody was more frightened than ever. *What had happened?*

"It will come back to you," the woman said. She brought a small wooden bowl filled with a viscous white liquid. "Drink this. It will make you sleep. And in the right time, it will all come back."

In the right time.

For days, Carmody was overcome by a strange lethargy,

as though even remembering was too much trouble. She was content to lie all day and all night on her pallet, under a blanket—it grew surprisingly cold at night in this place, wherever it was. And as she grew stronger, she began to stir, to notice those around her.

Besides the Healing Woman—who was called Otobil—there were perhaps a half dozen others who shared this mountain hideaway. Luisa, a shy, dark spirit of the woods. Gomez, a square brutish-looking man with fierce independence glaring in his eyes. Gomez followed Otobil with his eyes always, and seemed almost to anticipate her thoughts. And there was Ramon, with a thin, tormented face, and lighthearted Felix, owner of a rich, rolling laugh.

Carmody's body was healing, but her memories eluded her yet. Dimly, she was grateful for the respite of not knowing. She had been brought here nearly dead, they told her, and her dreadful injuries could have resulted only from some anguish too dreadful to contemplate. And her mind had, quite simply, shut the truth away while flesh healed, bones mended. But soon, she would have to face whatever was now hidden.

Otobil had been away for a day and a night, and when she returned she came to drop beside Carmody on a rude bench made of a mahoe log.

"I've been down below," she began. "There is much stirring. Have you remembered any?"

"Not too well," Carmody said slowly. "Somehow it doesn't seem worthwhile to try. I'm here, and I'm getting well. I remember that I was captured by soldiers. And I remember something about a prison, but no, that was Ralph in the prison." She turned to Otobil. "Was I in prison?"

"You were," said the woman calmly, as though prison were a common place. "And they took you into court, and the judge—"

"I remember him! A fierce, crazy old man with his wig awry."

Otobil nodded approvingly. "And he said—?"

"To the colonies with you," Carmody repeated as

though in a trance. "I hear they die soon out there anyway."

It began to come back to her then. The convict ship, the Tolliver plantation. Aurelia Tolliver. And that mad impotent man, whose inability to function as a husband had driven his wife into the arms of another, had festered in him until his desire turned aside into raging destruction—

"And Aurelia died," Carmody said after a long time. "And then—"

She covered her face with her hands. Her hands were almost healed now, except for the crooked little finger. It was nearly straight, but not quite; even Otobil's skill could not make the shattered bone whole again.

"Then?" prompted Otobil. "Best get it out into the open. Lest it fester inside, and no man can heal it."

"Then—he wanted to marry me, his wife's handmaiden, he said, like Abraham and Hagar, and he came at me and I could have killed him. I had the dagger—the letter opener, you understand. But I didn't. I didn't kill again. And then I think I fell."

Ruthlessly, Otobil cut away the concealing barriers in Carmody's mind. "He struck you, again and again, judging from the shape of the bruises. I think he must have used his fist. And then when you fell down the stairs, escaping from him—"

Carmody interrupted. "I couldn't see, that was it. I woke up and it was black and I couldn't get my eyes open. But I got to the door—"

"The verandah door," said Otobil. "Bonwit told me they found you at the bottom of the stairs. You had crawled under the shrubbery, do you remember that?"

"No," said Carmody. Otobil probed no more, adding only that Bonwit and the others had brought her up the mountain, and saved her life.

"For what it's worth," said Carmody sourly.

They sat together for a long time, Otobil resting from her trip down to the lowlands and back, lending Carmody as much of her strength as she could.

"Only one thing I don't know," Carmody said at last. "How long ago was it? When I was in prison?"

"The Duke's Rebellion was over four years ago."

Four years! It was as though the calendar had been stretched out of shape, making days out of years, and years out of hours. Strange, but she would get used to it. And, if she tried, she could probably remember it all. But why should she? She was taken care of here, safe, and those around her would protect her. They had been slaves, but they had belonged to the Spanish, and when the English had taken over Jamaica thirty years before, the Spanish slaves had escaped to the mountains. A generation ago, and no one dared to try to get them back.

Some day, though, and that day must come soon, Carmody would have to consider what she would do. But not now. In the right time, as Otobil often said.

"Just one thing," said Otobil, as she rose to her feet. "You said just now that you didn't kill *again*. Believe me, your secret is safe with me. But there may be others who are not so discreet. Be careful."

Kill again?

Carmody's memory flooded back with a vengeance, once it started, and Waldo's look of astonishment was before her inner eyes, and herself holding the mammoth pistol in shaking hands, while the sound of the shot resounded in the room and blue-gray smoke rose from the barrel.

The days flowed on, one running into the next. Carmody began to take her turn cooking the simple meals for them all, and because it helped to pass the time, she asked Otobil to teach her about the healing remedies. She mixed salves, she learned how to tell one herb from another, and soon she was in charge of drying certain special plants. She did not want to move away from the safe mountain haven. She had been so laden with responsibility for what seemed a very long time, and the agonizing decisions she had made—even though she would make the same ones again—had taken their toll.

Perhaps, she thought, all the things that had happened to her in the last four years were the atonement that was exacted from her for her sin. Breaking God's laws—that was what Tolliver had said about his wife. But she, too, was guilty.

Well, Otobil had the word for it. Whatever was to be, would be. In the right time. And that time was not yet.

Then came the day when Carmody's peaceful existence was shattered. She was drying green pimento berries over a slow, slow fire built of lignum vitae, when she heard voices approaching. Immediately, all the inhabitants of the mountain top seemed to merge into the shadows, and, looking about her as she ran to shelter herself, Carmody could not distinguish any of them from the trees and rocks that hid them.

Carmody recognized the curious clop-clop sound as the footfalls of one of the tiny donkeys that ran wild on the island. The footsteps came closer and closer, and finally stopped, still out of sight.

Creaky noises then, and Carmody could envision what must be taking place on the trail. The donkey halted, the rider slipping off to come the rest of the very steep way on foot, leading his mount. Bringing supplies? Visitors were rare except when the Healing Woman's services were needed, or when another slave escaped from an agonized life under English masters.

The footsteps began again, slowly. Carmody peered anxiously toward the notch in the rock where the head of the trail emerged.

Before anyone came in sight, a voice rang out cheerily. A robust, feminine voice, speaking in English rather than the liquid dialect of the slaves. "Holla, anybody here? Don't worry, I'm alone! Can't do anybody a parcel of harm!"

Bewildered, Carmody left her shelter and stood gaping. That voice she knew, but it was long dead! It could not be Lucy's voice.

But it was. Lucy herself appeared from behind the last jutting outpost of rock that hid the encampment from view. Carmody cried out. How glad she was to see this round-faced, apple-cheeked woman who had grown up in neighboring Somerset! There was a touch of home about her and Carmody had known many on Oaklands who were of the same sort—honest, full of practical common-sense, and cheerful.

Carmody embraced her wholeheartedly. "I thought you were—" She realized how tactless her words would sound, and stopped, but Lucy herself supplied the missing word.

"Dead? Aye, that's what they all think. But I simply faded away from the field one day, and they didn't miss me until nightfall. Of course," she added practically, "I first asked if they was any serpents on the island, and when I heard there were none that bite with poison, it was just a matter of waiting till my chance came."

She told Carmody how she had wandered alone in the forest, seeing always the mountains towering above, sometimes cloud-hidden, sometimes starkly blue-green against the sky. Until someone found her and led her to Otobil. What a vast conspiracy of silence there was among the Maroons, as the Spanish ex-slaves were called. It was as though two separate civilizations existed in the same place, each carrying on their business independently, each aware of but ignoring the other's existence.

Carmody could not blame the mountain-dwellers. That other life below, as she knew only too well, was full of strife and ugliness, unhappiness, and even evil.

Whereas up here—peaceful enough, but around the campfire that night, listening to Lucy regale the others with news she had gathered in the course of her errands, Carmody suddenly realized that she must leave the highlands. Lucy had found her niche here, traveling back and forth from mountain to plantation, weaving a secret network between exiles and the world below.

But Carmody did not know what work she had to do in the world, and she must seek until she found it. The purpose of her life was all mixed up in her mind with self-punishment for her crime, her sin of murder—and although she couldn't unravel the different strands, she knew there was a strong cord drawing her inexorably toward the world again.

She looked up to find Otobil's eyes fixed upon her. Sad, but yet Carmody read approval too, in them. Otobil could at times almost worm her way into Carmody's inmost thoughts, so it seemed, and this must be one of the times. Carmody smiled shyly back.

All things happened in the right time, Otobil was fond of saying. And Carmody knew she must simply wait until the right time was revealed to her.

Surprisingly, the right time was now.

Carmody's mind had wandered away from the talk around the campfire, but now she was jerked back. Lucy was saying, "And so the new King—"

"The new King?" interrupted one, a man called Major, who had come from a neighboring mountain camp.

"William they call him, and his wife Mary. Yon pair make a great couple, they say. She's the daughter of the old king."

"What happened to the old King?"

"They do say when he heard William was marching to London, with his thousands of men, he went out the back door, to to speak, and he's in France."

Carmody could almost see it. The troops marching from the coast where they had landed in force, taking the same road, or nearly so, to London, with martial step and sunlight glinting on the weapons. And poor James Scott—how pitiful his small, untrained, unarmed forces seemed now. She sighed heavily.

"But the thing is, the new king has pardoned everybody that was in the Monmouth rebellion."

"Everybody?" Carmody leaped to her feet. "You? Me?"

Lucy grinned, a smile that bunched up her cheeks and closed her eyes in good-humored wrinkles. "Both of us, Mercy."

Later, when most of the company had sought their austere beds, Carmody said to Lucy, "What are you going to do? Go back to Somerset?"

"Nay. What would I do there? My man's dead. There was a time when I fair hated him for the trouble he brought on me, but that's gone now. This is a strange country, Mercy, and I never dreamed I would end up in a place the likes of this. In truth, I never dreamed there *was* a place like this. But I'm used to it now, and I've got friends."

A silence fell between them. Gomez moved around the campfire, covering the embers for the night, seeing that all was safe. Soon, Carmody knew, he would tiptoe silently to the head of the trail, give a low whistle to alert the sentry below, and there would be an answering whistle. The trail was guarded, night and day, by men who would not be seen unless they chose to be.

"What matter is it," Lucy said, "whether I dream of Somerset and live here, or go back where my friends are most of them gone, and dream of these mountains? Best I stay here."

Carmody reached out to cover Lucy's hand with hers. How well she understood the woman. The existence she had once known—the mellow bricks of Oaklands, the employees on the estate, even Harriet Paine—she could not go back and find them all the same. And—when Lucy called her Mercy, she remembered that the amnesty would not run on murder. Not even, she believed, if that murder was committed to save her own life.

"No, I can't go back," she mused, not knowing she spoke aloud.

"Then what?" It was Otobil, joining them in the spreading moonlight. "You are welcome here, Mercy, to make your life with us."

"I know that," said Carmody, slowly, picking her way among the strange new thoughts that opened up before her. "But I just can't stay. This life is for you, Otobil. You're needed here. And you too, Lucy. You've carved out a new life for yourself, and you fit in it. Somewhere there's such a life for me. I must believe that."

A life where she might, some time in the far distant future, hope to lay the ghost of Waldo Rivers at last.

Otobil nodded. "I understand," she said softly. "You must go. But how will you get along?"

"I thought once of going to the Carolinas," Carmody confessed, dreamily. "Or some other of the colonies."

Lucy objected, "But that takes money."

"I've got some." She looked at both her friends. "Truly I have. A man owes me money and maybe I can get it back. It's enough to buy passage on a ship away from here, anyway."

"Money?" echoed Lucy, and then, practical as always, "Who is he?"

"Howard Vickery. If he hasn't left the island. If," Carmody began to count up the barriers between her and her golden sovereigns, "he has much himself."

Lucy said shortly. "He's got it. I hear he's doing well. Or so he calls it."

"What do you mean?" asked Carmody.

Suddenly Lucy yawned. "I'm sorry. I'm sleepy enough to fall off this seat. We can all sleep better tonight, can't we, knowing we're not convicts any more!"

Even after Otobil followed Lucy to bed, Carmody sat at the fire. She planned her next move, and then discarded that first plan for another, only to find flaws in the second. At length, she gave up. A plan would present itself, and she would get her two sovereigns back from Howard Vickery, and then—she did not know.

But she would—in the right time.

4

Felix guided Carmody along the secret road winding down from the mountain stronghold of the Maroons, leading the way until she knew they were very close to the shore. The sea was up. The waves rolled in with a peculiar, ground-shaking thunder, and overhead the palm leaves fought their endless tournaments with wooden sword-like clattering.

Suddenly her guide raised a thickly-leaved branch of some nameless shrub, and motioned her to pass under it. She did, and at once stood on the hard-packed ground that served as a road. It was the road, Felix told her, from Port Royal.

"That way," he pointed to the east. "Right next here is the plantation you come from."

"Tolliver's?" she said, instinctively stepping back toward the shelter of the hidden path.

"Never mind. You're on Vickery land right now. Just go along there to the gate."

Carmody stood for a moment and oriented herself. If that way lay Tolliver's house, then the cove before her was where she had waded out into the clean, silvery water.

She turned to thank Felix, but he had gone more silently than a whisper, and she was alone on the road. She turned her back on Tolliver's, and started down the road toward Vickery's gate.

Howard Vickery was indeed doing well, so much she could see from the road. She judged she had walked along

212

his land for more than half a mile before she reached the driveway to the house.

It was just after noon. The steamy heat rose oppressively around her, and she felt suffocated in the lowland humidity. The mountain air had been cool, fresh, inspiriting. Perhaps she had made a mistake in leaving the security of that refuge. She could have made some sort of life there instead of the unknown future she now faced. But she had made her decision, and now she must live with it.

She opened the gate.

The house she approached on the winding drive could have been a twin of the Tolliver house. All lowland houses were built to take advantage of the morning and evening sea breezes, the air whirling through the rooms which opened to the verandah that ran along the front of the house; a balcony above served to ventilate the bedrooms upstairs.

There was a moment just before Carmody raised her hand to knock at the front door when she almost turned and fled. But she heard footsteps inside, and the moment was gone past redemption.

Howard himself stood in the doorway. He stared at her as though he could not believe his eyes, and she was conscious of the primitive simplicity of her plain gown.

Wordlessly, he opened the door wider, and she stepped into the cool, dim interior. It was a welcome relief from the strong sunlight, but a blinding contrast.

"Here," he said, "let us go into this room. If it's dusted."

"I won't notice," she promised. "Besides, it's too dim to see."

He guided her through a door opening off the entry hall, and waved vaguely toward a pair of chairs at the far end of the long room. She began to make out details of her surroundings in the tenebrous dusk. Where it had been high noon along the road, here it seemed the last moments of twilight. But it was only her fancy, she told herself, noticing with some surprise the sparseness of the furniture—

two chairs like rocks in a meadow, a tall chest against one wall, a long table against another.

"Let me offer you something," Howard said. "Something to eat? A drink of something? But—" He gave up trying to make polite conversation, and simply blurted out what was uppermost in his mind. "Tolliver was frantic when you disappeared. Where have you been?"

"Away."

"With the Maroons, no doubt. Well, I won't ask any more. You're free, of course. You've heard of the amnesty?"

"Yes." She found it difficult to put into words what she wanted to say. Her carefully rehearsed speech had flown out of the window when she came to the point, and her courage waned. She was not accustomed to beg for money, even though it was rightfully hers.

"What are you going to do then?" he asked.

"Go away somewhere. Not back to England. I thought the American colonies, maybe."

"Virginia? A good place, I suppose. I've got some property there, although I've never seen it."

They talked a little. He was watching her carefully now, sitting opposite her so close that if he reached out he could touch her knee.

"You're not in jail," she commented with a little laugh, remembering Edward Tolliver's threat.

"You saved me from that, at least," he said. "I have my plantation back. I've acquired that estate in Virginia I mentioned, and I hope it is worth the price the fellow set on it when he threw it into the pot."

"You won it, gambling?" She could not keep her disapproval from her voice.

"A friendly game now and then." He changed the subject airily. "You know Tolliver has drunk himself under the table. His wife's death seemed to take away his reason for living."

Carmody wondered what Howard would think if he had seen that terrible fight in dead Aurelia's room. Tolliver had certainly thought he had a reason to live, that night.

Could it be possible that the island grapevine had not informed Howard of the incident?

"But I understand you fell down the steps," Howard said, unconsciously answering her thoughts. "Badly injured, so my people told me. Are you recovered?"

"Entirely so. Well enough to leave Jamaica, as I said. But I do need money, and I came to ask for a return of my loan."

"Ah, yes. The two sovereigns."

He rose and began to pace around the room while she waited, tense in her chair. Was he going to deny his words—that they were a loan? Would he refuse to pay her back? She would have no recourse in the courts.

"You see this house, Mercy? It was my grandfather's, and my father's. I lost it when Tolliver foreclosed on it. The house, the plantations that go with it, my slaves. Tolliver took the slaves he thought I prized most, and left the others to till the fields. But there weren't enough hands to keep up the place. So the plantation ran downhill. Pastures full of that damned sensitive plant. Indigo—the crops weren't cut in June, so that they took only one crop a year out of the fields."

His step grew shorter, faster, revealing his unsatisfied anger. At length he stopped near the windows that looked out, through jalousies, onto the verandah.

"But why would he do that?" Carmody queried. "That's no way to make money."

"Ah, now you sound like a landowner," Howard said. "I wonder who you really are, Mercy Holland. What was your life like, back in England?"

She moistened her dry lips. She had nearly given herself away. *Landowner*, he had said, accurately. It was Carmody Petrie of Oaklands who had asked that question.

"Mr. Vickery," she began, stirring in her chair. It was a simple matter of two sovereigns, she told herself sturdily. Either he would repay them, or he would refuse. In either case, she must not stay here.

"You want the sovereigns. I'm coming to that. I just wanted to tell you that you brought me luck that night. You saved me from prison, and with that loan of yours—

no matter how little I deserved your thanks that night—I was able to get back on my feet again."

He forestalled her questions. "No matter how I did it. I began to remake my fortune. I redeemed my plantation—not all my slaves, but most. And the fields are beginning to produce what they should again."

"I'm glad you have your ancestral home again," Carmody said stiffly. She knew how much that would mean—at least how much it meant to her. But she rose, pulling the shawl across her shoulders. Her dress was uncomfortably low-cut at the neck.

"Come, let me show my house to you."

Over her protests, he insisted upon taking her through the rooms downstairs. The large living room they were in, a vast dining room next door. Across the hall, another room dreadfully similar to the library she had been trapped in, that night at Tolliver's. And a smaller room behind it, which, Howard said, he used as an office.

There was something unpleasant about the rooms. An aura of decay, of dust, of neglect—but something more, as though ghosts whispered in the corners. An unwelcoming house, she felt, under a spell cast by old, remembered sorrows. She shivered, but he did not notice.

"There was a chest there once," he said, pointing to a place along the living room wall, when they had returned from the tour. All along the walls, in every room, there were signs where furniture had stood before—a lighter rectangle along the wall, where the paper was not faded so much. Unpainted squares on the floor, where furniture had stood.

"Tolliver," snarled Howard. "He sold the best pieces. The ones my grandfather had imported."

"I'm sorry," she said sincerely. How like Oaklands, where Ralph had almost wrought a similar disaster!

"Mercy Holland," said Howard, "you have a strangely aristocratic carriage for—a convict. And those eyes—I can see why Tolliver thought you had bewitched him. Why he—well, no matter."

"Mr. Vickery—"

"Now then, my name is Howard. Mercy, listen to me."

He was going to give her a dozen reasons why he could not repay her money, she expected. So when he resumed, she was astonished.

"Mercy, you're responsible for my getting all this back, in a way. Marry me, and it will all be yours."

"Wh-what did you say?"

"Marry me. This house needs a woman to run it, you can see that. And you'll have all the gowns, the jewels, anything you want. You're good luck to me, you know."

He must be joking. This island had strange influences on men, driving them lunatic in odd ways, she decided.

"I suppose you are short of cash—" she began.

"You think that's it?" His smile twisted unexpectedly. He wheeled and went to a drawer in the highboy standing against the wall. Rummaging in a drawer, he came back to stand in front of her, forcing her to look up into his face. "Here. Two gold sovereigns. I would not have thought you would settle for so little, when you could have so much. Or does the fact that you have to take me spoil the bargain?"

Suddenly, he seemed touchingly vulnerable. She had not thought she could be so moved again by any man, but something inside her, long suppressed, began to stir.

"No," she said. "It's just so—unreal."

"Unreal? You'll find I am very tangible indeed. I must make arrangements. But first—"

He took her into his arms, possessively, and looked down into her face. "Gold sovereigns," he said huskily, "but silver eyes."

Then his lips found hers, and she felt her long pent-up responses sweeping back like a consuming tidal wave. She reached up to encircle his neck with her arms, pressing herself against him, feeling with awakened remembrance the thickness of his clothes through her thin gown.

Another time, a different man, but the same kindling, instinctive response—

His eyebrows lifted in surprise, and somehow that gesture brought her back to herself. She stiffened and began to pull away. She felt his arms relax, his lips left hers, and inside her every fiber was screaming—don't leave me now!

He steadied her on her feet, letting his hands linger on her shoulders. "Well!" he said. And she could see speculation in his eyes. Well, she had not pretended to anybody that she was untouched. But even Howard must never know that it was James Scott, late Duke of Monmouth, who had taught her the winning ways of men. For then, her identity would be laid bare.

"Special license," Howard was saying. "We can be married at once. I know the right hands to drop a coin into."

A marriage was not a wedding, Carmody thought with some regret. She would not now go back to wishing she could have been married in the little stone chapel in the village, with old Tom ringing the bell, and her friends and neighbors waiting outside the church to wish happy the new Lady Rivers. She was a realist, and she knew that even if her own hand had not lifted the pistol, that marriage was never destined to happen. Waldo had fallen out of love with her when Ralph's derelictions became common knowledge. Indeed, once in a while she wondered whether he had ever intended to marry her.

But she would have liked Otobil, Bonwit, and Lucy, and Iletha and Ascar, and even Jassy, to be with her now. Instead, there was no one to witness her marriage except fumbling witnesses brought in from the street.

And she was now Mrs. Howard Vickery, who had come to her marriage with a dowry of two golden sovereigns. She had stayed in Port Royal for the three days it took to make arrangements for the hasty ceremony. She had improved the time by, at Howard's direction, ordering a new wardrobe. His choice for her was flamboyant, but he did not even blink at the cost, and she ended by feeling she was luckier by far than she had even dreamed of a week ago.

After the afternoon ceremony he had brought her home. The house had been dusted and cleaned, and the smell of beeswax filled the air.

Howard introduced her servants to her, and she had tried to greet them with assurance. She knew how important it would be to gain their confidence and trust, and she knew she could do it. But not with Howard hovering at her elbow, speaking for her.

The house still held its sad aura, and she doubted, now, whether she had acted wisely. To marry a stranger simply because his kiss aroused memories—put into such simple words, the reasons didn't seem heavy enough in the balance. It was a simple truth in the end. She didn't feel able to run her own life any more—it was too late to change her mind.

"Sorry, my sweet," said Howard, taking her upstairs after dinner—a meal served in near silence, and eaten by a silent bride who could not throw off her depression.

"Sorry?" she said, lifting the hem of her new gown as she climbed the stairs, Howard's hand tightly under her elbow.

"That I couldn't take you off on an ocean trip. Your wedding voyage will have to wait. I've got too much afoot here."

"Yes, you hinted at dinner of some plans," she said.

"Just now," he answered, opening the door to the bedroom she had not yet seen, "there's only one plan I have in mind."

The bedroom was barely furnished. A double bed, covered by a thin coverlet falling to the floor on either side. Two chairs and a wardrobe clearly brought in from some other room, hastily, and set not quite square with the wall.

A robe of thin muslin was laid out on the bed, and a pale yellow night shift beside it. The sea breeze had come up and the gauzy white curtains at the windows billowed cloud-like into the room.

Carmody looked around her in dismay. Howard was lighting the candles on a small table near the bed. "Not much of a room," he said, with surprising viciousness in his voice. "Tolliver again. He took everything I prized and destroyed it."

Too much bitterness, she thought. What was he thinking? That Tolliver could be in his thoughts, particularly when everywhere they turned there was evidence of his ravishing hand, was certainly understandable. But that was months ago, and surely a bridegroom could forget for a little while.

She looked at her husband, trying to puzzle out his mood. His eyes were shadowed under his tawny eyebrows, and she could not read their expression. He shaded the flickering candle flame with one hand and looked at her, steadily, probingly.

"Why did he hate you so much?" she ventured at last.

"Don't you know?"

She shook her head.

"He was a vicious, ruthless, possessive devil," Howard said, his voice calm. Underneath, she could swear he was trembling with rage.

"And now he's mad, and I suppose that's revenge enough."

Carmody moved to the shadows on the other side of the bed and sat down heavily. Absently she gathered up the robe and shift, and piled them on the pillow near at hand.

A strange marriage, she thought—a strange wedding ceremony, hustled through as though the words were meaningless. And an even stranger man to share her bed.

But she was grateful to him for his rescue of her—for this amounted to a rescue, she thought. From uncertainty. From making a ragged way for herself in the world.

The trouble was she didn't know what kind of life was in store for her now. But she was on the verge of a discovery about it, she thought, and with a sudden determination she began unbuttoning the tiny buttons marching down the front of her wedding dress.

She finished unbuttoning her bodice, and stood erect to let the dress fall to the floor. Carefully, clad only in her shift, she folded the new dress and laid it neatly over one of the two straight chairs.

She turned back to the bed. Howard stood between her and the robe she was reaching for. How silent the man was! she thought.

"Now, Mistress Vickery," he said, a hidden laugh lurking around his thin lips, "you must admire me for my forebearance, the other day in the hall. I have been thinking of nothing else these three days. In fact, ever since I saw you one night in the cove where I used to meet Aurelia." His lips twisted in scorn. "Thinking of nothing but your trollop's eagerness to come to my bed."

He sat down on the side of the bed where she had sat only moments before. The candle flickered on the table on the far side of the bed.

"Trollop's eagerness!" she repeated, bewildered by the sudden alteration in him—the contempt in every line of his face. He spread his knees apart and jerked her to him, pulling her off balance. She steadied herself by placing her hands hastily on his shoulders.

"If you hate me so," she cried out, "why did you marry me?"

"I married a bride willing—nay, greedy, for my embraces," he said mockingly. "You did surprise me, you know, when I kissed you. But also, I expect a lady to grace my table, meet my friends—a lady, mind you, with a decent reserve." But then his scorn collapsed. "Oh, Mercy," he cried, abruptly burying his face in the valley between her breasts, "who are you? A witch? You've set my senses swimming!"

Suddenly he threw himself back on the bed, and Carmody's precarious balance was gone. She fell on him, gasping. He fumbled with the hem of her shift, and—thinking of the exorbitant cost of it—she forestalled him by pulling it over her head, and dropping it beside the bed.

Howard's mouth was hard, probing, demanding upon hers, and she sobbed for breath. She suddenly was not on his hot bed, but far away across the sea, with James Scott forcing her back against the bunk in the cabin of the *Helderenburgh.*

Not caressing hands on her now, though, as his had been. These bruised, crushed, *hurt.* And, shamefully, her own body reached out to meet him, taking punishment, absorbing it and even demanding more of him until the tiny spring deep in her was touched, and tension was washed away in the flood of grateful release.

"So," he said sometime later, "as I suspected. I am not the first."

"I never said you would be."

"Well, it can't be helped. It makes no difference now. If I asked who, would you tell me?"

"No."

"More than one?"

"Would it make any difference?" she parried. "I'm married to you, and there's no one I regret."

"And no one you will yearn for in the future, either. Remember that."

He rolled away from her. She feared he might be angry at her refusal to tell him about the first man she had known.

"Howard?"

"Yes."

His voice was cold, and she raised up on one elbow to look at him. "I want to tell you, it was not Tolliver. He tried—"

To her astonishment, he began to laugh. She thought, I have never heard him laugh before. Not like this. A cruel, mocking laugh, like a slap in the face.

She fell back, and turned away from him. Just now, when she would have welcomed a comforting caressing arm around her, all she heard was the sound of jeering.

He stopped abruptly. "My sweet, you're crying! Did I injure you so much?"

His forefinger traced the tears down her cheeks, and he gently turned her face back towards his. "Look at me, Mercy," he said. "Believe me, I was only laughing at Tolliver. Of course, he tried—you are a delicious handful for any man. But don't you see what was funny?"

She gulped back a sob, and shook her head.

"That's all Tolliver could do. *Try.*"

"I know Aurelia *said* so. But he claimed it was her fault."

"Not Aurelia's fault," said Howard. "At least, I wasn't impotent when she turned to me. And now—it's poetic justice that you, too, turn to me, is it not?"

Her stunned revulsion at Howard's obscene triumph over his enemy Tolliver, a triumph using her as a weapon, made no impression on him.

"Now," he said, with a wicked chuckle, "let us continue with our honeymoon."

The honeymoon lasted exactly three days—and three punishing nights.

The fourth day, Carmody walked down the broad stairs in a bemused state of mind. The night before, she had finally been forced to protest her husband's ferocious love-making, and now she began to worry about his reaction.

This morning she had examined her new clothes, hanging in the broad wardrobe, and wished that she liked them better. The impressive collection of gowns contained more furbelows than she liked, and almost all were lower-cut on the shoulders than she was comfortable with.

Fortunately, she had insisted—after Howard had left her alone with the dressmaker—on one simple muslin dress, cool and white, with tiny embroidered flowers daintily spread over the fabric.

She put it on now and descended the stairs with a resolve forming in her mind to order more of this kind of simple garment.

Howard was standing in the doorway of the living room. She was rudely jerked from her planning when she caught sight of his grim and forbiddingly stern expression.

"Where did you get that rag?" he demanded.

"You dislike my choice of gown?" she said, quietly.

"I bought you everything you need. That—that *thing* you're wearing makes you look like a schoolgirl. What I do not need is a naive child here."

"You think that is what I am? Then your behavior with me is even more scandalous."

A sly smile crossed his handsome face, but did not reach his cold eyes. "I know better. You've been bought and paid for, at least once before. But I do not lose my possessions easily, and you are mine now."

She was stung. "Bought and paid for? You asked me to marry you. I am your wife, not your mistress. Remember that."

"I remember. It is a mere detail. The price of a wife is

a bit higher than a mistress, I'll concede that. Two golden sovereigns, to be precise."

"You're unfair!" she cried out, anguished. "You asked me to marry you. I thought you wanted me, at least a little. It would have been easy enough to pay back my loan. You didn't have to—debase me, the way you do."

For the first time she noticed how cruelly his thin lips could curve into a sneer. How had she thought him vulnerable? She wondered uneasily what he was thinking. Certainly she had misread his thoughts so far.

"I always like interest on my money. You'll turn me a profit yet." Suddenly his harsh laugh rang out. "Your face is open as a pane of glass, Mercy. You have not learned to conceal your thoughts. Don't worry, my dear. My wife belongs to me—and I have not the slightest intention of allowing anyone else the privileges that are mine. Not even for profit. So rest assured. You need not fear alien hands on you."

Uncannily, he put into words the fear that had risen in her, and then wiped it away. But it was a revelation, that she could even suspect him of dealing so despicably with her.

Howard did not refer to her dress again, not then. Instead, he gestured imperiously for her to accompany him into the living room. Once there, he studied the room as though he had not seen it before.

To divert her racing thoughts, Carmody tried to see the room as it would be when she finished with it. For she certainly would not leave it with worn straw matting on the floor, and stained wallpaper. There should be curtains at the windows—some gauzy fabric would be best, to let in air and light and yet afford some privacy to those inside. She must wait until he was in a better mood before she asked for funds to start refurbishing his house.

"You're not listening, Mercy," Howard was saying, and guiltily she started. "I was saying, I want the house refurnished, redecorated."

Amazed, she looked at him. Perhaps he was jesting with her before, when he said those terrible things. Perhaps he was teasing—

"Howard, how delightful! I do think it's too bad that the house has been badly neglected. I will certainly enjoy making the rooms look their best."

"I am glad to hear that you're agreeable to my wishes," he said dryly. "But I think you misunderstand me."

She was too intent on the vista of planning that was opening before her—a chance to allow her creative talent to bud again and blossom into a work of value. She had not heard the warning note in his voice.

"Mercy, perhaps you had better make a list."

"A list? A good idea."

"Before you fly away, let me give you the general directions for your efforts."

She turned faintly puzzled eyes toward him. "I don't think I understand you. Is this not to be my task?"

"And have it all turn out like that muslin thing you're wearing? I think not."

Her growing dreams wavered, and then faded. He would not let her decorate her own house. Why?

Uncannily, again he echoed her thoughts. "I'll tell you why, Mercy. We will be having many guests, of a kind that will not appreciate dainty ladylike furnishings. Especially things like the curtains that I am sure you already have in mind—thin veils of voile, probably. Yes, I see I am right. Truly, Mercy, you will have to learn to control your expression. I will not have you giving away my guests' secrets."

"What kind of guests are these, with dreadful secrets?"

"Men—and occasionally women. Who want a place to sit at a table and play cards. Or other games."

She revolved his words in her mind, and came out with the only possible answer. "Gambling."

"Precisely. And I will not have you strolling behind the players and signaling—all innocently, of course—the other players at the table."

"I think you will find yourself mistaken, Howard. I will not be strolling behind your guests, innocently or not. I will have no part of gambling, Howard. I have seen far too much of the misery and disaster gambling is responsible for, and—"

He took her wrist, and stopped her with a sudden, vicious pressure. "I advise you not to tell me what you will or will not do. You are my wife, and you will do exactly as I say. Just as my hounds do, and my field hands. You are as much my property as they are, and you will do well to remember it. Now here is the list of the things you will do, beginning today."

In four weeks, the gambling palace—for it was so lavishly furnished it was a veritable palace—was in full swing. The two large rooms at the front of the house were crowded every night, and the noise of shouting and laughter seemed at times almost to make the walls quiver.

For Carmody, every night she came downstairs to preside over such gaiety, dressed ornately as Howard instructed her, it was a fresh descent into the lower regions that the vicar back home had often spoken of. A torment everlasting, he had said, waited for those who have broken the Law. And she had broken the most binding, the most universal of all laws—taking the life of another human. Now she was punished, in every way she could imagine. The only reprieve was that after the third night of their marriage, and her protests, Howard had not touched her again.

If she had feared that she herself might be one of the attractions Howard offered—in spite of his assurance to the contrary—she soon found, that her role was purely decorative. She was expected to smile and say pleasant, but entirely harmless things—more like a talking doll, she thought resentfully, than anything else.

But a doll prized, at least in public, by its owner.

Soon she began to sort out the various patrons of the gambling tables. Several men from the town she knew. An aide to the Governor, for one, who came in late at night and would not look at her, as if by not meeting her eye, no one would know he was there.

A few women came, too, surprisingly. And all of the gamblers, long, short, thin, ladies or men—all had the same look in their face, a universal expression that Carmody thought she would recognize for the rest of her life.

A gambler's face.

An obsessive look, one that swerved neither to right nor left, but focused only on the gaming table, the dark green covers providing stark contrast to the brightly colored playing cards with their plain white backs.

She thought she could have worn her muslin gown, or even nothing at all, and no one bent on his game, or the dice, would even have noticed her.

After a month, the edges of shame and of torment began to be blunted with repetition. She was not required to take an active part, only to greet guests at the door, keeping up the fiction that this was a private house and she was the hostess. She moved through the rooms, still playing the part Howard had given her, of seeing to refreshments, making sure that the guests had everything they needed to make them comfortable, and allow them to risk even higher stakes.

She became acquainted with the "regulars," those who came night after night. And when they did not appear, somehow she missed them.

So when Captain Samuel Short from Virginia came puffing up the three steps to the verandah, she greeted him almost gaily. "Well, Captain, we haven't seen you for nearly a week. I hope nothing is wrong."

"Nothing that a little luck won't cure, Mrs. Vickery," said the captain. He smiled back at her, but an element of tenseness, of anxiety, lay at the back of his little eyes.

She waved him into the house, almost catching his sleeve to beg him not to risk more than he could afford to lose, but she let the moment pass. She was glad she had not yielded to impulse, for when she turned to look after the captain, she caught Howard's eyes on her, cold, with unmistakable warning in them.

She turned away quickly. She tried to remember what she knew about Captain Short, almost as though she had some presentiment of events to come. He was past middle age, grizzled in beard and hair, but with great bushy eyebrows like black bars of fur straight across his eyes. He did not own his own ship, she knew, but served as captain for one of the Tennant ships that came to Port Royal to load mahogany and logwood.

The Tennant enterprises were based in one of the continental colonies of England—Virginia, she thought—and there was supposed to be a good deal of wealth in the Tennant family. Some old patriarch, she supposed, sitting like a spider in a corner of the Tennant web, sending out threads to all the world.

How fanciful, she thought, fiddling with the cords of the red velvet draperies—Howard's choice, the red velvet!

Carmody was in a restless mood. The heavy curtains cut out the sea wind, and the heat, with so many people inside, grew suffocating. With a quick glance around to make sure that Howard was not watching her, she slipped through the door at the far end of the room, onto the open verandah. The cool breeze breathed upon her hot forehead, and she leaned against the side of the house, careless of her satin, low-cut gown.

Far out, through the intervening trees, she could catch a glimpse of the sea. The moon was not full, and the light it shed on the heaving waters was obscure and faint, giving rather a luminescence that touched briefly on the waves and slipped into the dark troughs, a light that promised more than it revealed, and was surprisingly alluring. She could almost picture herself upon that sea, going as far as the southern horizon, and perhaps dropping over the edge of the world, as sailors of olden times believed.

Far from Howard Vickery, she thought, tightening her lips. I must get away, far away—but there was no possible way. She lingered, unwilling to leave the dreamlike mood of moon and sea, lingered too long.

When she returned to the stifling rooms, she realized at once that something had happened. The players at two of the tables were so intent on their game that they ignored the sound of raised voices, but toward the door a little group of spectators peered out into the hall beyond. Picking up her skirts, Carmody ran to the door, and pushed through into the hall.

Howard was there, of course. And facing him, with a heavy pistol in his hand, was Captain Samuel Short.

"You owe me something!" the old man was shouting. "You got to let me play. Get my money back."

Howard teetered casually on the balls of his feet, looking indolent, but Carmody knew he was poised to move like a striking snake. *Stay back, Captain!* But the cry was only in her mind.

"Give me the gun," said Howard, calmly. "You don't need it. Unless to shoot yourself with."

"Aye, you don't take blame here, do ye?" said the little man, nearing sobbing. "You don't admit that your dice are loaded, your cards crooked. That Van John game of yours, nobody wins but the house. But you don't put up a sign to warn of dangerous reefs, do you?"

Carmody didn't hear the rest of his tirade, suddenly wondering if what Captain Short said could be true. Was the game he mentioned by its colloquial name—really, Vingt-et-Un—was it crooked? Were the dice loaded, cunningly inserted lead pellets making them fall in certain ways?

Unable to move, with one part of her mind she knew that she despised her husband more than any other creature she had ever known—he was taking advantage of men infected by the disease of gaming, and stealing from them, for stealing it was, if the games were dishonest. And with the other part of her mind she watched Captain Short wave his pistol, watched Howard advance, his eyes fixed hypnotically upon the Captain's, and when he was close enough, snatching the pistol from the Captain's hand.

"I should unload this," said Howard, "lest a babe in the woods like you do yourself some harm with it—or, worse, somebody else. But, why should I? You don't have nerve enough to shoot anybody, or you would have pulled the trigger just now."

Don't goad him into something desperate, begged Carmody silently, even though a wayward imp grinned at the edge of her mind and said, *You'd be free then.*

But not like that, she could have wailed. Not like Waldo, to die by violence, before her eyes. She couldn't bear it.

Captain Short was gone, then, slipping away like a shadow at noon. Like the shadow that Howard had made of him.

Howard drawled, looking at the spectators in the door-way, "I think we might as well get back to our pleasure. Mercy, my dear, order drinks all around, on the house."

His charm was never more evident, she thought. His brilliant smile at her appeared, to their guests, full of his convincing charm. And only the muttered undertone, as she passed him on her way to do his bidding, said other-wise. "Don't meddle," he said, uncannily anticipating the protests she had in mind for later that night. "This is my affair, not yours."

By the time a half hour had passed, the episode with Captain Short might never have happened. But it was not over.

Carmody needed to think. Could she find out if Howard's gaming tables were dishonest? If it were true, the discovery might show her the way to freedom. Her mind turned over fanciful plots—but none of her schemes would serve her purpose. She went through the open front door onto the verandah. What good would it do if she did find out? There was nothing she could do to change things—no way to get away, clear off the island. Going back to Otobil might help, but she feared that Howard would find her, even there—

There was somebody on the porch, illuminated by the light from the tens of candles lighted in the hall, streaming out through the open door.

The man, recognizable in the light, was Captain Samuel Short, or what was left of him, she realized suddenly. The eyes that had looked at her so worriedly, earlier that eve-ning, now looked hollow and empty. The man himself had gone away somewhere, driven by Howard Vickery into flight, leaving only this shell.

Before her frightened eyes, Captain Short lifted his right hand and pointed the pistol at his temple.

"I'll leave him something he can't explain," the Captain muttered—and his finger moved on the trigger.

With a shriek, Carmody leaped at him, hand out-stretched to strike the pistol away from its target. Her scream startled the Captain, and he hesitated, too long.

Her hand struck his with all the force she could muster. The pistol discharged.

She heard a sobbing moan, and knew it was hers. The sound of the shot deafened her to all else for a moment, and she watched bewildered as people rushed from the house, and—the Captain did not fall to the ground.

She had succeeded!

His attempt foiled, his main drive gone, Captain Short submitted numbly to those who took custody of his person. Howard said, clearly enough for all to hear, "You're a heroine, my dear. Come away inside, away from all this."

His words were kind, but his fingers bit deeply into her arm. She was scarcely aware of constables arriving, of gamesters leaving, of the house growing quiet, the candles blazing down on disordered tables, dirty glasses, chairs akimbo and overturned.

Howard never released his grip on her. She protested a little, but he ignored her. Not until he had marched her up the stairs and thrust her into her bedroom did he say a word.

"What made you interfere like that?"

"Interfere?" At last she was coming out of her numbness. "Howard, the man was going to kill himself!"

"And what difference would that make? Now, you've set the cat among the pigeons. I could do with a little less meddling from you."

"The man would have killed himself on your doorstep! Think what a scandal that would have brought on you!"

"Now he is still alive. Thanks to you. And now he will be able to tell somebody about the dice he said were loaded, the game he thought was rigged. And if he tells the right people, then—" He shrugged his elegant shoulders. "You see what you have done to me. I did not know your spite ran so deeply. "

"Believe me, Howard, it was not spite." She wished her voice sounded as strong as she felt. For she heard her words tremble and hoped he wouldn't take it for weakness, but for the rage she knew it was. "I find it difficult to believe that anyone would believe you—ran a crooked game,

I believe the phrase is?" She contrived to insert a mocking note into her voice. "And why would I try to betray you?"

His face was a cold mask. "I don't know, my dear, but I advise you not to try. In fact," he said musingly, "I should perhaps point out to you firmly the error of your ways. For instance, I should like to see a little more cordiality toward our guests."

"Allowing them to kill themselves, if they choose?"

"Exactly so," he said. "We must not interfere with another's destiny."

She longed for him to go. Hadn't he said enough? He hadn't even been in her bedroom, certainly not shared her bed, since the third night after they had been wed. At first she had been too proud to question him. Then, suspecting that he visited the slave quarters frequently, she was relieved. She had taken him too much for granted, though, and she made a mistake.

Thinking she would indicate her longing for sleep—it was past three in the morning—she began to unclasp the diamonds around her neck. Laying the jewels on the dresser, she turned her back on her husband. She kicked off her slippers. She unfastened the jeweled pin that held her bodice together, and turned to say a definite goodnight to him.

He watched her with the same derision she had seen when he glared at the unfortunate Captain. "You hate me, don't you, Mercy?" he asked conversationally.

"Yes!" she said in a burst of honesty. "I do."

"Then it is time to point out to you that how you feel toward me is no longer relevant. I must teach you to obey me." He continued, imperturbably, "Come to me."

"No."

He moved swiftly. He was around the bed, gripping her shoulders with his strong hands, before she could move. Too late she guessed his intention.

He ripped the dress from her, with a long, tearing sound. She cried out, "Don't touch me!"

"You should thank me for ruining the dress I bought, since you hate it so much," he said, his voice dripping scorn. "Here, let's get rid of the petticoats, too," he said, savagely tearing them off, hurling them to the far corner of the room. "Now, stand there. Just the way you came to me, except for that rag you wore. And this is the way you will leave me, without even that rag. But you'll never leave me, Mercy."

In panic, she struck out at him with her fists. But though she fought valiantly, and silently, she lost ground as he forced her back, hurling her onto the bed with a muffled curse. He fell heavily upon her, his woolen jacket chafing her skin, and then, suddenly, his jacket and ruffled shirt, and his breeches, were no longer between them. He pinioned her flailing hands beneath her, and although her whole body writhed in outrage, he possessed her ferociously, in a tearing, irresistible phallic rush.

When she could do no more than lie, sobbing, under his crushing weight, he removed his bruising mouth from hers and said, "You hate me even more now." She tried to free a hand to rub her lacerated lips. He said, "Stop whimpering. I'm not through yet."

Much later, Carmody risked opening her eyes. Howard had rolled away from her, at last, and a tremulous relief touched her. Glancing at his averted face, she believed his frenzy had spent itself.

His features were cold, passionless. Then he lifted himself on his elbow and let his appraising eyes travel slowly, insultingly, over her. "No more fight in you? You surprise me. I suppose you're entertaining thoughts of revenge. Forget them, my dear. In law, a wife can't be raped by her husband. I can beat you, starve you, anything I wish. But I think you hate this"—he gestured—"the most."

Her blazing eyes told him how heartily she agreed with him.

"That's more like it," he said approvingly. "A worthy opponent." He was no longer angry. But she feared him more—his implacable, icy mood was not human. "Since I think," he said with a judicial air, "you would still defy me, if you could, I must make sure you have learned your lesson."

"Leave me alone!"

"Still defiant? I must risk your hating me even more," he said with a wolfish grin, "and this time, I won't be tender and considerate of your softness, as I was just now."

5

WHILE Howard was working off his insensate fury on the body of his wife, Captain Samuel Short was indeed making trouble.

The Captain had talked to the right people, nameless in general, and a searching inquiry into Howard's business was about to get under way.

"Thanks to you," Howard said scathingly, when Carmody crept, numb and aching, down to breakfast the next morning. "I see I should have taken you in hand before."

"Don't try that again," Carmody said quietly. Her eyes were sunken in her head and staring, as though they had looked into a pit of crawling, obscene things—as indeed they had.

"Truly? You frighten me," he said, raising an eyebrow. "Pray don't do away with yourself, Mercy. My reputation really would suffer, with two attempts at suicide at my door."

"There are other ways," she said darkly, vaguely.

"Oh, come now, Mercy," he said with a chuckle. "You enjoyed last night."

"*Enjoyed!*"

"All women have a secret longing to be violated. You're fortunate that I understand this. Force is the natural way of it."

"You *beast!*"

"I must admit, your resistance was a spice that I found

235

delightful," he said, gleefully. "You have possibilities that I've overlooked."

He left the room, contempt in his gleaming eyes as he said, "Don't wander too far away, Mercy. Not even in your thoughts."

Howard had his hands full in Port Royal, defending himself against the Captain's accusations, reassuring his old customers and enticing new ones. The house would be open again, he told everyone, in less than a month.

Carmody moved in a dangerous state of near shock. The bruises on her mind were less easy to heal than the others, and sometimes she believed that she would never feel any different—never feel anything but this terrible not-alive state. She took to planning an escape to the mountains, to Otobil, who would protect her, and went so far as to put a few things together in a scarf, but the servants seemed always in the hall and she could not slip by them. She finally realized that Howard had set them to guard her.

Ten days after the dreadful night, Howard sent word to the servants—not to her—that he would be delayed overnight in Port Royal. She had taken to avoiding Howard, hiding in her room as much as she could. She bolted her door every night, but she knew that if a strong determined body hurled itself against the door it would splinter, and there would be no protection, not anywhere.

But the night that he was away in town, even though she could have slept safely, she was more restless than ever. The moon was now at the full, and it was said in Dorset that the full moon "did strange things to folk, driving them daft." She felt suddenly carefree, knowing that Howard's eyes did not watch her this night.

She wandered aimlessly around the garden, listening to the rhythmic beat of the surf. It exerted a pull on her, like the moon upon the tidal waters, and she drifted toward the shore. There was a suggestion of a cove beyond the house, and she had often come here, not to bathe as she had once before, in another cove, but to look across the placid water to watch the ships sleeping on the harbor waters.

The Vickery plantation was not far from Port Royal itself, and this enhanced its appeal to Howard's victims—no, she must call them guests, lest he become angry again.

And it was near enough to see, even though from a distance, the tall ship masts raking the sky, the bare poles showing above the trees screening the actual waterfront from her eyes.

She reached the shore this night. It was bathed, as she always liked it best, in the silver light that glimmered starkly against the black ebony of the shadows. Black and silver, a monotone of color, but peaceful, the surf gentle upon the sand.

She found an outcropping of rock that made a kind of shelf, and sat on it, pulling her knees up to keep her slippers from the wet sand. Her pale gown blended into the moonlight, and she sat quietly, letting the moving water speak to her of infinity and blessed peace.

Peace. She longed for it as she once longed for the exciting streets of London.

Far out on the horizon, the white sails of a ship hull-down glinted in the moonlight like foam topping a wavelet on the shore. The cool moistness of the air bathed her face, smoothing out the lines of fear and of suffering that had etched themselves in the last weeks.

The quiet serenity moved her, lifting her spirit into a realm of calm, away from all passion. The escape she ached for, formed tortured little schemes to attain, was there before her eyes.

If she walked out far enough, the sea would receive her, and she would be enfolded forever in the placid depths, in a remote tranquillity that would erase all thought.

Another time, in another cove, she had taken off her slippers and her dress. Now she gave no thought to anything but her need for the sea. She stepped into the water.

Steadily she moved, the water laving her thighs with a gentleness she had not felt recently. The sea fought her dress, holding her back. With dreamlike patience, she unfastened the thin muslin gown and lifted it over her shoulders, and dropped it unheedingly. That was better—

The waves lapped against her hips, against her waist.

She reached her hands down to cup the water closer to her. She moved beyond the shadow of the rock into the moonlight and continued steadily toward the deeper water. The sand was hard and ridged on the bottom of her slippers. Soon, her unsettled mind told her, soon you will be away from that hell behind you.

Waves lapped at her chin. She took another step.

A rude voice in her ear shattered the quiet. "What the hell!"

This wasn't the peace of the sea, she thought, puzzled. She was deceived again. Is there nothing that is as it seems?

She was not alone in the water. Rough arms, hands under her chin, were holding her up, moving her backward, toward the shore. She cried out, but there was no sound. Nothing but heavy breathing in her ear.

It was not Howard. She did not know how that could be, but she knew it was not Howard, and there was no more fight left in her. Whatever happened, it could not be as bad as if Howard had found her—

She looked up into a worried face, angry now that the danger was past. The face of a complete stranger. "What do you think you were doing?" he demanded, exasperation lending an edge to his voice. "You could have drowned out there."

"Better if I had," she whispered.

He had brought her to the shore, and laid her on the sand as gently as a mother lays down a sleeping child. She leaned against his shoulder. The moonlight streamed through palm leaves, making a strange mottled pattern on her white skin—

She sprang away from him, and he laughed—a full-bodied laugh of rich amusement, and reluctantly she joined him.

He went away and came back with something sodden dangling from his hand. "Here," he said. "Your dress, I believe? I wouldn't have seen you if this hadn't come floating to the shore over there at my feet."

She stood in the shadows and pulled the dress over her head, struggling to pull the wet clinging cloth into place.

"The dress," he added, "convinced me you were not a mermaid. And I had to investigate that dark object too far out in the water."

Deep laughter underlay his voice, she sensed, and in her bruised mind she knew there was strength in him, too. She was over her madness, for the moment at least. Over the moment when escape seemed so easy. And back in her personal hell.

"Or are you?" her rescuer insisted.

"Am I what?" Carmody said with a start. She had not been listening.

"A mermaid. No, I think you must not be. I never heard that they had voices."

She owed this man something. He had done what he thought best for her and possibly, in the unfathomable scheme of things, he was right.

"Have you met many?" she asked.

"Mermaids? No, not really. They don't sport except in tropical seas like this one. Although I have heard of one who left the Baltic Sea to live ashore."

She laughed. "Anyone would leave the Baltic Sea, one would think."

"How right you are. And yet passion ripens best under a moon like this. The Baltic would never recognize it as the same moon as theirs."

"Don't speak to me of passion," she burst out.

"I meant nothing," he said, quickly contrite. "Is love a better word?"

"There's no such thing as love," she answered, and suddenly knew she had come to believe the truth of that statement. "Love masquerades behind other faces."

There was a little silence before he said, "And other faces are all ugly?"

"Ugly as sin."

After a moment he said, very gently, "Ugly as that bruise on your breast?"

"Oh!" It was a piteous cry. She began to tremble in belated reaction—to her abasement at the hands of her husband, to her nearly successful escape into the depths of the sea and her unwanted rescue. But most of all she cried because a man was gentle with her, his voice full of solicitude, his actions even respectful.

Once started, the tears flowing in rivulets down her cheeks, she could not stop. Later, when her sobs died away, and her convulsive weeping was done, she realized she felt better. Exhausted, empty, but ready to believe that somehow she would escape, and she knew she must wait until the way became clear to her.

She heard a huge sigh nearby in the shadows.

She gasped. "You haven't gone!"

"How could I? Not until I knew you would not slip back into your natural element. You see, I know the ways of mermaids."

Carmody was immensely grateful for the stranger's restraint. She was in no mood to fend off probing questions. Besides, the strange tie that held them—rescuer and rescued—must be broken at once. It would be a poor return to expose this Samaritan to Howard's vindictiveness—it would be dangerous for both of them.

"You needn't worry," she told him. "I stay on land from now on."

He sighed. "You are in truth a lady of the land. No mermaid could speak so," he acknowledged. "And I must apologize for intruding upon your privacy."

"Please don't apologize. It is I who am where I should not be. But," she added with faint curiosity, "you are not native here on the island?"

"Merely a passing traveler. I have business with a man who lives along the road here, and I thought to find him at home. I fear I will not locate his house tonight. I must wait until daylight and come again."

Suddenly suspicious, she demanded, "A man along here?"

"A despicable rogue," agreed the stranger, "whom I will take great pleasure in—teaching a lesson to."

She realized then that the man's face had been in darkness all the while she had been talking to him. She was aware of his broad shoulders, the power in him as he had stepped gracefully across the sands, and his competence in pulling her to shore. She also knew the delicacy of his feelings as he had stepped some feet away from her, so she would not be frightened of him. But she would not recognize him again—that brief moment when he laid her on the shore had passed too soon.

She would have asked his name, but she dared not. She was convinced he meant Howard—the description certainly fit! Let it be, she decided—just the two of us, disembodied voices now in the night, who meet, share a crisis, and part with a friendly salutation, no more.

"I must go," she said at last.

"How sad you sound," he commented, and he added impulsively, "you must have known trouble—your recent endeavor shows that. And—other signs." The bruises, as he had remarked, were still vivid on her fair skin. "But whatever lies ahead for you, I wish you well."

Carmody swallowed the lump in her throat, and managed to say with grace, "I thank you, sir. I am truly grateful to you. And I should wish you happiness, and success in your endeavors."

He made no move to help her as she rose to her feet. She made her way across the soft sand, alone, until she stood in the shadows along the edge of the road. Still in shadow, she said softly, toward the darkness where she knew he waited, "Goodnight," and did not wait for his answer.

It had been a strange encounter—and the strangeness of it lay, she thought, in the fact that she had felt safe and free with the man whose face she had not seen. That deeply resonant voice she would recognize anywhere, she knew, and—she did not know exactly how to put her thoughts into words, but—it was a friendly meeting without overtones of man and woman, desire and retreat. A simple meeting of equals.

It was hard to put it out of her mind, she found, even after Howard came back from Port Royal in a triumphant mood, ready to reopen the gambling house.

Carmody clung to that one interlude of peace and made

a little space for it in her most secret thoughts, a place she could retreat to when things grew unbearable.

She spared a little time, in what she castigated as sheer weakness, to think about what might have been, if she could have erased the past that she carried on her shoulders like a galling yoke. Would there be something she and the stranger might have built, together? Then, having savored in her imagination her private vision, she put it aside, as one lays away a cherished garment in a pomander of rose petals and spices.

The gambling rooms opened again three weeks to the day after the closing caused by Captain Short's accusations. Howard's fury with Carmody had abated, replaced by a constant grumbling about the loss of income caused by the shutdown and the expense of bribing officials to forget the Captain's foolish babbling—as he called it.

He did not attempt to assault her again. The weeks since that fateful night had blunted the edge of her revulsion, simply through habitude, seeing him always around, an awareness that he did not even think of her, scarcely noticing her presence.

That evening, as the servants lit the luminarios to light the way from the road—making a magical pathway of flickering yellow light, promising much to those who came to challenge the goddess of Chance—the house took on new life.

The furniture was again polished, the windows were freshly washed and clean curtains hung at them. The rugs, so heavy it took six of the men to manage them, had been taken out and thoroughly beaten.

The door to the verandah stood invitingly open to the perfumed night air. The jasmine at the corner of the porch had come into bloom, and the sea breeze carried the fragrance into every corner of the rooms, banishing the smell of soap and beeswax.

Yet, Carmody thought, as she moved upstairs to repair a small catch in her glittering gown where one of the beads had just been torn off, it was a fevered excitement that she felt, more highly charged with delirium than she remembered from other days in the rooms below. Perhaps it was only the reopening excitement. Perhaps an omen of trouble ahead.

She could not tell, only that it seemed to her they were riding breakneck for a jump, one too high for anyone to take.

The excitement, because she despised the gambling house and all it stood for, was too much for her. Suddenly lightheaded, she stopped halfway up the stairs and clung to the railing with both hands. Dizziness swept her—she remembered she hadn't eaten all day.

She exerted all her will to fight back a stunning wave of nausea. She ached to lie down in the dark on her bed, and sleep. But Howard would come to find her, and he would be angry. Fear of him drove her up another step.

And then she heard the voice.

The voice that had come to her out of the shadows by the sea, that night when she had so nearly drowned herself. The voice, she thought now, feeling the hair stirring on the back of her neck, that she would never forget.

Below her in the hall, Howard was playing the part of gracious host to a newcomer. The man she was now seeing for the first time in light was taller than Howard, and less broad in the shoulders. Strength and power in his controlled grace she had noticed before, and she saw now that his face was calm, with brows that swept up at the corners like wings. There was authority in every gesture, even the way he stood.

Her gaze upon him must have conveyed a message, for suddenly he looked up and saw her where she stood, transfixed, upon the stairs. He gave no sign that he recognized her, and yet she felt a current strong as a tide flow between them. She swayed slightly, and then, a flush suffusing her pale cheeks, she turned and sped up the stairs, along the corridor, and bolted her bedroom door behind her.

What was he doing here? Was he a gambler? Or had he found out who she was and come to see her again?

The questions ran along the corners of her mind like mice in the wainscoting. She sat on the side of the bed while waves of sickness overwhelmed her and then, after a while, receded. She remembered at last that Howard would be sending to find her, and she sprang to her feet with a sudden cry. He never wanted her out of his sight while the house was full. She bathed her face with cool water from the basin on the commode.

Would the stranger still be there? Suddenly fearful that he might be gone, she hastened.

He had not gone. When she descended the stairs, she discovered that she must have been gone a long time—long enough so that Howard had replaced his hired dealer, and sat on the opposite side of the round table, facing the stranger. The other gamblers for once had forgotten their games—giving clear sign that the two men in their midst were engaged in a titanic struggle.

The game was Vingt-et-Un—the same game that Captain Short had claimed was dishonest. And money was piled in heaps before the stranger.

Howard was livid with fury. She could see his hands shaking, and a telltale vein throbbed along his temple. His eyes glittered as he concentrated on the cards. Carmody dared not get too close—she feared to distract the stranger. A part of her exulted at the sight of Howard, losing drastically—not so much the money, but his reputation for good fortune rode on this game.

Carmody never pretended to understand the game—but she knew enough to thrill when the stranger laid card after card face up on the table, and with every turn of the cards, more money changed hands, all of it joining the substantial pile of gold in front of the stranger.

She dared stay no longer. The excitement bubbling in her was bound to spill over. Howard was unaware of her presence for the moment, although she dreaded the time when the company would depart, leaving her alone with him. She could not be here when that moment came.

The stranger had not glanced her way. But suddenly she knew he was as aware of her as she was of him. And then, he spoke. "Does this break your bank, Mr. Vickery? Or shall we continue our play?"

Abruptly Howard stood up, jarring the table so that the

little gold piles toppled. The light caught the sovereigns on the table, winking triumphantly, so it seemed, and Howard snarled, "Whom do I have the honor of entertaining? Or are you the devil himself?"

"No devil," smiled his adversary. "Merely a man who feels indignant at your methods. Driving a poor old sea captain to lose his way among the sharks on land, after forty years of braving them at sea."

"Sea captain?" queried Howard, although the light in his eyes told of his dawning suspicions.

"Captain Samuel Short," said the stranger, "a good man, until he moved out of his element."

"He came here of his own free will," said Howard between clenched teeth. "I didn't drag him in here."

"True. But he might have won, as I have—*if* the cards had been honest. Or if he had insisted on a new deck, as I did. But I wrong the sharks by comparing you to them. We've talked long enough." The stranger was scooping up his winnings and dropping them into a leather bag. "I must get back to my ship."

"Your ship?" sneered Howard. "I suppose you are Short's first mate, or supercargo? Do you plan to buy the Tennant shipping line with your winnings?"

The stranger laughed. "Not even one of their ships," he assured Howard, amiably. He was at the door before he looked back. "I'll be in Port Royal for a week. If you have a wish to talk further, ask for me aboard the *Sea Queen*. My name is Mark Tennant."

"Mark Tennant!" It was only a whisper from Howard. The owner of the shipping line that valued the services of Captain Samuel Short had come himself to vindicate his man.

And although Mark Tennant had directed his last words to Howard, Carmody knew he meant them for her. If she wanted him, she knew where he was and the next move was up to her.

It was inevitable that they would meet again.

After that night on the beach, Mark had walked through her dreams more than she liked. Now, she knew she walked along the edge of a precipice. She was drawn to him as she had never been to any man. She needed desperately to see him, to talk to him. And yet—what good could it do? She paced back and forth in her bedroom, trying to put her confused thoughts—not thoughts, she amended, *yearnings*—into some sort of order, hearing the subdued chatter of the still stunned gamblers as they left, listening fearfully for the sound of Howard's footstep.

But he did not come.

The next day she busied herself with homely everyday tasks. She straightened out her drawers, refolding the thin chemises, the muslin petticoats. The cotton thread stockings—

She seized upon the opportunity offered her. She needed new undergarments, and Port Royal was where they were to be found. It was merely coincidence, she told herself, that Mark Tennant's ship would be lying in the harbor, or that he himself might be strolling along the waterfront.

She stopped in Howard's office to ask him for money for her shopping.

"Money?" he said sourly. "After that affair last night, it's a wonder we've got any left."

Just the same, he opened the desk drawer where he kept his cash, and fished out a few coins for her. "I'll be surprised if anybody shows up tonight."

Incautiously she retorted, "Nobody wants to play if they think the house is crooked."

He glared up at her, piercing her with his cold blue eyes. She faltered inwardly, with the remembrance of his anger still churning within her. "You think it was a dishonest game?" he said in a low, menacing voice.

"Howard, you know I don't know anything about gambling. I only repeat what I heard some say last night, while the game was going on."

"So." He nodded briefly. "He'll pay for this, of course."

"He?" she said, striving to keep the rising note of alarm from her voice.

"Tennant. The man who was brazen enough to turn my wife against me in my own house."

"He had nothing to do with it, Howard. I don't want to know anything about your game. Gambling itself is bad enough. If your game is crooked, leave me out of it."

"Your face would give me away in a moment," he said. "If, of course, the cards were really marked. Which I wouldn't admit."

"Oh," she said, trying to appear casual. "Who is the man, anyway? Tennant, you said?"

Howard was unusually communicative, and she should have been warned by it. "From Virginia, the colony on the mainland. He's wealthy. Several of his ships are right now in the harbor. And that idiot Short was one of his captains. I wish I'd known that sooner."

He saw the perplexity in her face, and added, "Tennant's got the reputation of standing up for his men. But then, I'm glad it happened. I've figured out how to take care of him. And so, my dear wife, enjoy your shopping."

Dismissed, she went out the front door to the waiting chaise. If Howard had figured out how to "take care" of Mark Tennant, she thought uneasily, it would not be in fair play, not in gaming at the green-covered tables. Somehow her thoughts ran along the lines of knives and sordid dark alleys. And Howard was capable of doing just that—perhaps even hiring someone to catch his enemy unaware.

As the carriage approached the limits of Port Royal, she knew she must find a way to warn Mark. The road ran along the curving waterfront, and she looked out with consuming interest at the ships in the roadstead. She knew little of ships, and she could not distinguish one from another. She sank back against the cushions in disappointment. There was no way to reach Mark. She dared not send word to him. Her servants, including Gunno on the perch of the chaise, were loyal first to Howard. And it would be only a matter of minutes after she returned home this afternoon before Howard would know every move she had made.

The recollection of his raging fury came back to her in vivid pictures, making her stomach churn uncomfortably.

She closed her eyes for a moment, deliberately banishing her memories.

And when she opened them, feeling the carriage stop unexpectedly, she looked straight into the deep blue eyes of Mark Tennant!

Carmody could only stare at him, taking in his laughing eyes under the daredevil flyaway eyebrows, and the amused quirk to his lips. Another of her mental pictures, no doubt—

This phantasm could speak. "Mistress Vickery, I think?" he said formally, for the benefit of the coachman, but underneath was laughter. "I had not expected the happiness of seeing you again, not after my winnings at your table."

"My husband's table," she corrected him. It was important to her that he know how unwillingly she served in Howard's establishment.

He bowed in acknowledgment of her correction. She thought swiftly, trying to find an innocuous way of warning him of Howard's intentions, conscious of Gunno, who was standing no more than three feet away. But she could not seem to find a way—and she could not let him go, not just yet.

"I believe you told my husband," she said, "that you have a ship here in the harbor. Which one is it? I think that ships are such lovely things."

He laughed. "Seeing them lie like birds on the waters, they are beautiful. But when you see into the hold, they are not so ethereal. But, of course, you must have come to Jamaica by ship."

He was skirting dangerously near the unpleasant reminders of her past—the past that kept him from her, raising an invisible barrier that, far more than Howard's claim, was impassible.

She must move on. To linger longer, here on a public thoroughfare, would be inviting trouble. To her relief, Mark seemed to read her thoughts. She could not have taken the first step away from him, but he smoothly lifted her hand from where it rested on the low door of the carriage, and brought it to his lips.

"Mistress Vickery, my pleasure," he said, releasing her

hand. He looked at her a moment longer, sending her, she thought fancifully, a portion of his strength. Without volition her lips formed the words, "Take care," and she saw a glimmer of understanding pass over his face before he touched his hat and strode away.

Suddenly, she felt ill. The waterfront buildings tilted and then righted themselves. Faintly, she instructed her coachman.

"I've changed my mind, Gunno. It's really too hot to shop. Please drive home."

The message came two days later. Nothing had happened to indicate that Howard had been told of the chance meeting, and even his attitude seemed indifferent. How grateful she was for indifference, and how strange that her life should have come to such a low ebb that indifference was a prized boon!

The gambling rooms were open as always every night. But they were less crowded, and she began to realize that the debacle the other night was beginning to take its toll. Mark had not claimed that the house dealer was cheating. Not even when Howard himself took over the deal. But Mark had spoken of calling for a new deck, and the implication was obvious.

A ship's officer appeared in the doorway, two nights after her meeting with Mark in town. His brass buttons were brightly polished and his coat was of fine material and well cut. Howard brushed her aside, hurrying to greet the newcomer.

"Never been here before," the officer said. "I hear you have some games of chance going."

"We certainly do," said Howard. "Cards or dice?" His eyes narrowed, as though suddenly wary.

"Oh, dice," said the man. "Cards mean nothing to me."

"What ship are you from?"

"The *Mary Rose*. Just arrived in port from Boston. First thing I did, I asked about where there would be some good fun."

"The *Mary Rose*," mused Howard. "Strange, there's something familiar about you. Have I seen you in town recently? But no, you said you just arrived." Suddenly brisk, he added, "Let me introduce you to our tables of 'bones.' "

Howard's jocularity had worn off by the time he returned to Carmody's side. "Mercy, he's not from one of Tennant's ships. So don't expect anything special from him."

"Why should I? I know nothing about your business." She was suddenly alarmed.

"My business, don't forget it. You're part of it. If something happens to all this, it will be your bad luck as well. I saw the way Mark Tennant looked at you the other night. I'm used to seeing men lust after you. But your face—it gives you away, every time."

"He's a gentleman, that's all," she said sturdily. "And you wish me to be polite."

"Polite, yes. But you were looking at him as if you were starving and he were a bag full of candy. I'm warning you, Mercy, don't tempt me too far."

He turned away. She glanced covertly around to see whether anyone had observed their vicious little exchange. Howard had smiled all the while, but she knew she hadn't been able to hide her fear of him. She caught the eyes of the newcomer, the ship's officer, and his look was full of meaning. She could not decipher his message before he turned to concentrate on the dice.

She avoided him all evening, making her way through the rooms, threading her way among the tables, pausing here to order more drinks for the players, stopping there to watch the play as though she enjoyed the game, but all she could see was her mental picture—a moonlit cove, the quiet sea, and a strong voice with the lilt of laughter beneath, as though the owner of that voice looked upon life without illusion, but with good humor.

Not until the evening was over, and the guests were crowding the door in departure, did she see the officer again.

He was engrossed in stuffing his winnings—substantial, Carmody noticed—into a little leather purse, and didn't look where he was going. He bumped into Carmody and dropped his purse on the floor. Coins rolled in all directions, and with a mumbled apology he stooped to retrieve them.

Carmody quickly knelt to help him. "Hard enough to win," she laughed, "without throwing them away."

"Hard enough to win here," said the man, "as I heard before I came. But it can be done."

He looked at her under cover of their joint effort to find all the coins. "Mistress Vickery," he whispered, "don't make a sign. I am told to tell you the mountain road near the white cross."

"What?" she breathed. Her heart lurched and then began to race.

A pair of feet came within her line of vision, and she looked up to see Howard glaring down at her. The well-known look of jealousy fired his glance, and she thought with a sinking feeling that he must have overheard. And then the last guest had gone and Howard closed the double doors.

"Come now, Mercy," he coaxed. "Cheer up. We've made a pile tonight, and it looks as though our troubles may be over."

"Troubles?" she echoed.

"That officer tonight lied. I know I've seen him around town for some time, and he tried to make me think he's just arrived. But he's not one of Tennant's men, so we can all sleep well tonight."

"I must say it makes a nice change to see you cheerful again," she said with relief.

"Well," he was almost gleeful. "I've got over that fit of anger. I'm not such a bad fellow after all."

She gave him a level glance. "How can you say that, when you know what you've done to me?"

"What I've done? I've furnished you with a very comfortable living. Good food, although I must say you're looking too thin. A very extensive wardrobe." Deliberately he went on, "And my protection. To see that you don't give way to your foolish impulses, my dear. To—chastise you, if I need to."

"Is that what you call it?"

"I have no doubt you would use a shorter word. But I

told you that word has no legal existence between a man and his devoted submissive wife."

He reached out to touch her, his finger on the low-cut neck of her gown, tracing the edge of the fabric with a touch like a living flame. She forced herself to endure his touch without giving him the satisfaction of seeing how she cringed away from him. "No overwhelming desire for me, Mercy? Well, I must be content with my rejection." He sighed heavily, mockingly.

Hardly daring to believe that she was free to leave, she started up the steps. He stopped her. "By the way, if by some fate you need my attentions this night, don't expect to find me in my room. I will be down in the slaves' quarters, where I usually spend a little time every night. But of course, you wouldn't know. Not having missed me enough to search for me."

He laughed then, a wicked sound that chilled the blood in her veins. He was soon out of sight, toward the back of the grounds. Her husband, finding his pleasures with the slaves! Instead of resenting his waywardness, she felt a great burden lift from her shoulders. This night, at least, she need not fear him.

And this night, of all nights, she needed to be sure he would not interfere.

The white cross that the ship's officer had mentioned was on the secret path to the mountains, not more than a mile from the house. Carmody stood on the verandah for a long moment, sheltered by a jasmine vine, and listened to the sounds of gaiety from the shacks at the back of the grounds. She was overcome with a sudden dizziness, but she forced herself to breathe slowly while the feeling passed, and then she hurried across the garden, searching along the hedge for the gap that would set her on the path that intercepted the mountain road. From that fork it was only a little way to the white cross, a shrine erected by a grateful native to give thanks for what he thought was a miraculous escape from death at that place.

The path was narrow and precipitous, and though she moved carefully, suddenly the dizziness she had fought on the verandah returned to overcome her, and she fell, nauseous now, to the ground.

Afterward, she sat spent and gasping for breath, her back against a friendly rock, while her thoughts flapped around her like black vultures coming out of the silent skies in search of carrion.

The truth was clear and shattering. The nausea, the dizziness—it must mean only one thing.

That night when Howard had used her so brutally, his savage attacks lasting until the faint light of dawn showed her the terrifying outlines of his distorted feral features, had resulted in more than bruises in her mind and livid marks on her body.

She was carrying a child.

She sat a long time leaning against the rock. It was the final catastrophe—she could regard it as nothing else. A child conceived in hatred and violence—what would it be like? What chance could it have? And—more selfishly—how could she ever escape now?

And how could she bear Howard's gloating eyes on her for the months ahead, knowing how she hated him, triumphing daily over the trap he held her in?

"Mercy, Mercy, are you here?" The moon-shadows had moved far along the path, and Carmody startled at hearing her name called.

The soft voice was a woman's, not Mark's voice, and she was glad. Hours ago she would have given her world to see him, to hear his voice again. But now, she had nothing to give him, nothing but the shame she could not share.

"Mercy," came the voice again, and this time she knew it.

"Lucy!" she cried out in wonderment. "How can it be you?"

Her friend's hard dry hand took hers, and she said simply, "I came to say goodby."

"Goodby? You can't go! Just when I need you most!"

"It is too dangerous to stay here on the island. There's a price on my head, you know—for helping our friends up the mountain. I was nearly captured by the dragoons two days ago."

"How dreadful!" Carmody was fonder of Lucy than of anyone else she had ever known. "Just knowing you were up the mountain has been a comfort beyond believing. But how selfish I really am. You must go. And I have nothing to give you, nothing save all my love."

"Save some for the babe," said Lucy surprisingly.

Stunned, Carmody said, "I just realized it myself. How do you know?"

"The look in your face in the moonlight," whispered Lucy. "But you are not happy about the babe?"

Carmody heard the anxious love in Lucy's words. She would not let her go with an added worry. It was enough that she had her own escape to think about. Carmody lied, "Oh, yes, Lucy dear. I am. It was just such a surprise, that's all. Tell me what you'll do?"

"Sailing tonight. A sailor I know from home—never mind how he found me, too long a story to tell—but he won a great gaggle of money tonight." Lucy's chuckle was happily indulgent. "All he was supposed to do was give you my message."

The officer was from Lucy, not Mark. But she would not have missed saying goodby to Lucy, not for anything. A few more words of farewell—

"I must hurry. The *Mary Rose* sails on the tide—"

And Lucy was gone.

6

CARMODY stumbled across the garden, thankful that her hazardous descent from the trail was at an end. Guided by the waning moonlight as it filtered irregularly through the palm branches, she had begun to hurry in despair: all the windows in the house were lighted!

There was a dark red glow through the velvet draperies of the gambling rooms at the front of the house. Faint yellow, veiled by thin curtains, showed from the rooms at the back. There was even the raw, unshaded primrose of the tallow candles in the kitchen wing—

A cold hand clutched at her heart. Had Howard missed her? Was the hunt up for her? What explanation could she give? That she had gone out eagerly, expecting to meet her husband's greatest enemy? Or the truth—that she had said farewell to a woman wanted by the dragoons?

She would have to think of something!

Obscurely, she decided it would be better to enter by the front door—farthest away from the mountain trail. Perhaps she could dissemble sufficiently— And suddenly the thought came to her: she was carrying his child! Surely he would spare her for the child's sake!

Regaining a shaky assurance, she marched up the verandah steps and along the house. She threw open the door, and heard, amazingly, an ominous click, like the cocking of a pistol. She froze on the threshold.

"Stop right there!" came Howard's voice, unnecessarily

warning her. She could not have moved if her life depended on it. "Oh, it's only you."

He let the hand holding the pistol drop to his side. In a flurry, she stammered, "Whom did you expect, Howard? Please put the gun away. I'm deathly afraid of them."

"Oh, is that true?" he said, an odd note in his voice. "Well, stand away from the door, Mercy. I must admit I am relieved to see my wife returning. I wonder where you have been. No matter, don't answer me. I wouldn't believe you would tell me the truth, anyway."

"I don't lie to you."

He ignored that, a small smile playing at the corner of his thin lips. "My dear, spare me your protests. Your whole life is a lie. You married me, protesting a sort of affection. But the truth is you have a poisonous dislike of me. Would you really like to leave me?"

"I loathe everything you are. But don't worry. I'll be here for a long time."

He raised one eyebrow in that way he had, turning a polite mannerism into a sneer. "I am glad you have loyalty, if not love."

"Not love. Nor loyalty, either. I will be here because your child needs the support of his father."

She had not planned to tell him in such a bald fashion, but the words had come out almost without her knowledge. She could see him revolving her news in his mind, probably trying to discover a trick in it.

"No trick," she said, wearily. "You judge everyone by yourself, Howard. There are people who are straightforward, honest. Try to believe that, if you can."

He nodded. Then, amazingly, he gave a wicked chuckle. "You see what your temper gets you into? Poor judgment all the way, Mercy. Inviting my—attention, so to speak." He threw back his head and laughed, an ugly, braying noise. "And now you're trapped, because you saved an idiot from killing himself. That's the greatest jest of all." Callously he added, "This should prove a convincing lesson, Mercy. Don't trifle with me."

"*My* temper!" she shot back. "Whose was it—"

"Now, now, my dear, don't be crude. If you had not interfered with the Captain, you would not be in your present interesting condition."

It was as simple as that, to him, she thought morosely. It was her fault. And the amazing thing was that he believed it. He truly believed what he said.

She lifted her hands and let them fall again, hopelessly, by her side. Finally, she remembered that she had not found out the reason for the illumination, and above all, for the manner of her welcome. "Why the gun, Howard? You surely aren't afraid of me?"

"Perhaps I should be," he said, with that odd note in his voice again. "But the fact is that your good friend Captain Short has escaped from the jail where he was enjoying life as an attempted suicide. Somebody provided him with sufficient rum to build up his nerve, and he broke out. Overpowered a guard, if you please. And rumor says he is coming here."

"Here!"

"To pay me back, so my informant says. Although that's ridiculous, because he has already paid me." Howard laughed harshly. "I never thought to have an heir."

And then, suddenly, as if from nowhere, Captain Short stood weaving on the threshold of the open doorway where Carmody herself had stopped only moments ago. Howard's pistol was again steady, its little black eye pointing directly at the captain's chest.

The captain had a knife. His gun must have been taken away from him, but somewhere he had obtained a knife, and now he held it levelly toward Howard. The candlelight flickered along the keen edge like a living flame, promising destruction if it could reach its destination.

But Howard's ball would hit him first, before the knife could even get near him. "Stop where you are, Short," said Howard, warningly. "I'll kill you if you take another step. You have no grievance against me. I didn't invite you to come and gamble here. You're supposed to be a grown man, and you're acting like a child."

Carmody could see that Howard was trying to calm the Captain, divert him and weaken his resolution. She was surprised, because he seemed to be taking pains to spare the man.

She glanced at Howard, almost smiling. But the look in his eyes destroyed her new-found hopes. He glared at Short with an evil light in his eyes, a light almost insane. She shivered, and could not stop. It was the same look she had seen on his face the night he had attacked her.

She knew now—he meant to kill Captain Short!

Murder him, really, because a knife was no kind of weapon against a primed, loaded, and cocked pistol at short range. Somehow she must stop this—this insane duel.

She fixed her eyes on Howard. She would be able to tell the moment he intended to pull the trigger, and in that moment she would do something—

Silently she inched sideways toward the center of the hall, closer to Howard. Her long skirts swayed in the breeze sweeping through the open door, and the swirling movement of the fabric disguised her sidling movement.

Howard's voice droned on, insulting now, goading Captain Short into taking that one step forward that would, in Howard's mind, justify his shooting.

And then, so fast she almost missed it, there was a quick movement of the captain's hand. He had made his move, performing the sleight of hand trick that sailors know well—and Captain Short, completely sober, now held the keen knife by its tip. She had almost reached her husband, but she would be too late.

"You slum-conceived bastard!" Howard cried, and in that moment Carmody saw his finger tighten on the trigger. Her raised arm struck his pistol hand, and at the precise moment that he fired, his aim was ruined. The tinkling of glass somewhere spoke of a broken mirror, and, too swift for the eye to follow, the knife sailed unerringly through the air for Howard.

But the blow that had saved Captain Short's life also saved Howard's. The knife, which would have found its victim's heart, struck deep into his shoulder, instead.

Carmody had a brief impression of the captain's stunned look of disappointment, realizing that his prey had escaped his revenge, and then Howard's angry fist—raised in fury against her meddling, and propelled by the sudden maddening pain in his shoulder—struck out at her savagely. The smoking pistol was still in his hand, and it caught her temple, slashing a deep gash even through her coiled hair.

Howard's animal cry rang in her ears as she fell, stunned, losing awareness of everything but the ringing in her head, and the sudden sharp, ominous pain twisting through her abdomen.

With faint surprise, she dreamed of Lucy's honest face, worried brown eyes. But it could not be more than a dream, for Lucy was away, far away, on a mountain top somewhere—no, no, on a *ship*.

It was too much effort to open her eyes. Everything hurt. Her head wore an iron band, tightening each time she swam up to consciousness. And somewhere inside, a deep sorrow, unnamed, but undeniable, wept forlornly.

Soft voices lingered at the edge of awareness, and she could not draw them closer. Not for a long time. But at last, she opened her eyes.

She was in her own room, the gauzy curtains billowing at the windows—at least she had had her own way in furnishing this room—and the sunshine lying on the faded grass matting.

"My head—"

"Ah, you're awake then," Jassy said. "We thought you wouldn't ever come back to us. We'll give you something for that head, now."

"Jassy! Where did you come from? What—what has happened?"

"Don't you fret any."

"Don't put me off." Carmody tried to lift her head from the pillow, but the surging pain forced her to drop back with a gasp. Memory came back as sharply as the pain—the captain and his knife, Howard and his pistol. Carmody herself, Howard's hand lifted to strike her, and—

"My baby?"

"Lost. But you're here. And that was something we

wouldn't have counted on. A terrible time you had. Out of your head."

Fear crept in and settled among Carmody's foggy thoughts. "What did I say?"

"Nothing," lied Jassy valiantly. "And besides, no one was here but just me. I shooed them all out, so I could use the Healing Woman's remedies she taught me. I'll give you a potion for that head now."

The potion smelled nauseating and tasted worse. But after she conquered the heaving of her stomach, and swallowed all of it under Jassy's stern eye, she felt better. She slept almost instantly.

When she awakened, her thoughts ran on Lucy. How far they had traveled, Carmody thought idly. Six years ago, Lucy and her man—whose name Carmody never did learn—were living happily in a small village in Somersetshire, the affairs of London remote from them, and never dreaming they would be caught up in a mad whirlwind of rebellion.

And Carmody herself, preparing to turn Oaklands over to her brother, engaged to Waldo Rivers, had been content in her anticipation of a placid future.

Now—Lucy off with the tide and a new love, and Jassy, who had shared with Carmody the care of Aurelia's last days, was living up the mountain in that hidden world of the Maroons.

The potions, and other nameless remedies, worked marvels, and Carmody recovered fast, almost too fast. She would have liked to linger in her room, secluded from all duties, floating along on a sea of idle lethargy, numb in her emotions, apathetic in her thoughts.

She did not know how long it was after that night— probably no more than a week—when Howard came to see her for the first time. She had heard that he had not come while they despaired of her life. Nor had he come to cheer her convalescence. When he appared now in the doorway, she recognized how favored she had been by his absence.

Whether it was the harsh sunlight upon his features, or perhaps the new and disillusioned eyes she saw him through, he had lost much of his handsomeness. A suggestion of fat lay beneath his chin, and little pockets pouched under his eyes. He carried his arm in a sling. Just a thin dusting of age and care, she thought suddenly, and I see him the way he will look in ten years. The thought of ten years side by side with Howard made her quail.

"Enjoying yourself?" he said with deep sarcasm. "I wonder the revelry downstairs of an evening has not disturbed your rest."

It was strange, but she hadn't noticed any sounds from the gambling rooms, and said so.

"I've lost another week's income. I should bring you up to date, here in your convent, so to speak—I'm sure you've been longing for news of my wound. It is healing. But not well. That stupid Jassy tried to treat the thing, but I wouldn't let her touch me." With a malicious chuckle, he added, "I sent her to practice her arts on you. I hear she's escaped again. Too bad."

Defensively, Carmody flared, "You see how I am recovering. Perhaps you should have let her treat your wound."

"A witch like her? Never." He studied his wife for a moment. "You look well enough. Tonight we reopen. I will expect you downstairs at the usual time."

"Howard! I can barely stand. Let me rest a while longer. In a few days, I'll be better, I promise you."

He considered her, with a sneer gradually forming on his face. "Two sovereigns. I should have doubled your loan and sent you on your way. I'd have been better off in the long run."

"Make me that offer now," she countered tartly.

"Thanks to you," he told her, "I need all the assets I can muster. You're one of them—dubious, of course, but the best I can do on short notice. I will expect you tonight in the entry hall to greet our guests. And, remember, I expect a smile on your face and not a word about what happened."

He slammed the door behind him. The pain of his wound still rasped along the edges of his temper.

She wondered what had happened to the captain. She

hoped he had got away. He was captain of one of Mark's ships, and Mark would take care of him.

Mark, she thought, picturing his strong face in her mind—and realizing that the picture had never really left her—would take care of those who belonged to him.

And she could never belong to him, become part of his life. Never.

She wondered if the *Sea Queen* had sailed.

The door stood wide open. Carmody had found a small chair and placed it in the entry hall. She sat gratefully, her garnet skirts billowing around her. The lights of the chandelier above blazed as fiercely as ever, but she noticed that the candles were tallow, and not the expensive wax tapers used formerly. The soft black velvet of the night lurked mysteriously just beyond the door, held at bay by the candles, but still making its dark presence felt.

On such a night had she escaped this house, traveled to the shore, and embraced the welcoming sea. That seemed to have been in another life, so long ago that it was like a dream. A dream of peace, of a safe haven—

"Where is everybody?" said Howard, entering the hall from the room she had once thought of as her living room.

"It's still early," she said. "You know the big rush always comes after eleven."

"Have you been asleep?" he asked dryly. "It's past midnight."

Something was greatly amiss. Past midnight, and not a single gambler had shown up. Not one.

"Why?" she whispered.

"My guess is that word has gotten out that this is an unhealthy place to visit. Captain Short certainly spread the word around. I heard he took ship just ahead of the authorities. Good riddance."

"But it was more unhealthy for you," she pointed out tactfully. She said nothing about her own injury, her own loss. The still unhealed gash on her temple was artfully covered by a loop of hair.

Howard paced back and forth like a caged tiger. "Well,

it was a gamble," he said after a while. "But then, all life is a gamble. We gamble on luck. We even gamble on love. And that's always a loss—because love doesn't exist. Not much more than luck exists."

"But there have been winners here, many of them. And luck certainly was with them."

"But not with the losers, Mercy. And they can't believe that luck deserted them. They insist that it has to be crooked cards, loaded dice—anything except that luck finds them unworthy of winning."

"And were the dice loaded?" Howard was in a mellower mood, she noticed, a mild mood, like despair when hope is gone and there is no longer any use of fighting. Somehow she needed to know whether Mark was right when he had implied that Howard twisted the odds in his favor.

He gave a sudden snort of laughter. "Of course they were loaded. And there's more than one way of marking cards, too—ways that don't show up on the white backs. You have no idea how clever your husband is, Mercy."

"Clever," she smiled, concealing her scorn. His admission only confirmed her conviction. Her contempt was complete. She was not bound to him any longer—not since the night his blow had caused her to lose his child. She did not care what happened to her. "So clever," she continued, "that your arm is in a sling, and pains you badly. The house is empty, no one comes—that's clever indeed."

His face darkened and he lifted his hand to strike her. But another thought crossed his mind, and diverted him for the moment.

She decided to walk more warily, dreading a repetition of his earlier violence. She wanted no more hostages to fortune. She was truly afraid of him, afraid for her life.

Then, surprisingly, he laughed. "I don't suppose you have two more sovereigns tucked away somewhere? I could use them."

Lightly, she said, "If I had them I would give them to you all over again. As a gift this time, not a loan."

"And not collect them again? That's wise of you." He was silent such a long time that she finally spoke.

"What would you do with the sovereigns, Howard?"

"Supposing you had them, of course? Well, I would gamble again. And get it all back, my plantations, my slaves—"

His words struck a chill in her. "What do you mean, get it all back? You did that once."

"Now, I need to do it again, my dear. You have brought me nothing but bad luck."

"You don't believe in luck."

"Every gambler believes in luck. Sometimes he has to help it along a bit, but the luck is always there, good or bad. And I've lost the plantation again. There's nothing left."

"How could you?" she wailed.

"These furnishings cost plenty. I've gone out on a limb for the money to pay off the winners. That's why I had to resort to cheating—to keep even. They were winning more than I was taking in. And now tonight—after they've taken it all, they don't give me a chance to win it back! They're dirty rotten dogs, every one of them. I've a good notion to leave them all to whistle for their money. Jamaica doesn't appeal to me any more. I can't pay the bills if I'm not here, now, can I?"

Rapidly he was working himself into an unreasoning frenzy. She sprang to her feet in alarm. The sudden movement caught his eye, and he stopped in mid-oath.

"Don't worry, Mercy. You're safe enough. I won't molest you—strange word to use about one's wife, don't you agree?—not tonight. It would be too easy, no sport at all. You're nearly swooning right now. If I laid so much as my finger on you, you'd faint. Another night, Mercy. A night of my choosing. Count on it."

The authorities in Port Royal, acting under instructions from his creditors, would waste no time in proceeding with their steps against Howard Vickery, now that his business was at a standstill.

"Like vultures!" snarled Howard.

"Perhaps it's only self-preservation," Carmody said quietly.

She was emerging from the state of mental paralysis

that she had lived in for the last five weeks, since Captain Short had made his threat to kill himself. She thought she had plumbed the depths before this. She thought that the true horror of this life with Howard lay in that it appeared so serene and prosperous on the surface, but when one looked beneath, there was all sorts of writhing rottenness.

"You don't have to live this way," she said now, trying to shore up his obvious despair. "You can ask for more time, and sell some logwood, open up those two tracts. There is plenty of mahoe yet."

He looked at her in mild surprise. "My factor would be well advised to discuss my business with you, I see. How familiar you seem to be with the running of an estate."

The remark hung in the air like a poised sword suspended by a thread. In her desire to help him, she had nearly given herself away. Surely by this time Mercy Holland's identity should be as much a part of her as her breath, her pulse, but sometimes, inconveniently, Carmody Petrie crept through the chinks in her armor, and one day—

If she were discovered, the gallows would loom before her, and suddenly, now, sitting with her brutish husband at breakfast in a land alien to her birth, listening calmly to his story of financial ruin, she discovered that she did not want to die.

Life held promise, a chance to create, to build a life of service—and she marveled at the strength of her conviction. Where had it come from? A month ago, she could have died, willingly, hopelessly. Two weeks ago, she had waded purposefully into the sea.

Now, knowing that Mark Tennant walked in the world, she was sustained by a frail sliver of hope that had crept into her, huddling for warmth in her—

"But what you don't understand, Mercy, is that I no longer control that logwood tract. Nor the indigo fields."

"Mortgaged, I imagine?"

"Sold, I should have said. Outright sold. The mortgages cover—other things."

"Tell me, Howard. Tell me all of it."

He watched her with sly, smiling eyes. "I think not. The element of surprise is always piquant, don't you agree?"

She would not beg. Perhaps he was just trying to frighten her, and would laugh at her alarm. And all the time he had made accommodation with his creditors—

She believed in the existence of the rapacious creditors. Howard owed far more than he could repay, she was sure. But she did not see what advantage it would be to them to confiscate his property, including the means to repay them in full. If Howard did not run his tables—and business would likely pick up soon—then he could never come up with sufficient money to pay his bills. It seemed only sensible for the creditors to hold back and give him another chance.

But her hopes were rudely dashed into oblivion in a few hours. Shortly after lunch—a lavish meal as usual, with no sign of austerity—she heard the sound of wagon wheels on the oyster shell road. The clop clop of horses on the drive!

She ran out onto the verandah, and stopped short in sheer astonishment.

It was a caravan! Wagons, heavy plantation wagons, each drawn by two great draft animals. And the line of wagons came to a halt in front of the center verandah steps. The lead driver sat his perch stolidly, glancing at her once, and then staring straight ahead of him.

"What is the meaning of this?" she cried, knowing her voice sounded shrill. She could not believe the deadly sinking feeling inside her that told her the truth. "Leave here at once!"

"I'm afraid they can't do that, Mistress Vickery," came a crisp voice from the side of the verandah. Coming up those steps was a fusty little man with papers in his hand and a shrewd look in his eyes. "Not at once, anyway. Not until they're loaded."

"Loaded? And with what, pray?"

He gestured vaguely toward the interior of the house, dim in the shadow beyond the open doors. "Here are my papers. I am empowered to take all of value from this house in settlement of certain obligations." His voice was singsong like the clerk of a court. In fact, he looked more like a clerk than anything else—dusty, apologetic, adamantly doing his job.

"Let me see the papers."

"I would rather give them to Mr. Vickery, ma'am."

"He is not here." She held her hand out with insistent authority, and reluctantly the papers changed hands. "I'll be glad to read them to you," he offered.

She flashed her eyes at him, and did not answer. She scanned the papers quickly. The extent of the disaster was hard to believe. These papers must be mistaken—Howard could not have been so foolish!

She said, "I can't believe these details are right. Surely my husband did not purchase *all* these items on credit."

"I'm sorry, ma'am,"—the man was sincere—"truly sorry to cause you discomfort. But you see, it is as it says in the papers. For six months he has paid nothing on his obligations. And my superiors have given me my instructions. Believe me," he burst out, "I wish with all my heart I didn't have to do this to you!"

She thanked him with a smile. She sighed once, and then waved her hand toward the interior, giving him permission to enter.

Where was Howard? Would he come back raging at her, expecting her to have held off a court clerk with a bundle of official papers? An ugly little thought came to her—he had spoken of leaving the island. Could he already have gone, leaving her to face the bailiffs?

From somewhere toward the back of the wagon caravan came half a dozen men of muscle and power. She could hear barked orders inside, and soon, through the double doors, a stream began to flow—a stream of men carrying furniture from the house. When the first wagon was loaded, the driver flicked his whip and the horses began to move, dragging the heavy load toward town.

Howard had apparently not paid a cent toward the cost. Six months, the clerk had said. That was before her marriage—that must be why he had not repaid her loan of the two sovereigns. Instead, he had offered marriage, and why not? It had cost him nothing. She had even added to the appeal of his enterprise.

Out came the great round tables, strangely different now that their green coverings were folded up and carried by another man. She should rejoice at seeing those grossly tempting articles removed from her home.

My home! A bitter twist curled her lips. She had never had a home here.

But then came the little gilt chairs that stood in the entry, chairs that she thought beautiful. They carried out chests, candlesticks—

She whirled and went inside to the clerk. "Your warrant runs not much farther, sir," she warned him. "The furnishings that were here in the house already are not included in thg unpaid purchases."

"I was told to take all the furniture in the house, ma'am."

"I cannot allow you to take my husband's possessions in his absence. I fear you exceed your authority."

Stubbornly he shook his head. "I was told—"

She interrupted with authority. "I will call my servants to prevent you from touching anything except what is in these two front rooms and this hall. Believe me, I am not afraid of you, and I am anxious that my husband not be angered."

Surprisingly, he capitulated abruptly. "I've heard that he has a foolhardy temper," he agreed, "and I doubt not that you would bear the brunt of it. I wouldn't want it on my conscience that I was the fault of trouble to a lady like you."

He whistled up the men, and said, "I've got to go back to the office and check on a few things. Wagons full?"

"Aye, most of them."

"Then off with you." He added, almost gently, "I will come back tomorrow, and trust that Mr. Vickery himself will give permission for me to do what I am required to do."

He bowed stiffly, as though his days were spent among people who bowed to him, and vanished.

Suddenly weak, Carmody felt her knees sagging, but there was no place to sit down. Not a chair, not even a bench was left.

She needed fresh air. Following an impulse to get as far away as she could from the empty rooms, she went down the drive, the shells crunching beneath her feet, until she reached the road. The cove would give her rest, and she hurried toward it.

The cove did not look the same in daylight. The golden sand met the soft white-topped turquoise of the sea. Far out, the water was deep blue and, even farther, green.

The rock outcropping that thrust out into the water was damp with flung spray on its outer point. She dropped wearily on a dry section of the uneven ledge.

Her mind flowed away and, like the tide, left odd jetsam behind. Where was Howard? How had he spent the money, if not to repay his debts? She had thought her gowns and jewels were purchased by winnings, and given to her to adorn the role she was forced to play. But the legal writs said that her possessions were forfeit, too.

Suddenly she laughed. The thought occurred to her that there was one gown that they would not take back—the green satin that Howard had torn from her body. Would she need to explain the absence of one gown? Or, even worse, produce it in its shredded condition?

My husband is an impatient man, m'lord, she could say, eyes cast down demurely. Or even, You must ask my husband to explain how considerate he is of me, m'lord, so considerate that he doesn't even allow me the task of unfastening my dress fasteners!

Mischievously, she said to herself with a chuckle, Let him squirm out of that one!

"That's a good sound, ma'am!"

She came down to earth with a thud. A man in fairly rough clothing stood on the strand, and after a bewildered moment, she recognized him—Captain Short!

"Only you're not a captain now?" she said, noticing the lack of brass buttons on his coat.

"Not no more. Mr. Tennant got my money back, though. You knew?"

How well she knew that Mark Tennant had cleared the board and put it into his bulging pockets! But he must have turned his winnings over to his employee. Former employee, she amended.

"But he says—very nicely of course, ma'am, and he's

right, too—that he can't trust my judgment. Not if I go ashore on a gambling spree. It's a disease in my blood, ma'am, that's the truth."

She nodded. "I know how it is for some people."

He watched her silently for a moment. She felt the breeze pick up a stray russet curl and tickle her cheek with it.

"Just came to—I need to say thank you, ma'am, for saving me the other night. I would sure have made a fool of myself had I really shot the bast—the villain, ma'am. But I lost my ship—the *Sea Queen* sailed without me. I had to sign on as third mate and it's a blow to a man's pride. But I've never killed a man in cold blood, so to speak, and I thank you for saving me from it this time."

She regarded with affection this gnarly little man, nervously shifting his weight from one foot to the other while he spoke his inner thoughts—a rare undertaking for him, she guessed. Also, there came the vaguest hint of a dawning plan—

"Your ship is in the harbor now?"

"Aye, the one I'm signed on," he said, carefully.

"Sailing when?"

"After midnight, with the tide."

Glancing guardedly at her, a suggestion trembled upon his lips, but he could not quite dare to voice his thoughts. And in her turn, she could not make a decision—even if the opportunity slipped away from her like sand through open fingers—not until she had talked again to Howard. He was her husband, after all, and while she feared his physical violence, yet she had made certain promises to him. And she could not kick him if he were a broken man.

"Good sailing," she said at last. "And I hope you get your command back one of these days."

"Aye, Mr. Tennant is a fine man to work for," he said, and giving a half salute, he turned and walked in his rolling sea gait along the beach, up to the road, and out of sight.

7

WHEN Carmody returned to the house, an ominous quiet greeted her. There was not even the distant sound of slaves moving in the kitchen.

The devastation wrought by the bailiff's men was like a physical blow as she entered the hall—so might Oaklands have looked, but for her.

The downstairs rooms—the two at the front of the house—were bare to the walls. The dust of their emptying danced lazily in the sun rays, and already the house seemed to take on an alien air. She no longer belonged here. Her role, if she could have put her rambling thoughts into words, was solely as a part of the gambling operation. That was why Howard had married her. Since the gambling was gone, she should be gone too.

But since she, and not the furniture, could talk—might talk too much about the sickening secrets these walls held—he might not be willing to see her leave.

An unexpected noise from the back of the house startled her. She followed the sound to the room Howard called his office.

He was sitting behind the desk, a set of keys in his hand. He didn't hear her approach. "So," said Carmody, seeing his guilty start at her voice, "you decided to come back." The empty rooms had brought Oaklands vividly to her, and by a trick of her mind she imagined she was surveying a younger brother who had gambled Oaklands away. It was a full turn on the wheel, she thought, hearing

271

her voice now as Ralph must have heard it then, chiding, dictatorial, disgusted. But she couldn't change it.

"I didn't know they were coming today," he said. "I thought I had another day."

"To do what?" Carmody pursued. "Run away altogether and leave me to face the bailiff? I suppose I was foolish to expect better treatment from you."

"I wouldn't run away, not from my beautiful and submissive wife," Howard jibed, regaining his confidence. "I thought we might take passage away from the island. I swear I am tired of this tropical heat. Will you go with me?"

"I'm surprised you have passage money left."

He tapped a tin box in the open drawer beside him. "My nest egg," he said with a sly grin. "I thought we might return to England. The climate there is better suited, and I understand the stakes in London run quite high."

"Can't you forget this awful gambling? It's brought nothing but disgrace. How do you think I feel seeing our possessions carried out on men's backs? The shame of knowing that nothing we have used has been paid for?"

He smiled, surprisingly, a strange gloating smile that suddenly set off an alarm bell in her mind. He did not act like a man who had just lost everything. On the contrary. He seemed to wear the cloak of a man who has a secret, cherished jewel, hidden where no one could find it, but who cannot keep from boasting about it. And whatever use he would make of his "jewel," he would be ruthless.

"Even my dresses," she went on, anxious that he not read in her face her sudden suspicion. "And what will they say when they ask for that green—" Too late she realized she was treading on unsafe ground. The green satin gown she should not have mentioned.

"I have a solution, my dear, if the absence of one gown bothers you. Let us give them another one to worry about."

"Don't come near me!"

But Howard was always faster than she realized, and she hadn't a chance of escape. She was so tired, weaker than she thought, and now she simply stopped where she was and let him come. His hands on her shoulders, he looked down into her eyes and said, "You're recovering your beauty, after looking really quite drawn for some weeks. I regret your recent illness. If you had not allowed your beauty to fall away, your silver eyes would have bewitched my customers again and we would still be in business. You really don't know how beautiful you are, do you? You don't know—"

He bent to kiss her, and then with rising interest slid his hands down to the small of her back to press her closely against him. His lips wandered to her hair, and he murmured words she had never heard him say, words of endearment and surprising tenderness. But so much did she mistrust him that she stiffened automatically, not able to believe anything she heard from him, wondering only when the moment would come when his caresses would turn to crushing violence.

"If only things had been different," Howard was murmuring in her ear. "There was nothing we couldn't have done together, Carmody. I could have learned to love you, as I never loved anyone in my life."

She sagged against him, her head swimming. She had left her sick bed too soon, but he had insisted. All futile, so it seemed. The bailiffs had been armed with their instructions even before the house opened last night.

"Poor child," he said. "I'll let you go. For now. You dislike me so clearly that I am not sure I should let you continue in such an unpleasant state of mind. Perhaps I can change your opinion of me, one way or another."

He let her go, and took her to the door. Opening it for her, he said, "Best rest before dinner. I *think* there will be dinner."

"*Think?*"

"You asked me earlier what I was doing all day. I was in Port Royal, watching most of my slaves being sold at auction, to satisfy my debts. At least some of my creditors will sleep more easily tonight."

She climbed the stairs slowly, clinging desperately to the railing, feeling his eyes upon her back. She was free of him for the moment, she thought, grateful for even such a small breathing space. She knew she could not endure his violent lovemaking—aside from the sheer brutality that it seemed he could not control, she loathed even the touch of the man.

What could she do?

She walked as in a dream to the bed, and simply fell onto it. She managed to kick off her slippers, but she could not for her life have taken off her dress.

Her head still swam from weakness, from the fear of him just now in the room below. But he had been gentle for the moment, and perhaps he could be coaxed to re-form a little—

She did not want him, reformed or not.

She had seen what he was capable of. She knew his fundamental contempt for his fellows, his lack of scruples. However, marriage was final. She was bound to him. And while she could live apart from him, she could not make any kind of new life, except a solitary one, in the future. She could welcome that—just to live alone would be heaven.

The laughing face of Mark Tennant passed before her closed eyes, and she knew she lied. Howard, she loathed and feared. Mark, she wanted—at least to know him better. And Mark was forever out of reach.

The words ran through her mind—Howard had been at the slave auction, watching them sold. A farewell to the slaves he knew well, from all the nights he had spent in their quarters. With only one? Or were there many who had vied for the master's favors? Carmody had never asked.

And Howard himself, saying to her that he could have learned to love her, stuck in her memory like a burr. What had he said exactly? *There was nothing we couldn't*—how did it go?—*couldn't have done together, Carmody.*

She sat bolt upright in bed, her head reeling.

Carmody.

Had he said her name? Had her fevered imagination distorted what she had heard? Again she went over every word in her mind.

He had called her *Carmody.*

And that meant that by some means she could not guess he had learned her real name. That explained the odd note in his voice—*your whole life is a lie*. There was no chance that he would not have learned her entire secret, including, besides the interim with James Scott, the murder of the man she had expected to marry.

And her husband was not one to keep a secret, if he saw an advantage in it.

Panic, like a great rushing of wings, beat upon her mind. She could not think. She sprang out of bed and ran to the door, but she did not lift the latch. She must consider first what to do. Instinctively, she knew that if he caught her this time, his revenge upon her would be—she heard someone sobbing, and, in a moment, knew the piteous mewling came from her own throat.

Knuckles rapped at her door. Her hand was still on the latch, and she jerked as though the iron seared her.

Her tongue clove to the roof of her mouth, and she could not utter a sound. Howard! What did he want of her now? She hurried silently back to lie again on the bed.

"Mercy!" he called. "Dinner is ready. Come and eat with me."

She forced herself to answer. He must not be allowed to become impatient. "Please, Howard," she answered, her voice satisfactorily steady. "I'm too tired now. I'm lying down. Go ahead without me."

"All right," he said without comment.

She heard him go down the hall, then his footsteps faded away. She must not lie longer on the bed. She was so exhausted that she feared to drop into a slumber she could not afford. She must plan.

She pulled a chair—how fortunate the bailiffs had left before reaching the second floor—carefully to the window, and sat, feeling the rising sea breeze brush her face with cooling fingers.

She must plan, but she despaired of ever grasping coherence out of the jumble in her numb mind. Howard called her Carmody, let's start with that. He had wondered several times aloud about her identity—"You walk with such noble grace," he had told her once. She was not noble, but being gently born also left an unmistakable mark touching the body and the spirit within—so it was always said.

And obviously he had made it his business to find out about her. How long had he known? She remembered his comment that very morning about how familiar she seemed with running an estate. So he knew about her struggles at Oaklands. She was positive that whoever told him that much would have told him the rest—the Duke, her return to seek Waldo's help, the pistol ball that had ended Waldo's life.

And he intended to use it against her.

She was sure of that. Perhaps not today, not even tomorrow, but some day he would force her to do something so abominable that he could not extract obedience from her in any other way.

How many intermediate steps would there be on the way down to that lowest level, where he would say, Do this or Carmody Petrie will hang. And would she say, at that ultimate moment, I don't care to live any longer? And then face an ugly, smirching trial?

No, she shuddered, I couldn't live through that.

It was still not moonrise. There was little sound outside the house now, and she realized with a start how much the noises of the slave quarters had become a part of the background of her life. Now, there were only one or two left, she supposed. Enough to cook the master's dinner tonight. And perform whatever other acts the master might need to comfort him.

And even, she resumed the thread of her thoughts, though she herself hoped she would refuse that final threat—what about the events in between? Where would her own conscience demand that she stop? And with sudden penetrating insight, she knew that the place where she said No, on the descending ladder, would be the occasion of Howard's threat to Carmody Petrie.

So that her degradation—and there was no doubt that Howard would lead her ever downward—was to be measured by her own revulsion.

She must leave.

Suddenly she knew that she must not lose a moment. She must get right away, and now.

She jumped up from her chair, and too late remembered to be quiet. She listened long, but there was no sound from below. It must be later than she thought. The moon's rising rays now touched the tops of the royal palms surrounding the house, and faint light filtered through to the ground beneath.

In this faint light she saw a welcome sight. Her husband, walking with purposeful, but unhurried, steps across the garden toward the back of the grounds. There must be at least one slave left!

Or maybe he was setting a trap—

Her hands hurried, feeling the fabric beneath her hands in the wardrobe as she recognized by touch and discarded most of the garments Howard had bought for her. The thin white muslin was hers, and she took it out. There was a similar dress of a darker color, and that one she slipped on in place of the one she had worn all day. She fastened it with trembling fingers.

The thin white dress she folded. A single pair of shoes—one more suited to outdoor wear than the slippers she usually wore. Petticoats, shifts. A comb and brush. No jewelry. She could not know what Howard had given her and paid for, and she would not take anything else, no matter how much she might need the money.

Money.

She finished her packing, such as it was, and searched for something to carry her clothes in. A maid had brought up fresh linen two days ago, and finding Carmody sleeping, had left it for changing the bed another time. Without a qualm, Carmody dumped the sheets to the floor, and set her own garments in the basket.

Her cloak, thin, but a green which was a dark shadowy color at night, over her shoulders, one more pin to hold her heavy hair better, and she was ready.

Money, she remembered again.

Carefully she opened the door. There was nobody in the hall, only dark shadows in the corners where the moonlight had not yet invaded. She listened. There was no sound.

Her ultimate goal was not clear, but the need for money, if she did not have it, might become an obsession. She set her basket down at the front door, and hurried back to Howard's office. If only he didn't have the keys in his pocket—

She dared not light a lamp. This room faced the back of the grounds, and a light would be noticed. Her hands spread out in front of her, she moved cautiously into the room.

The desk should be right about—here! she thought as she fell against it. Her hand stretched out to catch her balance, and landed on something hard. Beneath her hand she could feel metal—with rising excitement she felt of it, square, metal, and with a lid that miraculously opened up.

Howard's cash box!

He had not then been as much master of himself as she had thought, not if he left his cash box on top of the desk, and unlocked.

Unless it was a trap.

She froze, listening, but all she could hear was her own heart pounding like a military drum, summoning troops to the charge.

She touched the contents of the box with the tips of her fingers. Coins, cool and remote. Her quixotic impulse was to find two gold sovereigns, and leave the rest. But she was always practical. She lifted a few in her hands. Four of the heaviest and six of the others she kept, dropping the rest, with reluctance but with conscious virtue, back into the box. Even in her need, she would not take more than her right.

She could see fairly well in the dark now, she found, as she picked up her basket and eased through the front door. Outside the house, it was much lighter.

Port Royal lay to the left, and she turned in that direction. Not more than two miles to walk, and the road was fairly good. She walked silently on the road's grassy edge until she was well away from the house, and then stepped out in a countrywoman's stride that she hoped would last until she reached the town.

But what then? What would she do when she reached Port Royal? She had no friends there to shelter her. If she were to count all the friends she had in the world, she could, on one hand, and have fingers left over.

Lucy, escaped and free in a new life.

Ascar, Bonwit? Not true friends. Well-disposed, but only to the limit of their ability. And, of course, she could not ask for help from them. They had already risked their lives for her.

The lights of the town grew larger and more numerous as she neared. The only sound she had heard till now was the soft slipslop of her shoes on the hard road. Now, faintly, came the indeterminate hum of many people, in the streets, talking softly at open windows. Singing and brawling in the waterfront taverns.

Little shanties loomed in the shadows, stretching away on either side of the road. She was in the outer limits of the city.

In the back of her mind a plan had been forming, and now, close to the place where she must put it in motion, she stopped in the shadow of a ceiba tree, and considered her scheme. She must get away, that much was certain.

Right away from the island. And her traveling must be by ship. It was late at night, and shipping offices were closed. But even had it been high noon, she could not have entered one. It was too dangerous.

She must get to the waterfront and somehow find a boatman who could take her to a ship sailing to—anywhere. Anywhere but England. Perhaps even Captain Short's ship—

One step at a time. She took a deep breath, and emerged from the sheltering shadow of the ceiba tree.

At the first lane that looked broad enough to be a street, she turned right, toward the water's edge. There was surely action enough here, judging from the raucous sounds of revelry.

Her heart failed her. She stopped at the corner where

the waterfront cobbles met the dirt lane, and got her bearings.

On her left, stretching along the entire length of the street, were taverns, waterfront dives where torches stood atop poles outside the doors, and the doors themselves stood open throwing rectangles of light into the street.

Men in twos or threes, arms around each other's shoulders, stumbled out of one door and staggered a few steps away into another, so much the same in appearance that it hardly seemed worth the obvious effort to walk.

She must stay as far away from that side of the street as she could.

She turned to her right, and looked out over the harbor. The ships rode on the quiet water, seeming asleep, each with only a lantern at the stern to light the wayward crew as they returned. And on the cobbled street itself were racks of empty wagons, waiting in the dark for new ships to come in, unload their cargo and load up again with the wealth of Jamaica—coffee, indigo, sugar, allspice, lumber.

She moved closer to the water's edge. The street ran along a high curbing, and the cement wall below was studded with great iron rings, rusting in the constant briny dampness, but sturdy enough to moor and hold great ships. Below the top of the curbing there was shadow, but not deep darkness. The moon was beginning to illumine the harbor, and its light was reflected from the gentle surface of the water into the crannies in the wall.

In the gloom beneath the wall small boats nestled, waiting, no doubt, for the revelers. Suddenly she was taken back in memory to another waterfront, to a Dutch-hulled ship in the harbor, and an obsession in her mind. She shook her head to banish the memory. The movement was noticed from a boat that was tied, not with the rest, but a few yards away where a stunted tree surmounted the harbor wall and sent out a straggly collection of branches.

She heard with her quick ears a sound from the shadow of the tree, the clearing of a dry throat, the subdued clink of boat chain, pulled back into the boat. Oars tickling the water, featherlight.

And the boat emerged into the half-light and headed toward her.

For a moment she could not move. But she must, she must! Who knew what manner of creature was pulling the small boat toward her? But she took a deep breath and told herself—perhaps it is a man who can get me passage on one of those big ships, lying quiescent under bare poles. So she stayed where she was and watched the boat approach, warily.

There was something purposeful in the boat sculling directly toward her. She lifted her skirts in one hand, nervously ready to flee. One more yard, she thought, without a sound, and I will flee in unreasoning panic—one more yard.

"Mistress Vickery?" The voice, coming softly over the water, was a mere breath of sound.

"Yes?" She could hardly speak in her astonishment. "Who is it?"

"Sam Short, ma'am. At your service."

Delirium. It must be. She had only dreamed that she had walked for miles, carrying her few possessions, and now to be called by name on this savage waterfront where she was intrepid enough, or foolhardy enough, to venture—it could have no remote connection with reality.

But the boat touched its prow to the wall, and the man at the oars quickly fastened a line to a ring—where already three boats were moored—and leaped goat-like up to the cobbles where she stood.

"Captain *Short?*" she cried. "I longed to find you, and instead you found me. Are you real?"

"Real enough, ma'am. Now I take it you're looking for a ship out of here?"

"Yes. But you knew already. You were waiting for me?"

"Ma'am, you have no idea how much gossip there is in this place. I don't partake of it, of course," he added virtuously, "but—no matter for that. Here you are, and yonder is the ship that's sailing tonight."

"Around midnight, you said, with the tide," she confirmed. "That is the ship I would like to sail on. I have little passage money, but enough perhaps to pay my way to the next port. Oh, can you help me? It—it would be worth something to me."

She reached out to clutch the sleeve of his seaman's jacket. She looked up into his face, trying to read the answer in his expression. But all she saw was a certain satisfaction, as though an assigned task, difficult at best, had finally been accomplished.

"Never fear, ma'am."

He turned away and stepped down into his boat. He picked up a lantern from the bow and fumbled with it until a soft beam fell upon the thwart. Then he lifted the lantern and swung it in the air. She did not notice the answering blink of light from the ship farthest out in the harbor, almost at the entrance.

He set the lantern down. "Now, ma'am," he said, reaching his arms up to her, "if you please."

It seemed a long way across the harbor. She noticed that they kept to the shadows along the western arm of the harbor until they were nearly opposite the farthest ship. Then, with a deft movement, he veered the boat to cut across the mouth of the harbor, and fetched up in the murky lee of the ship.

It had been a darksome trip. Her boatman refused to talk. "How did you happen to be there waiting?" she asked once, but he only said, "Orders." And that one word alarmed her so she fell silent.

But the questions raged unanswered in her mind. Whose orders? Was this a trap of some kind? Would she be shipped off to some noisome jungle coast and made to entertain seamen roaring off the coast with crude appetites a-whet?

Could it even be that the authorities had sent for her to stand trial again in Winchester, this time for murder?

Could it be—?

One thing was certain. She was not going to board a Dutch vessel and strike a bargain with the Duke of Monmouth. How strange life was! A series of echoes, moving in a circle. Then, Oaklands, ripe for ruin—now, Vickery furniture carted away in bailiffs' wagons. Then, a bargain and an initiation that, after the first strangeness and pain of it, had at least been endurable.

Now, she could not fathom the future. Not even the next hour. She could only keep on, enduring, taking whatever came, burying all the hopes, the draggled dreams—

"Here you are, ma'am."

A rope ladder dangled over the side. Hands helped her from below, and hands pulled from above. Her basket, held for her to make her ascent easier, was restored to her.

And all the while, few words, and no lights at all. A furtive business. The deck gleamed faintly in well-holystoned smoothness, the moonlight touched briefly on rail, on anchor chain, on sharply outlined bulkheads.

Figures swarmed around her, suddenly, apparently by a command she did not hear. A strange feeling possessed her. This was a ghost ship, upon a ghost sea—and she half expected to see Charon the ferryman turn his grinning face to her.

The ship would sail out onto the broad waters, and go as far as the limitless horizon, and she would find—

Captain Short had positioned her by the rail on the port side and told her to stay there. "We've got some work to do before we get under way, ma'am. You'll not be in the way here."

The work was going on around her. She was aware of it, but only at the fringe of her mind. The anchor chain rattled in the hawsehole, the windlass creaking loud enough to be heard in Port Royal and beyond.

The sails were going up, smoothly, to catch the breath of wind, and she could feel the tilt of the ship responding to wind and to the tide, just now on the turn.

She had timed her arrival most fortunately. The tide was at the full, making it easy for her to clamber into the boat, and just in time to catch the ship almost at the moment of sailing.

They were moving.

The tide, slowly at first, and then gathering momentum as it ebbed, lifted the ship buoyantly on the breast of the water, and carried it through the entrance to the harbor.

The sails, set partly at first, now soared up to the high

yards, and snapped as the wind filled them, like a farewell salute to the mountainous ridge they were leaving.

The ship stood out from the harbor and then, sails full and gleaming in the moonlight, set her forefoot down in the strong winds and began to run down her easting.

Carmody had stood too long at the rail. But she dared not venture from the spot in which she had been placed. How weary she was! Her emotions had been stirred up, simmered, and entangled so that she could not think.

Fear, and despair. Fear of Howard, and despair over her future, now that Howard knew her secret.

She looked down, hypnotized by the waters rushing past, making a constant hissing noise as the ship sped from the harbor.

She had not slept well since—truly, since the first days of her marriage. More than four months ago, now. Somewhere aboard this ship there must be a bed!

To ease a sudden cramp in her foot, she shifted her weight with a sudden wincing cry of pain. She clutched at the rail and half turned away from it.

The moon fell fair upon her face. It also outlined a man standing not ten feet away from her. How long had he been there?

"Ah!" she gasped. "You startled me."

Still the man said nothing, but she began to realize that she had seen that figure before, and somehow it was in a position just like this, lounging gracefully, totally at his assured ease.

It came to her where, and when—and who.

"I am glad to see that you recognize me, ma'am," came the laughing voice she had heard so often in her dreams. And then Mark Tennant added, "May I welcome you aboard my ship, and trust that we will have a safe and uneventful voyage?"

Book Three

VIRGINIA

1

MARK turned slightly, letting the moon fall full upon his face.

Sheer astonishment held Carmody speechless. She must be dreaming! Her hidden thoughts must have somehow taken upon themselves sufficient substance to march through her slumber, so solid she could reach out—as she did now—to touch him.

"I'm real enough," he said. There was a laughing note in his voice, an underlying note that spoke of high zest in every living breath, sheer exuberance and vitality, enough to carry both himself and another on the flowing tide of adventure.

She had heard that note often enough, in her waking dreams—seeing again the animation that danced in his eyes while he turned over card after card, that pivotal night in the gambling room.

And now here he was, living and breathing, wearing a jacket that felt real to her fingers: she stroked the length of his sleeve, feeling hard muscle beneath the fabric.

"Come, Mistress Vickery," he said softly, "you know I am real." Then suddenly, "Was it such a struggle to get away? What is it that shadows your face so that you look at me with swimming eyes?"

In truth, her tears were very near to brimming over. "Don't be kind to me," she said in a voice so low he had to lean toward her to catch the words. "I—I'm not used to it."

She had not expected to sound so pitiful. She gulped, and hastened to retrieve her dignity. "I should not have said that," she added quietly. "It was only that I did not expect to see you. I do not understand how it happens that you are here on this ship. I thought you had left long ago, when the *Sea Queen* sailed."

"The *Queen* was loaded and sailed. My business is finished, of course—beneath our feet the hold of the *Nancy* is full of bags of indigo, and other ships will be here to load the timber I bought. I did expect that you might soon need a quick way off the island, so I stayed. I owe you a great deal."

"Me? You are mistaken. I have done nothing for you."

"In the person of my captain. Sam Short was on the verge of becoming a murderer, and he tells me you prevented that. At some cost to yourself."

"How could you know that—about the cost?"

"You underestimate the island communication system. I marvel at it myself, even though I know how it works, and have even at times used it to my own advantage. As in this case. But it's still uncanny."

The ship sailed on. She knew little about the technical details of managing a sailing ship, but she could see that more sails had been raised, and they now filled with the strong breeze out of the west. Their full rounded curves shone silver in the moonlight, and the heaving wake sparkled in light and darkness. Jamaica was only a darker smudge now against the western sky, and she saw with thankfulness that this ship was the only one on the broad face of the water. Howard had not yet, apparently, discovered her absence.

Would he follow her? Or would he simply write her off as a bad gamble? It would be time to think of that tomorrow, or the next day, or next month. Just now, it was enough to know that she was safe from him for tonight.

And tonight was—tonight, and she had escaped. As the Gospel said, Sufficient unto the day is the evil thereof. Tomorrow could take care of itself.

I think I am rambling, she thought, and did not know she spoke aloud, until Mark said, "You're too tired to think at all. I'll show you your cabin, and you can be assured of a good rest."

He picked up the basket she had set on the deck, and escorted her down a hatchway into a lower level. The cabin he showed her into was small, and it smelled recently scrubbed.

Mark lit the lamp, and watched it for a moment as it swung safely in its gimbal. For a fraction of a heartbeat, she was taken back in her thoughts to another ship's cabin, another oil lamp swinging, just so, and she turned frightened eyes to Mark.

"Your expression tells me much," he said, suddenly stiff in his manner. "On my part, I will tell you that you have nothing to fear from me. Nor from the crew of my ship. Not tonight, nor any night. May you sleep well."

With a swift movement he had vanished through the door and she was alone.

She sank down onto the narrow pallet that served as bed, and dropped her face into her hands. She sat thus for a long time, so it seemed, hardly aware of her surroundings.

Her thoughts scampered like coneys in the rocks, too swift to recognize, flickering like will-o'-the-wisps luring her on to catch one, only to find it vanishing in her hands. She was unutterably weary. Faces swam before her closed eyes—people she had known, people she had only seen, the inhabitants of the gambling rooms, faces that looked alike, masked, as it were, by the lust for gambling.

And her own expression? Always easy to read, Howard had said. And now Mark. She must have shown him the fear she had felt in that other ship's cabin—for that was what he read on her face. Whereas it was only remembered emotion. Here, she was not afraid. Nor would she ever be afraid of Mark.

In fact, she darkly suspected that she would run to meet him halfway—more than halfway.

Slowly rocking back and forth in her distress, she became aware of the sounds of the ship. She was rocking in the same rhythm as the ship, meeting the great swells of the sea, rising to top the crest of the wave, and sliding gently down the other side as the crest passed beneath the keel.

The high hum of the shrouds, taut in the strong breeze. The slap of water against the hull of the ship, the hiss as the ship slid through the waters. Sounds that were reassuring, competent, safe.

She rose from the bunk, and searched for her night shift. She could not find it in the smoky light from the lamp. She gave up the search. What difference did it make? Suddenly her eyes closed even while she stood, one hand on the hinged table fastened to the wall, and she nearly fell, already more than half asleep.

She took off her gown, and like a child let the garment lie where it fell. She simply could not find the strength to fold it neatly.

She was asleep the moment her head touched the pillow.

The second day out from Port Royal, Carmody was getting the feel of the ship so that she no longer moved in jerky runs from one handhold to another. She was slowly realizing that her escape from Jamaica, from Howard, was real—that she would not wake up to find this, the ship under her feet, the limitless horizon, only a dream.

The wind tugged at her hair until she devised a tight knotting of her scarf, confining the deep red tresses securely, and leaving the clean lines of her cheekbones and the sharp line of her jaw to catch the bright sunlight. She was too thin, the delicately shadowed hollows of her cheeks giving her a poignant look under her slanting silver eyes.

She found a spot on the deck, in an angle made by a bulkhead and a cargo hatch, where she could sit sheltered from the weather, and out of the way of the crew.

It was there, on the second day, that Mark sought her out. He stood a little way from her, waiting until his shadow fell across her lap and she looked up. "May I join you?" he asked.

"Of course," she said, feeling a sudden flush of pleasure burning her cheeks.

"Are you satisfied with the food aboard my ship?" he asked abruptly. The ordinary question surprised her.

Solemnly, she nodded. "Much better than the last ship I sailed in."

"I am sure of it. Oh, yes, I know how you came out from England. I have heard much of what has already happened to you. But I am wondering whether you have given thought to what may lie ahead."

"No," she said finally, with a shake of her head. "I haven't any idea what I should do. Besides," she added quickly, suddenly amused, "I don't even know where we're going!"

"Their Majesties' colony of Virginia. My cargo must be delivered first. Then—" He frowned. "You can make arrangements there for your desired destination. If you are not pleased to settle in Virginia."

"I really can't say yet what I should do." She had spent her hoarded sum of energy simply in escaping from Howard. The next step was one she could not yet imagine. She closed her eyes and did not see Mark's thoughtful frown.

The motion of the ship altered, becoming more choppy, and when she opened her eyes to look it seemed that the surface of the water took on a sort of oily look, as though spilled tallow was spreading. Far out on the western horizon—the ship was sailing north now, and had since that first dawn—lay a grayish-blue smudge, and the sun drew a thin veil over its face.

But Mark seemed not to notice, and, guided by his calmness, Carmody leaned back against the bulkhead and sighed with contentment. Far from worry about her future, she was for the moment acquiescent, and said, "I wish the voyage would go on forever. Always sailing, never arriving."

"I understand that. But when would you build something, a memorial to leave behind you?"

She was startled. "I haven't heard a sentiment like that since—well, since I left my home. I worked at building something, Mark. I spent my whole girlhood learning to manage the estate, building up what my father had neglected, until I got the farms doing very well indeed."

Her voice died away. Finally, he prompted her. "But you didn't stay?"

"No. I made the land prosper, to turn over to my younger brother. He was away at school until he came of age to take over his inheritance, and by now, I should imagine, there is nothing left."

"Gambling? That's the quickest way to ruin."

"More than that. My brother gambled, it is true. Using for stakes other people's lives, as it happened."

"Yours included?"

"Mine, naturally. But, of course, it was my fault."

He waited silently, but his very lack of comment was companionable, trustworthy. She felt instinctively that he would not blame nor censure. And she felt a need of someone to talk to.

"I treated him like a child. Sister knows best, I thought. Well, sister finally was forced to extreme measures, and now I suppose it was all for nothing."

Useless to give herself to James, to get Ralph out of that jail. Only to end up in jail herself, after shooting Waldo. And yet she would do it all again, she thought.

"It seems hard," she said, more to herself than to Mark, "to have given up those three years to the estates, to build something of value, and then have it rejected out of hand. I don't see any reason to build again. No," she added with sudden determination, "I just want to sail on, without ever landing. I wish this ship would never come to port."

"Hush!" said Mark sharply. "Do you know what you're saying? Don't let the sailors hear you."

"Why not?"

For answer he pointed to the western horizon. The clouds that had been lying innocuously on the horizon now had reared up to cover a quarter of the sky. The front edge was like the unhemmed edge of a newly woven blanket, fluffy and thick, and rising fast, as though an invisible hand pulled the blanket over the expanse of sky. A chill wind struck her, and she shivered.

The ship began to pitch in earnest. "Best come below,"

Mark told her. "The men will have need of all the deck room without watching out for you."

"You'll come with me?"

"I can lend a hand here for a bit," he said. "All I can do is take in sail, but that's what's needed now."

He took her down to her cabin, and said, "I'll come back to you when I can. Don't worry. This voyage isn't going to end here and now. We'll land, and at our proper port too. You and I have a good deal to talk about. For one thing, you don't know the first thing about love."

She heard his fast stride taking the steps two at a time, and then the sounds were all overhead, on the deck, the sounds of the scurrying crew taking in sails, clewing them up, helping the ship shake herself and turn to meet the foe head-on.

The storm hit.

Carmody had been pacing in the small cabin for perhaps an hour when the wind first struck the *Nancy*, laying her nearly on her beam ends for a heart-stopping minute before she began to right herself.

The gale rose to an eldritch shriek, increasing in volume until Carmody could hear nothing else, not even the cabin door as it banged to and fro, smashing the latch so that it could not be secured again.

She had lighted the lamp after Mark had gone, to dispel the unpleasant darkness, but now, seeing it swaying wildly, she hurried to blow out the flame before the lamp escaped the gimbal altogether.

It was almost as if, with the extinguishing of the lamp, James Scott, Duke of Monmouth, sat beside her in the stygian dark. He had not been the first male to take advantage of her—no, her father had done that. Then Ralph. But James had been the first to awaken her senses with his sure, expert Stuart touch. Practiced, so smooth that it revealed long experience and little deep feeling, yet he had been gentle, affectionate, even loving—as much as his shallow character would allow. Howard was the opposite—brutal, beastly, cruel, savage. And he would not ever touch her again; she would die first.

But Mark—what had he meant by his cryptic remark? Not know about love? She thought, wryly, I've known all I need to know. An appetite of the moment, an automatic instinct of the senses once awakened, never truly stilled. And, used as she had been, she could only consider love as degrading. None of the men she knew—from father on down to Howard Vickery—had looked at her as a person, not as an individual with wants and desires of her own, with thoughts that were valuable, that were prized because they were hers and no one else in the world could have just the same combination of thoughts, ideas, of personality.

What did Mark know about love? Nothing she did not already know, in one form or another. Fiercely, she struck her fist on the side of the bunk. She realized how much she had hoped that somewhere there would be something shiny and new, colored like the rainbow, bringing ineffable happiness. That something she had called once, because she did not know what else to call it, love.

And—born of the mystery of their meeting, the current that she thought had flowed between them the night of the card game, even the instinct that had led him to wait for her, to send Sam Short to the wharf in case she should need him—she had thought that Mark might bring her to that *something*.

But he had said only words that promised—what else could he have meant?—some foolish trivial difference that in the long run would amount to the same thing: a staking out of claims, of possession, lasting for the moments that her senses ruled her mind, and no longer.

He could have left that unsaid, she thought morosely. She did not need to brood in advance upon disillusion. Time enough for that after he had come back to her. There was no escaping, not from a ship at sea where he was the owner—not from a ship in the throes of a mighty storm.

She could not sleep, nor did she want to. The din in her ears was deafening—worse because she did not recognize the sounds for what they were. Instead, she read into the live flexing of the ship's timbers, bending to great seas, the meaning that the hull was being rent asunder.

The scream of the wind, the heavy pounding of waves on the deck, the curling hiss as the green seas broke over the waist of the little ship.

In the dark, wedged in a corner of the bunk, huddling herself together in as small a space as she could manage, as if to try to make herself too small for the storm to notice, Carmody felt water coursing down her cheeks. She touched the tip of her tongue to the moisture, and tasted salt. The sea, breaking in at last?

Only tears. Crying for something lost.

And crying in deathly fear. The ship rolled from side to side—or rather, to starboard and, more and more reluctantly, back to a safely upright keel. Then came the time when, inevitably, the ship did not respond. She lay over on her beam, rail doubtless under water—so Carmody pictured in her mind in the fearsome dark—and lay there, too torpid to move.

And then, she heard the cabin door flung back against the bulkhead, and Mark was beside her. His hands groped for her in the dark.

"Mercy, where are you? We've got to get topside at once. Come on, no time to lose!"

He found her, touching bent knees, arm, shoulder, pulling her away from the only safe corner she had found.

A little whimpering sound close to her ear, and Carmody recognized with a kind of remote surprise that the sound had come from her own lips. "Come *on*, Mercy!"

He pulled at her, and she resisted him as if she could not bear to trade her newly won safety in the dark corner, like a cave that just fit, for whatever lay outside.

Even Mark was an intruder, trying to pull her away, away to destruction—

And then, just as he had braced himself and got his arm around her shoulders, tugging methodically at her as one pries a clinging sea creature from a rock, the ship began to move.

Move, miraculously, away from the deep. A movement

sluggish, stirring, bringing her lee rail with a sucking noise out of the sea.

The *Nancy* had saved herself!

Mark sat down suddenly in the bunk beside Carmody. He pulled her to him, forcing her teared face into the collar of his sodden jacket, both arms tight around her.

He held her thus, steadily, sturdily, for a long time. He moved once, to pull a blanket from the bunk and tuck it around her, putting its free end around his own soaking shoulders.

A long time afterwards, feeling her take a deep, shuddery breath against his chest, and move her face away from his jacket, he said softly, "A long time ago, when I brought you down here, I told you you knew nothing about love. What you know as love is something that has been done to you—with your consent, maybe, but not with your whole self. It means nothing. Like a beating to a child, orders to servants—anything like that. Something you have no control over."

He held her carefully, giving her all the reassurance and steadiness that he could, simply by being there.

Gently he continued. "Love—the real thing, I'm speaking of now—is sort of like a spiral. I've thought about this a lot. My parents had a perfect marriage, and they died within a week of each other, as they would have wanted. I hoped some day I would be lucky enough to find what they found. So I've thought about it."

He fell silent, and finally Carmody managed to get the blanket away from her face, and say, loudly against the still howling storm winds, "You said a spiral?"

"You meet someone who attracts you, let us say. Then you begin to skirt around the outside of her personality— or his, it works both ways. You learn each other's mind, hopes, and eventually you trust enough to share your dreams. And after all the special sharing, the learning of the other's heart, I suppose you could say, then you have arrived at cherishing—and I think that's the key to the special kind of love I mean. The special kind I want for myself."

She was silent for so long he thought she must have

fallen asleep. He smiled wryly—so far had he gone with no other woman. Never before had he felt so impelled to explain, to expose his innermost self to possible ridicule or—even worse, as now—to have his words produce a boredom of such colossal proportions that one would fall asleep in the middle of his speech.

He moved involuntarily, and Carmody stirred, sitting up and throwing off the blanket. Faint light appeared in the porthole.

"You're wet," she said. "I didn't realize how cold you must be. Here."

Over his protests she took the blanket and said, "Take off your jacket." Then she wrapped the blanket around him. "I suppose there's nothing hot to drink, but perhaps later there will be."

She wasn't asleep, then, he thought. But she said nothing! What did she think of him?

And as if reading his thoughts, she said, "There was a time, Mark, when I would have given my soul for such cherishing."

She reached over to touch his hand lightly with her fingertips. The light was growing in the little cabin, a gray murky storm-wracked light, sufficient for her to see the hollows where his eyes lay, under those wing-soaring brows.

"But I lost my soul for much, much less."

The storm abated swiftly, its fury spent. And when Carmody followed Mark onto the canting deck, she was amazed to see that the sun was rising, a brooding red color crossed by bars of receding charcoal-colored clouds. The sky overhead was still fretted with trailing cloud-wrack, but the wind was gathering up the tatters and hustling them away to the southeast.

She clutched at the rail. She was not prone to seasickness, she had discovered—possibly her Viking ancestor had bequeathed her his sea-steadiness. But it was difficult to stand erect, unaided, on the angled deck as the ship heeled.

As she glanced over the deck, she saw that the night

had not left the *Nancy* unharmed. She knew little about ships, but she knew a broken mainmast when she saw it. There were tangled shrouds like a skein of yarn used as a kitten's plaything, and in a corner of the deck, two injured men.

The men she could do something about, thanks to the weeks spent on Otobil's mountaintop. It was difficult to set a broken arm, with makeshift splints, while holding spasmodically to a handhold, but eventually she managed it. The application of ointment and bandages, with her torn petticoat and the small jar of salve she had made under Otobil's direction, went better.

She leaned back on her heels to survey her handiwork. Potter, the injured seaman, held one hand gingerly under the splinted arm. "Feels better, Mistress. You've done a fine job."

"Best get it looked at by a real doctor," she advised him. "When we get to shore."

"Nay, I've seen doctors' work. End up with one leg shorter than t'other, an arm all bent out of shape. Ruins a man's life, sometimes, the doctors do."

She smiled at her patient. "I think we're all lucky to get out of such a storm alive."

"Aye, we could have gone to the bottom, and I thought we would more 'n once."

The other patient, who had a nasty gash in his hand, was quieter, but she judged he would be all right. Certainly there was nothing more she could do for him, but cover him with a blanket and let sleep and the application of salve do their work.

She stayed where she was after her two patients had been helped away and watched the work parties cut at the tangled lines, stitching torn canvas together, and beginning some sort of hard groaning labor toward the base of the toppled mast.

Her head swam, and she realized she was starving. She hadn't eaten for hours, and she guessed that even the galley crew would be working on deck to get the ship in order again. What she wouldn't give for a hot cup of tea!

As though she had spoken aloud, she heard footsteps

beside her and a mug of dark, bitter brew, steaming, was placed in her hand.

Mark dropped to sit on the deck beside her. "Cook's busy so I made myself useful."

"I should think you'd be working as hard as the rest of them," she said, gratefully sipping the bitter tea. "It's your ship, isn't it?"

"I'd just be in the way," Mark said. "The captain is competent, and I'd embarrass him, waiting for him to give me orders. Besides, I'm not much use."

She cupped her hands around the mug, and felt the warmth invade her fingers, and creep through her body, comforting and, surprisingly, giving her new strength.

At last she sighed, letting the last drop fall on her tongue, before she set down the empty mug. "What a cup of tea will do!" she laughed. "I'm truly grateful, sir."

She glanced at him, and instantly sobered. His face was drawn and pallid, and in spite of the chilly wind beads of sweat dotted his forehead.

"Mark!" she cried. "You're hurt!"

His smile twisted with pain, but there was still a sort of gaunt amusement lingering in his dark blue eyes, just before they closed and he toppled head first into her lap.

Her scream was torn from her lips and hurried away to mingle with the low-flying storm wrack, but she heard neither scream nor wind.

Mark's head lay heavily in her lap, and she could not find the cause of his collapse. He was injured, so much was sure, but where?

Carefully she laid back the dark hair, curling roughly around the temple, and saw the ends of her fingers were bloody. The gash was long, and the bruise beneath it was severe. She probed delicately, letting her fingertips see for her, as Otobil had taught her.

She was satisfied that there was no deeper damage. But she could not treat him here. She looked around wildly for help, but all were intent upon their strenuous tasks, saving the ship, bringing her under control again rather than wallowing helplessly, dismasted, in the trough of the great seas.

She must do it alone. Carefully she extricated herself from the inert weight of Mark's head and chest, and managed to roll him over on his back. She wedged him between two timbers, the ordinary use of which she could not fathom, and set to work.

Carefully clipping away the dark curls, she laid bare the skin, ready for the healing salve and the bandages. Somewhere someone sobbed, and she realized that it was she herself. Crying for what? She knew the answer to that, even while her fingers rubbed salve, closed the gash, and did the other things that were needed. Fortunately she had brought the blanket from her cabin, the blanket that had sheltered them both in the night. He had been chilled through, then, and it must have been afterward that some wide-swinging spar had struck him. He would be lucky indeed if he did not end up with a congestion in the lungs. Her medicine for that she had not been able to bring along.

He opened his eyes once, wide with shock and a sort of child-like wonder. He moistened dry lips before he could speak. "Mercy? I didn't dream?"

"I'm here," she said heartily. "I'll stay with you, don't worry. Now go to sleep."

"Stay forever?" He clutched a fold of her skirt with his fingers, but he was asleep before she could answer his question. Stay forever. How long a journey she had made to find what she wanted above all else. Until last night when she came to rest in his arms, like a storm-driven gull reaching haven, he had made no attempt even to touch her—yet he had made love to her in a more shattering way than if he had attacked her. A proving, intimate promise he had given her—a sharing of mind and spirit as well as the fusion of flesh. A total commitment was what he would demand of her, and he would be satisfied with nothing less from the woman he loved.

An exciting prospect—truly a wonderful prospect. It would have been—it *might* have been the adventure of her life. But she could not allow herself even the indulgence of thinking about what might have been.

Mark stirred, his hand hot beneath her cool fingers as

she crouched beside him. She soothed him, and he lapsed again into sleep, or unconsciousness—she could not tell which.

She could do nothing else for him now but sit by his side, holding his hand, soothing him when he stirred. Nothing else but think. She knew she could not burden him with the secret that walked with her, commit him to sharing the secret or betraying her. And yet she had dared share the first step, telling him a bit about Oaklands.

She huddled beside him as the long afternoon wore on. The ship now boasted a jury-rigged mast, and scraps of sail were hoisted on halyards already strained. But as the wind blew more steadily, and the captain gained confidence in his makeshift gear, the ship tacked toward the port it had set sail for.

And with the setting of the proper course for the ship, Carmody knew that there was no proper course for her—only to drift at the whim of whatever winds that came.

In one day the danger of pneumonia was past for Mark, and the second day he was able to take a bowl and a half of broth.

She was content, then, to sit near him, holding a tight rein on her compelling need to touch him, to see his dark blue eyes turn often to her, like a compass needle seeking true north.

At length land was sighted—the Capes, through which the *Nancy* would travel onto the broad waters of Chesapeake Bay. And then?

"I have an idea," Mark said.

He had sent for her, and she came gladly. But she crouched on the deck a yard away from the pallet where his men had made him comfortable, rigging an awning against the sun, shifting his pallet to be out of the wind.

"A wonderful friend of mine," Mark said, his voice still weak, but the spirit behind it as strong as ever, "Lady Anne York owns the plantation next to mine."

She searched her memory, and found what she was looking for. "I thought you said you did not know who had bought the land next to yours."

"That's on the downstream side. A fool of a kid inherited it, and promptly gambled it away. Well, Lady Anne lives on my other side."

"Alone?"

"Yes. I don't know much about her family, but she is a wonderful woman—she's nearly fifty, but she runs her plantation with a hand as strong as a man's. She'll be glad to have you."

"Have me?" Carmody was very quiet, but her thoughts were loud and furious. Like an unwanted object—like cleaning out an old attic—like—

"Don't get excited, Mercy," Mark said, a glint of humor in his eyes. "Only until you get on your feet and decide what you want to do. I can't take you in, you know that. Not that I don't want to, because I do. And one day—you will come to me, Mercy. I don't know yet how we'll clear things away, but we will. Trust in that."

So it was settled, at last. She really had no choice. She could not go far with her handful of coins, even though the small store was still intact. Mark would not take passage money from her.

She was forced to agree that she would trespass upon Lady Anne's hospitality, for a little while at least. Until they could clear away a few things! How could she clear away the memory of a crime such as hers? Now that Howard knew who she was, she could not, *dared* not, link herself to Mark in any way. The taint that stained her was hers alone to live with, to repent. She knew that, whatever might happen to her, Mark must remain untouched, to live his own life—to share his precious dreams with someone else, not her.

She would stay with Lady Anne until she found a way to escape—again.

The storm had driven them far to the north and it had taken more than a week for the *Nancy* to make up the time that had been lost. So as the ship reached across Chesapeake Bay, the captain dispatched his fast-sailing pinnace to carry word ahead that they would dock at Mark

Tennant's own wharf the next day. Mark sent word to Lady Anne to meet the *Nancy*.

The Tennant plantation wharf stretched out into the river at an angle that allowed sailing vessels access to the structure at high tide; unloading had to take place rapidly, before the tide fell below half, and as the ship warped into its berth, at least two dozen men swarmed down to be ready at the dock.

There was the usual calling back and forth across the narrowing stretch of dark water, the whistling of lines put ashore and snugged around bollards, before the ship nudged the wooden wharf and settled easily, ready to be relieved of its cargo.

The sailors went about their own tasks with dispatch, swirling around Carmody as she stood at the rail like creaming white water around a stone in a stream. Once again she admired the discipline that prevailed on Mark's ship, the competence of his captain.

It was not time for her to go ashore. She had leisure for the moment to watch the activity. From the deck, elevated above the shore line, she could see the broad stretch of rough lawn sweeping up from water's edge to a house, half-hidden on the hill. The trees that abounded on the slope were old and straight as cathedral pillars, breaking into luxuriant foliage at their crowns, different trees from the ones she had grown accustomed to in Jamaica. She looked in vain for palm trees, for the misshapen silk-cotton, the majestic logwood.

Instead she recognized oaks and beeches—the trees of a more temperate climate, like Dorset, familiar, and from happier times. Was it an omen? Perhaps she was really, at last, emerging from the nightmare. She looked around her with renewed interest.

A double line of workmen cleared the cargo from the ship, one line coming to the wharf to load, the other already laden and starting back on the well-beaten path toward the top of the hill and down the other side to the outbuildings. They sang a strange rhythmic work song, not unlike one she had heard on Tolliver's plantation when the indigo was harvested.

Already most of the deck was cleared of debris from the storm wreckage, and the hempen bags of spices that had been brought up from a leaky hold below deck.

The foreman watched his crew for a little while, directing by a mere gesture of his hand. Then, satisfied that things were going as he wanted them to, he stepped aboard the ship.

Mark introduced him to Carmody. "Mistress Vickery, may I present my good right arm, Digby. He speaks for me on all occasions. Nearly all, I should say. Some occasions I reserve for myself!"

Digby gave a queer, sidelong glance at Mark, and for a moment Carmody had the thought that her name was not unknown to the foreman. But of course the pinnace would have brought word to the household here. She smiled at Digby. "I am sure you speak well in Mr. Tennant's behalf."

"All of us here set his interests above our own, ma'am," said Digby.

"Your interests are my interests, too," said Mark quietly. "It is that simple."

It was a new facet to Mark's personality, she thought, to see him here in his own land, with his own servants around him. There had been genuine welcome, even love, on the face of even the lowliest workman, and she surmised that Mark must be an excellent master—much like the kind of man that Oaklands would have needed, instead of Ralph.

Her mind seemed to run on Oaklands, and the reason, she guessed, was the great oaks sheltering Mark's house. But where Oaklands was sheltered from the world by its trees and the hills surrounding it, this house of Mark Tennant's dominated the scene, standing imperiously on the top of the hill, watching the trees march down to the busy wharf where the prosperity of the plantation culminated.

She tried, but was unable to visualize Ralph's features in her mind—it was as though he had been a picture in a book, nearly forgotten after she closed the cover. And she thought dourly that the turn she had taken in her life, the weighing of her own person against Ralph's sanity and the safety of the people of Oaklands, had been a futile mistake.

She was so wrapped in her own thoughts that when Mark spoke to her she was startled. In her thoughts she had been Carmody.

"Mercy, where have you been?" he demanded, half-amused. "Far from the James River, I would guess. Lady Anne is here, and we must go ashore now. Ready?"

As ready as I will ever be, she thought, feeling her heart sink at the thought of meeting that formidable lady who was to take her in charge. Suppose they didn't like each other? It was a masculine vanity, she suspected, that led Mark to believe that any friends of his must be friends of each other, but it was not always that simple.

He smiled reassuringly at her, his eyes lingering long and warmly. "We'll work something out," he promised her in a whisper, his flyaway eyebrows quirking, "even if we have to sail to the south seas to be together."

As she set foot upon the wharf, feeling the solidity under her as unsettling as though the wooden dock rocked wildly beneath her feet, she saw a woman on horseback, waiting and watching from part way up the hill. Another rider, a man, stood a little apart from her.

It was always a disadvantage to look up at someone on horseback, she reflected, and that was probably why the Normans were able to dominate the peasantry. She had not thought how her people at Oaklands must have felt, as she rode among them, not until now.

Lady Anne had been brought up with courtesy bred in her very bones. She clearly recognized Carmody's quality, for as the girl approached, Mark at her side, she slid from her saddle to the ground. A groom, watchful and quick, took the reins almost at the moment her well-booted foot touched the ground.

"Lady Anne," said Mark, "this is Mistress Vickery, about whom I wrote to you. She has had rather a bad time of it lately."

"My dear, I am glad to see you." She put out both hands to take Carmody's, and smiled in quick approval. "Mark, I see you did not exaggerate her beauty."

Carmody took note of the thin, fine-boned aristocratic face, tanned from long hours in the weather, her riding hat covering most of her hair except for the little white curls that escaped from the dark hat. She looked a decade younger than her fifty years. And more than the whipcord thinness of the woman, the wiry build that spoke of endurance and strength, Carmody saw the lurking compassion in the dark eyes, kindness that probably would be gruffly denied if she were accused of it.

Even more than kindness, Carmody sensed a solid integrity, an honesty that she could trust and find it never failing. Impulsively she smiled back at Lady Anne, and murmured words that were appropriate.

"Mark," said Lady Anne, beckoning her companion forward and introducing him. "My nephew, Jermyn Fox, has come to stay with me for a little."

Clearly Lady Anne doted on the young man. Her shrewd eyes softened as she looked at him. Carmody had only a swift impression of shyness, hidden under charming manners.

Mark was welcoming Lady Anne's nephew cordially, but his attention soon returned to Carmody. "I'll send Mercy to you in a carriage. I am afraid she came away without proper clothes for riding—"

His voice trailed away as he caught the message that Lady Anne was sending him. Carmody, too, saw the message flash between the two of them, and knew it meant trouble. Lady Anne did not like her, Lady Anne could not take her in—but why?

"I am sorry, child," said Lady Anne. "I recognized your name when Mark wrote me. I came as soon as I received your note, Mark. The pinnace made good time."

"Lady Anne, you are avoiding the point," said Mark uneasily.

Carmody could not breathe. Her name? But Mark had never known her real name. How could he have sent it ahead, and why? And yet, Howard had known her real name—and she did not know how he had discovered it.

She looked wildly around. Had Lady Anne come with bailiffs in her train? To take her back to stand trial in

Dorset? She could not bear it. Rather the ship had sunk—except for the others, who did not bear her heavy guilt.

"Come here," said Mark's strong voice in her ear, a hand under her elbow. "Too much sun, Mercy. Come, I'll put you here in the shade."

Carmody forced her eyes open. She would not cringe before the majesty of the law. She had killed Waldo, and sooner or later she would pay for it. And she would meet whatever came with dignity.

Lady Anne was saying something incomprehensible. "I tried to keep him from coming, Mark. Believe me, I did not inform him the *Nancy* was about to dock."

Lady Anne gestured, and Carmody's eyes flew to a man she had not seen before. He had moved now from the shade into the edge of the sunlight, so that the brilliant light beat down on his blond head.

"No, Mercy," said a familiar, hated voice. "You will remember that I have my own ways of—finding out things." He smiled wolfishly. "Welcome to Virginia, my dear wife."

2

THE sun went in and the shadows covered the earth, but when Carmody looked again, nothing had changed.

The sun shone as brightly on Howard's yellow hair as before, no one had moved, and no one even seemed to know the nature of the trap that closed in around her once again.

No one but Mark, whose swift intake of breath hissed in her ear.

"How—how did you get here?" she faltered at last.

"I was shocked to find that you were gone, Mercy," he said, teetering on the balls of his feet, and thoroughly enjoying the sensation he was making. "The only ship out of Port Royal was the *Nancy*, bound, as they said, for Virginia. So I took ship, too. Imagine my surprise at finding I had arrived before you. But even with the storm blowing you out of your way," he added, his meaning clear, "I am sure you had a more pleasant trip than I did." His eyes traveled deliberately from Carmody to Mark. "Much more pleasant."

She opened her mouth to protest, but Mark forestalled her. "See here, Vickery, you're out of line. Nothing happened on that voyage, and you malign your wife badly."

"Ah, yes, so you remember she is my wife? I am rejoiced to hear it."

"Howard!" Carmody found her voice at last. "For heaven's sake, don't make a scene! Everybody's listening!"

"Do you find it embarrassing? Especially in front of

Lady Anne?" Suddenly Howard's face darkened. "Remember this, Mercy. The countryside knows, now, what you are. A piece of damaged goods."

Without warning Mark swung at Howard, too swiftly for Digby to stop him. Carmody heard a muffled exclamation from Lady Anne, but everything happened in a sort of blur. Mark landed only the one blow before Digby and Felton held him back, but it was enough to send Howard sprawling on the ground. When he rose to his feet, rubbing his jaw, the look in his eyes was murderous.

"You will pay for that, Tennant," said Howard in a deadly quiet voice. "As you will pay for all the other times you have stood in my way. Remember that. And remember, too, that if I see you on Vickery ground, you will be shot—like a marauding dog around a sheep pen."

Mark strained to free himself, but Digby and black Felton restrained their master. Howard's eyes glittered, but apparently he deemed it better to leave while he could still play the injured husband. He turned to Carmody.

"Now, Mistress Vickery, if you please?" He clutched her arm just above the elbow in fingers that still held his terrible rage with Mark. Steering her toward the carriage that she had not seen before, she could hear his breath whistling through his teeth, in the way that she had long ago learned boded no good for anyone.

"Just a moment!"

Lady Anne's carrying voice stopped them. She strode across the short distance that separated her from Carmody and her husband. She looked at Howard for a moment. Her expression was unreadable. Then she turned to Carmody and took her hand.

"Remember, my dear, that my home is always open to you. At any time of the day or night. Without ceremony." She flicked a glance, sharp as the end of a whip, at Howard, and said, to Carmody, "For *whatever* reason."

Carmody wished that Lady Anne had not made her warning to Howard quite so plain. Howard's resentment would be swift and physical, with Carmody as an object. But she managed a faint, "Thank you," before Howard handed her into the open carriage and joined her on the seat, picking up the reins.

The carriage had started up the hill and turned down the long drive from the Tennant house, passing through a double row of great oaks, before Howard spoke again.

"We will have much to talk of, Mercy," he said, his voice surprisingly calm. "But it can wait until we get home. To Vickery Hall. How well you must have listened to me, my dear, to remember that I held property here. Or did you forget after all, and just arrive here by chance?"

She looked away. She could feel her lips quivering with rage and despair, and dared not answer him. She had come so close, so close to being free of him, but the dark influence of her husband had once again come to brood over her.

She let the hopeless darkness sweep over her spirit, numbing her into a cocoon where nothing Howard said could hurt her. But even after they drove up their own driveway, similarly planted with trees forming an arching canopy over them, but littered with the previous winter's fallen limbs, he said nothing.

The carriage drew up to the front door. She stepped at last to the ground and looked about her in dismay. The house was handsome in its proportions, much larger than Mark's had seemed to be. A house of mellow brick, made, she learned later, of bricks carried from England in the holds of sailing ships as ballast, removed when the bales of tobacco and cotton were shipped back.

The imposing front steps up to a great front door were broad, beautifully shaped, but lacking paint. One step was broken at the end, and Howard guided her around it safely.

At the door she turned and looked back down the drive. The last way of escape, she thought, and there was no way she could use it. No place to go except to Lady Anne's, who would shelter her. But at what a cost! Carmody could not bring Howard's vengeance down upon anyone else. Already, she had made Mark an enemy of Howard's.

"We're home, Mercy. The word has a nice ring to it, don't you agree?" He pushed past her into the great entry hall, containing a stairway winding up into the shadowy second floor.

A thin layer of dust covered everything, and the floor had not been swept. The banister was gray until she ran a tentative finger over it and discovered the rich mahogany beneath the grime. She sighed shortly.

Howard laughed. "Once again I bring you to a house that, to say the least, lacks a woman's touch. Had you ever thought, Mercy, that your mission in life is simply to set a house in order?"

He threw open a handsome folding door, painted white, into a neglected drawing room. Here at least some effort had been made to keep dirt and decay at bay. There were dust covers over the furniture, and a heavy linen bag hanging from the ceiling must conceal a chandelier. Slatted blinds were drawn so that outside light filtered in faintly and lay in narrow bands upon the bare floor. The rug that no doubt covered the floor in better times lay rolled up against the inner wall of the room.

There was a stale smell of ancient wood ashes, dust, and quite possibly dry rot in the chairs.

"Well, here it is, Mercy. Your new home. The servants are arriving shortly, unless their ship too has been caught by the storm. But you will have plenty of slaves to do your bidding."

"How long have you been here?"

"Three days. While you were out disporting yourself on a healthful sea voyage."

Her eyes blazed at him, and she felt a return of her rebellious spirit. He could do no worse to her than he had already done, and she simply could not fight him. There was no place to go.

But she was not yet conquered. And by him, she never would be, she vowed. He could treat her body as he chose—he had the legal right. But he could never touch the glow inside that was the essence of Carmody. That frail flame was her own, to give or withhold, her own individuality that she would cherish and nurse in secret.

"I suppose it is no use to tell you that Mr. Tennant means nothing to me."

"No use whatever. You see, my dear wife, I watched you that night when he tricked me at cards. You never could disguise your feelings. Too bad I didn't realize you were willing to jeopardize your good name by eloping with the man."

"You had already ruined my good name," she said bitterly, "with your cheating and your obnoxious gambling den. Making me no better than a tawdry come-on for your victims."

Surprisingly, he chuckled. "Well, I suppose you could look at it that way. But that's all past. All behind us. Now, Mercy, we have something better to do. And we will do it together."

She stiffened, and backed away from him. He laughed aloud. "Don't worry. I'm not going to put a hand on that lovely, frozen body of yours. You're just not good enough. No, you will sleep alone in your icy solitude. There are, however, certain duties I will expect from you."

Warily, she watched him, ready to retreat. She did not believe him. "What kind of duties?"

"Nothing you can object to. I have grander objectives now. The gambling is all in the past. I've got a foothold here in this colony, and I find it much more to my liking than steamy Port Royal. And there is more to gain, too."

"I don't understand you, Howard. Why do you want to keep me? Why don't you just let me go on my own way?"

"Then who would refurbish my house, direct my servants?" he asked in apparent surprise. "And where would you go? Who would want a woman of such tarnished reputation? Don't think I wouldn't come after you again, Mercy, for I would. Even changing your name won't help you. I will keep what is mine, *Mercy*, make no mistake about it. I will—protect—you very well indeed."

Carmody sank into a chair, grimacing at the faint cloud of dust that rose up around her. Howard had finally left her alone, but she was past the point of caring. Her muslin gown was badly worn, and stained with salt water. The small basket she had brought with her from Port Royal stood neglected in the hall, but there was little in it except another pair of slippers, a few jars of ointments and medicaments, a shawl, and two fresh undergarments. Nothing to suit an occasion such as this.

The lady wore the latest fashion in gyves, she thought morosely, matching fetters upon wrist and ankle. But not upon her spirit!

She was dimly aware of sounds elsewhere in the house—the carriage taken around the outside drive to stables, somewhere in the rear and out of sound now. A door slamming at the back. Voices.

Voices? She had thought she was alone in this house, except for Howard. She should have known better. Howard would never willingly turn his hand to labor—and someone had to cook his meals, feed and rub down his horse. Of course there would be a servant.

She sat there, thinking of nothing, feeling her weary muscles grow slack, her head start to swim. She dozed for a time. If Howard were true to his promise to leave her alone, she thought finally, she could exist. Not live, not enjoy her days, her years—but, exist. And somehow, that in itself promised much. To live in the same world that held Mark Tennant—well, she would survive.

A shadow darkened the doorway, and she glanced up with new apprehension. But it was only a servant. "Mistress Vickery, I was told to come in and light the candles."

"Of course," she said automatically. How long had she sat there? The sunlight no longer slatted across the floor, and the blinds no longer held back the daylight.

The servant lighted the candles on the mantel. The brass holders did not reflect the light, as they must have done once. Carmody vowed that they would shine as brightly as they had when they were new. And not in the far distant future, either.

She could see the servant now. A waddling fat woman, with a face as kind as Ascar's, and a worried expression on her face now, as though she expected to be blamed for all that was wrong in her world.

"I'm sorry about the state of things," the woman said in her soft voice, creaming around the edges, and rich. "They call me Prissy. But they wasn't anybody to tell me how to do, nor anybody to care after I did it."

Carmody hastily summoned her charm. "I'm sorry you had to be alone," she said, sincerely, "it's always unsettling not to know what is going to happen, isn't it?"

At the genuine note of sympathy in her new mistress's voice, the woman visibly relaxed. "I've got some good soup in the kettle, ma'am. Can I bring you a bowl?"

"Please do," said Carmody. "And don't worry. We will let things go tonight, but in the morning we will see what needs to be done."

Prissy was as good a cook as existed in Virginia, Carmody thought, and won the woman's undying affection by saying so, as she was shown upstairs to the bedchamber that was to be hers.

"I've tried to keep the rooms up here in case they were wanted," apologized Prissy. "Just now I put new sheets on the bed and aired the room. Dusted some."

She set the candle down on the small table next to the bed. There was no tester, Carmody saw thankfully. After seeing all the other signs of neglect in the house, she could not have slept under a tester doubtless full of ominous creatures.

As it was, a fresh meadowsweet fragrance came in the open window, with no curtains to screen out the breeze. She found her basket on a small chair, and, smiling, told Prissy that she would need nothing more for the night. "Sleep well," she said, and was rewarded by a brilliant flash of white teeth.

She would get along well with Prissy. It would remain to find out what Howard wanted of the house—how much money she had to deal with, and when the other servants would arrive. More hands were needed inside the house than hers and Prissy's. And already Carmody's mind, renewing itself because it must in order to survive, was leaping ahead, past the refurbishing of the house, to the trimming of the trees along the drive, the neatening of the grounds—

She laughed aloud, a strange sound in her ears. Even as

the door of her dungeon closed upon her, she was already planning how to make it more livable!

She did not sleep for a long time that night, missing the regular swaying of the ship, the singing of the shrouds, the long dip and rise of the deck beneath her feet.

Seeing always the laughing face of Mark in those days of free sailing before the wind. And she knew that without Mark, her life would be like an empty house—sad, unloved, and cold.

She was like Prissy, she thought, not knowing what was going to happen next, but, knowing Howard, she was sunk in dour foreboding. In the morning, she would ask him just what he intended.

"My intention," he said the next morning, "is to become a Virginia planter. No more, no less."

She could only stare at him. Finally she ventured, "This does not sound like you, Howard. No Vingt-et-Un? No risking everything on the throw of a loaded die?"

"Not any more," he said. "My gamble is simply to make you love me. And I know what appeals to you. I'll give you all the things you ever wanted. Jewels, carriages, a house full of guests—"

"I don't want any of those things."

"I didn't think so," he said surprisingly. "But you see how conventional I have become."

"What do you want of me?"

"Ah, down to business at once. I like that. No vaporings, no screaming that you hate me—just the deadly look in your eyes that conveys your unmistakable loathing. Too bad that your hate is so much more intense than your love."

"You never had my love," she said, daring the truth.

"No matter. What I want from you, dear wife, is an appearance before the world of a certain domestic tranquillity. And that means before the world, before Lady Anne, Tennant, everybody. And in return—"

He was silent for so long that she prompted him. "In return?"

"In return I will give you free hand to put the house in

order. And if you're a good girl, I might even let you do more. I had word this morning that the ship with our household staff has docked in the Bay. When they come, you'll have all the help you need. I suppose that you will want to spend money."

"I assume there will be necessary expenditures."

"Any amount," he said airily. "There is a sufficiency of funds."

"Where did you—"

"Another condition, my dear," he said, suddenly forbidding as he rose from the breakfast table and threw down his napkin. "No questions. Of any kind. Agreed?"

The only question she wanted an answer to was one she dared not ask him—*when can I go free?* The answer, of course, was simple—never.

"Agreed," she said, and signalled to Prissy for more coffee.

In the next days, she went through the great house, making lists. She had the feeling that she had done all this in another existence, that her life was coming round upon itself like the spokes of a wheel. The wheel had turned from making lists of things to pack in her wedding trunks, of things to be done for Ralph's coming-of-age party, revolving now to making lists of endless tasks to be done to put Vickery Hall in order.

And the strange thing was, whether Howard intended it or not—and of course he did not intend anything of the sort—this was the best possible healing that she could have had. The years since James Scott had left Carmody in that haystack, saying a bittersweet goodby and leaving her with the two sovereigns and a few light-hearted memories among all the bad ones, the years of convict toil and worse, had left her a different person from the one who had made out lists at Oaklands.

At night Carmody's dreams haunted her—the good times as well as the bad. And in the morning she would wake to the cheerful, affectionate face of Prissy, who would not delegate to anyone else the laborious climb upstairs to her mistress's room bearing a tray of hot cinnamon toast and a cup of rich chocolate.

And her day would start again, keeping the dreams at bay for a little. Her solution was to drive herself until she dropped, until she would be too tired even to dream.

And so the house put its own healing arms about Carmody and held her fast, lulling her into a feeling of security. But when the refurbishing was complete? She could not bear to look ahead.

At length the bad dreams went away, and she seldom dreamed of anything more troubling than which shade of damask to choose for the curtains in the dining room, or which girl to set to work mending linen.

Seldom—but when she woke troubled, and limp with weariness, she knew she had dreamed again of Mark Tennant.

Carmody had the house to herself much of the time. Howard came and went, hardly bothering to tell her even how long he would be gone. And she really did not care.

He lived up to his bargain of not bothering her, and she responded by asking him no questions. She did wonder, of course, what he could find to keep himself busy. He had no interest in the growing crops, nor, so far as she could tell, was he gambling.

She finished the downstairs rooms. The living room— she would have called it a drawing room at Oaklands— glowed in soft tones of blue and ivory, with a touch of deepest red in a loose cushion or two to bring the room to life. The dining room shone now with polished wood, gleaming silver and warm brass.

The previous owner of the house had spent care and money on the furnishings. Someone had loved the house—bringing to it the best French china, the finest of drapery and upholstery fabrics. All that was needed, truly, was to clean, clean, clean. And mend.

A small room behind the dining room she had chosen for her own use. She changed it to reflect her own personality, and retreated to it like a haven in rising storm.

For a storm was coming, she was sure of that.

No matter how changed Howard seemed to be, how generous with money, how straightforward in keeping his bargain with her, she stepped daily in fear that something, somehow, would trigger the lurking tigerish temper in him.

When that day came, she did not recognize it.

It started out calmly enough. Howard had come home the night before from Jamestown, the capital of the colony, a hard day's ride away from Vickery Hall.

Waving aside her offer of a late meal, he disappeared into the room he used at the far end of the hall from hers. His light burned late into the night, and she slept little. His mind was clearly full of scheming, and she dreaded the issue, whatever it could be.

She found out at breakfast.

"I should like you to dress properly to pay a call today," he said. "You received the gowns I had sent from Jamestown?"

"Yes. I would have let you know they had arrived, but I did not know where to send word."

He flashed her a warning glance. She was treading too close to his privacy. "Never mind," he said, deciding to overlook the subject. "You've told me now. We will leave in an hour."

She dared not ask where they were going. Even when they trotted down the long driveway, cleared now of fallen limbs, the long grass suitably mowed, and turned to the left, Howard remained silent.

They passed the boundary stone that marked the end of Vickery land, and now they were passing Mark Tennant's estate. She dared not think of Mark, feeling Howard's eyes turned speculatively on her. Were they going to turn in here, drive up the long lane to Mark's house on the river?

For the first time she began to regret her agreement with Howard—it was hard not to ask questions, not when her very nerves cried out in alarm. Was Howard planning harm for Mark?

She was convinced that Howard had never forgiven what he considered the injuries inflicted upon him by Mark—not only helping her to escape Port Royal, but also before that, in abetting Captain Short, and in exposing Howard's crooked table. It did not occur to him that his own devious schemes had brought about his downfall. It was easier to blame someone else, and he blamed Mark for his ruin in Jamaica.

He said now, "Did you think I was going to deliver you to Tennant? Vain hope, Mercy. I will never, while I live, allow you to leave me. Nor, of course, will I allow you to dally with Mark Tennant."

"I don't suppose you will ever believe me when I say he has never touched me—not in the way you mean."

"No," he said simply. "I don't believe you. It's your fault, you know. Strange how an odd assortment of features can be put together in such a fashion as to drive men mad. Even Tolliver began to believe he could become a man again. You inspire men to heights they never dreamed of," Howard said, laughing without amusement. "And I am the lucky man to own such a galaxy of charm, rolled into one woman."

He leaned forward, speaking in a lower voice so that the coachman couldn't hear. He put his hand on her knee and looked into her face. "Now, Mercy, listen to me. You are a worthless woman, trash, fondled by every man that comes in sight of you, from the Duke on down to the opportunist living in that house we just passed. I don't want you—not after he's pawed you for a week or more on his ship. He's spoiled you for me, and I won't forgive him for that."

Wearily, she repeated, "He never touched me."

"You mean a man can be with you in a narrow space for ten days, and not take you? Don't make me laugh. It's not possible."

"Don't judge every man by yourself," she retorted.

His hand tightened, painful and hot on her knee. "I may forget my promise to you, right now. The coachman would look the other way."

For a breathtaking moment, he stared hypnotically into her eyes. She could see the yellow feline specks moving at the back of his light eyes, reflections of an unhealthy fire consuming him.

His hand moved up her thigh, and he watched her, waiting for her reaction. She stiffened, steeling herself not to show any emotion. Simply his physical nearness sent her nerves crawling along her skin, but she could not show weakness—not to this man, who battened on the unprotected.

The silence grew between them as his hand stroked the cloth of her skirt, making it taut so that he could feel her warm flesh quivering beneath his fingers.

"You will ruin the drape of my gown," she said, glad that her voice stayed fairly steady. "I don't know where we are going, but doubtless you wish me to appear at my best."

He held her eyes for a long moment before he smiled with tight lips and took his hand from her. He sank back opposite her, and said, with an attempt at lightness, "If we had been going to Tennant's, I would have enjoyed seeing you step down from the carriage before his eyes all pink and tousled from my lovemaking. But—another time."

She pulled away and huddled in her corner of the seat, thankful that Howard had released her so easily.

They had reached the next estate along the road beyond Mark Tennant's. The carriage turned in between great stone gateposts, and began the long journey up the driveway to a house hidden by beech trees.

This was Lady Anne York's! She must be mistaken. Howard knew he was not welcome here—Lady Anne had told him so with great firmness that dreadful day when the *Nancy* had docked. She had been too sensitive to send any kind of word to Lady Anne. If she had reassured her as to her own safety, this would have been disloyal to Howard. And while Carmody had no feeling for him, he was yet her husband and she could not denigrate him. A slight flicker of amusement told her that he would take care of destroying his own reputation, and never even know how he did it!

The carriage pulled up before the door, and Howard, not waiting for the assiduous footman who had scampered out of the house, jumped to the ground. Turning, he put his hands around Carmody's waist to lift her from the seat. He smiled down at her as he set her down, looking like a devoted husband in the gentle way he handled her, but the smile did not reach his cold eyes. He said in a low whisper, "Mind what you say. I will be watching every move you make, remember that."

He released her, and tucked a curl beneath her bonnet in a proprietary gesture. "Another time, Mercy, you will not be able to hide behind the appearance of your gown."

Her heart plummeted. The truce was over, and she would have to rely on her wits. They had not been sufficiently sharp before to save her, nor—she feared desperately—would they be now.

Lady Anne, frowning and grim, was already on the portico to greet her uninvited guests. For a dreadful moment, Carmody feared that Lady Anne would send them away, not even inviting her inside. Her cheeks burned in anticipation, and perhaps it was the sight of her obvious embarrassment that made Lady Anne relent.

No matter the reason, her face relaxed its rigid lines and with civility—but not enthusiasm—she opened the door wide and bade them enter.

After that one moment, when Lady Anne balanced on the knife-edge of decision, her welcome was faultless. It turned out that they were not the only visitors Lady Anne was entertaining at the moment. She ushered Carmody into a drawing room that seemed full of people—Lady Anne's nephew Jermyn, and four others whom she barely saw.

For the other person in the room was Mark Tennant, and from the first startled moment when their eyes met across the room, the world and all its denizens fell away into nothing.

If Carmody had any doubts that she had for the first time in her life loved someone, loved a man so much that her life was worthless misery without him, this moment resolved all her doubts.

She tore her glance away from him—remembering that Howard was watching her like a cat at a promising mousehole—and turned to listen to her hostess.

To appear to listen—that was the best she could do. For she could hear her blood thrumming in her ears, feel a tight band holding her breath—and then the moment was over.

"Mr. Worth, and Mrs. Worth—Mrs. Abbott, Mr. Abbott, and you have met Mark Tennant, and my nephew."

She tried to sort them out in her mind, dwelling with absurd attention on each detail as though she would be required to paint their portraits when she returned home.

Vernon Worth, a substantial planter, heavy-jowled with good food, an air of solidity. One would be safe with him.

His willowy wife Genevieve, who obviously adored her husband.

Prudence Abbott, a managing person, bustling, and full of shrewd common sense which shone placidly from her eyes.

And Charles, her husband. Tall, thin, spare, stooped. A scholar, no doubt, who allowed his wife to run their family—she found out later the Abbotts had six half-grown children—their plantation, and probably himself.

And, clinging to the smallest things, so as not to think of the overwhelming presence of Mark Tennant, Carmody bent her mind to her companions. She glanced half fearfully at Howard, but to her relief he seemed not to have noticed her momentary abstraction when she first caught sight of Mark. Perhaps Howard, too, had been taken by surprise. She surmised he would not have brought her here, if he had known she would meet Mark.

But there she was wrong.

"I hoped you would be here, Tennant," Howard said. "I think we are all concerned with some of the things that are happening here in the colony, and it is good to discuss them together."

Howard was aware, then, that Lady Anne had guests, and that there was a serious reason for them to be together. And whatever the reason, Howard had not been invited. Lady Anne had made that clear on the doorstep. Carmody longed to sink into the floor.

Worth said, his voice a deep rumble, "We have been discussing them, it is true. But is it possible that you have something new to add? You see, sir, your reputation has preceded you."

Howard nodded. "I am glad of that, sir," he said untruthfully, "for it saves me some trouble. I know I am new here, but my holdings are substantial, and my tobacco will make a good crop this year."

"Tobacco means much to all of us, Mr. Vickery," commented Lady Anne.

"Of course. What I had in mind was that we need a spokesman to talk for us in the government."

Someone broke in dryly, "We've thought of that."

Howard ignored the interruption. "I have just come from Jamestown, and there is news that may benefit us."

Carmody's mind wandered. She was dimly aware that Howard was putting forth arguments he considered cogent on the subject of government, tobacco, prices, and concerted efforts to control their own affairs without government interference—but his words meant nothing to her. The men listened stolidly, without comment.

She could not look at Mark, not without alerting Howard that her protestations of innocence were, at base, false. Mark had not made love to her, not in the way Howard suspected. But he had made her his, put his seal on her, in a much more subtle way. She ached just to be with him. She longed to be able, without fear, to trace the line of dark hair along his high forehead, to smooth away the frown that lay between his wing-like eyebrows. She was looking at her hands folded in her lap, but she could see clearly the vulnerable, hungry look Mark had allowed to appear on his face before he clamped on the wooden mask he wore now.

Yes, she had seen, for one moment, the same yearning, leaping between them. They belonged together. But she dare not even speak to him lest she rouse Howard's savage jealousy.

Lady Anne served comfits and wine, and at length Howard gave the longed-for signal. Too promptly Carmody rose to her feet. This had been perhaps the longest day in the history of the world, and yet even the longest day seemed to have an end. She preceded Howard from the drawing room, speaking to the people she had met only that afternoon, and meeting with a kindly smile from Genevieve Worth, and an anxious concern from Prudence Abbott, who pressed her hand in friendliness.

If things were different, she would have been glad to know them better, and she thought they accepted her. But she could only falter her farewells, and seek the haven of the coach.

Not until the vehicle was in motion, swaying on the long driveway toward the sandy road, did Howard speak. And then it was only a chuckle at first.

"Set them on their ears, I did!" he crowed. "News to them that I've been busy these weeks."

"Busy doing what?" she responded, automatically.

"I didn't think you were listening. I saw that look between you and him. But don't worry. He won't be around long to enjoy whatever you choose to bestow on him."

Her eyes flew open in sudden alarm. "Not long? What do you mean?"

"Never mind. I noticed that they all seem to accept *you*. Did you notice? I did. You're their kind, all right. I had that figured right."

"What does that mean? It sounds as though you're planning to use me—again. I thought that was all over with."

"Now why would you think that? I use all my assets the best way I can. You're well-born, a gentlewoman, and I have need of those talents. To lend me respectability."

She covered her burning face with her hands. She could not bear what he was doing to her. To take her best virtues, and degrade them to his own purposes, was more than she could abide. To deceive people who were kind to her—

"I won't do it," she said. "I don't know what you're aiming for, but I will be no part of it."

"What is Lady Anne to you?" he countered. "She's just an old crow, who thinks she knows it all. Well, she won't be so high and mighty forever."

"You're crude!"

"You've had a pretty easy life. Suppose you had to scrape for even a crust of bread to keep you alive when you were seven years old? Suppose that you had to fight the rats for rotten garbage in the alleys? No place to sleep at night except under a bridge—there was a whole colony of us underneath the arches of London Bridge. And all the fools just ripe for plucking, with their superior airs and their slow minds. You learn to take what you can get pretty early, I can tell you."

The bald tale of his childhood moved Carmody. Impulsively she touched the back of his hand in sympathy. He turned his palm upward and gently imprisoned her fingers. She was content to leave her hand so, at least for now.

Whatever he had become was not entirely his fault, then, and she must make allowances for him. But she must not let him ruin the innocent people she had met that afternoon. She knew little of them except that they were unsuspecting, little believing the urbane surface of Howard Vickery covered the slum-spawned monster she knew.

And she must pay attention to Howard's plans, understand what he was scheming, and prevent him, if she could.

"If I am to be part of your plans, Howard, shouldn't I know what they are?"

The tentative gambit didn't work. He crushed her fingers before he let them go. "And let you run shouting to everyone what you've found out? Not a bit of it, my sweet. You will do what I tell you from time to time, no more, no less."

He left her to eat dinner alone, and climb the stairs with her candle to bed, later. She was weary, spent with emotion, and even now she could not think how to cope with Howard and his malign designs. She did not even know what he intended.

He had not changed in the slightest since the bad days in Port Royal when she had learned what he was—a gambler, cruel, lashing out at anyone near at hand. Making them suffer, even as he had suffered as a child of the streets in the evil slums of London.

Only by degrading others could he climb upon them and show himself to be superior. Only by twisting them, making them beg—

She sighed hugely, and opened the door to her bedroom. She closed it behind her, and latched it. She touched her candle to the unlit tapers on the table just inside the door.

Crossing the room to the candlestick at her bedside, she lit the two candles there, and then turned—

She shrieked. Howard was sitting in the big chair drawn up before the empty hearth. "Light the rest of the candles, Mercy. We need to talk a bit."

Obediently, with shaking fingers, she lit candles on the mantel, and on the low table next to him. She glanced up as she did the last, seeking to find some clue in his expression. But his eyes were yet in shadow.

"Talk?" she said at last. "What about? And must you lie in wait for me? You could talk to me any time."

"But this is so much more pleasant, is it not? Remove your dress. I should not want to muss it."

So it had come! Blindly she went to the wardrobe and took out her thin robe. Carefully, making the task last as long as possible, she took off her dress, placing it on a scented hanger in the wardrobe. She reached for her robe. From the chair—at least he had not moved!—his voice came lazily. "Take off the rest of your clothes, Mercy."

She clutched the folds of the robe before her and stared at him, with fear-widened eyes. Then she remembered that she was determined not to show him that she was frightened. It would take some doing this time, for she was petrified.

"Shall I do it for you?"

Hastily she turned her back and dropped the rest of her clothing to the floor. She thrust arms into sleeves and tied the robe tight around her waist before she turned to face him again.

"Come here."

Step by step she crossed the room. "Sit there, Mercy." He indicated the chair opposite him and she sat hesitantly on the edge of the seat, poised for a flight she knew would be useless.

"I will not tell you what I have planned. But we will go to Jamestown next week. I have taken a house, fortunately in better condition than this one, and I will expect you to entertain."

"Like Port Royal?" she said. "Lure your victims in?"

"No need for that," he said with a chuckle. "They will

ruin themselves. All I need to do is pick up the pieces. But one word to anyone from you—"

He rose to his feet and jerked her up to stand before him. With rough hands he tore away the belt and drew the robe from her shoulders, letting it fall to the floor. She stirred as though to run, but he held her shoulders tightly and she could not move. Then, his hand still on one shoulder, he set her away from him, as though—she thought, humiliated—she were a slave on the block.

He nodded. "Delectable," he said, letting his gaze run hotly over her. "A prize even for a royal bastard. But a trifle shopworn." His eyes examined her greedily. Her chin up, she forced herself to face him bravely, her mind numb with dread, feeling his attention move, burningly, from the hollow at the base of her throat, down, lingeringly, over her breasts, to the slim waist, and on—

"Was the traitor Duke the first to look at you? The first to explore here, and *here?* Never mind. He's dead, and you are merely—part of my inventory, shall I say?"

He shoved her and she fell into the chair. He strode purposefully to the door, leaving her shivering from fear.

"Another time, Mercy," he laughed. The sound sent an icy finger down her bare spine.

3

DURING Howard's many absences, it had seemed natural for the workmen to come to Carmody for instructions, and she learned much about the running of a Virginia plantation. The operation had its own ways, far different from Oaklands, but equally satisfying to her.

Building something—that was what Mark had spoken of. She could see her work now in that light—but without Mark there was no virtue in it.

After the night when Howard had examined her like a stock buyer, and rejected her, he had not come near her. He had spent that night, she strongly suspected, in one of the slave cabins. At any rate, he had left the house and not returned until dawn.

A few days later—Howard having departed on one of his unscheduled trips—she decided to ride out to look at a tobacco field that had been planted late and was slow in maturing. She rode alone, assuring Quint, the foreman, that she would not leave Vickery land. "I'll be safe enough!"

She was, in spite of herself, learning to love the Virginia land, the sloping fields rolling out before her to wooded hillocks beyond. The oaks would turn a burnished russet in the fall, she was sure, and the beeches—not the copper beeches she knew from home—would turn, so Prissy had told her, pale dry yellow and drop their three-cornered nuts that the pigs loved so much, and fattened on.

Different from Dorset, of course, and harsh in its dampness, surrounded as the peninsula was by waters. But the land responded exuberantly to care, and she felt a countrywoman's oneness with the ground beneath her feet, the vast fields, heavy green leaves flourishing under the sun. The gentle rolling contours of the land.

Only when Howard was gone did she feel secure. He was given to unannounced departures and, worse, unheralded arrivals. His business was a mystery to her, and she dared not ask questions. He had served notice that his promise to let her alone meant nothing, and she knew, quite simply, that she could not live through another such night. Her body might endure, but her spirit would perish. Only here in the open fields could she find some measure of peace.

She stopped to look at the tobacco field. It was maturing fast now, and she was glad she could count on this crop too. The repairs to the house were costing more than she expected, and it was a matter of pride to her now to pay for the extras from the plantation itself. She did not want any more of Howard's money. She suspected that she would not sleep at night if she knew the source of his sudden and unexplained wealth.

Satisfied with her fields, she glanced at the sun. High enough yet—plenty of time before she was expected back at the Hall. At the far limit of the last field was a knoll, covered with tall oaks and shielded by a windbreak hedge of bramble rose at the foot of the rise. She had never ridden that far, and now she set Dally walking in that direction.

The wild brambles had turned red, providing a rich-looking border to the woods. She walked Dally along the edge of the field searching for a way through the hedge. The sun was warm, and the shade in the copse looked invitingly cool.

She had almost given up finding a way in when she saw in the soft ground of the field a hoof print—and just beyond, a barely noticeable gap in the hedge. Someone had been here, and recently, too. Within the last few days.

The hoof print gave her pause. Far from the men at Vickery Hall, no one working in the fields, she was totally alone. She could see through the hedge, but not clearly.

She could—and probably should—go back to fetch Quint. She was still on Vickery land, however, and, foolhardy or not, she had a right to be here.

But as she slipped to the ground and wrapped Dally's reins around a branch, she quailed a moment. She listened intently. The only sound was Dally's snorting protest, and a hoof pawing the ground. Far away a late thrush sang. Overhead one limb creaked against another, sounding startlingly like the rusty hinge on a warped door.

She stepped through the hedge.

She had moved into an alien land. Beech mast covered the floor of the woods with a russet carpet, yielding and soft under her booted foot. The hush of peace descended on her, as though she had left trouble behind her, and evolved into a state of serenity.

And yet it was only the place that was serene. She herself was not. A cabin stood just before her. A deserted cabin? Surprisingly, the door did not droop from its hinges. Nor were the hinges perceptibly rusty. She listened again, but there was only the stillness that unmistakably means that no one is there.

It was odd that no one had mentioned the existence of this cabin. The windows were shuttered, giving the minuscule structure a guarded, enigmatical appearance. What secrets were concealed inside?

The door latch moved under her hand, and, silently, the door opened. The cabin consisted of one room, with a loft of rough-hewn boards reached through an open trap door in the ceiling. It was dark except for light coming from a slit where the roof was damaged.

The room seemed to have been recently swept, although there was no furniture. The table and chairs were long ago taken away for use somewhere else, leaving marks on the board floor. A built-in bunk occupied one wall. A fieldstone hearth with a narrow chimney was opposite.

Empty, but not deserted. It was a private place, with a clandestine atmosphere of its own. A place of rendezvous, she thought—no slave would come near here, certainly not after dark, and the candle, standing on the floor in an old tin plate, was a sure clue that the cabin was visited by night. And tucked in a corner near the chimney, on the floor, where it could easily be missed in the dark, lay a small scarf of expensive quality, such as women wore around the neck of their riding habits. This was a dark green, like her own. She touched her throat to reassure herself that hers was still in place.

Carmody left it there for its owner to retrieve, and emerged from the cabin. Dally was restlessly whickering. She mounted and rode back to the plantation at a slow lope, thinking about what she had seen. At first sight she had thought to find a broken-down building that she could set to use as a storage place for tools, perhaps, or even temporary shelter for a part of the coming crop.

Now, knowing that someone was using it, she knew that she would have to investigate further. As long as she was responsible for the plantation, she could not allow the question to go unresolved. There was the danger of fire, for example—she shuddered at the thought of that foolish little candle in its tin plate.

Carmody drew within sight of the plantation buildings, and made up her mind how to proceed. She would say nothing to anybody, except to Quint. She had come to rely on his sober good judgment, his ability to keep his own counsel. She felt they understood each other, and although they had never put this into words, she thought she could read in his level dark eyes a matching respect for her.

Now he had apparently been watching for her. As she loped up the last slope to the stable, down the wide lane between the fields of tobacco, he popped out of the stable half-door, and came to take the reins as she slid from the saddle.

She was too intent upon her recent experience to notice that he was uneasy. "Quint, I've found a cabin in the woods beyond the west field. You know the one I mean?"

Something flickered in the back of his eyes, as he nodded. But she could not be sure, for when she looked squarely at him, his face was impassive as always.

"Someone's been using the cabin," she said. "Do you know who?"

"No, ma'am." Quint led Dally into the stable and began

to rub her down. His voice was muffled against the mare's flank, and she could not read his expression. "Prissy says it's haunted."

Suddenly she remembered that always the servants knew far more than the master or mistress about what was going on. Somehow she must cross the gap that yawned between them. She waited, but Quint said no more. In his forty years, more or less, he had learned the value of not volunteering information. And while usually this was a help to Carmody, just now it served to work against her.

"Do you think the cabin is haunted, too, Quint?"

His reply was evasive. "Haunts don't need lights, but then haunts make their own rules, too. Might be this ghost is afraid of the dark!" He dissolved into a series of gulping giggles that annoyed Carmody. She watched him working with Dally for a moment. Somewhere in the stable another horse snorted and stamped a hoof on the wooden floor. The smell of hay was dusty in the air, seemingly one with the harvest time that was upon them—the dry turn of the season, ripening all the growing things to maturity before the breath of frost killed them.

She sighed and returned to the house. She saw nothing of the building before her, her mental images being far more real. The clean floor, the expensive scarf—had she been wise to leave it?

She imagined some unnamed woman returning home to find that her scarf was missing. Perhaps it had been given to her by someone—not the man of the rendezvous—who would notice its absence. She would have to return to the cabin to find it. Carmody could picture the panic if the woman dared a return visit to her trysting place and could not find the scarf. Perhaps she would ride back to her home, however far that might be, searching the bramble bushes, the low branching trees, the ground beneath, hunting in vain for the green scarf.

No, Carmody was content—she had done the right thing to leave it there. It was useless to speculate on the identity of the woman using the cabin. Or the man, either. Quite likely the cabin was known to many a neighbor, most of whom had lived in the area much of their lives. And how convenient the surreptitious meeting place would be—on someone else's land, compromising neither one of the couple.

Carmody entered the side door to the house, holding her riding skirt off the ground with one hand, and then pushed open the door to the back entrance hall, which divided the main body of the house from the kitchen wing. It was narrow, holding coats and boots in season, and a mat on which to wipe wet and muddy shoes.

Prissy met her, a troubled look on her face. "Hear you been to the cabin, ma'am."

"How fast news travels, Prissy!" Carmody was not pleased. "I have only this minute returned."

"Word got back 'fore you did." Prissy stood in her way, uncompromising and stern. "Not safe to go there, ma'am. Best give it a wide go-round."

"No? I found it perfectly safe." She chose to ignore the prickling feeling she had known before she resolutely pushed her way through the hedge. "It belongs to this plantation? Then no one has more right there than I do."

"Right, may be," muttered Prissy stubbornly. "It's the haunts that don't pay mind to who owns it."

"Ghosts?" said Carmody, suddenly amused. "Prissy, there aren't any ghosts. Not there at the cabin, anyway."

Skepticism shouted aloud from Prissy's face, and Carmody added, "The haunts are real people."

"No, ma'am."

"Someone has been there in the cabin, Prissy. I tell you I saw a real candle, and a real scarf. And someone swept the cabin with a real broom. I saw the marks on the floor."

"Yes, ma'am." Prissy would not look at her, but shuffled her feet. "But it's a danger place, it is."

"Don't worry, Prissy. I'll be all right." Prissy waddled back to the kitchen, mumbling words that Carmody shrewdly suspected were an incantation against ungodly spirits. First Quint, then Prissy. Her discovery of the cabin had disturbed more than the spirits!

In the entry hall, Carmody stopped. Halfway down the hall were two doors, set opposite each other in the wide walls. One, on the right, led into the mammoth kitchen, with rooms beyond it, stretching down the hall toward the outbuildings beyond. Carmody watched Prissy waddle through into her domain.

The other door opened into the grand entrance hall, just under the graciously wide stairway leading to the upper floor.

She noticed mechanically that the door to the back sitting room was ajar, and a welcome breeze gusted through. She moved toward the stairs.

Howard stood on the bottom step, as though to ascend.

"You're home!"

"Obviously," he said. "And, equally obviously, you have been inspecting our property. You find the crops growing well?"

There was a light in his eyes that she did not like. But she answered pleasantly enough, "Yes. We will have nearly a shipload of tobacco next month. Perhaps we could send it to Bristol this time. I believe we would get a better price there."

"Do as you like. It matters not to me," he said indifferently.

"How long have you been home?"

He eyed her for a stiff moment. She was suddenly reminded of a hare paralyzed by the steady eye of a ferret. Then, she amended quickly—No, more like the ferret itself, ready to spring. But there was no reason for him to pounce on her, she thought, grateful for a clear conscience for once, and in truth she might have imagined his sudden stillness. At any rate, it was gone in a moment, as he waved toward the door.

"I just now came in," he said. "Have you been anxious for my return? Don't answer that, Mercy. I can read your face, as always. Please forgive me, Jamestown was excessively hot and steamy. I must confess, I am looking forward to my bath and a change of clothing."

He bowed courteously and ascended the stairs. Her thoughts ran along familiar lines, now that he was home. Would he be in for dinner? She would have to notify cook. How long would he stay?

And—more importantly—what unpleasant surprises would he have for her this time?

He had allowed her much freedom with the plantation, she realized, and her fear of him, with nothing new to feed upon, was slowly abating. It was not a hard life he had brought her to—but for a breath-taking moment she felt the old knife of memories twist in her breast.

Mark—how much she had lost by not knowing him first! By not being able to come to him, where her heart told her she belonged. There had been a time, aboard ship, when she had clung to Mark in that wildly pitching vessel, and—if she admitted the truth—longed to die there in his arms. It was a foolish thought, but the alternative was this long, long journey without him. Alone, beset by her fear of her husband and the vows she had taken with him, and beset too by the knowledge that even if she were not married, she could not go to Mark with clean hands. She would, of necessity, bring only trouble to him were her identity discovered and her crime brought home to her.

Of the two reasons, she thought realistically, the bond between her and Howard was the weaker, and often during the solitary nights she could have forgotten it altogether.

She was dimly aware, as she clung to the newel post, letting her grief for what might have been possess her for a time, that a servant had gone upstairs to Howard, bearing a great pitcher of hot water. She wondered idly how the servants had managed so quickly to divine his wishes and bring the needed water for his bath. But, of course, Landers, Howard's manservant, would harry them on. At last she climbed the stairs, and regained the privacy of her own room.

Howard had returned, he told her later, to inform her of his Jamestown activities. "When the new Governor arrives from London, we will want to be in residence. I have taken a house—I thought you were not listening when I told you before."

"Oh, Howard! Not moving again!"

"No, no. Just for the season, Mercy. And not for several weeks yet. But I thought it well to make sure of a house suitable for my noble lady—well-born, gracious and courteous—a credit to me and a fitting ornament of the Governor's court." His vulpine grin flashed momentarily. "You see, my dear, your usefulness is just beginning."

It was useless to protest. She kept her eyes fastened on her plate but her food remained untouched as he continued. "The house is brick, of course. I will not live in a wooden house—not in Jamestown."

"Why not?"

"It's been burned twice. Once in the early days, and again, no more than fifteen years ago, by rebels."

He went on to describe the house. "Already furnished, my dear, so that you need take only the slaves you will want. You can make do with whatever china and linen is there."

"Who lived in the house before?" she asked, pretending interest. "It might give me an idea of how well stocked it is."

"Some Englishman who thought the governor's staff was a permanent fixture, instead of coming and going at the whim of the planters. The last governor left in something of a hurry, and his deputy, whose house we have, must have scampered for safety with only what he wore on his back."

"I thought the deputy governor was a local man, and not from London."

He nodded approvingly. "I am glad to see you are keeping your ears open. I told you that you could be a great help to me. I wonder whether I should—no, I think I will not confide in you, not just yet. Your face is far too expressive, and I dare not chance my plans being revealed prematurely."

Tartly, she retorted, "That must mean that your schemes are not suitable for open knowledge."

"How well you know me, my sweet. Pray ring for more coffee."

She rang, automatically, and Prissy appeared with a pewter pitcher of steaming coffee. When she had departed again, Carmody said, "I imagine that you want to be deputy governor. But for the life of me, I can't imagine why."

"You are quite wrong, my dear. It is Mark Tennant who wants the appointment."

Heart pounding, she leaned against the straight back of the chair. "But what good is it? Simply an ordinary job full of troubles and no rewards, is it not?"

"My dear, leave the reasoning to me. Suffice it for you to know that I will not seek the office. Let Mark work for it, let him make his plans for all the good deeds he is going to perform for the Virginia planters. I will support him to the best of my ability. And I ask you to remember that. I will do everything I can for Tennant, up to a point. Even you can find no fault in that."

The messenger arrived only hours after Howard had ridden away. This time he had told her he would be gone for several days—"Try not to spend too much money," he advised her. "I'll need everything for a certain investment."

She knew better than to ask questions, and she truly did not want to know. Whatever investment he planned to make could only mean some kind of trouble.

The rider came in at a canter. "Lady Anne York wishes you to call upon her," the man Flint told her. "She asked me to say please come, and please hurry."

"Hurry! Is she ill?"

"No, ma'am. There are some ladies with her, and I was told to say they would like you to spend the afternoon with them."

If Howard's plans had not unsettled her, she might have thought twice about accepting such an informal invitation. It bore every earmark of ill-considered haste, not like her impression of Lady Anne at all.

But anything was better than the company of her own thoughts. She hurried to change into her riding dress, tied on her dark green scarf, and mounted Dally to make the short journey to Lady Anne's.

To her surprise, Flint led her not to the front steps, but around the side of the building to a door almost hidden in creeping ivy. She glanced askance at the servant, but his expression was unchanged. He opened the door for her, and, hesitantly, she stepped inside. Lady Anne's arrangements were odd, at the very least!

Lady Anne herself was just inside the door. "My dear, I am so glad you agreed to come. I did not quite know what to say in my message, and left it only to your kindness to indulge an old woman."

She led the way into the entry hall, through a door behind the staircase. From a room beyond, at the front of the house, she could hear women's voices, rising in genteel hubbub, over the clink of teacups. At least that part of her hostess's message was accurate—there were ladies with her.

But Lady Anne turned aside and opened a door just opposite the place where they stood. "In here, my dear," she said, "you will find someone whose acquaintance you already have made."

Carmody entered alone, and the door closed on her heels. Mark stood at the window.

"Mark!"

He turned and held out his hands. She rushed to take them, and in an instant she was engulfed in his arms, his coat rough against her cheek.

He stroked her hair, tumbling off her riding hat to the floor, her scarf slipping after it. Neither of them noticed. A long time passed before he gently set her aside and looked, smiling, into her upturned face.

"I must know that you are all right," he said softly, "before I go."

"Go? Oh, Mark, where?"

"You should ask why, shouldn't you?"

"All right, then," she said, searching his face for some indication of his thought, pulling him down to sit beside her on a sofa. "Why?"

"Because I can't abide being so near to you, and yet knowing you are beyond my reach. Not to see you every day, waking and sleeping, in happiness, even sharing your sorrow—" He broke off and laughed briefly. "Sounds like a marriage vow, doesn't it? My thoughts do run along that line."

Her hand moved convulsively in his. "But, Mark—"

"Hush. I know. But I have decided that I must put half the earth between us, before I will feel safe from temptation." He stroked her fingers ceaselessly. "If you knew how many times I have saddled my horse to ride over to see that you are unharmed."

"Oh, no!" she cried out in alarm. "That wouldn't help."

After a moment, he said thoughtfully, "That's what I surmised. You see, I remember the bruises, the night we met. Dark, ugly." His face twisted. "My very existence rubs him, doesn't it? Don't answer me, your face reveals a great deal. And I must not give you too many secrets to conceal."

"When are you leaving?" she asked at last, her voice so tiny he could hardly hear it.

"With the tide. Lady Anne was kind enough to furnish me this opportunity to see you, in a way that would be safe for you." He searched her eyes. "You *are* safe?"

"Oh, yes. He—leaves me alone," she said, not quite truthfully. But she dared not think of that frightening night, after their visit to this very house, when Howard had threatened to violate her, only to toss her aside like a torn shift. Mark needed no unhappy thoughts to keep him company on his long journey.

"Mercy," he said, "will you go with me? We've sailed together before, and you didn't have to worry about fighting me off, did you? Could you come with me this time?"

"Sail with you?" Her heart leaped with joy at the thought—and, laughing, she daringly added, "You'd probably have to fight *me* off!"

He lifted her fingers to his lips and kissed them one by one, giving her time to think. Too much time. "I can't go, Mark," she said. "Believe me, I would bring you only unhappiness, and even worse."

"How could you?" he argued. "We'll go first to Santiago, around the Horn. Then to the islands beyond. He could never find you. And I would protect you well against him."

But who can protect me against the ghost of Waldo? she thought mournfully, and could not speak.

"I would not urge you to break your marriage vows, believe me. This must be your decision. But those vows hardly exist, do they? We belong together. You know that?" He lifted her chin so that she was forced to look at him. "Don't cry," he said gently. "I'll find a way to—"

He stopped short and she was grateful. She could not go with him, carrying her crime with her, so that always she would look over her shoulder in a strange port, looking for the minions of the law, set upon her trail by Howard in his savage jealousy.

She could not bring disaster upon the man she loved— the only man she would ever love. This, at least, she could do for him—send him away, far out of Howard's reach, from the consequences of her own murderous act. Set him free of her.

"My darling, look at me. Mercy, you belong to me if ever a woman belonged to a man. One day, we'll be together, no matter what I have—" He broke off sharply. "Enough," he said, pulling her to her feet and holding her for an instant. "Wish me well." He kissed her gently, lingeringly, on her forehead, and in a few quick steps was gone.

The rest of her afternoon was, indeed, spent among the teacups with Lady Anne's invited guests. Prudence Abbott, Genevieve Worth, Bel Gannon, Lady Anne herself. The chatter was mild, general, and totally beyond Carmody. She heard, but did not listen to, talk of crops, of children, of house slaves, of husbands' peccadillos—I could tell them a thing or two, she thought darkly, about that.

The pulse that beat in her temples, the breaths she took, ragged at the edges, all spoke of grief. Mark was going over the sea, as far away from her as he could. And, eventually, she knew she would rejoice that Mark was far away from whatever Howard might plan to do to him, that Mark was safe. But just now, she was aware only of irreparable loss.

The tobacco crop was ready for shipping. The ships that contracted for carrying to England came to rest at Tennant's wharves, and loaded produce brought long distances from inland plantations and warehouses. But the local planters—Lady Anne, Mark himself or, now, Digby, Vernon Worth, Arthur Gannon, and Carmody—planned to load directly from their wagons into the ships.

Carmody planned to oversee the loading at the Vickery barns, but Howard insisted that she join him at the wharves.

"You said you had no interest in the crops!" she protested.

"That was then. Now I want to see the tobacco aboard," he told her. "Perhaps I can make a deal with the captain."

"What kind of deal?"

"I need you along to see that I don't get cheated," Howard said. "See how valuable you are to me? The captain may not want to give me a fair price."

"You're going to sell the tobacco outright?"

"Of course. Money in the hand is better than a fine crop at the bottom of the sea. Besides, I need the money right now."

"I counted on that money to run the plantation!"

"Too bad. I have need of it."

"For that investment, I suppose!"

His eyes flashed and she knew she had gone too far. He said, "Exactly so."

The broad landing area was alive with people: the workers trudging along in their singsong work train; the ships' crews stretching their legs, while the stevedores stowed the produce; small boys, women, dogs from the neighboring plantations down to catch a glimpse of the excitement when the great ships came in to dock, and when they pulled anchor and warped out into the swift ocean-going current of the river.

Howard went in search of a ship's captain he knew, and Carmody was left alone. The wagons would be coming soon, but her work was over now. Howard would take care of the delivery of the crop, and pocket the proceeds. She wondered, idly, what his investment might be. Land? Shares in an ocean-going ship? He was so secretive about everything!

Vernon Worth and his wife came to chat for a bit, but,

upon seeing Howard returning to her side, they made excuses to move on. She must get used to it, Carmody thought with wry humor—any friends she might make would fade away like morning fog when Howard arrived.

Charles Abbott and Lady Anne were together. Carmody, alone, slipped over to greet Lady Anne. "Thank you," she said quietly, and Lady Anne understood at once.

Howard joined them, visibly jubilant, and Carmody guessed he had sold the tobacco without her help. Lady Anne chose not to leave at his arrival, but she spoke only to Carmody. "I so enjoyed our visit the other day, with Mistress Worth, and the others. You were kind to join us. We need a young face at our teacup gossips."

Howard was alert at once. "A tea party? And only for women! Too bad. I am sure we would all enjoy an evening of visiting, one day soon." His hint to Lady Anne was broad and blatant, but she was not to be cozened into offering the man she despised an invitation to her home. She looked levelly at him and snubbed him. "Good day, Mr. Vickery. And to you, my dear," she said, turning to Carmody. "By the way, you left your green scarf behind. I remembered to bring it with me today, on the chance that I might see you and have an opportunity to return it."

So saying, she handed Carmody the folded green cloth. Carmody thrust it into a pocket, saying farewells. She could not remember leaving it behind at Lady Anne's, but her mind had been so full of Mark and his imminent departure that she could have left more than a scarf behind and never missed it.

Inevitably, it reminded her of the green scarf in the cabin, and the unprotected candle in the holder on the floor. The woods surrounding the cabin were dry as tinder, and fire was a worry always.

Three days after meeting at the Tennant wharves, Carmody finally hit upon a plan to safeguard the cabin.

"Quint, we need the cabin on the knoll to store tools. Too far to bring the plows back every night until we get the west fields sown again."

Quint eyed her sullenly. "Can't."

"Can't? Why not? Cut a wider gap through the hedge."

"Cabin's got haunts. No man will go near it."

"Only people—real, living, breathing humans—have been using the cabin!"

He refused to answer. He also refused to move the farm tools into the cabin. "No, *ma'am!*" he said. "*I'm* not afraid, but I can't do it alone. And they just won't go. No help from them."

She suspected Quint was more fearful than he would admit, but she knew he was immovable. "All right, I'll prove the cabin's not haunted. Next time a light is seen there, tell me. We'll all go together, and you'll see. Real people, Quint."

It never occurred to her that Quint and the others might be more afraid of real people—the ones meeting in the cabin—than of ghosts.

Her original plan, to fill the cabin with smaller implements, making it unusable for trysts, had failed. But if a posse of a dozen men noisily descended in the night upon the woods, the lovers would have time to escape, and be warned against returning. She was well pleased with the way it was turning out.

That afternoon, three hours after Howard left the house, she heard a noisy tumult coming from the drive. The very tone of the voices she could hear told her something was amiss. She ran to the door.

Vernon Worth stood on the porch, his hand raised to knock on the door. His face was grave. His broad shoulders blocked her view of what was behind him. "I'm sorry, Mistress Vickery, to bring you sad news. Your husband has been shot."

"Shot! But how—"

Carmody pressed trembling fingers to her lips to still the insistent questions that prodded for expression. She opened the door wide to admit two servants, bearing Howard on a makeshift trestle. He was unconscious, his head lolling to one side, and blood still welled from a wound near his heart, although he was alive.

The hall was suddenly full of servants, wide-eyed with curiosity, nearly exploding with excitement, drawn by that unexplained swiftness that spreads bad news with the wind.

Carmody spoke briskly. "Prissy, we'll make up a bed in the study there. Call Thill to help you. Bring the cot from the closet under the stairs. Landers, show these men where to take Mr. Vickery. Gently as you can. No, Jenny, he's not dead, stop wailing so. The rest of you, go on about your tasks. You'll know what's happened as soon as I know. Dess, run upstairs and get my basket, you know the one, with the salves in it. Hurry now!"

In a short time the hall was emptied again. Landers was already directing the trestle bearers to the study. Carmody turned to the two neighbors who were still standing in the hall, clearly troubled and worried, and equally uncertain as to whether to go or to leave.

"Mr. Worth, Mr. Gannon. Thank you for bringing my husband home. I must see to him now, but I beg you to stay. You must know I have much to ask."

Vernon Worth, as she expected, spoke for them both. Indeed, glancing from the corner of her eye at his companion, she wondered whether Arthur Gannon could have spoken at all. He appeared ready to drop, probably from sheer nervous excitement. Certainly he was strung up tight as a violin string, and one more turn of the peg might break him.

Vernon said with heavy dignity, "We will stay, of course, until you can tell us the extent of the—the damage. We will try not to get in your way." She had not thought Howard was so well-liked that two of his neighbors would wait, fingers fidgeting on hat brims, until they were assured he would be out of danger.

"I must go," she said quickly. "You may find the drawing room comfortable. Through that door. I will send someone with refreshments."

In the room Howard called his office, Carmody found Prissy and Thill finishing up, the cot now spread with fresh linen. The clean, cool scent of lavender drifted through the room from the stored sheets, but she was only half-conscious of the fragrance.

"Thank you," she said to Prissy. "The gentlemen are in

the drawing room. Will you see to their needs? And then come back."

Carmody dropped to her knees beside Howard. The pallor of his face was alarming enough, but it was the deep red stain, still spreading as she watched, that riveted her attention. He had lost a lot of blood, and that could be dangerous.

"Landers, help me here. I dare not move him until we stop the bleeding."

He held the heavy cloth of the jacket as she snipped away at the fabric, having difficulty where the blood had matted the fibers. The next half hour went by. She was concentrating entirely on the wound, bared at last—an ugly black hole that was like an unwinking malevolent eye in the reddening flesh around it. She must work fast to counteract the possibility of infection—

Only when she had applied the cloth binding over the tight pressure bandage, to keep it securely in place and staunch the bleeding, did she look up to thank Landers and Dess. Then she saw the two servants who had brought Howard home. She did not know them, and in fact she had forgotten they were there.

Struggling to her feet, easing the cramp in her knees from her long kneeling, she thanked them for their help. "He will be all right. I think the salve will prevent infection. As you noticed, the bullet passed clear through without touching bone, a very fortunate occurrence. Landers, can you see that these men receive some refreshment? I am sure they must be weary."

The men moved Howard to the cot, where he lay unconscious, breathing heavily. He would wake after an hour or so, and he would feel the pain from his shoulder then, severely. She studied the face, so innocent in sleep, all the lines that showed the character—or lack of it—of the man erased, and now he seemed to her to look as he must have done when he was twenty. If she had known him then, would things have been different between them?

There was no way she could tell. But that was in the past, and he could not go back. Even as she watched, some deep pain must have touched him in his sleep, for he frowned and shook his head slightly, denying something. Perhaps he was reliving the moment just before he was shot.

Her thoughts took an abrupt turning. He had been shot at very close range, and that meant Howard knew who had shot him, and, no doubt, also knew why.

She signalled for Dess.

Dess said, shyly, "He'll be all right, won't he?"

"Yes, he will." She wondered whether the maid had a real affection for Howard, but she couldn't ask.

"It's only that if he die we all get sold again," Dess volunteered.

Carmody hadn't thought of that. "Don't worry," she said. "He will be all right. Can you watch beside him for a while? I must go see Mr. Worth, if he hasn't become impatient with waiting."

Vernon Worth gave no sign of impatience when she entered the drawing room. Instead, he crossed the room to meet her.

"How is he?" he asked at once. Then, searching her face, he said, "I don't know what I'm thinking of. Let me ring for something for you. No? Then, at least sit here. This has been a great shock to you, to open the door and find your husband in such condition."

She sank into the chair he indicated, and suddenly realized that her emotions had wearied her as much as the task of caring for Howard. Shock, yes. And a great worry. What had Howard done now? What hornets' nest had he prodded with a too-short pole?

She realized that Mr. Worth was talking quietly, giving her time to recover her self-possession. She managed to gather her dignity and smiled at him by way of thanks.

He was a square-shouldered, heavy man whose bulk made his height unnoticeable. But he was fully as tall as Howard. His chin was strong and square and gave one the feeling of strength, and, in some strange way, of integrity. So, too, did his habit of speaking seldom, but to the point. And his slate grey eyes watched her with genuine concern; he pulled a chair near to her.

"Ah, you are better," he said with real satisfaction.

"Yes, thank you. I owe you and Mr. Gannon a debt for finding my husband and bringing him to me with such care. Am I wrong as to how it happened? Did you in truth find him?"

"I can tell you what I saw," said Mr. Worth, suddenly evasive. "I found Mr. Gannon on my drive, riding in haste to fetch me. He gave me to understand that the situation was extremely serious, so I called two of my men. They laid a door over a cart, and we followed where Gannon led us."

"Yes?" she prompted him. "And you found Howard?"

Her glance strayed to Gannon, standing with his back to her, looking out of the window. But, noticing the dejected sag of the man's thin shoulders, she guessed that he saw little but his own thoughts.

"We found Howard." Mr. Worth hesitated, glancing at his friend at the window, then went on, more deliberately, more heavily. "He was along the line between the Tennant place and your own land."

"Shot?" The word was a mere whisper.

"Shot."

"But then, how did Mr. Gannon happen upon him?" she said slowly. She consulted the map she drew in her head of the various plantations. Vickery land adjacent to Tennant land, near the wooded knoll hiding the cabin. Beyond Tennant land, Lady Anne's acres, and on up the valley lay the others—Gannon's among them. But Vernon Worth lived to the east, in the opposite direction.

"And why not come directly here to tell me? To get help?" It seemed to her that Gannon must have gone past Vickery Hall to seek help from Vernon Worth.

"I think Arthur wants to tell you something." said Mr. Worth.

His voice had authority in it now, and suddenly Carmody was seized with a feeling that what lay heavily in the air in this room, what knowledge the two men shared would in a moment be hers, as well—a knowledge that might very well be one more faggot added to the pyre of shame that Howard had burdened her with.

She knew no details—but somewhere deep inside her

mind was the conviction that she could express only in the simple phrase: What has he done now?

"Yes, Mr. Gannon?" She turned her silvery eyes to watch him, feeling a quivering of sheer nervous dread inside her. He turned from the window, and she almost gasped when she saw his face. The dark eyes were sunken beneath his bushy eyebrows, the cheeks unnaturally hollowed. He looked as if he had not slept for days, waking through the night hours to feed his spirit upon some nauseous fare.

"I shot him."

A long time went by before Carmody could speak. Then, she could merely echo his words. "*You* shot him? Why?"

She could think of myriad answers to her simple questions. She discarded one after another. But none of the answers she considered was as fantastic to her mind as the one Gannon spoke now.

"He took my wife away from me."

For an astounded moment, Carmody could not bring to mind a clear picture of Bel Gannon. Then arose the pale pointed face underneath a cloud of fair hair, china-blue eyes with a perpetual expression of astonishment in them—

The idea was so outlandish that she barely managed to restrain the rude retort that trembled on her lips. Impossible! she would have said. But then she reflected, seeing the genuine worry in the usually calm eyes of Gannon's attorney and friend, Vernon Worth, that it was entirely possible that Howard, for whatever twisted motive he might summon up, had seduced that fluffy, addlepated little woman. Surely, Carmody thought, I know Howard well enough to know that seeing Gannon's misery would be reward enough for him.

But she was a loyal wife, if far from loving, and she told the men who stood before her, looming over her as she sat in her low chair, that she was sure Mr. Gannon must be mistaken, that Howard was too much the man of honor to treat a neighbor so, and, as she showed them out of the front door, she said in dismissal, "I'm sure you're wrong."

Mr. Worth said, "I hope so. A scandal would be a bad thing just now. With the new governor coming, we must not show a rift in our ranks."

When, several days later, Carmody related the details of this interview to a convalescent Howard, he laughed aloud. "I wish I had seen that," he said. "You lie so poorly I'm sure you convinced nobody."

"Don't you care?"

"Only for my reputation," he said. "To have anyone think that I would spend a second glance on a creature like that vixen—did you ever notice how much like a fox she does look?—is an insult to me. My taste runs to finer quality than that."

Something in the tone of his voice jarred her. Not the crude words, nor the crass, animal description of Bel Gannon—but a more subtle note that she had heard before, a note that told her, as if he had screamed it aloud from the gallery, that he lied. And he called her a poor liar!

She turned startled eyes toward him. He was staring fixedly at her. "After all," he said coarsely, "the seal of a Stuart, even a bastard Stuart, assures the presence of quality. And I will say, I have no complaints."

Her blood chilled and sank to her toes. She watched him like a rabbit spellbound by a ferret. She could not move, not even breathe. In a moment he would call her murderer, and then—

"Howard—" she said faintly, hating the unbidden note of pleading in her voice.

"Bring me some laudanum," he ordered sharply. "My shoulder hurts like fury."

It was two weeks later that Landers came to find her alone in the drawing room after dinner. She had lit the candles to dispel a melancholy that was more mental than actual, and the fire burned cheerily on the hearth. But her thoughts were gloom-filled. Howard was much recovered, nearly back to normal. Saying he was weary, he had gone to bed early this night. She could be grateful for that, she supposed.

Her thoughts moved along paths that in the past weeks had become well-trodden. Mark was safe. Nothing Howard could devise could touch Mark, aboard one of his great ships, sailing south on the trade winds. And she could be at his side at the rail, his arm securely holding her—

She deliberately buried her memories. Memories of denial, dreams of bliss that would never be hers. But they came to life again and again, and again.

She could not bear her thoughts. So when Landers appeared in the doorway, he provided a welcome interruption.

He seemed consumed with suppressed excitement as he spoke. "Mistress Vickery, the haunt's there again!"

Then, seeing she was puzzled, he explained, "The light's showing at the haunted cabin again. The girls down below are so scared they're under the beds with the covers pulled over their heads." He lost his assurance. "You did tell Quint, ma'am, that you wanted to be told the next time the ghosts showed up."

She seized upon the diversion as a welcome alternative to her mood of the evening. "Yes, Landers. I'm afraid my thoughts were ill company, and I was not thinking clearly. Yes, of course. Saddle Dally for me, and I'll go at once. Rouse the men to go along. We'll see what ghosts there are, and I wager they have hands and feet like the rest of us!"

Her spirits lightening, she hurried up the stairs to her own room. Hastily she slid out of her stiff gown and donned the welcome riding habit. She dressed with nervous fingers, and hurried to where Landers was waiting at the stables.

Carmody kept her horse at a slow pace down the lane, with Landers trotting just behind her. She had begun to think that she might be foolish, jogging out into the dark night with only the stars overhead for illumination, to investigate a so-called ghost light in a deserted cabin in the woods.

She peered at Landers. It was too dark to see his face, but she became aware that his hands fidgeted on the reins and he twisted often in the saddle to look over his shoulder. Yes, Landers was excessively nervous. No doubt he wished now he had not been so eager to bring her the news she had asked for.

"Where are Quint and the rest?" she asked.

"They're coming. Quint's got to do some strong talking."

"You lead the way," she instructed, after a moment. "I'm not sure of the lane in the dark." Besides, although she didn't put it into words, ahead of her he was not so apt to turn and gallop back to the stables, leaving her alone in the windy dark.

Following the broad, bulky shape of the field horse and its rider made the journey easier, and now her eyes were used to the dark.

The wind was rising, shaking the autumn leaves into clattering sound, like a thousand soldiers stamping and murmuring, far away. Overhead, against the sky, the oaks moved, fitfully blacking out the lower stars. Landers was walking his horse. They must be getting close to the cabin. She peered ahead. The woods loomed, a darker shadow, and she knew where she was. Landers stopped.

"We'd best walk from here. Don't want to give notice that a whole army is coming," he said with a rare flash of humor.

She let him tie her mare. She kept her eyes fixed upon the woods ahead, to keep her bearings. There was no light.

Thre must be a light in the cabin! She had not delayed so long that the temporary tenants would have finished their dubious business and departed, she was sure. And if "they" had come on horseback, she believed she would have heard them departing.

Had they heard her and Landers? In that event, the quest for the ghost lights would be fruitless this time, but perhaps the intended warning would suffice.

Carmody moved ahead now to the end of the lane. With hands stretched out before her, she realized painfully that she had found the thorn hedge. She crept stealthily along it, her right hand keeping in touch with the hedge. The woods spoke with their own voices in the wind, a deeper, sonorous note underlying the crisp chatter of fallen leaves. Once something passed along her hip, as though someone had flung tiny pebbles at her, and she started, smothering the cry of alarm that sprang to her lips. But it was only the whirling wind, sportively playing with fallen leaves, spraying them across her riding skirt.

She breathed again.

Far away a horse whickered. The sound was cut off sharply, as though a compelling hand had been clamped over nostrils. Landers was still with the horses, then! She wished she had chosen a braver escort. Where were Quint and the men? She looked back the way they had come. Far away she thought she heard a voice, quickly muted. They must be on the way.

She edged along until her hand met emptiness. She had found the gap in the hedge. Easily, too—a good omen.

And there was the cabin.

She stood before the building, irresolute, uncertain of her next step. She could see now why the light had not shown before. The shutters had been closed—a sensible precaution.

But no precaution could prevent the candlelight from outlining the ill-fitting door in a yellow rectangle.

Should she knock? Should she simply walk in unannounced? What would she find? No, no, she told herself. Not *what*. Who. She stepped boldly to the door. Under the slight pressure of her knuckles, raised to rap, the door swung open.

She blinked in the light of the candles—after the darkness outside, it seemed brilliant. And she must be dreaming, she thought unsteadily, for Mark's dear face floated before her, as it so often did in her sleep.

"Close the door, Mercy," said Mark's loved voice, the amusement always there, but this time betraying also a shakiness that spoke of much more.

Obediently, she closed the door, setting the latch down hard. The click exploding into the silent room told her she was awake, and Mark was truly here.

He held his arms wide, welcoming, inviting, and with an inarticulate cry, she flew to him.

"Oh, Mark!" she cried, half sobbing. "I've missed you so! Why didn't you let me know you were back? But of course, you couldn't!"

She knew she was not making sense, but the ultimate sense was to be here, safe in the arms of her beloved Mark. At first, she sensed a little restraint, but it was gone before she could be sure. She drew back to look up into his dear face. There were new lines around the corners of his eyes under the flyaway brows, speaking perhaps of long days at sea looking at far horizons. But the new lines bracketing his full mouth told of battles of self-discipline, of opposing forces warring within him. She traced them with her finger, half-fearful lest Mark prove an apparition after all.

"Nay, love, I'm real enough. Can't you tell?" He held her close then, caressing her shoulders, bringing his strong hands down her back to her hips, pressing her close against him.

"Mark, darling, we mustn't—I'm so confused—" she protested, half laughing, but she did not move away. Not until he murmured a word in her ear that slowly crept into her mind, bringing an aura of poison with it. "Note?" she said. She pulled back and peered at him through narrowed lids. "I thought you had sailed. I would not have sent you a note."

"I did sail. I got as far as Trinidad, and I knew I couldn't stand to be away from you. So I came back."

"But you spoke of a note."

"The note that came by messenger this afternoon. Telling me you would meet me here, I—" He clutched her arm. "You didn't write the note?"

"Didn't you know? But of course, you wouldn't know my hand."

"I don't like this." He frowned. They had been talking in low voices, but now he whispered. "Were you followed?"

She shook her head. "Only Landers. And that," she concluded bitterly, "should have told me everything. He is Howard's man."

"A trap, then," said Mark grimly. "I must get you out of here."

She watched him, her eyes wide, as he considered what to do. He picked up a candle, and handed it to her. "You have a right to be here, on your own land. I'm the intruder. Blow out the candle, and I'll slip through the door in the dark. You'll be all right then."

"Mark, I'm so sorry."

"Don't worry," he whispered. "I should have asked questions. But all I could think of was that you wanted me as much as I wanted you. Now—"

"I was tricked too, Mark. But I thought you were safe, out of his reach." And while she gazed at him, realizing Howard's trickery but not understanding why, the door behind Mark was smashed open, banging against the wall, and she knew the answer.

"Here is the proof I promised you," said Howard Vickery, his voice gritty as sand, his words hard as boulders. "You see, Gannon? Jermyn? It was not Gannon's wife and I here in this cabin, in secret illicit rendezvous. It was my own wife and that impeccable man of honor, the peerless Mark Tennant!"

4

THE moon hung in the east like a golden ball, as the ill-assorted quartet rode away from the cabin. The moonlight touched the tops of the trees with amber and its effulgence lighted the path before them.

Carmody huddled in her saddle, turning up her collar to hide her face. And yet it was an automatic gesture, useless under the circumstances. Far louder in her mind were the hoofbeats of the four horses, muffled in the loose sand, like funeral drums muted in mourning.

Appropriate enough, she thought—mourning for the trouble she had brought upon Mark, riding, now, no doubt, hard for his own stable. But while her mind registered the muffled beat of the horses, the spasmodic and brief talk around her, it was only a part of her that knew these things.

There were questions—how did Howard know she was at the cabin? The answer, of course—he planned the rendezvous, forging a false note to Mark, sending Landers to lure her to the cabin. Why? To smear Mark, and to show himself in the role of an aggrieved innocent.

Questions, all of them with answers. And a part of her wondered, and listened, and filed away what it heard to come back later.

Just now, even the nerves along her skin clamored, and her heart pounded as though it would burst, shattering her into a thousand grieving bits. She felt she was being shaken into pieces, literally, by her screaming nerves, her throbbing emotions, like a swelling wave still poised, unspent. Her desperate thoughts.

And yet, outwardly, she must present no new and alarming aspect to the three men who rode close to her, almost as though guarding her as their prisoner. As prisoner she was. Now and forevermore.

Gannon broke the silence. "Wish Vernon had come with us."

Howard agreed. "But we're enough. You asked for proof, Gannon. You were the one who must be convinced, not Worth. But Jermyn too can testify, if need be."

Jermyn cried out sharply. "Testify! I can't do that!"

"No need to," soothed Howard. "I think we must all understand that this is not to go any farther. Now that I think of it, I believe it was wise not to have Worth with us. As it is, we can keep this secret among the three of us. And surely Tennant won't say anything. He dare not."

Gannon said stubbornly, "I think we ought to tell the whole countryside about this."

"No!" said Jermyn, too loudly.

"I agree," said Howard pacifically. "Everyone has secrets—not harmful secrets, but just nobody else's business. You agree, Jermyn?"

The part of Carmody that was listening thought that Howard was in an unexpectedly jovial mood, displaying little of the righteous indignation of a man nearly wearing a cuckold's horns.

They said little more until they reached the lane that would lead Gannon and Jermyn to the main road. The moon shone now, much paler, but far more illuminating than the misty orange of its first rising.

"Remember," said Howard, as they paused before parting, "we have a new governor coming, one of the Puritan kind. And his wife is even worse, so I'm told. The Dutch king has made his mark already." He chuckled. "We must all hang together on this, and keep our scandals to ourselves. Remember, Gannon, it's my wife who is involved this time. And you have already indicated that shooting is the proper act for a gentleman to protect his own good name."

"I said I was sorry," mumbled Gannon, reining his horse into the new path. It seemed almost as though he were sorry to be wrong—as though he thought Howard was a fit target for his bullet, even though he weren't guilty of this particular offense.

"Then we're agreed. Not a word of this to anyone."

Satisfied with the mumbled assents from his witnesses, Howard bade them farewell and prodded his horse into motion, touching Dally's flank on the way. Carmody and Howard rode the rest of the way in total silence, except for an odd snatch of humming now and then from her supposedly betrayed husband.

Not until she regained her own room, with Howard following just behind her, did she face him. She lit the candle on the bedside table. She became aware of the strangely triumphant expression in his eyes, a victory he could not hide, and knew she must be wary. He had prepared a pitfall somewhere here, and she must not fall into the trap.

"How could you shame me this way?" she began in a low voice that trembled in spite of all she could do to control it. "How could you—"

"Break in on my dearly beloved wife in such a compromising situation?"

"Oh, Howard!" she cried in disgust. "That's not true!"

"Oh, I agree. You did disappoint me, my dear. I expected to find you *in flagrante delicto,* I think the term is. I should have enjoyed your guilty protests, aimed at covering up the bare truth."

"Your jesting is ill-timed."

"Quite right. I could not resist. But surely, Mercy, you must see that I could not have Arthur Gannon spreading the rumor that I had seduced his wife, now could I? And if you had my interests at heart, as one must confess one expects from one's wife, you would have understood that."

"But it is the truth, isn't it? That you were meeting Bel there?"

"Not only there, my dear. Anywhere else the foolish woman wanted. I must confess, though, I don't find the floor of a hovel as appealing a setting as I hoped you and your friend would. I wonder why you held back?"

"You couldn't begin to understand." The blandness with which Howard was treating this deception he was perpetrating on Gannon stirred her, and she clawed verbally as instinctively as breathing. "You haven't the capacity to understand. And the terrible thing is that you don't even feel guilty. You don't care that you've lied to Gannon, that you sneer at the woman you've brought so low as to care for you. I assume Bel must have convinced herself she's in love with you. Surely nobody could endure you simply as a pastime."

She had lost all caution, and she could have bitten her tongue as she saw the effect her words had on Howard. From being bland, seemingly uncaring, now his brow darkened and he bent a fierce look upon her that portended nothing good.

"And you don't have the excuse of loving me, do you? And yet you endure me. It can't be your vows," he said, pausing in the act of taking off his jacket, as though to consider the problem carefully. She had seen him do this before, feeding his anger deliberately until it was strong enough to burst any bounds he might place upon it. "You have paid little enough heed to your vows before this. I know—I have been mistaken all this time!"

It was a grotesque parody of delight that he assumed, grimacing in a ghastly travesty of a smile— "You *do* love me! How delightful. And you cannot wait to hurl yourself into my arms. Come now, Mercy, let me see whether I can sustain the proofs of your devotion to me."

She gaped at him. She could not believe her ears. "Howard, have you no feeling of decency whatever?"

"Decency? A strange word, coming from you."

All the time he was talking now, he was taking off his garments, one after another. First his coat, blue velvet with gold braid and gold-colored buttons. The ruffled shirt, revealing his bare chest, white in the candlelight as far as the line of his throat where the sun had reached all summer long. And red, puckering where the bullet—Arthur Gannon's bullet—had torn through muscle and sinew.

"Mercy, I fear you lag far behind me in disrobing, and I warn you I can be impatient." His voice throbbed, and, her ear acute to intonations that she knew well, she knew that now was almost too late to escape.

But she had to try. "Howard, you are not recovered yet. You will do yourself an injury."

He dropped his last garment, and advanced toward her. She did not think she could bear his hands upon her, his lips ruthless upon her lips where she could still taste Mark's gentle sweetness. She looked wildly about her.

She lunged for the candlestick and held the dripping candle like a dagger before her.

"It's no use," he said, with a wicked chuckle. "Mark enjoys you—why not your husband?"

Panic seized her. For a moment, she was nearly out of her mind. Blindly she tried to evade him, but he thrust clawed fingers into the neck of her riding jacket and pulled. The rending fabric sounded like a scream, and in blind panic she threw out the hand that held the candle—

A sharp curse tore the air. Suddenly it was dark and she was free. Howard leaped back from her, and words dribbled from his lips.

"You—" The words that followed made no sense to her. She hardly heard them, hearing only the heavy panting of her own gasping lungs. She crouched, awaiting his next onslaught, but there was the noise of Howard falling against a chair in the dark, even a moan, and the door opened. Howard stood profiled in moonlight reflecting through a window somewhere and faintly outlining his naked body. And he closed the door behind him.

Spent, she could not move. Her thoughts raced, waiting until he came back, but he did not come. Finally, trembling so she could hardly stand, she tottered to the door, and bolted it.

She groped on the floor for the fallen candle. She found it, the end still warm. And flat—as though it had been pushed, extinguishing the flame, onto bare flesh, possibly onto not-yet-healed tissue. When she had thrown out her hand to save her balance, she had forgotten she still held the candle.

She could not bring herself to light the candle again.

She removed her torn clothing and fell into bed, exhausted in mind and body.

The next morning, Howard joined her at breakfast and behaved as if nothing had happened. Once again, he had managed to bring his emotions under control, but always, she knew, they lay as dangerously dormant as a sleeping volcano, ready to erupt and overflow to bring destruction to everything they touched.

The only sign that the events of the night before had not been a particularly vicious dream was that his left shoulder seemed larger than his right, as though a bulky bandage had been applied awkwardly to a wound, straining the jacket.

But before she could finish her coffee, and leave as graciously as she could, he said, apparently idly, picking up a remark from the night before, "It is strange to discover people's weaknesses, I find. Strange and sometimes profitable. Some people have the most ordinary weaknesses of the flesh. Gannon, for example. His weakness is this idiotic doting on that foolish woman. He would be far better off without her. He has a good mind, he could do well, but he must scourge himself wondering where she is and what she is doing and how she feels about him—all the whole sordid mess."

"I feel sorry for him."

Howard went on as if she had not spoken. "And then Vernon Worth. He is too incurious to have any weaknesses."

A smug little smile played around his thin lips. He was a bewildering mixture at best. At worst, which seemed to be more and more often recently, he was vicious and brutal. Carmody put no stock in his promise not to tell the entire peninsula between the rivers about Mark. No matter that Howard's wife would be equally smeared. That did not matter. She had only a glimpse once before of Howard's consuming hatred of Mark Tennant. She had dreadfully underestimated it. Now she was beginning to catch its foul outlines, and her heart sank as she thought of the dreadful consequences to Mark's standing in the colony if Howard's filthy insinuations gained currency.

She must do what she could—whatever she could—to keep her husband in good humor. She was intent upon her resolve, and missed the next part of what he was saying.

"The entire colony will be scandal-free, believe me. They will all hang together, keeping their little secrets hidden, at least until the new governor's term is over."

"Lord Monteith?" she asked brightly.

"Nothing but an old woman. And Lady Monteith is worse. Even the late and unlamented Cromwell would have been hard put to satisfy Lady Monteith's moral scruples."

She must have looked aghast, for he chuckled. "Have no fear, my dear. You and I are a happily married couple. And we have no worries about our little scandal coming out, for everyone has his own little fears. I could tell you things—"

But he did not, and she decided that he was merely trying to impress her. For he changed the subject then, and she began to think of all that must be done in the next few days. There was much to do. Within the week they would be moving to the house in Jamestown, to be on hand for the new governor's arrival and the festivities that would inevitably accompany his advent.

"And, of course," Howard was saying now, "the appointment of his new deputy will be the source of much interest."

Something in the ring of his voice told her that there was significance in his news. She was not wrong.

"It is the idea of this new governor to appoint someone from the colony to serve as deputy governor. To present the colonists' view of things, so it is said. And I understand," he continued, "that an honorable man by the name of Tennant—Mark Tennant, I believe—is running far ahead of other claimants for the position. That day—the day when your lover takes office—will make you very happy, won't it, my dear?"

Her newly resolved determination to keep Howard from becoming irritable and unstable flew out of the window. "How can you let your petty dislike of a man stand in the way of that appointment? It's for the good of the colonists!"

"And the colonists, my dear, don't matter a damn to me. Mark has a lot of support, you know. All the worthies of Virginia are for him. It looks like a foregone conclusion."

"You hate him, don't you. Why? He's never done anything to you."

He looked at her in surprise. "My dear, the reason is very simple. He exists. But never mind, I know the Governor will name him."

If his words were meant to reassure her, they failed of their intent. It was like believing the happy smile of the crocodile, just before some dreadful violent move by the beast of prey.

But yet. she consoled herself, if Lady Anne and Vernon Worth, and even Charles Abbott, stood firm, insisting upon Mark's appointment, all could yet be well.

She knew she was too optimistic, but she could not abide the alternative. That she, who loved Mark more than her life, should be the instrument of his downfall, seemed grossly unfair.

And yet, my girl, she told herself, where did it ever say that life was fair? Nowhere, not that I ever read.

It was that afternoon that Lady Anne York came to call. Carmody came to meet her, barely restraining her astonishment. Lady Anne had never before come to Vickery Hall, and Carmody was sure the dislike that Howard often expressed toward Lady Anne was reciprocated, full measure and running over.

She rode up the drive, under the great oaks, not quite at a full gallop. She sat erect in her saddle as though she were yet a girl. Carmody found it hard to believe that the woman was nearly fifty. She was possessed of an ageless beauty, and certainly, her bone structure would add to that beauty as years went by.

Carmody peered anxiously from the window. If Lady Anne were not alone, if she had brought her nephew with her, then Carmody would quite simply abandon her duties as hostess and flee to the haven of her room. She could not face Jermyn. Too vivid in her mind was the picture of his frowning, distressed face witnessing herself and Mark in a secret trysting place.

But Lady Anne was alone. How much had Jermyn told her? With any luck he had kept his own counsel. Carmody waited for Lady Anne on the broad portico, apprehensive for her first words.

They were ordinary enough. One of the stable boys came running to take the reins, and Lady Anne gave him instructions to walk her spirited horse. "I won't be staying long, so don't stable him."

She came up the steps briskly. "Mistress Vickery, this is not a social call." Her face was set grimly and the friendliness she had shown before was gone.

Carmody quailed. Jermyn had talked then, breaking his promise to Howard, spreading her shame at least one stage farther. But, what business was it of Lady Anne's? Surely, Mark was free to dally where he chose.

Carmody gathered her forces to meet the unexpected challenge. "I dare say it is not. But I cannot see what business we might have."

The woman's rigid face relaxed perceptibly. She stood beside Carmody on the portico. Somehow she gave the impression of towering over everyone around her. Perhaps it was her aristocratic bearing, carrying herself proudly as though disdaining even the earth beneath her narrow, expensively booted feet. Or the long thin face with the excellent bones, speaking of generations of careful breeding.

Lady Anne was seething with fury. Carmody stifled a gasp and automatically stretched out her hand in protest. It was a mistake. Lady Anne stiffened indignantly, and stepped back. The hand that still held her riding crop jerked convulsively. Clearly the woman was strongly agitated.

"You and I have no business, Mistress Vickery. Unless you share your husband's counsel."

"No, I do not. If your business is with him, I know nothing of it. I will send word that you are here. But there is no need for us to stand here. It will be more comfortable within."

"I doubt it." Lady Anne's words were insulting, but Carmody believed they referred only to her business with Howard. Secretly, she thought that Howard, in a way she could not imagine, had crossed the path of the formidable Lady Anne. And this time, she exulted, Howard had met his match!

"Your husband is a scoundrel," Lady Anne told Carmody. "He has led Jermyn into gambling, you know. I will pay Jermyn's debts, of course," she added, stepping into the hall, "but I will see that Jermyn doesn't gamble again." She peered into Carmody's shocked face. "Didn't you really know?"

"No. I didn't know." It was beginning over again—the gambling, the lying, the cheating—

And while Carmody didn't care what Howard did to himself—and she dared not, for her life, literally, protest the degradation he brought to her—she did care very much what he did to others. Partly, of course, because inevitably she was believed to be to blame. And in a real way, perhaps she was. She had lost the thread of Lady Anne's words—something about Howard's friendly games? And Arthur Gannon's house, where they played?

She would try to put it together—but later. Just now Lady Anne was halfway to Howard's study door. She said over her shoulder, "Don't interfere, Mistress Vickery, no matter what you hear. I plan to convince your husband to leave Jermyn alone, in any way I need to." She lifted her hand and the long thin thong of her little riding whip snaked in the air.

Carmody groped to find the chair in the entry, and sat, unheedful of her surroundings. Where was it leading to? And more important, when would it end?

More than once she had been close to ending it all. It had seemed simple, once, to walk steadily into the silver surf, to an ultimate union with the cool sea. But she had not been allowed such an easy solution.

And—irony of ironies!—it had been Mark who had saved her. She had brought nothing but trouble and shame to him, and he must many times have heartily cursed himself for interfering.

Carmody watched the closed doorway at the back of the hall, through which Lady Anne had passed. How long ago? Uncertain, frowning, she stared at the door. It came to her that she had not heard a sound from the study since Lady Anne entered. It was certain that Lady Anne had not had to resort to her whip.

Howard was perhaps—Carmody tried to picture the scene—cowering in his big chair behind the rampart of his desk, while the lady—

Carmody shook her head. The picture would not come to life for her. She admitted that she could not imagine her husband cowering. But she realized soon that whatever she had imagined, it was not even remotely accurate. She had no idea how long it was that Lady Anne was closeted with Howard, when suddenly the door opened and the lady emerged.

Not fuming, not in triumph, not looking like the daughter of a belted earl and kin, so it was said, to royalty.

Lady Anne emerged from her interview tottering, reaching out blindly with empty hands for support. Her face was ghostly pale and her eyes were deep cauldrons of misery.

Carmody was at her side in an instant. "What happened? Are you all right?" It was a foolish question. Of course she was not all right. The handsome woman who strode less than an hour ago through the hall was now a broken woman, showing her true age and more.

Her fingers closed futilely on empty air. She refused Carmody's offer of a carriage. "What if I do break my neck?" she said, her voice cracking. "Nothing matters any more. *Nothing.*"

Carmody watched her ride down the avenue. Even her slumped shoulders shouted defeat abroad.

Howard had come out on the portico. "Lady Anne left her whip behind," he commented, his eyes alive with satisfaction. "I wonder what she intended to do with it."

Full of Lady Anne's parting words, Carmody said waspishly, "To kill you, from what she said. Too bad she didn't!"

Howard weighed her in one comprehensive look. Then he laughed. "There's a spice to living after all, to be hated by two such proud, well-bred women!"

It took all of two days to accomplish the move to Jamestown, no more than thirty miles away. Carmody had no faith in Howard's words that the house was entirely furnished. She insisted on some china and pewter of her own, and of course food enough to furnish the household for several weeks, at least.

When she stepped through the front door, for a moment she could have believed she stepped into the front hall of the house in Jamaica, with a gambling room on either side of the hall. Here was the same red velvet, the same gilt girandoles in the hall, with a wavy mirror and a console beneath them.

She murmured, "Where are the tables?" but Howard only laughed.

The next day Carmody wiped her hot forehead, and remarked to Prissy, "If I had had any idea of what the place looked like! Prissy, this place is a *closet!*"

Prissy's good-humored grin was absent. She had dark suspicions about the rooms the servants lived in.

"But Mr. Vickery says that the town is all new since the burning, and everything had to be brought here from far inland to build with, so I suppose—" Carmody's voice trailed away, and she forgot what she was saying. The details of housekeeping could occupy her mind only fitfully. After the night when Howard had found her with Mark, ugly monsters roved through the chaos that seemed to be her mind these days—monsters of violence, assault, dreadful shame—her ever-lurking fear of Howard himself, the thoughts of Mark which tormented her.

She watched Dess, on a stool, evening the curtains on the rods, but her mind, as always, played around Mark. She had been tricked into going to that cabin, and Mark too had been deceived.

She had no illusions about Howard, not any more. She

was watched now, she was sure. The trouble was, she did not know which of the faces around her were masks, behind which were watchful eyes and tattling tongues.

She would have to be careful. Howard was an ever-present menace. His shoulder was still painful from the burn she had by chance inflicted on the sensitive flesh. He was only biding his time, she was positive. Even the air between them was heavily charged with foreboding when his light glittering eyes watched her every movement.

"I can't think why you want me here in Jamestown," she said. "You derive no pleasure from my company."

"On the contrary," he assured her. "You amuse me. Besides, I shall want to share my triumph with my wife."

His thin lips stretched in a sort of smile. She realized that Howard's face was the mask—and the servants only concealed bitter hatred and envy, consuming jealousy, and followed his example. The handsome, depraved face violence that heightened his sensual pleasure.

"Triumph?" She was cautious.

"Over all the high and mighty worthies of Virginia. And now, my dear, I must not tell you more. Your face is so easy to read—although I admit your detestation of me adds a piquant touch at times."

He touched his shoulder, wincing. An unguarded look lurked in his expression and for a moment she could see the urchin he had been, living by his precocious wits on the streets, feeding his self-love with fantasies of superiority, that he would one day grind "them" under his heel. She could have cried at the waste of his considerable talent, warped in the service of envy.

"I could have loved you, once," she said in a low voice, half believing she spoke the truth, "but there's no gentleness in you."

"Gentleness! That's for fools! Besides, where would I learn it?" he countered. "I suppose you feel that if you had met me earlier, you might have changed me? Disabuse yourself of the notion, my dear. It might give you food for thought if you meditated upon the proposition that you cannot solve the world's ills by yourself—by sacrificing, let us say, your innocent honor on the altar of your brother's sanity. Oh, yes. I know about Carmody Petrie. And that is why, my dear girl, nothing you do surprises me. Once a whore, always a loose lady. It is simply a matter of price, that is all."

And then, in a rare moment, he laid his hand gently on her drooping shoulder, and said, "You see in us the excesses—you give too much, and for the wrong reasons, and I take too much."

He lingered for the space of a couple of heartbeats, and then, saying no more, left her to contemplate the gloomiest thoughts she had ever known.

In a few days she found she was restored in body, if not in heart, and her body required fresh air. Hugging herself in a white woolen shawl, she ventured out to examine the grounds of the house that Howard had rented.

The house had a narrow front lawn, as was the fashion in England, but rather wider side lawns than usual. There was an oystershell walk around either side of the house, and the familiar crunching sound beneath her feet reminded her forcibly of Jamaica.

In back of the house timbered additions housed the few slaves they had brought along, and behind the kitchen addition stretched another much longer area where someone had tried half-heartedly to make a formal garden. The straggly yews had been planted, but died in the heat, and their ragged stumps stuck up like broken teeth in a comb. Between the unsightly files of dead waist-high trees was a walk not even paved with oystershell, but thick with the white sand that abounded on the peninsula between the York and the James.

Already the autumn was advanced. It was the first of November, and the malaria season was past. The cold airs gusted up the river onto this little neck of land that had seen the beginning of Virginia colony more than eighty years before.

There was a hedge, more prosperous than the yews, that outlined what she supposed was the limit of the ground belonging to the house. There were houses on either side, neither so grand as the one behind her, half hidden in the trees still clinging to their dessicated leaves.

Beyond the hedge, houses on more spacious grounds faced another street. Aimlessly she strolled to the hedge at the back, and saw that the yard beyond was equally as neglected as the one she stood in. Some other absentee landlord, no doubt, more interested in his plantations inland than in such city life as Jamestown could boast.

Suddenly chilled, she turned and hurried back to the house.

Later that same day, Jermyn Fox came to see Howard. But Howard was not at home, and Jermyn asked for her.

Carmody thought wildly of denying herself to him, but she hardly dared. She had not seen Jermyn since that night in the cabin, and she dreaded facing him. She walked these days on a knife-edge of danger, as cautious as she could be, not knowing where the pitfalls lay, nor which misstep might plunge her headlong into danger.

With hesitancy, she entered the drawing room, steeling herself against the bright, knowing look she expected from a witness to the scene in the cabin.

She had no need to worry. Jermyn might have forgotten the event, as far as his manner went. He had things of his own to worry about, as it developed.

"You husband is not home?" he asked with scant ceremony.

"He is with the Governor, I believe," she said.

"No doubt, no doubt."

"Do you think that is sinister?" Carmody tried for a light touch, for no other reason than to keep her darker thoughts at bay.

Jermyn shot her a glance full of meaning. "Don't you think so?"

"Truly, I don't know what business he has with the new Governor. You can imagine that my husband does not confide in me."

Jermyn fidgeted, obviously in two minds as to how to proceed. But apparently his need for information, for discussing the situation that ranked very high in his mind, proved stronger than any discretion he had.

Suddenly he threw out his hands in a gesture that reminded her forcibly of Lady Anne. "You know there's a great deal of unrest in the colony," he said

"I have heard complaints, certainly, about the price of tobacco."

"And other regulations that keep the planters from running their business as they see fit. But you are not interested in politics, I would guess. Certainly I am not, except as it affects Lady Anne. But the Governor has new ideas of cooperation—new governor, new broom. And maybe it will work."

"But you don't think so."

"Who knows? Just when you think you've got things coming along nicely, the way you want them, something blows the whole thing away."

Carmody could have said, "Don't I know that!" but she didn't. There were too many times like that—and all of them now gone as though they had never been. Not quite that, she amended—gone leaving only dross behind, like the wind-winnowing of olden times.

"The Governor may appoint the wrong man. That's what Lady Anne says, any way."

Carmody thought for a moment. "I don't know the men here very well, but it would seem to me that most of them think alike."

"Most do. And it is certainly everybody's choice to have Mark Tennant serve."

Something in his manner troubled her, almost like a warning bell. Jermyn was not through yet, and she had the impression that he was skirting the nub of the matter, and when he arrived, the nub would be black with rot—

"But, of course, your husband is opposed to that."

She nodded sourly. "But if everyone wants Mark—" she began, and then saw the pitfall.

Jermyn, watching her closely, nodded sagely. "You see it. The Governor's aide is inland now, sounding out the local opinion, and he will come back with Mark's name. But it won't suit your husband. I don't know what Vickery is planning, but he is devious. And you should stop him before he ruins us all."

"I?" She laughed aloud in derision. "Not I. There is no way I can stop Howard. But you could. You and Lady Anne—"

Her voice died away as she remembered the last time she had seen Lady Anne. Lady Anne had suffered a stunning defeat once at the hands of Howard Vickery, and she would not dare again.

"But you could," pointed out Carmody. "Perhaps Lady Anne would not want to stoop to deal with Howard—" She was talking more to herself than to Jermyn, and her absent-mindedness had led her into unfortunate words. "I mean only—"

Jermyn interrupted her. "I know what you mean. Whoever deals with your husband is going to get his hands filthy. Better me than Lady Anne, I agree. He ought to be soundly horsewhipped."

Lady Anne's intention to do just that, as her pitiful riding crop had plainly displayed, had faded. For the first time in days, Carmody began to wonder why. Lady Anne was afraid of nothing, so it had appeared. Extremely well-born, with powerful family backing, she could simply have crushed an upstart like Howard Vickery beneath her heel as one grinds out an intruding wasp. But she hadn't. Why?

Jermyn flicked his fingers, as though he could almost feel Howard's throat under his hands, squeezing out his life—

"Just like Lady Anne," Carmody remarked. "You have a few mannerisms like hers."

Jermyn said wryly. "When two people live together, are close, they pick up little habits."

Carmody said gently, "I would have thought it was rather an exhibition of family traits, held in common."

The look Jermyn shot her from under his hooded eyebrows shocked her with its naked display of torment. "Did we take you in with our deception? I wish your husband had been as blind."

She stared at him. She had no thought of uncovering anything, but now it was too late to pretend she had not seen the misery in his face. He seemed to have aged ten years. Much as, she thought, Lady Anne had suddenly become a middle-aged woman, so now had Jermyn passed a barrier, leaving his youth behind.

"I love her, you know. She is not my aunt. No kin at all, so there is nothing to stand in our way. But she will not marry me because of the difference in our ages. 'What would people say?' she keeps asking. 'I'm old enough to be your mother.' Nothing I say will convince her that the years don't matter."

"But how did Howard find out? And what can he do anyway? If you get married——"

"It's too late for that. Everyone in Virginia will know that we've—been living together, and that this nephew business was totally a lie."

He had tied the cord of the curtains into knots that would later take someone an hour to undo. But neither of them noticed it now.

"My idea, at that. To protect her. I'd do anything to protect her." He turned to leave. "I'm sorry to burden you with this," he said, belatedly contrite. "I thought you knew about us. Your husband told Lady Anne, you know, that he would blacken her name all through the colony unless she supported him for the governor's deputy."

"But she despises him!"

"She can't do anything else."

Suddenly he slammed one clenched fist into the other palm, in a vicious gesture of violence. "I'd kill him! Yes, I'd kill him today if I thought it would do any good."

Carmody said tartly, "That seems to be a universal reaction to the man I married. He deserves to be killed—how often I've heard it!"

"And I would guess you agree?" Jermyn said softly.

She evaded. "He is my husband."

"And we're all under his thumb."

Howard came back from the Governor's office late. He carried with him an aura of gloating triumph that boded ill for someone. Please God, not Mark!

"You brought the gold satin dress I bought you, didn't you?"

"You specifically asked me to bring it," Carmody answered coolly. "You did not tell me why."

"I wish to have you do me credit," Howard said, "at the governor's ball, three days hence."

She lifted an eyebrow. "Ball? In this town? Where will it be held?"

"In the governor's house, where else?" he answered irritably. "That's not important."

"Gold satin seems a little elaborate for tiny rooms in a swampy town."

He did not hear her. "You will be delighted to know that your old friend Mark Tennant will be there. And I wager he will remember the ball for many years to come."

"I'm sure he will," she murmured, feeling Howard's eyes probing her face.

"After he has left Virginia, that is. In disgrace."

Her eyes flew to her husband's face. "What—what are you going to do?"

"Ah. you express an interest in my plans, at last! I'm gratified. I must tell you about them, and you will tell me what you think."

She sat still, willing herself not to move, not to betray by the slightest gesture her dread of what she might hear. For armed by Jermyn's terrible confession, and the realization that Howard had no mercy, she feared to make Mark's situation worse. She had no clear picture of the disaster that waited for him. Jermyn had told her what he could, but of necessity that was not the whole story, for only Howard knew it all.

"Picture to yourself, Mercy, your friend Mark—deprived of the solace of your company—pinning his noble hopes upon the position of deputy governor to Lord Monteith. His ambition is raised toward being able to speak for his friends, obtain certain trade advantages for them—in short, throw his weight where he, in his great wisdom, thinks best."

Howard smoothed his fair hair back, and looked at her with his glittering light eyes.

"And the ball—all his friends, happy, congratulations raining on him. And your lovely eyes feasting on him from across the room—and the governor rises to make the expected announcement."

Howard continued to build up suspense, but she refused to express impatience. At length he tired of the game.

"And when the Governor names Mark Tennant—I shall stand up and announce that Mark's morals are so shoddy that he must be denied his heart's wish."

She should have expected this, but yet she had not. She thought Howard had used the cabin incident only to remove Arthur Gannon's suspicions. But his ploy, it seemed, was far more complicated than that.

"You promised not to tell that," she accused hotly. "Howard, how can you hold your own wife up to such shame?"

"Really, my dear, it is quite easy. You think that you are the only one who can hate. You've told me that you hate me—and, I will confess, quite likely with reason. But don't forget this," he added, his voice suddenly taking on a razor-sharp, deadly edge, "I have the same feeling toward you. You and Mark have romped disgracefully over my feelings, over my reputation, thinking that I am of no account, simply because you disapprove of some of the things I have done. You haven't even tried to understand my reasons. Not scrupulous, you say!"

He rose from his chair and crossed to where she was sitting. Taking her chin in his hand, he raised her face to look into his. "Fine words for a young woman who threw herself on a royal bastard and followed him all over Dorset, like a camp follower. Fine words from a woman who ran away from her husband, eloped with a ship owner who fancied her for the moment—scrupulous, you say? I could laugh for a week!"

He was feeding his anger again, lashing himself into a frenzy, and there was no way of knowing just what form that frenzy would take when it finally burst its bonds.

"What good is it going to do to denounce him?" she argued, trying to keep him talking until she could think of what best to do.

"Why, besides the shame that the man will feel at being exposed before his friends—the Governor and his lady are such rigid puritans that they will forbid him the capital. The Governor has sufficient interest in high places in London that the Tennant ships will go begging for cargo, and the whole prosperous structure that Mark has built will collapse. And, of course, the appointment will fall to someone else."

"And that someone else," she said shrewdly, "is you."

"Exactly so. So you see, my dear, why I wish you to wear the gold satin gown."

"And," she added, greatly daring, "you have support among the colonists themselves, I suppose. Lady Anne, for example?"

She had made a mistake. He wheeled and sent her a piercing glance."I suppose that sniveling boy was here. Did he try to get you to plead with me?"

"No, Howard, he didn't beg. Doesn't it matter to you that you've taken something that seemed fine to him and Lady Anne and trampled it into the mire? You've shattered two lives beyond repair. Don't you care?"

"They'll get over it," he said callously. "They don't matter." He seemed to look inwardly then, as though she weren't in the room. "They were in the way. I had to use Lady Anne to get to—"

Suddenly he remembered Carmody. "Lady Anne will support my claim to the appointment," he said in an entirely different voice, "and Mark Tennant will be humiliated. He's stood in my way long enough. He'll find out there's no room in Virginia for him."

She had badly underestimated the depths of his hatred. Mark had been born to all the privileges Howard lacked—reputation, education, a certain wealth. All these Howard had attained for himself. But the breeding Howard could never hope to acquire. So he must smash Mark's reputation, grind it into the dirt, and hold it up for the world to see besmirched.

And Howard had it in his power to do so. There was probably nothing she could do, but she knew she must try.

"Howard, let's go away. Back to Europe if you like.

You don't even like it here in Virginia. We can go to Europe, or one of the islands. We could—"

"And you would go with me? How touching! The sacrifices you are willing to make move me deeply." He laughed harshly. "It's too late, Mercy. The governor's aide is upland now, talking to planters—like Arthur Gannon. And Lady Anne. I understand she has secluded herself from society, now. And he will hear enough to convince him that I'm the man for the job after Mark Tennant is exposed as the hypocritical knave he is."

"You tricked him that night!"

"So I did. But—he responded to the note. Don't forget that."

"I won't ever forget how you used me. You wrote the note, you had Landers lure me out to the cabin. The whole incident was a dastardly trick!"

He filled his glass. "But don't forget—how strange I should be required to remind you!—that I did not shove you into his arms, as you were only moments before we entered." He smiled, satisfied at the reaction he obtained from her. "That fact, my dear, was written all over your face. So, you see, I am not to blame after all."

"I loathe you!"

"No doubt." He laughed shortly, and lifted his glass mockingly. "Let me give you a toast, dear wife. Here's to—true love!"

She slept that night, but it did her little good. Dreaming, the agonized faces she knew swam before her vision and faded away—all but Mark's: the deep blue eyes, dark as the deepest sea, his flyaway brows, angling up at the outer edges to give him a rakehell expression that matched, as she knew all too well, the spirit of the man inside. The sweet strong curve of his sensitive lips—the feel of them insistent upon her own. The touch of his strong hands—

She moaned in her sleep and woke, to dream again, waking. And in the morning, fog still thick against the window, she sat up in bed and dropped her face into her hands. She was the instrument used to despoil all that

Mark held dear. And she must, somehow, become the instrument to undo whatever she could.

All the day she pondered upon her decision. Her hands sewed, sorted linen, mended. Her lips spoke words of household use, directing menus, ordering brass polishing, the waxing of furniture in this rented house.

But her imagination played around the dear image of Mark, seeking escape for him from the fate Howard had so carefully prepared.

Twilight came, here in Virginia, with a softness unheard of in Jamaica, where night fell like a velvet blanket dropped suddenly upon the island. This afternoon the fog rolled up the river from the bay in gray woolly billows, blotting out the sun at first, and then methodically swallowing up the landmarks—the steeple of the little white church, the high ridgepole of the governor's house, the most pretentious in town. The upper story of the house across the street. Beyond the church, out of sight, was Mark's town house. Jermyn had mentioned the location to her.

Howard had departed on unknown business, late in the foggy afternoon, and she was alone when she realized that this was her opportunity to warn Mark. She could not divert Howard from his juggernaut destruction, but Mark need not be publicly humiliated—

Throwing her heaviest cloak over her shoulders, she made her escape from the house without being noticed. The fog was thinner, but it had an unsettling way of writhing back and forth on the slightest current of air, like hordes of people drifting aimlessly through the fading light.

The safest way to Mark's house was for her to go through the garden and down the rutted lane. It would be slippery in the damp, but she must go. It might be her only opportunity to see him before the ball—her only chance to warn him, beg him to stay away. She was not sure why Howard had told her his plans, but she surmised that he had expected Landers to keep her captive until the fatal night.

She stopped halfway down the walk toward the foot of

the garden, and turned to look behind her. No one was following,

The house loomed dimly in the increasing fog, and the lights seemed only faint yellow splotches, as though smeared on the gray bulk by a paint-covered thumb, at random. It was a ghost house, with ghost lights, and she moved in a haunted world. The wet fog on her face added to her sudden sense of moving in a silent, unreal world—a world where anything could happen. Ghosts of the past, specters of the future—

It was at that moment that the incredible happened.

Looming out of the fog at the foot of the garden, a dark shape at first, but in an instant coming close enough to recognize, a tall, familiar figure strode toward her—and she looked up into the face of Sir Waldo Rivers!

5

SHE was leaning against a very solid shoulder.

The world swung around her, whirling and tilting, and then, at last, righted itself. She looked up into the unquestionably living face of the man she had killed.

"Waldo?" she asked, shakily.

"I might ask in my turn, Carmody?"

She put her hand to her forehead. Her bronze ringlets were covered with moisture. She looked at the back of her hand as though she had not seen it before.

"It's wet," she said in a wondering voice. "I can't be dreaming, then, my hand is wet."

"I would doubt very much," Waldo said dryly, "that you would dream of me—outside of an occasional nightmare. My dreams, I must say, are probably more satisfactory than yours. Is there some place where we can talk? You'll catch your death of cold here."

Half laughing, half crying, she said, "Yes, we can go into the house. I think I can get us in without the servants knowing. I got out, you see, unnoticed. Let me hold your sleeve, Waldo, then if you depart when the cock crows I'll have something to prove to myself that you did indeed visit me here. Will you dissolve into a puddle at an appropriate time?"

"You're babbling, Carmody," Waldo said in genuine concern. "Come, let us find this house you speak of. Will the other servants betray you?"

"Other servants? Oh, no, they are as afraid of the master of the house as I am. But he is from home now, and perhaps—careful, Waldo, don't slip on the stones. I would be reluctant to see you die before my eyes a second time."

She did not know whether she continued to chatter, letting the meaningless phrases flow from her lips to cushion her against the catastrophic shock she had just experienced, was still reeling from. But at length they arrived at the door by which she had left the house.

She seemed to have lost all power of movement. It was Waldo who stretched out a gloved hand and pushed the door open. He helped her over the threshold, and closed the door behind them.

The square space in which they stood was small and enclosed, except for a door ajar into the kitchen wing, where there was the movement of servants, and the spicy warm aroma of bread baking. The light that came through the half-open door was sufficient to reveal the door on the left, leading into the main part of the house. Waldo looked a question at her, but in the dark, she did not see, nor could he have seen an answer.

The hand on his arm began to shake now, despite the sudden warmth after the chill outside. Truly alarmed, Waldo opened the door and pulled Carmody after him. They were in a dimly lit room that appeared to be a back sitting room. It was furnished comfortably enough, although far from elegant.

But the necessities of life were there, Waldo discovered, and he set about making use of them. He guided her to a chair before the fireplace, and stirred up the smoldering embers with the poker. He worked deftly with the fire for a few moments, and was rewarded by an awakening blaze that leaped, throwing the room into light, and showing Waldo where the brandy was kept.

Kneeling before her, he helped her off with her cloak, and removing her clogs set himself to rubbing her feet into warmth again. When he was satisfied, he poured a small glass of brandy for her. He hesitated, and then poured a rather larger tot for himself. The shock had not been Carmody's alone.

His hand shook only slightly as he brought the brandy

to her. He knelt again beside her and coaxed her into sipping the fiery liquid.

She was still shaking, her teeth chattering on the lip of the glass in spite of all she could do. She thought she would never be warm again; she could not even feel the heat thrown out by the blazing fire.

She sputtered over the brandy, but at length managed to swallow it all. Only then did Waldo take up his own glass and lean negligently against the mantel, for all the world as though specters moved at regular, almost unnoticed, occasions through his life.

"You were never this thoughtful before," she said, finally.

"I never had so little to lose," he countered. "Now, you're beyond my reach. I took some of the master's brandy. I hope you don't have trouble over it. Shall I wait and explain?"

"No need to do that. At least, as far as the brandy is concerned. But there is much more to explain to me, I think, and I should like to hear all of it before Howard returns."

He looked at her in stillness. At length he ventured, "Howard? You mean Howard Vickery, I assume—but first names?"

"I am Howard's wife."

It was a simple, bald statement, delivered in a flat, unaccented voice, but it had a startling effect on Waldo. "By Jove! I didn't know that. I thought he called his wife something else—Charity, Prudence? Some kind of virtue, anyway."

"Mercy. That's the name he married me under. But he has called me many other things."

She noticed that her fingers were entwining restlessly in her lap, and she forced stillness upon them. Suddenly she leaned back in her chair and looked up at Waldo with a ghost of the roguish smile he remembered so well. "How good it is to see you, Waldo! Even though you frightened me half to death!"

He grinned back. He left the mantel and pulled up a chair to face her. "I didn't expect to see you either.

Rumor said that you had disappeared after the battle at Sedgemoor. I knew you had survived that, of course, but no one could tell me what happened subsequently."

"It's a long story. I was captured, of course. Somehow I had another name. My maid's, Mercy Holland, you remember her? And there was a judge—Judge Jeffreys, and—I don't want to remember anything of those days, Waldo."

Her face was in shadow, the cheekbones prominently catching the firelight.

"You're too thin," he burst out suddenly. "You must have had a frightful time."

She nodded. "I survived."

He gave her a long, measuring look. "Yes, you would. You always will. You're even surviving the hell I imagine your marriage to be."

Startled, she glanced at him. "You know him."

"To know him is to despise him. You've changed, Carmody. Once you would have been curious as to what I was doing in your back garden. Or even what I'm doing in Virginia. But you haven't asked a single question. Not about me, or Ralph. Or even Oaklands, and I confess that surprises me. You loved Oaklands more than any person—your brother, or me."

"It's all so far away. As though I were in fact a different person from the one who shot you. I take it my aim was poor."

"Dreadfully so." He moved his shoulder. "Hurts a little in rainy weather. It's done no harm to my own shooting arm."

It was slowly reaching her understanding—the overwhelming relief at finding Waldo alive. At realizing, slowly but none the less surely, that she had not killed anybody. That she was in fact free of Howard's implied blackmail. That she no longer need cringe at the thought of being returned to London in chains, to be executed for the terrible crime of murder. No longer need she—

"But you said nobody knew what had happened to me after Sedgemoor. You must have told somebody what I did to you."

"I spoke your name to nobody, except to inquire about you after I recovered somewhat. Believe me," he said quietly, "I am not guilty of accusing you of shooting me, no matter what else I have done to you."

"But Howard knows—"

"He couldn't. Nobody knew you shot me that night. To my dying day I will regret the unforgivable thing I did to you, but I did not tell anyone. Believe me."

Strangely, she did. Howard had never in so many words said Waldo's name, had never threatened her with the consequences of her supposed crime—which was now no crime at all.

"The wicked flee," she murmured, "when no man pursueth. I have been foolish indeed. And for my great folly, terrible things have happened, are going to happen."

Waldo sat back in his chair, his fingers making a tent together. His widow's peak had begun to recede a bit, and even, she suspected, might be graying. "Now, Carmody, you always were one to shoulder the whole blame, whether it was rightly yours or not."

He was right, but it would be long before she could see the fairness of his judgment. She would go back in her mind to Waldo, to Ralph—to James Scott, and those things that had been done to her since then.

She smiled wanly at him. How good it was to have him here, alive. She discovered that she had a real affection for him.

"Comfortable, that's the word," she said. "Now, Waldo, I am sufficiently restored to ask. What were you doing in my back garden?"

"I came to see your husband. Don't worry. Even if he discovers me here, he will raise no fuss. I can guarantee that much."

"He is very jealous."

"But not so much as to spite him himself, I think. I came to Virginia, first of all, in the new Governor's suite."

"But how did you get into government service at all?"

He contemplated his fingers for a bit. "I was able," he said finally, "to do the late King James the Second a small favor."

She looked at him suspiciously, her silver eyes steady on him. "I see," she said finally. "You betrayed James Scott to him."

"The *rebel* James Scott," Waldo corrected. "My duty as a loyal subject of the crown. But let us not resurrect motives at this late date, Carmody. None of us can stand against the winds of change—you are a different, and very lovely, woman. And I—I have at last had the tables turned on me. Let us forgive?"

"Forgive," she agreed, glad her reluctance was not obvious.

"So one thing led to another, and eventually I found myself on the staff of Lord and Lady Monteith. And I am assigned to this God-forsaken strand at the beck and call of the world's most rigid Puritan."

Suddenly she was amused. "How did that happen, Waldo? You were always very quick on your feet."

"A folly of my own, my dear. I thought it was easier to marry money than to earn it. But you see, I married it and now I must also earn it."

"I'm sorry," she said sincerely. "I don't suppose I would know your wife?"

"On the contrary, you know her very well. She was Harriet Paine, before she married me."

"Harriet!"

From some forgotten niche in her memory came the recollection of Waldo's not too subtle questions about Harriet's wealth.

"She is still somewhat autocratic, I judge?"

With appealing shamefacedness, Waldo glanced at her from under thick black brows. "Totally so. You see, I no longer have secrets from you. I was desperate for money, and I married it. But unfortunately," he added with a grimace, "I had to take the lady too. I would never say that to another soul, Carmody, but you are, amusingly enough, my oldest friend."

Somewhere in the house a door opened. Carmody sprang from her chair and listened intently. It must have been the rear door, for the fresh current of air swirled cold and very close, fanning the flames in the grate, and carrying a hint of ginger from the kitchen.

One of the servants, she thought, and not Howard, after all. She could not trust Waldo's assurances that he possessed enough influence to dampen Howard's suspicious resentment.

"That is why you are in Virginia, Waldo," she resumed. "But why in my back garden?"

He hesitated. "How shall I say this? Your husband has certain goals, ambitions that he places a certain value upon. And he was in touch with me even before we left London to ask me to further these ambitions." He spoke slowly, and deliberately chose his words to convey the message he wanted her to receive without stating it specifically.

"And you came to report? Through the back door?"

"Not quite," he said, "although it must look that way. But in fact I have been into the hinterland, and certain things are going on that I thought he should know."

A silence fell between them. She could have asked further questions. Certainly there was much left unsaid. But she knew she could not alter Howard's course. And now all that was left to her was to warn Mark. That chance, too, had been blasted. But there would come another chance. It was too late to leave the house tonight, for Howard would surely miss her if she were not at home when he returned.

She must put her dire anxieties to one side. With a conscious effort, she returned to the present—Waldo was sitting across from her, watchful, intent. And *alive*. She summoned up a smile for him.

"Now, Waldo," she said. "What can you tell me about Ralph? I haven't heard a word about him since—"

Since the night she had seen him in the wretched jail at Lyme Regis. Since the night she had procured his freedom, salvaged his sanity, aboard the *Helderenburgh*.

To her total amazement, she found she did not care any more what happened to Ralph. Or even, it truth were told, to Oaklands. She had thought once she was at the hub of the universe, in the manor house at Oaklands. That was the core of her life, she had believed, and would be always, no matter where she went, no matter what happened to her.

How mistaken she was! There was far more in the world than Oaklands, and she had savored a good deal of it, and the taste in her mouth was bitter as rue.

She settled herself to listen as though to a tale of a stranger, as Waldo smiled. "At last, the Carmody I once knew. But yet, with a change. We have both altered a great deal, far more than I would have believed. But you ask about Ralph. He has managed to hang on to Oaklands, although at one time it was very questionable that he could. But he took seriously to drinking, and fortunately the alcohol made his brain sodden enough, so that all his schemes died on his lips. And your factor—Yarrow?—manages the estates without Ralph's interference."

There was, she discovered, a vestige of feeling for her brother. If she could have stayed on, she could perhaps have provided the stability, the strength that was so sadly lacking in him. If she had married Waldo, they might be sitting as they sat now, visiting comfortably before a fire, almost—but not quite—friends after all.

"What will happen to Oaklands?" Waldo asked curiously. "Your brother looks as if he will have no legitimate heirs. Plenty of bastards, I hear. He's seduced all the maids, some more than once from what gossip tells my dear lady." He smiled. "Harriet has her eye on the estate, you know. She's waiting for a chance to add to her holdings."

"If Ralph dies without heirs, the estate goes to some far cousin in the north of England, I think—Waldo, you look pleased. Don't you want Harriet to acquire Oaklands?"

"She's a miser, Carmody. Her holdings stay in her control. I get only enough to buy tobacco."

She contemplated him for a few moments, and then, knowing Waldo far better than she realized, she understood. "And so you are on the lookout for funds of your own!"

"A man has to live," he said simply.

A log burned through and fell with a dull plop into the coals, sending a shower of sparks into the air. She was grateful for this little space of time, a quiet reflective mood filled with nostalgia for the past, a past as remote as—as the Crusades! Soon she would realize her freedom, soon she would be able to flex her mind and realize that her only sins were of the flesh, not of the soul. Her hands were guiltless of murder, and——soon——she would feel her shoulders free of the dreadful yoke.

In a minute.

"This is pleasant, Waldo," she said ruminatively, "to sit here together, like old friends at a gossip. My governess used a phrase once—I forget now the purpose she intended—and I never knew what she meant, until now. She meant us, Waldo. *All passion spent.*"

He stirred in his chair. The mood was broken. He rose to his feet and looked for his cloak, finding it on the floor before the fire where he had dropped it unthinkingly in his concern for her. He fastened it at the throat with a heavily ornate clasp of silver, and came to stand before her.

He pulled her to her feet, and looked into her face with an odd expression, a mixture of affection and regret. "*Spent?* Don't you believe it. You're more desirable this moment than ever. I'm not given to foolish whims, like falling in love—but you've clung to my thoughts all these years, Carmody. And when I saw you there in the fog, I think my heart literally turned over."

He lifted her chin with one finger. "Those silver eyes, that freshness that circles you like a perfume—" He broke off with a rueful laugh. "Never thought I'd become so poetic."

"Waldo—" Impulsively she raised herself on tiptoe and kissed his lips. Her hand was on his arm for support and she could feel the sudden start as his muscles tightened.

"My gravest mistake, in a long mistaken career, was letting you go. But then again, you would have carried the burden of making a silk purse out of me. Maybe you could have succeeded, who knows? If anyone could have changed me, Carmody, it was you."

He held her briefly, then let her go. "If I can ever do you a favor, Carmody, believe me, I'll do it. Remember that. No, don't see me out. I can find my way."

He stopped at the door and turned. There was a wry twist to his lips as he spoke, voice roughened by emotion. "All passion spent, Carmody? Don't you believe it!" And he was gone, back into the fog whence he came.

His intention might not have been to comfort her, but she felt, as she had not for a long time, secure, like a child tucked into bed at night by loving hands.

Alive! Waldo was *alive!*

He had only a slight scar, he had told her, an old wound which pained him, like an old soldier's, only in dampness. Such as tonight. And he had never told anyone who shot him. Howard had no hold on her now—

Except his power to ruin Mark.

Things began to come clear in her mind. Howard was exceedingly sure that, after Mark had lost the appointment in disgrace, he himself would be named to the position. How could he be so sure, when there were other planters far better qualified? And better liked, for that matter?

True, he had Lady Anne's grudging support. And Arthur Gannon's need to make amends. But those two could not, by themselves, carry the day for Howard. No, he had to count on something more. And then, slowly, the pieces fit together. Waldo had a nearly obsessive need for money that was his own, and not his tight-fisted wife's. And Waldo had influence with the Governor.

The "investment" Howard had mentioned, into which he put all his gambling winnings from the private games at Arthur Gannon's house, all the proceeds of her tobacco crop—

No question—Howard had bought the appointment with a massive bribe to Waldo!

6

THE capital city of the colony of Virginia was built upon a small mound of land connected with the mainland by a thin neck of low, swampy land. The near-island thus thrust out into the current of the James River as it moved from highland down through the fertile Tidewater area to the salt water of Chesapeake Bay, washed the sides of the town of Jamestown, and limited the area on which houses and outbuildings could be built.

It was mainly for this reason that the Governor's residence was so modest. A mere two stories, a handful of rooms, and this night the reception was crowded into the two front rooms of the house, with a buffet supper laid on in one of the narrow side rooms.

The ever-present autumn fog swirled up from the river, wreathing houses and streets, sheds and carriages, with torn shreds of gray, bringing with it a damp that penetrated the bones.

Carmody, sitting apart from Howard in the carriage, felt the cold more than ever. It was strange, she thought—she could not tell whether the icy chill that pervaded her came from the fog outside, or, more likely, from the icy foreboding that filled her thoughts.

There was no escape. Howard had made that clear. He had watched her during the dinner that she could not eat, and even supervised her dressing. She had looked up once from her mirror and seen his eyes glittering in the half light where he sat, like a beast's kept at bay by a fire, a fire for which the fuel was almost exhausted. She had no illusions.

There was no one to help her. Lady Anne was worse than useless as an ally, and Arthur Gannon would not allow his wife to lift a finger for Carmody. The Worths? Lovely Genevieve and honest Vernon? She could not bring Howard's wrath down upon their innocent heads.

That was the nub of it—wherever she might turn, Howard would follow. And after tonight, she would never see Mark again.

He would think she was a tool of Howard's. He would believe—Howard would make him believe—that she had lured him there on purpose to put him into a compromising situation.

She saw it all so clearly. And the fact that she had been unable to warn him would certainly convince Mark, if he did not already believe the worst of her!

They were at the Governor's residence before she was aware of it, and Howard was handing her down from the carriage with exaggerated concern. Only the painful grip on her fingers told her he was still mindful of her. She refused to wince—now, she resolved, or in the future. She would not give him the satisfaction.

Inside the open door stood the Governor. The Earl of Monteith, peer of Scotland—a kindly man, harassed by a job he did not clearly understand. But he smiled kindly on Carmody, and she responded in kind. Perhaps help was here—but seeing the tired, pouched eyes, she knew that he could not help her.

Lady Monteith reminded her in a way of Harriet Paine, except that the Governor's lady appeared more generous of spirit, more genuinely glad to know people.

Assisting the Governor, standing nearby in elegant dark blue velvet, stood Sir Waldo Rivers. Carmody glanced at him, uncertain whether to recognize him in public, but he bent low over her hand, and smiled correctly. Inside the first room there was already a throng.

Lady Rivers—dear Harriet, once Carmody's best friend. Now she looked paler, more faded, all except her bright blue eyes. They pierced Carmody like little daggers.

"Waldo told me he had seen you. I was stunned," she said calmly. "Surely everyone thought you had been lost in the battle."

"As you see," said Carmody, "I was not."

"You must have had many adventures with the Duke. Of course, I mean as to the rebellion."

"Naturally. The Duke was in *many* things unfortunate." There, she thought—let Harriet wonder whether the Duke was successful with me, or whether I held him at arm's length for three weeks! She laughed inwardly. The Duke hadn't been patient for as long as three days from the time he first laid covetous eyes on her.

Arthur Gannon refused to meet her eyes, and even flushed faintly. He bowed, of course, but she saw his eyes fastened no higher than her bare shoulders, and she knew—oh, how she knew!—what he was conjecturing. She turned swiftly to little Bel.

"Whatever must you think of me?" Bel said, astonishingly. Her voice was too low for Arthur to hear, and Carmody responded in kind. "I think Howard has left many victims in his trail," she said, and could not refrain from adding, "Including me."

She swept onward, greeting people she had met—few enough, as it turned out. And no sign of Mark! Perhaps somebody already had warned him. Perhaps—it could even be that this was the favor that Waldo had promised her. But it couldn't be. Waldo did not know how she felt about Mark.

Mistress Worth caught her wrist. "Come and talk to us for a minute. I haven't seen you this long time. Tell me how you are doing with the winter stores."

Carmody was caught up in discussion of pumpkins in the storage houses, hams curing over hickory fires, bins of squash in the cellars—all the everyday things that she would ordinarily take an interest in. But not this night—not with heavy gloom settling on her so darkly that she was sure she must walk with her face in shadow. Where was Mark?

Home, she hoped devoutly. And perversely, the longer she could not find him, the more her senses cried out for him. Just to see his beloved face again, even though she could not come near enough to speak to him. She dared not, not with Howard's vindictive eyes watching every move she made.

Lady Anne appeared abruptly before her. The woman's face was lined and haggard, as though she had not slept, as though her dreams brought her frightening visions. She was dressed in ugly yellow, the color of mustard, which fought biliously with her tanned skin. It was as if she had purposely made herself as unattractive as possible, so that no one would suspect she held Jermyn's love in her old hands. No one, looking at her, could possibly guess that she inspired the feelings that Jermyn had confessed to Carmody.

"I think I must apologize to you," said Lady Anne. "I thought at first you were sympathetic to your husband's endeavors, but my nephew tells me otherwise." The word nephew was faintly stressed, and Carmody understood the message. Lady Anne was going to brave it out. She had come to the reception with her flags flying—with her *nephew* at her side.

Carmody smiled in genuine affection for this gallant woman. "You are quite right, Lady Anne. My husband does not consult me on the slightest details of his business." Anyone overhearing this exchange would find it completely innocent, Carmody knew. Jermyn, hovering nearby, let his worried face relax, and Carmody thought, Maybe they can weather this storm after all.

She hoped they could. Although she could not help but notice that Lady Anne's eyes followed Jermyn wherever he went, and the expression in his eyes in an unguarded moment would have screamed their secret aloud to all who could read.

The room was a press—Carmody could barely move through the crowd. Howard was not at her side, and she had not noticed when he disappeared. She heard in the distance the strains of violins, and the rhythmic underbeat of dancing feet. She started toward the source of the sound.

She moved through the throng. If Mark were here, she

must find him. There was still time to warn him, and it seemed desperately important—the last thing she could do for him. He was taller than most, and if he were in this room she must have seen him by now.

She emerged, somewhat breathless, on the far side of the first drawing room. She was standing in the open doorway, and the next room, as she had suspected, was full of dancers. The room was lined with spectators. There were many faces she did not recognize, planters and their wives coming into the capital to meet the King's new representative—uncomfortable in their best wear, a faint but unmistakable fragrance of cedar underlining the rarity of such formal occasions in the bucolic life of Virginia.

She searched for Mark among the dancers—he was not there, and suddenly, the overwhelming tragedy of this night, the culmination of Howard's vicious, insane envy and hatred of everyone more fortunate than he, overcame her. The tragedy, and her helplessness to avert the disaster, was poignantly underlined by the joyous faces of the dancers, the carefree merry notes of the fiddlers.

She was near to suffocating, from the overheated room, from her hopeless mission.

The door at the side of the room stood open to the night, promising cold, reviving air. She edged toward it, but before she reached her goal, Mark stepped through the door. His eyes blinked in the light, and she had time before he saw her to notice the look of worry on his face. She longed to smooth the lines away—

He caught sight of her. The light of recognition in his eyes mingled with another, fiercer spark that flared briefly and was gone. She hardly knew when the music stopped and a new set was made up. Suddenly she found herself facing Mark on the floor, and the dance started.

Under cover of the music, she whispered desperately, "Mark, you've got to get out of here!"

His strong hand guided her through a few steps before he answered. "What trap are you setting for me this time? A magnificent one, I suspect, since your instructions are given in person, and not through a note!"

Somehow, in all her imaginings, she had given short

shrift to the idea that he might be angry. Surely he must know that she too had been fairly caught in the deadfall that Howard had set for them both.

"You believe I sent that note?" she said, knowing her chin was quivering, but powerless to stop it. "I thought you would have more trust in me."

"Trust? The one woman in my life whom I wanted to trust, whom I believed in—I thought on shipboard that we had a special kind of love binding us together."

"Oh!"

"I don't know what happened, but I believed," he said as though she hadn't spoken, "that you felt the same way about me. That we were made to be together, and sometimes the waiting would be too hard. That's why I thought—what I thought," he finished lamely. "Smile, Mercy. This is a joyous occasion."

"Yes," she said faintly, "it is, isn't it. Mark, believe me. I will tell you only once. I did not send that note. I was brought to the cabin by a trick. I had no idea you would be there, no matter what Howard said. And I have been trying to warn you. You must not be here when the Governor makes his announcement."

She thought he did not even hear her warning. His arm tightened slightly around her waist, and he said, "I believe you. I believed you that night. But I've been so—tormented."

"Mark, you've got to leave now! You don't know what he's got in mind—"

The dancing stopped, the violins faded away. An expectant hush fell over the crowd and a surge of people from the next room crowded in. The Governor himself came in from a back door. Carmody could see movement around the little stage where the musicians had been playing—music stands removed, chairs scraped across the improvised dais.

Waldo was directing the clearing away, and when the stage was ready, he extended a hand to help Lord Monteith up. Carmody was caught where she was, people pressing upon her so that if she fainted, she thought ruefully, no one would know until the crowd dispersed, for she had no room to drop to the floor.

Mark was next to her. He put his arms around her, trying to protect her from the crowd. It was then that she felt suspended in time, like a fly in North Sea amber. For a long moment she hoped desperately that this moment would go on, and on, and on—held close by Mark, protected against all the world, feeling his warm breath upon her cheek, seeing his strong hands upon her wrists, so close to her that she could lean back her whole length against his long, virile body. A curious peace fell upon her.

The Governor was speaking. Waldo stood just a little behind him, deferentially handing him notes as they were demanded. The moment was at hand, but if she could savor every second of this little space of time, to carry with her against whatever was to befall her, she might, just might, survive.

The words of welcome from the Governor as host passed her by. Not until he had spoken for perhaps five minutes did he say a word that riveted her attention on him.

"The new proposal has been accepted on a provisional basis. After consulting with the planters, the good citizens of this colony, I have made up my mind. My assistant has been of inestimable help in sounding out the temper of the citizens—and I could not do better than to make my choice upon the recommendation of Sir Waldo Rivers alone."

He looked around him, beaming upon the people he had come to govern. And misguided from the very beginning, Carmody thought, by putting his faith in Waldo Rivers, an opportunist beyond compare.

There was not a sound in the room. She glanced around, looking for Howard. He was in the doorway between the two rooms. He seemed to be edging toward the dais, to be on hand, no doubt, for the announcement, so he could gain the stage quickly.

In the crowd she saw Lady Anne, hard-faced and grim. Jermyn, glancing at Lady Anne frequently, had not dared to stand too close to her, lest Howard's vitriol spill over on them. Bel Gannon, apparently wrapped in her own thoughts, was clearly oblivious to the proceedings.

She did not see Arthur Gannon. But beyond Bel, standing close to her, was Genevieve Worth, her arm through her husband's, but her worried eyes on Bel.

"The first choice of the colonists—of you all," smiled the Governor, "I am sorry to say is not available to us. He has business overseas that claims his attention, and so Mark Tennant has declined the appointment."

Now was to come the announcement that Howard had pledged his fortune for, the pinnacle of his nefarious schemes. She glanced at him. He had already made his way halfway to the stage. She could not see his face fully, only the angle from the side. But she could tell that the news of Mark's refusal—destroying Howard's chance to denounce him publicly—was unwelcome and unexpected.

But the main part of his ambition was about to be realized, and he could—she was convinced he *would*—say something that would still accomplish his defamation of Mark.

She could not bear to hear the words. She was standing so close to Mark that whatever Howard would say in his acceptance speech would be immediately proved, simply by the fact that at this moment of her husband's triumph, she was with Mark.

No matter that his arms held her upright in the crowd, that his body was positioned to protect her—it would look compromising to everyone whose eyes, directed by Howard's words, turned to them.

With a silent sob, Carmody broke out of Mark's hold, and slid away from his outthrust hand. She shook her head, and edged as rapidly as she could through the crowd. She must have looked wild, she thought later, since a way was made for her as she passed.

She regained the outer room, and found it nearly deserted. Taking a deep shuddering breath, her only thought was escape. This room was not far enough away from Howard's face, gloating even now in expectancy, nor could any place be far enough away from him.

A plan was forming in her mind, although she did not

recognize it. She could not go back to Howard's house—not tonight. If she could get away—

Get away, get away, thrummed in her mind. She went through the door to the outer room, and stood undecided in the entry hall. The door just opposite stood ajar, and she slipped through.

The Governor's study!

She could not stay here. But it was silent and deserted. Regretfully, she tiptoed across the room to another door. Easing it open, she was astonished to see a buffet table laid out invitingly. For the repast following the announcement, doubtless.

From here she could hear the Governor's voice droning on. He had not come to the point where he must say Howard's name. She did not want to hear, yet, perversely, she could not tear herself away.

"And so—" The Governor was winding up, raising his voice to suit the pinnacle of his speech—"I am naming the man who is, I am told, the worthiest of many worthy men. A little jest, here, with the name—I solicit your acceptance and cooperation for my new Deputy Governor—Vernon Worth!"

Vernon Worth!

Not Mark, who deserved it, but who had refused the onerous appointment. And not Howard, who had paid over his fortune to Waldo to buy it.

If Howard's temper, his mad envy, had been ungovernable before, his rage would be titanic at this betrayal. She had strong suspicions that Waldo, as he had done before, had simply taken the bribe and done as he thought best. Her dowry had gone the same way.

She had been doubtful of her next step. Now that she had no crime to expiate, she knew she could leave Howard. She had hoped to have a little breathing space to plan. The last time her impromptu escape had been abruptly ended, and she had vowed as recently as this very morning that when she fled again, she would make sure Howard could never find her.

Now all that was changed. There was no time left to plan. She must escape while she could, even if it meant sleeping this night in a haystack. It wouldn't be the first time.

She wheeled to go back the way she had come, through the entry—perhaps she could get the maid to retrieve her cloak before the departing guests thronged the hall.

Through the door that led to the dais, came Waldo. He raised a quizzical eyebrow when he saw her.

"Carmody? Sorry to dash your husband's fond hopes. But he really would have been a disaster in the job, you know."

She scarcely heard him. "Waldo, I've got to leave."

As though there were all the time in the world, he took a small pistol from his pocket and laid it on the Governor's desk. Suddenly he paused, looking at her in amusement.

"Dare I let this out of my hands, Carmody? It's primed and loaded."

She brushed the question aside with a wave of her hand. "Waldo, I'm desperate! I must get away, quickly, before Howard finds me. He'll think I persuaded you to thwart him, and—"

Waldo frowned. "I confess, I had not thought of that. Well, Carmody, I owe you something. Let me consider."

They were no longer alone. Lady Monteith slipped through the door from the buffet room. "They must not have eaten for weeks!" she exclaimed, horrified. "The way they fell upon the supper, I doubt there will be enough food!"

The Governor was just behind her. "It is my experience," he commented dryly, "that happy people eat best. So this proves the choice of Vernon Worth was the right one. I believe we can work together."

He became aware then of Carmody and Waldo. If he suspected anything amiss, he was too accomplished a diplomat to say so. Instead he bowed and said, "You are wise, Mistress Vickery, to wait until the first rush at the tables is over."

"If there's anything left," Lady Monteith pointed out.

The door behind them opened, and Harriet entered from the hall. She was cool and untouched, even though she had clearly battled the surge toward the buffet tables. "What a rout!" she said in her flat, monotonous voice. Then, as she became aware of the others in the room, she ordered, "Waldo, put that gun away! You know how I dislike them."

A strange expression flitted across her husband's handsome face, but all he said was, "I thought it might be needful to protect the Governor." But he made no move to pocket the gun.

It all seemed a strange echo to Carmody. Long ago, and far away, she and Waldo had stood like this, a table, and a pistol, between them. And then, too, she was desperate for help. Involuntarily, she put out her hand as though to push away the too-vivid memory.

"Curious, isn't it, how my mind runs on the past tonight," Waldo said dreamily to Carmody, as though they were alone in the room. "How stern Providence is, not to give one another chance! Probably one would make the same mistakes all over again, though."

Harriet said sharply, "That's blasphemy!"

Waldo looked up quickly, as if he had forgotten her existence. "Have no fear, Harriet. It is only my chancy mood. The fog in this benighted country plays strange tricks, sets a man out of himself."

They were all caught up in the spell of his strangeness. Even Carmody's desperation slipped to one side. This was a facet of Waldo she had never dreamed of. A regretful man, looking back on what might have been. And the strangeness reached out and enclosed Carmody too. She knew then that she was still numbed from the shock of seeing her victim appearing out of the eerie mist like a returning ghost. But he had no revenge to work out on her, as Howard did.

She sighed hugely, and came back to her own plight. She could not look to Waldo for help now, not under the suspicious eyes of Harriet and the Monteiths. She turned to go. She must find the maid and obtain her warm cloak. Then she must know where Howard was, to evade his kindling eye—

Howard was in the room.

Without a sound of warning, without ceremony, he stood in the door to the entry hall. His eyes were incandescent with fury. His face was set in rigid maniacal lines, like a rabid wolf leaping over the fence of the sheepcote.

Involuntarily, Carmody stepped back until she reached the side of the desk. Governor Monteith hissed inwardly—Carmody vaguely heard him. Lady Monteith spoke sharply in protest, and according to her usual habit Harriet remained aloof, like a spectator at a repelling but fascinating battle in the bear pit.

"Vickery," said Waldo in a lazy drawl. "I think you must have mistaken your way. The trough—or should I say the buffet table?—is through the rooms you just now traversed."

Carmody gasped. Waldo's words seemed unnecessarily provocative. Did nobody but Carmody herself know the unlimited range of Howard's insane rage? Couldn't anybody see that he was on the verge of exploding like an unstable fireball hurled down from a parapet?

She could not move.

Fortunately, Howard did not quite seem to know she was there. His burning rage was directed at the target of the moment, the man who beyond other men had cheated him. Even Mark must be forgotten in his concentrated anger at Waldo.

"I'm the man for that job, you agreed to it!" Howard cried. "It was to be mine! You cheat, you dirty, rotten—"

"Take care," warned Waldo in a suddenly deadly voice. "Watch that you don't overstep—"

"Overstep!" Howard's voice babbled on in words that made even Harriet clap her hands over her ears. Only Carmody stood unmoved while Howard's voice rose to a thin piping that was ugly, grotesque, more frightening than the obscene words he screeched.

Suddenly Lady Monteith's scream rent the air, drowning out Howard's babbling. Carmody jerked, and found her numbness departing.

Howard held a gun.

He was staring at the man who had betrayed him—who

had accepted his bribe and double-crossed him. And this time, Howard was not simply threatening. He meant to kill.

The next few minutes were confused. Carmody leaned forward, with no clear idea of what she was doing. In her mind was a cloudy impulse to shield Waldo. But she was prevented.

Waldo flung out an arm and struck her away. At the same moment, two explosions rocked the room, so close together as at first to be one long blasting report. But the shot fired closer to Carmody had come discernibly first.

The smoke from his pistol wreathed Howard's face, as she looked in fascinated horror. Like ghostly fingers, the smoke drifted, masking the glazing eyes. A look of surprise came to Howard's face, and then the emotion, the life of him, drained from his features like a physical thing.

Howard seemed to crumple, awkwardly like a stick figure, and as he fell to the floor, the final horror appeared. From the center of his embroidered waistcoat, the best his wardrobe had to offer in honor of the great announcement he had purchased, seeped an effusion of blood, staining the cream and gold brocade like a great red-bordered black eye.

It was so like the other time! She did not see the crowds of people straining to enter the Governor's office, to see what tragedy the shots signified. She could only see the body, not even wearing the identity of her husband any more—simply a dead body. She saw, but did not notice then, the glance given her by Waldo—a glance as if to say, Here's my atonement for my sins against you—I give you your freedom!

It was all out of joint, she thought feverishly—Waldo was alive and strong, and Howard was on the floor, dead. And her own hands were empty. Waldo had the gun.

Waves of faintness swept over her, and she knew her knees were buckling. Just as she slid to the floor in a faint, she heard Waldo's voice saying, imperturbably, "But I thought he was going to shoot the Governor, don't you know. And, of course, I couldn't allow that."

And then the darkness claimed her.

She was in prison.

She heard sounds around her, and knew she was lying on the fetid straw at Winchester. A feeling of hopelessness pervaded her. She was not alone, she thought. Surely that was someone sobbing, not far away.

A hand touched her shoulder softly. "Are you awake?"

The sobbing stopped abruptly, and she knew she had made the sound herself. She opened her eyes, struggling to raise eyelids heavy as lead.

Lady Monteith's kind voice spoke again. "Don't worry, Mistress Vickery. You are safe here."

Her eyes blankly searched the ceiling. She was clearly not at Winchester. No such cultured voice spoke in that prison.

"The Governor is taking care of everything. Your husband's funeral will be held this afternoon. Go to sleep."

The next time she awoke, she knew where she was. An upstairs room at the Governor's residence. No one answered any questions until she had eaten broth and bread. Lady Monteith stayed with her, making sure that every crumb disappeared. Only after that did she answer Carmody's timid questions.

"I feel as if I've lost years from my life. I don't remember," Carmody said. "How did I come here?"

"Your husband, poor man, lost his mind apparently. He must have wanted the position as the Governor's deputy very badly. He was convinced that some ghastly mistake had been made. He accused the Governor of terrible fault."

things, threatened him. But it was not the Governor's

She remembered then Waldo's strange look as he blew the fumes away from the muzzle of his smoking pistol. His amends to her for the wrongs he had done her, both directly and in an oblique way—to rid her of the incubus called Vickery.

And, of course, Howard could not now testify about Waldo's acceptance of the bribe.

But each person had his own conscience to light his way, and hers was comparatively bright. Not tarnished by

Waldo's death as she supposed, nor by whatever means she might have been forced to survive, escaping from her pursuing husband.

Waldo had saved her from all this—given her back her own life to live. She could not be grateful enough.

"Now, there's someone outside to see you."

Lady Monteith rose. She wore a faintly disapproving air, but the twinkle in her eye belied her manner. Surely she was a romantic, and just as surely, she knew love when she saw it, she thought to herself, opening the door to admit Mark Tennant.

Mark sat by Carmody's bed for a long time, content merely to hold her hand, stroking her fingers soothingly, letting his love for her show in his eyes.

Finally, he broke the contented silence. "I'm not going to ask what happened in the Governor's office, Carmody. Oh, yes, your identity is out in the open now. Lady Rivers saw to that—don't think I broke your confidence!"

"Harriet has an old grudge, I suppose."

Mark went on. "I know there was a reason for you to warn me, and I didn't take you seriously. But I should have. I was simply so miserable I couldn't think straight."

She leaned back against the soft pillows and closed her eyes. She could feel tears oozing over her cheeks, running down to her chin. Mark wiped them away.

"The Governor said you were leaving Virginia."

"I am. Carmody, once before I asked you to go with me. And you would not. Were you afraid of me?"

She shook her head. The long nightmare was over—and the fact struck her suddenly. Howard was dead! And she need never fear him again, never cringe from the lash of his epithets, never feel his vicious hands brutally punishing her—

Suddenly the years fell away. All the remorse for things undone, the regret for things done—the long years of striving simply to hold herself whole against the shattering blows that rained upon her—the dam that had held back and buried all these things now burst.

Like Pandora's box, the lid opened and all manner of things escaped. She began to sob, and then could not stop.

"Let it go," whispered Mark. "Let it out. That's it, let it all out."

When her weeping subsided into long shuddering gasps, she was in Mark's arms, and she buried her face deeper into his shoulder.

"You and I belong together, Carmody. Perhaps it's too soon to say this, but I want you to go with me when I sail. Virginia's going to be uncomfortable for us both for a while. Arthur Gannon has been busy gossiping, and Lady Rivers seems remarkably well informed about the late Duke's affairs. But, darling, I won't sail without you, not this time."

She revolved in her mind all the complications—her husband newly and violently dead. The plantation he left her to run. The obligations to do things decently in a decent society. A year's mourning, for example. A decent wedding in the little church in Jamestown. Perhaps putting the plantation up for sale and working with the new owner to see that the estate had its best care—

You love Oaklands better than me, Waldo had said.

It was true. But she did not, she knew with deep conviction, love Vickery Hall more than Mark.

Suddenly, feeling the comforting reassurance of his jacket cloth beneath her fingers, she knew she could never let him go without her. Never could she wait for him to come back, knowing that storms sometimes rage at sea, suspecting untold hazards in unknown ports—

Knowing that she was not alive unless she was with her own eternal love—

"Tomorrow, at the turn of the tide, Mark? I'll be ready."

The leaping gladness in his eyes was his only answer. That, and his lips long upon hers, gently searching, tenderly commanding—

Neither one of them heard the door open, and Lady Monteith thrust her head in. Nor did they hear the door close, as she said to the maid holding a pitcher of warm water for washing,

"Not now, Millie."

And then she said a queer thing, because she knew nothing of James, Duke of Monmouth, nor of the precious coins hidden in the Bible given him by the ladies of Taunton, nor the loan to Howard Vickery.

"Few of us, Millie," said the romantic Lady Monteith, with some regret, "ever find such—such a sovereign love."

The Governor's Lady—romantic, but also at base a staunch Puritan—led the way down the stairs, planning a small and *immediate* wedding, and never looked back.